THE N

THE SPLENDOR OF ORDINARY DAYS

"Vivid characters, humor, and touches of mystery create a delightful story that perfectly captures Southern small-town life."

—Mary Ellen Taylor, author of the Union Street Bakery series and *At the Corner of King Street*

EACH SHINING HOUR

"Heartwarming, refreshing, and often amusing, this touching novel about a likable yet conflicted new doctor sent to a rural Tennessee town is a rare gem. A bustling medical practice, a budding romance, and a passel of small-town dramas make this a rich read, but a decades-old murder mystery adds the icing on the cake. The pristine setting and lovable characters will make readers search for Watervalley, Tennessee, on a map and plan a visit."

—Karen White, *New York Times* bestselling author of *The Sound of Glass*

"A young doctor, marking time until he can leave a somnolent farm town for the bustle of a big city, finds more excitement in Watervalley than he bargained for—an alluring woman, or two; an unsolved murder, or two; a crafty banker who knows more than he's saying; and a cache of . . . well, I'll let you find that out. *Each Shining Hour* kept me reading far into the night hours!"

—Ann B. Ross, *New York Times* bestselling author of the Miss Julia series and *Etta Mae's Worst Bad-Luck Day*

"Come back to Watervalley for another endearing tale of Dr. Luke Bradford and the good folks of this small Tennessee town. Heartwarming and tender, *Each Shining Hour* is a bright and lovely story."

—Lynne Branard, author of *The Art of Arranging Flowers*

"You open this book and you can't close it. The characters are so realistic . . . a wonderful book."

—Night Owl Reviews (Top Pick)

continued . . .

MORE THINGS IN HEAVEN AND EARTH

"Told through the eyes of Dr. Luke Bradford, a newly minted MD, the story of the little town of Watervalley, Tennessee, and its inhabitants comes vividly to life. Jeff High's medical background gives him that cutting edge in the technical details of his tale, and his love of his native Tennessee and the human race shines from every page. Dr. Fingal Flahertie O'Reilly is delighted to welcome Luke, a transatlantic colleague to be fiercely proud of."

—Patrick Taylor, MD, *New York Times* bestselling author of the Irish Country Doctor novels

"The best of small-town Americana and the eccentrics who live there are brought to life in *More Things in Heaven and Earth*. This story warmed me, made me laugh, and then kept a smile on my face. It's delightful, compassionate, humorous, tightly woven. If you're looking for a feel-good read, spend an afternoon with Jeff High's novel."

—Charles Martin, *New York Times* bestselling author of *Unwritten* and *When Crickets Cry*

"A well-spun story of the mystery and microcosm that is small-town America. Jeff High skillfully captures the healing places, the hurting places, and the places where we so often find out who we are truly meant to be."

—Lisa Wingate, national bestselling author of *Tending Roses* and *The Prayer Box*

"One of the best books I've read in years. Really. And I read a *bunch* of books. This is the book you should give to your mother and your best friend at Christmas. After you read it yourself, of course. . . . High has a gift for capturing the humor of small-town life . . . captures the joy and richness of living where your family has sunk its roots deep into the soil. As I read this novel, I fell in love with Watervalley and its citizens."

—Southern Literary Review

"Engaging . . . just enough crisis and tension to keep a very simple but endearing story moving and moving! Highly recommended!"

—The Best Reviews

"A lovely novel that had me tearing up in the first chapter and cracking up in the second."

—Dew on the Kudzu

Other Books in the Watervalley Series

More Things in Heaven and Earth

Each Shining Hour

THE SPLENDOR OF ORDINARY DAYS

A NOVEL OF WATERVALLEY

JEFF HIGH

New American Library

NEW AMERICAN LIBRARY
Published by New American Library,
an imprint of Penguin Random House LLC
375 Hudson Street, New York, New York 10014

This book is an original publication of New American Library.

First Printing, October 2015

LIBRARY OF CONGRESS CATALOGING-IN-PUBLICATION DATA:

High, Jeff, 1957–
The splendor of ordinary days: a novel of Watervalley/Jeff High.
p. cm.—(Watervalley series; 3)
ISBN 978-0-451-47410-0 (softcover)
1. Physicians—Fiction. 2. City and town life—Tennessee—Fiction. I. Title.
PS3608.I368S68 2015
813'.6—dc23 2015014796

Printed in the United States of America
10 9 8 7 6 5 4 3 2 1

Set in Adobe Garamond
Designed by Spring Hoteling

Penguin
Random
House

Dedicated to the Wounded Warriors whose scars cannot be seen and for those who hope, pray, and wait for them to be whole again.

"They also serve who only stand and wait."

—John Milton, "On His Blindness"

THE SPLENDOR OF ORDINARY DAYS

PRELUDE

Watervalley, Tennessee. July 5, 1968

The ring of the bell was hard and furious, piercing the night and shattering the quiet depths of the small hours. It rang with a shrill quality of urgency and menace, hammering savagely, relentlessly, permeating the stagnant, suffocating air of the empty streets and shadowed lawns. The clanging brutally woke him from the oblivion of sleep. He leapt from his bed and ran to the window, anticipating an orange glow from the nearby downtown, but there was none. The fire was somewhere in the countryside.

He dressed quickly and ran downstairs. The kitchen light was on, his mother waiting. She stood by with folded arms and a pale, ghostly face of tacit worry. As he rushed to the front door, her timid voice followed him with the familiar words of caution. He stopped, walked back to her, and kissed her on the cheek. "It's your big day. I'll come back safe."

The blistering, brassy tongue of the bell continued as he sprinted the three blocks to the fire hall. One by one, the houses along the street were lighting up. Out from the dark vault of night, the town was coming alive.

At the firehouse, the pump truck was already out on the pavement, poised to charge forward. It was a spectacle of bulk and power, a rolling fortress of steel and rails and magnificent lights. The great engine was idling, forcing the warm night air to shudder and vibrate. Men were running, shouting, rushing to grab their gear, bumping chaotically against one another in a furious effort to slide into coats and boots. And above the roar and confusion was the thunderous voice of the fire chief. Standing on the rear mount bumper of the truck, he was yelling for them to come, now, now, now.

Eighteen and nimble, he was the youngest in the volunteer service. He moved among them effortlessly, geared up quickly, and was one of the first to mount the ride bumper on the side of the truck. He stepped on and grabbed the rail. As the others arrived, they regarded him with astonishment, questioning him.

"What are you doing here? Don't you leave in the morning?"

Sleep didn't matter to him. It would be a long bus ride to Fort Polk. He could rest on the way. Vietnam would still be there.

Half-suited men were still clumsily chasing the truck as it began to pull away, launching itself with the slow ebbing wail of the long siren. The truck accelerated quickly. The ride was wild, noisy, insane. He held the rail firmly, his heart pounding.

Soon they left behind the sterile streetlights of downtown and were bounding headlong into the black and desolate countryside. Men were shouting, trying to be heard above the deafening blow of the wind and the siren.

"Where is it?"

Another man answered above the din. "Out Gallivant's Crossing. Some farmer called it in."

The words shook him. This was an odd, sobering coincidence. He had returned from Gallivant's Crossing only a few hours earlier. He tightened his grip against the reckless and exhilarating lunges of the turns. They rode on, the truck pitching and heaving, slinging them in unison.

Someone shouted into the howling noise. "Is it a house?"

An answer came from someone down the line. "Not sure."

They turned onto Gallivant's Crossing and drove for several miles into the rolling hills and thick woods where only a few isolated farms dotted the vast black landscape. There the world slept, illuminated by a solitary barnyard light that cast its frail luster into the shadows. These far-flung islands of life seemed soundless, timeless, blissfully removed from the surge and clamor of the wailing truck. They roared onward, into the uncertain darkness.

He knew this road. And with each mile, each hill, each turn, his heart began to sink slowly within him, flooding him with dread.

Surely not there, *he thought to himself.* Surely not the cottage.

The truck slowed, its driver in doubt of the fire's location. They topped the last hill before Mercy Creek Road, and the glow in the near distance was easily discerned. The truck made the tight turn down the narrow chert road and advanced with what speed it could toward the blaze. Trees crowded the sides of the lane, their branches brushing against the men.

One of them shouted out, "This isn't right, boys. We're on the fringe of Mennonite country. What are we doing here?"

A cry came back. "Putting out a fire, you idiot."

"You watch, genius. They won't let us get close."

The truck emerged from the trees as the lane cleared on the left to a small flat meadow tucked neatly between nearby hills. The massive engine turned onto the long drive and stopped. One hundred yards ahead, lighting up the night sky, was a small frame house, burning furiously. They could see dozens of shouting men. His thoughts raced. Why had the truck stopped?

The men began to step off and gather in small groups, staring at the distant blaze. The fire chief walked leisurely down the drive. Two men in broad-brim hats came to meet him. After a short discussion, the chief walked back.

"False alarm, boys. They've got a bucket brigade going from a pond out back. They're just going to let the fire burn itself out and water down the perimeter to keep it from getting into the field."

"Anybody hurt?"

"Nah. Apparently the house was empty. They only use it for storage."

The chief turned and stared at the fire for a moment. "We'll stay for a bit . . . just stand by at the ready in case it gets out of hand." He paused and shook his head. "You know these Mennonite boys. They don't like outsiders getting involved, even if it's for their own good."

He stared at the chief and stood silently, his nauseating panic slowly replaced by a sullen, bitter resentment. He knew all about this abandoned house, but he said nothing. He only watched. He knew who had started the fire, and he knew why.

And he wasn't the only one.

For decades, they would keep their silence, blinded by their anger.

CHAPTER 1

Memorial Day, Watervalley, Tennessee

As a doctor, I tend not to be superstitious.

I don't believe in ghosts, or that eating an apple a day will keep you well, or that a rabbit's foot will bring good luck, unless you're a rabbit.

However, numbers might be the exception. I've come to think of certain numbers as lucky, others not. For me, six is an unlucky number, seven can go either way, and the luckiest number of all is three.

But that notion changed on Memorial Day. During my frantic rush to the softball field to save Toy McAnders's life, I painfully recalled my med school professor's lecture about the Rule of Threes. This was the lecture about death.

On average, the human body can live for three weeks without food, three days without water, and three hours after subthermal exposure. These lousy situations share one small positive. Typically, they don't involve panic. The mind has time: time to process, to plan, to hope.

Lack of oxygen is a different matter. The "game over" bell on an oxygen-deprived body is about three minutes. It terrifies us. We panic. It's in our DNA.

And panic is contagious. Watching someone desperately gasp for breath creates a sympathetic physical response. It's automatic. . . . Heart rate and respiration accelerate, pupils dilate, skin perspires, and panicked people tend to talk in high-pitched gibberish. Understanding them is like trying to have a conversation with Flipper. Unfortunately, being a doctor doesn't make you immune.

So as I was heading out the door on that Memorial Day afternoon, I was thinking about barbecued ribs and fireworks and the beautiful smile awaiting my arrival. The ring of my cell phone changed everything.

"Dr. Bradford! Oh, thank God! He can't breathe! How soon can you get here?"

Startled, I blurted my response. "Hello, hello, who is this?"

"It's Sarah, Sarah McAnders. I . . . Help us. Can you come! He can't breathe!"

"Sarah! Slow down. Who can't . . . Where are you?"

"At the softball park. He's not breathing, Dr. Bradford. He's choking! Oh my God! What do we do?"

I began to run toward my car.

"Who are we talking about? Who's choking? Is it Sam?" Sarah was the young mother of a one-year-old son.

"No, no. It's Toy! The softball . . . His throat . . . It hit his throat! Where are you?"

I was trying to keep calm, stay focused, but a dozen thoughts were fumbling through my head and the blasted car wouldn't start. I looked down and realized I was trying to use my house key in the ignition. Like I said, panic is contagious.

"Sarah, how long ago did it happen?"

"Just now! I mean, I don't know. Maybe a minute ago!"

If this was correct, it was the only spark of good news. Toy was her husband, a strong athletic man in his mid-twenties. I looked at my watch. The softball park was five minutes away. My hope was that Toy's windpipe wasn't completely closed. That would buy me time.

"Sarah, I'm on my way. I'm going to hang up and call the EMTs. I'll get there as fast as I can. Do you understand?"

"Yes! Yes! I think so. Please hurry!"

I squealed onto Fleming Street.

A quick phone call got the EMTs at the fire station moving. They would be only a minute behind me. This was the hazard of being the sole physician in a remote Tennessee town. When emergencies occurred, there was no bench of reserve players. With my staff nurse out of town, the EMTs and I were it.

Fortunately, the softball park was a direct shot out Shiloh Road, set apart from the downtown, away from either one of Watervalley's two traffic lights. I put my emergency flashers on and pressed hard on the gas pedal. I needed to calm myself, to think clearly. I ran various scenarios through my head, trying to anticipate what I would do upon my arrival. I checked my watch. A minute and a half had passed.

The air passage to the lungs, the larynx, is made of flexible rings and typically bounces back . . . unless the impact crushes it along with the hyoid bone, better known as the Adam's apple. In that case, there are hemorrhaging and swelling that force the airway closed. But swelling takes time, and time was what I, and Toy McAnders, needed.

The damnable Rule of Threes was hounding me.

There was little traffic. I managed to pass one or two cars. Thankfully, a few pulled over to let me by, recognizing my Corolla with its flashing lights. Again I checked my watch. Two and a half minutes had passed. I might just make it.

Then, everything stopped.

After rounding a curve less than a half mile from the ballpark, I had to slam on the brakes to keep from rear-ending the car in front of me. Stretched in a long line ahead was a row of vehicles at a complete standstill.

It was unthinkable. Traffic jams simply didn't happen in Watervalley, and yet at this ill-timed moment, that was what lay before me. The road ahead curved with woods on either side, limiting my vision. This made no sense. There were no police sirens, and dispatch at the fire station hadn't mentioned anything.

I pulled the Corolla into the vacant oncoming lane. After a hundred yards, I had rounded the curve far enough to see the problem. Ahead was a flatbed truck stopped in the middle of the road. Strewn everywhere were slatted wooden crates, each the size of a large suitcase. Some were flipped sideways, some upended, some busted. All were filled with chickens. Stacked and strapped onto the truck bed, the crates had apparently come undone and spilled over the road and shoulder, completely blocking traffic.

Volunteers were casually helping the farmer reload the crates. I laid on my horn as I approached. From around the corner of the truck, heads appeared with irritated faces at the impatient honking. A couple of men recognized me and began to walk toward my approaching car.

"What's going on, Doc?"

"You gotta let me through, fellows. There's an emergency at the ballpark."

They exchanged glances and immediately ran back toward the others.

"Make a hole, boys! Doc needs to get by!"

Time came to a standstill. I tapped my finger rapidly on the steering wheel, and in those dead seconds of waiting, I started to feel that heavy-throated, sickening apprehension that everything was going south. Panic was overtaking me, screaming into my consciousness. Too much time! Too much time!

By now the EMT van was behind me. Six minutes had passed since Sarah's call, twice the threshold of the Rule of Threes. I was sweating, short of breath, consumed with a nauseating reality: Toy McAnders was probably dead.

I finally passed through, accelerated down the ballpark entrance, and pulled directly onto the field, where a large crowd circled the pitcher's mound. The EMT van followed. I slammed on my brakes, burning long ruts in the grass. In one fluid motion I grabbed my physician's bag and was out the car door, running headlong toward the center of the crowd. Instinctively people moved aside, availing a large opening. I halted in midstep three feet away from Toy, stunned at the sight before me.

Toy McAnders was seated on the ground against a stack of athletic bags. Protruding from the small of his throat were two large drinking straws. Sarah was standing beside him, a hand covering her mouth. A woman I had never met was on her knees next to Toy, calmly giving him instructions. Blood covered the front of his shirt, but he was alive.

The woman was intermittently dabbing a cloth around the tracheal opening made in Toy's neck, trying to check the bleeding. The setup was gruesome and unnatural looking. He had a weak consciousness and was struggling to breathe. But he was alive.

I dropped to a knee on Toy's opposite side.

"I'm Dr. Bradford."

The woman, who looked to be in her mid- to late thirties, nodded and continued to address Toy's mild bleeding as she spoke.

"This fellow looked away after a pitch, and the softball caught him square in the throat. Smacked him pretty hard. At the four-minute mark, he lost consciousness. I made an incision over the suprasternal notch and a lateral incision into the trachea, enough to get the two straws inserted. From what I can tell, heart rate is about one twenty, jugular pressure seems good, respirations are around thirty. It looks bad, but I estimate only about thirty milliliters of blood loss. I had to use my pocketknife, so he'll need an antibiotic. He lost consciousness for about ninety seconds, long enough for me to insert the straws."

She wore jeans and a T-shirt. She was small in size but athletic looking with brownish blond hair cropped in a pageboy. She had methodically given me a thorough medical report—clearly something she had done before.

By now the EMTs, Clarence and Leonard, were beside me with the gurney. We quickly lifted Toy onto it and into the van, where we could fully monitor him for transport to Regional Hospital in the next county.

Once Toy was loaded, I turned to the woman, extending my hand. "We haven't met."

"Karen."

She didn't offer a last name. "Nice work, Karen. You probably saved his life."

She pursed her lips and nodded.

Clarence called out to let me know they were ready to go. I turned and spoke briefly to him. When I turned back to Karen, she had been absorbed into the crowd.

I tossed my car key to a fellow I knew and asked him to move the Corolla to the parking lot. "Leave the key in the ignition," I said. "If I'm lucky, someone will steal it." I hustled to the ambulance, and we took off.

During the ride, Sarah McAnders explained what had happened. After Toy's collapse, amidst all the panic and shouting, the mysterious Karen had appeared from the crowd and spoken calmly.

"Ma'am. If you'll let me, I can save him."

At the time, I didn't know anything about Karen. None of the EMTs knew of her either. But something in the way she carried herself: something about her orderly manner in the face of such a traumatic event, gave me a clue.

CHAPTER 2
The Clinic

Nobody liked Luther Whitmore, including me. He didn't have anything nice to say to, or about, anybody. He'd as soon spit on them.

Nevertheless, during a medical exam, I always try to look past the hard exterior that people sometimes exhibit. With me, they have to be honest, open, vulnerable . . . and it scares them.

So every time Luther visited me at the clinic, I approached him with this simple, accommodating mind-set. I would patiently hear him out. I would listen, and assess, and look: into his ears, into his eyes, and into his soul. And I always came to the same conclusion. He was a mean jackass . . . no redeeming qualities whatsoever. Nope, I didn't like him.

He was also the owner and editor of the local newspaper.

Luther came to the clinic on the Tuesday afternoon following Memorial Day. Admittedly, I didn't want to be there. Outside, it was a cosmic, perfect day, and I was yearning to be part of it. The valley and surrounding hills were displaying the last of a glorious spring. Everywhere the landscape was painted in rich, thick hues of green, the flowers were at their pinnacle, and a sweet, intoxicating breeze floated in the air.

Throughout the day, I had stolen moments to step out the clinic's back door and absorb what I could of this splendid existence. I couldn't get enough of it. But the clinic staff giggled at me behind my back. They knew the real reason for my exalted state. I was in love, floating euphorically, and eager to be with her at day's end.

First, however, I had to deal with Luther.

I had been told that in his youth, Luther was a strong, powerful athlete. Now, he was a tall specter of a man with a large, bald head, prominent nose, and pointed chin. His face was invariably framed in a sour sneer, accentuated by bushy eyebrows that hung gloomily over the deep sockets of his eyes. He gazed upon the world like a vulture, hungry for the next victim of his critical tongue. Luther's only virtue was his penchant for truthful, unbiased reporting. Then again, Watervalley was not a hotbed of scandal, given that the majority of the police reports involved parking violations.

So, I took a deep breath, rose from my office chair, and proceeded across the hall to exam room one, which now could be appropriately thought of as the lair of the dragon.

"Hello, Doctor. 'Bout damn time."

And so it began.

"Nice salutation, Luther. And just when I thought you couldn't get any cuddlier."

There was a weak knock on the door followed by the timid entrance of Nancy Orman, the clinic's kind and corpulent office manager.

"Sorry, Dr. Bradford, sorry. I just need to get this cart out of here." She proceeded to grab the small supply bin used to stock the exam rooms. I stepped aside as she snatched it and backed out the door. All of this fell under Luther's leering scrutiny.

"Humph. A woman that big ought to make a beeping sound when she backs up."

I rewarded him with stiff silence as I perused his chart. Luther got the message.

He sat on the exam table, looking straight ahead, regarding me out of the corner of his eye. When he spoke, his curdled tone smacked more of inquisition than inquiry.

"You still got the gate key to the lake, Doc?"

He was referring to Moon Lake, a small slice of heaven that sat atop a treeless hill in the northern part of the county. The property had belonged to Luther's family for generations. But when Luther had inherited it forty years ago, he'd had it fenced, padlocked, and posted with no-trespassing signs. Why, no one knew. It was a grand and curious mystery. Even though I shared the burning curiosity about why Luther had so spitefully closed off Moon Lake, I had held on to my inquiries for a simple reason. I enjoyed a special status with respect to Watervalley's most enchanted spot. I had a key.

Several months back, in a rare act of kindness after I had helped cure him of hemorrhoids, Luther had lent me the key. Something in this exchange seemed symbolically in keeping with his personality.

"I do have the key. You want it back?"

"Nah, keep it. Just don't let anybody in there to fish. You're too much on the wussy side to be much of a fisherman yourself. Doubt you could do much damage on that account."

"Yeah, sure. Anyway, I, uh, I appreciate your letting me have it. It's a nice place to visit from time to time."

"Well, if you want to turn that gratitude into something tangible, you could have the place bush hogged. It's getting pretty overgrown."

I continued studying his chart, speaking vacantly. "Bush hogging is not exactly in my wheelhouse, Luther."

He rubbed his chin, still regarding me with a tired disdain. "Yeah, I figured. Eh, don't worry about it. Just a thought."

"So, Luther, are you still smoking?"

"I'm down to two packs a day."

"And how's your alcohol consumption?"

"Not more than a fifth a night."

"Hmm. I see. And last time you were here, I gave you a low-cholesterol-diet plan. How have you been doing with that?"

"I tried it for a couple of days and decided to hell with it."

"Nice."

"Hey, look. I still don't drink coffee. There ought to be some points for that. All coffee does is make people do stupid things faster and with more energy."

"Tell me, Luther. Do you lie awake at night just waiting for a heart attack to happen?"

He glared at me with poorly masked contempt. "Ah, get off my back, Doc. You and I both know that except for my cholesterol, my annual physical and blood work last year weren't that bad. Passed my stress test, had a clean colonoscopy, and no prostate issues. I'm fit as a damn fiddle."

The worst part of Luther's venomous response was that he was right. Simply put, Luther had excellent genes. If med school had taught me anything, it was that poor genes were almost impossible to fix and great genes were hard to mess up. Lifestyle is a huge factor in good health, but genetics is the trump card. Despite his deplorable habits, Luther's DNA had made him ridiculously bulletproof. He even had good teeth. And, true to form, he was pretty arrogant about all of it.

I exhaled and offered him a thin smile. For the life of me, I didn't get Luther. I couldn't understand his rotten nature. Continued coaching would be pointless.

"I heard you and the Chambers girl are dating?"

My answer was clipped. "That would be correct."

"Well, good for you. She's kind of a looker. Women are enough of a pain in the ass. They shouldn't be ugly on top of that. The ones that are should just stay home."

"Sounds like the making of a great editorial."

Luther grunted in response. My mind went immediately to his ex-wife, Claire. They had no children and had recently divorced. She was another odd chapter in Luther's story.

Claire was from California. They met and married when he lived there for a couple of years after serving in Vietnam. Claire was actually a lovely, engaging soul. Given Luther's hard personality, people wondered what in the world Claire could have been thinking when she married him and why it took her forty years to divorce him. Most folks concluded that instead of California, they had met on a deserted island with no hope of rescue. That would explain Claire's impulsive decision. Either that, or she had a mother she wanted to get back at.

Luther spoke with an air of barely concealed contempt. "By the way, what was the Mennonite fellow doing here?"

He was referring to a patient I had treated earlier. Luther had likely seen the man departing. A modestly sized Mennonite community bordered the northern part of the county.

"Luther, I think that comes under the 'none of your business' category."

"Humph, seems a little out of place. Maybe the black-hat boys should just pray a little harder."

"I see. And you know this from experience?"

Luther turned to me with a lecherous grin, quoting scripture. "'If you diligently heed the voice of the Lord, I will put none of the diseases on you which I have brought on the Egyptians.'"

"You know, Luther, somehow when you quote Exodus, it doesn't have the same appeal as when my pastor does." I had been quick to respond, but even I had to admit that considering he was such a jerk, Luther's knowledge of scripture was impressive. I refocused the conversation.

"So, what brings you here today?"

"My eyes. I seem to be losing vision in the center."

Finally, here was one thing about Luther that I did understand. Loss of central vision is the hallmark of macular degeneration, a disease that causes blindness in the middle of the visual field, leaving only peripheral vision. This would explain Luther's constant glancing from the side and perhaps even the higher-than-normal acidity in his remarks.

I did a thorough eye exam, including a test called the Amsler Grid. My suspicions proved correct. Luther had early onset of the disease. I prescribed some medications and recommended a strict follow-up schedule. In spite of Luther's noncompliance on all of my other medical recommendations, I gathered he would be diligent with this plan of care. Luther wasn't dumb or lazy. He was just mean.

And so it was I witnessed the first chink in the armor of Luther Whitmore's seemingly infallible genetics. Age and disease were a great leveler of the arrogant, and perhaps in the months ahead, I would be seeing a humbler, kinder version of Luther.

Then again, I doubted it.

In either case, actually liking him would remain a monumental task.

As he departed, I was thinking how pleasant it would be if Luther was abducted by aliens. Who knew—maybe he already had been. That would explain a lot.

It was nearing five, and I was expecting Christine, my beloved and beautiful girlfriend, to arrive at any minute. She had called earlier to tell me she had some exciting news and would drop by after work.

I returned to my office to gather my things, including a medical journal with an article I wanted to read. It was somewhere in the stack of magazines I'd tossed on the floor behind my desk. I was bent down on one knee looking for it when there was a simultaneous knock and opening of my office door, the typical entry of Nancy Orman.

"You have a visitor, Doctor."

I continued thumbing through the journals, thinking it odd that she would announce Christine. "Sure, send her in. I'm expecting her."

I was engrossed in looking for that blasted article, still on my knees behind my desk, when I heard the door open again. I spoke without looking up. "Hey, beautiful. Want to go grab some dinner?"

Christine didn't immediately respond, and there was nothing but stale silence in the room. So, I turned and peered over my desk.

Gazing down at me with a rather confused expression was Karen, the woman I had met at the ballpark the previous day. "Well, thanks for the offer, but I've already got a date with the Laundromat."

CHAPTER 3
A New Doctor

I stood immediately, hastily endeavoring to recover some portion of my dignity. "Oh, hi. Well, this is awkward. Sorry. I was expecting someone else."

She offered a cautious smile. "Yeah, I think I had that one figured out. Hope I'm not interrupting anything important?"

"No, not at all. I was just finishing for the day. I, um . . . I don't think I caught your full name yesterday."

"It's Davidson. Karen Davidson." She extended her hand in a crisp, exacting manner, and we shook firmly. She was attired in weathered but well-creased khaki pants and a rather frilly white blouse. The two items didn't quite go together . . . as if she had started to play dress up and had then given up on the idea.

"I came by to introduce myself. Actually, it's *Dr.* Karen Davidson. I'm a veterinarian. I've bought out what was left of Dr. Ingram's practice. I'm going to be here full-time."

"Well, congratulations and welcome to Watervalley." Charlie Ingram was Watervalley's only veterinarian, but he lived in the neighboring county and held hours in a satellite office here only one day a week.

Karen nodded, her lips still pressed in a slightly nervous smile. "Thanks."

"That was an incredible thing you did at the ballpark. I don't believe I got a chance to thank you."

"Oh, I just did, you know, what I thought I had to do."

"I know Sarah McAnders wanted to get your name. She called some friends at the park during the ambulance ride, but no one could find you."

Karen looked down sheepishly. "I left right afterward. It just, I don't know. It just felt sort of odd when it was over, like everyone was staring at me."

"I'm sure they were. What you did was rather heroic. . . . Pretty big news for a place like Watervalley. Matter of fact, you just missed Luther Whitmore, editor of the local newspaper. I bet he'd like to interview you."

A cringe twisted her face as she inhaled through clenched teeth, making a slight hissing sound. "Are you talking about the fellow in the black suit I just saw in the parking lot?"

"Sounds right."

"Gee, I thought he was a mortician. Just as well I missed him. Anyway, I don't much care for the spotlight."

"Yeah, that was Luther, all right. He's not exactly Mr. Sunshine. But I'm sure the paper will want to do a write-up about having a new vet in town. I don't think you will be able to avoid the spotlight completely."

She nodded. "I'm okay with that. How's the fellow from the ballpark doing?"

"Toy McAnders. He's good. We took him to Regional Hospital. He'll come home tomorrow."

I studied her for a moment and decided to pry further. "So, how long have you been in town?"

"I actually just arrived yesterday morning. I'm staying over at the B and B till my stuff arrives." She fell silent, seemingly unsure of what to say next. I spoke again in an accommodating voice.

"I have to admit, Karen, I'm a little curious. I'm guessing vet school didn't teach you how to do an emergency cricothyrotomy?"

She shrugged. "Hardly. I was in the military for fifteen years. Army medic. I went to veterinary school after I got out. I graduated this spring."

"Well, that explains a lot." This news came as no big surprise. With her ramrod posture, crisp speech, and reserved manner, everything about Karen Davidson reflected the enamel of military service. I gauged her to be in her late thirties and, while she was a pleasant, modestly attractive woman, her short haircut and minimal, if any, makeup telegraphed that she was either uninterested or unpracticed in accentuating her feminine side. She was polite and plain and seemed content to remain so.

"Well, I have a lethargic but lovable male golden retriever who will be excited to know that you've arrived in town."

"What's his name?" There was a notable lift in her voice.

"Rhett. He's an adopted stray. But he's turned out to be quite a character."

"They're great hunting dogs, you know."

"I'm sure that's true for the breed in general, but I'm not so sure Rhett could get vicious with a bird or a rabbit. He'd probably just trash-talk it a little and let it go at that."

"Well," she said warmly, "I look forward to meeting him."

"So, I take it you've introduced yourself around town some. Have you been by the Farmers' Co-op?"

"Yeah, I, um, I went by there earlier today and met a few of the guys. They were, well, polite."

The trepidation in her answer was obvious. "I take it you have some reservations about how that went?"

She paused and scrutinized me for a moment, as if weighing what level of confidence she wanted to engage with me. "It was okay. I think they weren't sure what to make of a woman my size taking on half-ton cows and pulling calves. Nobody said anything, but I could read it in their eyes."

"They can be a little tight-lipped at first, but they're good people. Just give it some time."

Karen smiled faintly. "I hope so. The cat and dog business will probably pay the light bill, but it will take a fair amount of large-animal practice to cover rent and food. Eating may be optional for a while."

I liked Karen Davidson instantly, but she was an odd mix. Her skillful handling of the crisis the previous day attested to a self-confidence that didn't seem to translate to social settings. Nevertheless, she had an easy sense of humor, and I detected an inborn toughness. Her awkward mannerisms only added to her distinctive, albeit peculiar, charm. I was about to speak again, when there was a knock at the door. It was Christine.

"Hi, am I interrupting? I can wait in the lobby."

"No, not at all. Come on in. I want you to meet someone."

A tall and athletic brunette, Christine Chambers had grown up in Watervalley, gone to college in Atlanta, and stayed there to teach in a private school for the last several years. She had returned to town the previous July, near the same time of my arrival. We had been dating since December, and what had started as a tenuous relationship had blossomed into a full-blown romance. I loved her, profoundly. She was intelligent, independent, and strikingly beautiful.

Neatly dressed in a summer top and white shorts, she smiled at me adoringly.

"Karen, this is Christine Chambers. Christine, this is Dr. Karen Davidson. She's a veterinarian and is setting up a full-time practice in town."

Christine's engaging response was warm and natural. "Oh, that's wonderful. It's so good to meet you."

Karen, however, responded awkwardly with only a swallowed "Hi."

She seemed off balance, saying nothing further and simply standing as if at attention, intently assessing Christine, who was a good five inches taller. When Karen spoke again, there was a childlike innocence to her unfiltered declaration. "Wow! You really are beautiful."

Christine shot a puzzled glance in my direction. "Well, thank you. It's very sweet of you to say so."

Karen now realized the inappropriate bluntness of her statement. "Oh, I'm sorry. That probably seemed out of place. I was just going on what Luke said earlier."

Christine smiled graciously before slowly rotating her head in my direction. "Okay, seriously. You can find nothing better to talk about?"

I started to raise my hands in a gesture of explanation, but Karen spoke first.

"No, no. He didn't say anything about you being beautiful. Actually, he called me beautiful, but he thought he was talking to you."

This didn't help.

Christine folded her arms, clearly trying to make sense of Karen's words. But nothing was fitting. Finally she laughed out loud.

"Okay. Good . . . I think."

Karen regarded me with a mortified face of apology. The misunderstanding was all quite laughable, and I offered her an obliging smile and a shrug of dismissal. But that did little to ease her embarrassment.

She took a deep breath. "Well, I think I've done enough damage here for one visit, so I'm going to head along. I need to find a Laundromat and maybe a little bit of my dignity. Luke, good to meet you." She regarded Christine sheepishly. "Christine, good to make your acquaintance. I hope to see you again soon."

Christine smiled sweetly. "Good to meet you as well. Welcome to Watervalley."

It looked for a moment like Karen might snap to attention before exiting, but she caught herself and walked briskly out the door, apparently eager to make a hasty retreat.

I turned to Christine, prepared to explain in detail what had transpired before her arrival, but before I could say a word, she grabbed my shoulders and planted a delightful kiss on me. She spoke with affectionate resignation. "Bradford, just . . . don't even try."

"Try what?"

"To explain."

"You don't want to hear the details?"

"Seriously, it's okay. Apparently you and Karen both have that socially inept doctor gene, so weird conversations are just bound to happen. I understand. I really do."

"Okay, I have a question. Why is it I get the third degree anytime that pharmaceutical rep, Michelle Herzenberg, visits me, yet you give this misunderstanding with Karen a pass?"

"What, the blond Swedish meatball? You can't be serious, Bradford."

"Karen is blond," I added defiantly.

"And a lovely person and apparently quite intelligent . . . although she could use a little coaching on her wardrobe."

"So, what's the difference?"

"Herzenberg does everything she can to come off as a woman of easy virtue."

"Should I be looking for a woman of difficult virtue?"

"Not funny, Bradford."

"Let's go back to the socially inept doctor gene comment. You know, if I thought about that statement long enough, I might take serious offense."

She mused over my words for a moment and then playfully began to straighten the collar of my lab coat. "Mmm, you could. But I bet you won't."

"And why is that?"

"Because there are better things you could be doing than complaining."

I frowned, making a low noise of disapproval.

She lifted an eyebrow and smiled impishly. "Give it up, Bradford. You're not fooling anybody."

I responded in mock indignation. "That's not true. I'm almost fooling myself."

She draped her hands around my neck. "Anyway, Karen seems nice, although . . . is it just me, or did she seem a little on the tomboy side?"

"Yeah, she's definitely that—ex-military, a medic, no less."

"Really?"

"Yep. She's the woman who saved Toy McAnders yesterday."

"Oh wow. Is that right?"

"Seems odd, doesn't it. Yesterday she saved Toy's life, as cool as a cucumber, and today she gets flustered making introductions and small talk."

"I guess she's more comfortable with animals. I can relate."

I was searching for a clever comeback to her obvious dig, but my mind was in a flutter. Christine did that to me. I shook my head and hummed her name softly. "Christine, Christine, Christine . . ."

Suddenly, she stiffened and regarded me with surprise, as if my calling her name was magical to her ears. "Am I missing something here?" I asked.

She seemed delighted, but offered only a dismissive smile. "No. No, it's nothing." She looked down, but her face was still radiant, animated, faintly amused.

"Anyway," I continued, "when we talked earlier today, you said you had come across something really big."

Her eyes twinkled with excitement. "Yes! It was something I found while helping Mom clear stuff out of our attic for the community charity yard sale."

"What was it?"

"Guess."

"You finally found Waldo."

"Funny. Get serious."

"Well, give me a hint."

"It's something from the past, very intimate and personal."

"I don't know. Sounds like a training bra."

"Bradford, you need to rethink your definition of 'get serious.' Last chance. Make it count."

"All right. Let me think. Youuuu found . . . a box of VHS tapes, including all nine seasons of *The X-Files*."

"Okay, that was pretty random, and no."

"So, what was the big discovery?"

Christine paused. Delighted, she searched my face for a moment, as if dreamily pondering some great secret. Her eyes grew soft, and there was an elated, almost triumphant quality to her voice. "I, Luke Bradford, found my old journal."

I smiled kindly, doing my best to hide that I had no idea why this was such a big deal.

EXCERPT FROM THE JOURNAL OF CHRISTINE CHAMBERS

My Journal, May 17, 1998

Dear Mr. Wonderful:

I dreamed of you today.

Your voice floated on the wind from beyond the hills. It drifted down the high slope of Akin's Ridge and found me on the rolling sweep of green on Bracken's Knoll.

I was there, in my favorite place . . . sitting in the soft clover beyond the crest, out of sight. The bees were there, too . . . buzzing, circling, busying themselves with spring. I sat with my arms around my knees, wondering, listening. But I wasn't listening for you. I wanted to hear the music of the falling water; the sweet, soothing sound it makes echoing up the slow rise from Snow Creek.

I closed my eyes and could hear the birds chattering. The breeze carried their notes across the tops of the grass. I shut my eyes even harder and waited, listening for the soft, delicate purr of the water and wanting the sound to wash over me like it always had.

Instead, I heard you, pushing your words over the distant fortress of tall trees, intruding upon my secret world.

You were calling my name.

The bees heard you too. They stopped their endless buzzing and lingered, sleepily hanging on the small white crowns of clover. The birds in the trees quieted and cooed distantly, shying away from their constant piping. Everything in my world was waiting, watching . . . and changing.

I told you to stop it. I didn't want to hear you right now. . . . Wasn't ready to hear you. . . . Wasn't prepared for my world to change. I wanted to hear the hum of the bees, the songs of the birds, the endless pouring of the water. I wanted to feel the fresh, clean warmth of the sunlight, to be lost in the sweet, fragrant smell of the clover. I wanted everything to be like it had always been.

Then I heard your voice again . . . and it was beautiful. It fell softly like a lullaby. There was magic in it of things unfelt, things unimagined, things yet to come that were tender and sweet and delightful, and I began to dream of you. It was wonderful . . . so that's the name I will give you.

I knew then and there, sitting in the clover of Bracken's Knoll, that someday I would hear your voice and I would know you. Someday I would see you, maybe in a crowd or standing in a doorway. And you would be the one who whispered my name, the one I heard, the one I would always love.

Who are you, Mr. Wonderful? What will you look like? Where will we meet? I listened, but you wouldn't say. You only called my name, telling me you were there.

And so I dreamed of you for the first time.

I dreamed of you today.

The sun grew hot, making me thirsty. But I didn't cup my hand and drink out of Snow Creek like I used to do when I was younger. I'm changing. Everything about me is changing. I'm older now and know better. Next month I'll be thirteen. So, I waited.

I will wait for you too, Mr. Wonderful. I will wait.

Twilight came and I started for home. But as I made my way across the open fields, I could still hear you, your voice, sweetly, magically calling my name . . . "Christine, Christine, Christine."

CAC

CHAPTER 4
Memories and Memoirs

"Can I make a confession?" I asked Christine.

"Sure."

"I'm glad you're happy to have found your old journal, but I'm not getting the significance."

Christine continued to regard me incandescently, with an odd mixture of fondness and curiosity, but her thoughts seemed miles away.

"Okay, Chambers, why all of a sudden have you invoked the cone of silence?"

My question brought her back. She sat in one of the wingback chairs, still absorbed with a tender, ruminating smile. "I was just thinking about something. It was fun to find my old journal and read what I wrote in my early teens."

I slouched in my chair, gazing idly at the ceiling. "Hmm. Let me guess. Probably a lot of stuff about hating braces and boys being dumb."

"Well, I never wore braces, so you're half-right."

"And when do I get to read this tell-all of your enchanted youth?"

"Bradford, you are not getting anywhere near my journal."

"Ouch, definitely hit a nerve there. Now I really want to read it."

"No chance, Buckhead boy."

"Hey, speaking of which, I have to run down to Atlanta sometime. All of my family furniture is in storage, and I want to get a few pieces moved up here."

I was an only child. When I was twelve, my parents died in an auto accident, after which I lived with Aunt Grace in her stately Buckhead home until she too died, the summer before I started med school. After I graduated, I signed a three-year contract with Watervalley. In return for my services as the sole doctor, the town would pay off my med school debts. I was also provided with a furnished house only a few blocks from the clinic. But some of the furnishings were rather dated, and I had a huge inventory of heirloom furniture in storage, left from my parents' estate and Aunt Grace's house.

"While I'm there," I said, "I'll try to locate my old journal. If I find it, we can swap."

Christine appeared unenthused. "I seriously doubt that would be a fair trade. What did you write about?"

"Hmm, mostly sports and girls." I paused briefly and added, "And girls who were good sports."

"Shocker."

"So, did you and your mom find many things for the yard sale?" Every year around the Fourth of July, several of the churches and civic clubs in Watervalley sponsored a huge charity yard sale to help out some benevolent organization.

"Yes. A ton of things. I don't think anyone has been up there in the five years since Daddy died. Lamps, an old sewing machine, tennis racquets, camping gear, and a bunch of my grandmother Cavanaugh's vases and china that were packed away back in the sixties."

"And an old journal."

"And an old journal."

"I have to admit," I said, "you've made me curious." I leaned forward, propping my elbows on my desk. "Okay, Christine Ann Chambers, time to confess. What deep, dark mysteries are hidden in those pages?"

Folding her arms, Christine eased back in her chair, wearing a flirtatious expression of stealth and amusement, her eyes full of secret warmth. "Not happening, Bradford."

"Oh, I see. So that's how it is, huh? Well, no matter." I slumped back into my chair. "Actually, besides my journal, there are three pretty important things I want to find in the Atlanta storage."

"Oh?"

"Yep. There's a box of old family photo albums and some of my mom's jewelry that I want to bring back with me."

Christine nodded thoughtfully. "Your mother's jewelry . . . hmm." She unfolded her arms and tucked a strand of her long brown hair behind her ear. Given the intensity of our relationship, I was sure she was curious about the mention of my mother's jewelry, but she was tactful enough not to ask. Her voice was tender and accommodating.

"Well, that all sounds very sweet. I'm sure it would be nice to have some family photos and some things of your mom's around you."

I stared at the bookshelves that lined the walls of my stately office, formerly the library of the antebellum home turned community clinic.

Christine's words conjured my best memory, my mother. Evelyn Bradford was a slim, tall, elegant woman with sandy hair and sky blue eyes, traits that I had inherited—except perhaps for the elegant part. I remember Aunt Grace, my dad's sister, once telling me that my mother had the prettiest legs she had ever seen. My mother was an only child and had come from a modestly wealthy family in Atlanta. Yet when my father, a doctor like myself, had set up practice in a rural Georgia community, she had willingly embraced small-town life.

In all my memories of her, whether sitting at a Little League game, going out for an evening, or working in her flower beds, she always wore a pearl necklace. As gracious and approachable as she was, there was something in my mother's private definition of herself that wanted to hold on to the aura of her Buckhead upbringing, a keepsake of her roots. I wanted to find those pearls.

I did, in fact, have definitive plans for some of my mother's jewelry. But I was far from ready to divulge any particulars. The musical sound of Christine's voice pulled me from my momentary trance.

"Luke, what is the third thing you're hoping to find?"

"Excuse me, the what?"

"The third thing. You said that besides your journal, there are three things you will be looking for in storage."

"Oh yes." I nodded and smiled softly. "There's something very special, something very dear to me from my younger days that I want to give you."

Christine leaned forward in her chair. Her entire body language seemed to be melting toward me in an expression of yielding endearment. She spoke in a pleased, excited voice. "Oh, and what would that be?"

"My old Beavis and Butt-Head T-shirt."

The pencil she sent flying only barely missed me.

CHAPTER 5
The Sisters

There was still plenty of warmth and daylight to be enjoyed when shortly after five we walked out to my car. Since Christine was a schoolteacher and off for summer break, we had a delightful flexibility in scheduling our time together, which of late had become a daily expectation. We laughed at ourselves about this new reality. I was thirty and Christine was in her late twenties . . . both of us old enough to have developed very independent lives. Yet our hunger for each other's company had become part of every day.

"Listen," I said, "I've got a house call to make in about an hour. You want to grab a bite to eat before I go?"

"Sure? Is the house call anything serious?"

"Nah, just following up on something. It's out past Gallivant's Crossing in the Mennonite community. Let's drop by the bakery. Estelle may have some wraps left over from lunch."

Christine climbed into the passenger side of my convertible, a 1960 Austin-Healey. I could never have afforded such an expensive second car had it not been willed to me by one of my patients who passed away. Watervalley's local mechanic, Chick McKissick, had beautifully restored the classic roadster.

I drove the few short blocks to the downtown square and the newly opened Sweetlife Bakery. Connie Thompson, my saintly, stern, and unexpectedly wealthy housekeeper, and her flamboyant sister, Estelle Pillow, were the owners.

Despite her sixty years, Connie was a lively, robust black woman with a brilliant mind, a no-nonsense demeanor, and a heart of gold. Soon after my arrival the previous year, she had agreed to keep house and cook to help me make a smooth transition as the new town doctor. After a rocky start, she had become a beloved friend. Now she came to help out only once or twice a week, but we still enjoyed an endearing relationship.

Estelle was in her early fifties and had recently retired from a professorship at Vanderbilt University to return to Watervalley and start the bakery. Originally, Connie had been less than enthusiastic about the new business, but eventually she had warmed to the idea and had become a silent partner in her sister's venture . . . at least, silent in the figurative sense.

I parked the car in front. As we entered, I noticed something odd down the street. Luther Whitmore had just walked out of the Tilted Tulip, Watervalley's local flower shop, and was carrying a bouquet of daisies. With his face framed in its familiar scowl, he walked straight to his car, oblivious to the rest of the world. Luther's buying flowers for someone was pretty much on par with a sign of the Apocalypse. I turned and followed Christine inside the bakery, curious about what I had just seen.

We found Connie and Estelle in the kitchen; squared-off with arms folded, they were engaged in a highly audible and enthusiastic discussion. In any other setting, this would be known as yelling, but with these two, it was daily discourse laced with a peculiar, underlying bond of affection.

"Estelle, sweetie! I know that technically corn bread is bread, but I don't think we should put it with the ciabatta and the baguettes." Connie was in rare form, lecturing her younger sister.

"Well, I can't believe my ears, Constance Grace. You're talking about Momma's corn bread recipe. It was so good people wanted to write poetry about it."

"Oh heavens, girl. Cousin Shirley tried to get Momma to make it for a wedding cake. Everyone knows it's good. But you're putting it in the wrong display."

It seemed that both sisters were masters of speaking passionately under a facade of detached indifference, as if a breezy boredom were crucial to the art of arguing.

Estelle still wasn't yielding. "I'll have you know I went through a very meticulous process to determine where to put the corn bread."

Connie regarded her skeptically. "Mmm-hmm. And what process was that? The one potato, two potato, three potato method?"

"Constance, you know when you start talking like that, it only means there's no logical basis for your argument."

"Estelle, honey, I'm just saying the corn bread ought to be with the chess pies and other Southern baked goods and not in the artisan breads display. It's just not efficient."

This insight deflated some of Estelle's bluster, and she hesitated for a moment. I suspected she finally saw the wisdom of Connie's assertion but wasn't quite ready to acquiesce. She responded with a reserved voice and raised chin. "We'll see. Efficiency takes time."

With that pronouncement, she walked triumphantly across the kitchen and back out to the front of the store. As she passed us, she offered a gushing and engaging "Hi, you two," to Christine and me, flipping her hand in a sprightly manner and radiating a bubbly smile as if addressing an infant in a carriage. The two of us grinned, doing our best to muzzle our outright laughter. As always, Estelle and Connie's exchange lacked any real sting of hostility. It was their norm for spirited conversation.

Meanwhile, Connie had removed her glasses and was rubbing the bridge of her nose. She stared straight ahead in bewilderment.

"Mmm-mmm. Efficiency takes time. I'm going to have to dwell on that one for a while." She shrugged, gushed a short laugh, and turned to us. "So, how are you two lovebirds?"

"Hungry," I responded. "And sorry about barging in on the business meeting, but it was just too entertaining to walk away from."

Connie cut her eyes at me and spoke with her usual deadpan intonation. "Mmm-hmm. Do tell." She shook her head in exasperation. But then, just as quickly, she exhaled another abrupt laugh. "It's just my crazy sister, the *pain de boulanger*, being a pain in the you know what." The hint of a smile remained at the edges of her mouth.

My close relationship with the two sisters afforded me carte blanche access to the treats of the bakery. I casually grabbed one of the newly frosted cupcakes from a nearby worktable. "Ah, come on, Connie. Admit it. Estelle is a load of fun. She's such a personality, it's kinda hard not to love her."

Connie dropped her chin and regarded me from above the top of her gold-inlay glasses. "Why wouldn't anyone love her personality? She has several to choose from."

I took a bite of the cupcake and handed it to Christine. Connie spoke again.

"So, big plans for the evening?"

Abandoning any pretense of good etiquette, I spoke through my half-swallowed bite. "Not really. I need to make a house call out in the Mennonite community and work a little of my magic. We thought we'd grab a quick bite first."

"Mmm-hmm," Connie responded in low reprimand. "Not if you choke on that cupcake first. Where are your manners, young man?"

I swallowed and continued. "Jacob Yoder came by today and asked me if I would come check on his dad. Apparently his father's eyesight has gotten worse, but he refuses to come to town to see the doctor. So, looks like the doctor is going to see him."

"Well," Connie responded, "that's certainly good of you."

"Maybe. Truth is, I've never seen a Mennonite village. Thought it might be interesting. What's the difference between them and the Amish?"

"The two are ecclesiastical cousins, but the Amish are less adapted to modern technology. Even so, the Watervalley Mennonites are an Old Order community and pretty basic."

"So, no phone, no lights, no motorcar?"

"Yeah, something like that. Anyway, busy day at the clinic?"

"Not too bad. Looked down a few sore throats, put in a few stitches, and did a physical on a rat in a black suit."

"Oh, so Luther came by to see you?"

"That obvious, huh?"

"His liver finally telling him that he's not immortal?"

"No. Genetics didn't take a holiday when Luther was born. He's got a chink or two in his armor, but otherwise he's pretty indestructible."

Connie nodded. She knew that I wouldn't divulge confidential patient information about Luther, despite how much I disliked him. "Those superpowers must have come from his mother's side. She was a tall, handsome woman. His father's people, on the other hand, were a little different. You shake that side of the family tree and a few nuts fall out."

"Did his father run the newspaper, too?"

"No, Luther inherited it from his mother's side. His father farmed and had a place near the Mennonite settlement out by Moon Lake. Luther grew up out there. His dad battled lung cancer, so they sold the farm and moved to town when Luther was in his early teens. The family kept Moon Lake to be a homesite for Luther . . . not that he's ever wanted to live there, the way he's got it all fenced off."

"I know. Why in the world did he do that?"

"Your guess is as good as mine. Claire, his ex-wife, and I were friends. Even she didn't know. Said he never wanted to talk about it."

I shrugged and let the matter drop. Luther was a curiosity, but he had occupied enough of my world for one day. "Anyway, I was hoping there are a few wraps left over from lunch? Mind if we grab a couple before I head out to the promised land?"

"Check the back fridge and help yourself. We're about to close up."

"You and Estelle have big plans this evening?"

This evoked a despairing slump from Connie. She spoke in a breezy monotone. "Oh, yeah. Estelle and I are observing our Tuesday night ritual. We make spaghetti and watch old Elvis movies. She sits there and giggles, and I contemplate setting myself on fire."

After raiding the fridge, we bid Connie good-bye and made our way back out to the front of the bakery, where Estelle and her assistant, Louise Fox, were cleaning up for the day.

Louise was my next-door neighbor on Fleming Street. In her early forties, she was a widow raising a brilliant, albeit quirky, thirteen-year-old son named Will. The sudden loss of her husband more than a year ago had left Louise in a spiral of alcoholism and imminent bankruptcy, but a recent turn of fortune had restored the family's financial standing, and with Connie's help, Louise had recovered from her struggles with addiction. She smiled warmly at me as we entered.

I left a twenty on the counter, waved, and headed for the door, but not before Estelle, who was more touchy-feely than airport security, came over and grabbed me.

"Now, sugar, you know you can't leave here without giving me a squnch."

I played along with enthusiasm. "Oh, I wouldn't dream of it."

Estelle was a half foot shorter than me, and despite being rather portly and fifty, she had a lively, pretty face. She approached from the side and wrapped her arms around me in a gushing hug, making a deep "mmm-mmm" sound.

She addressed Christine. "Now, don't be getting jealous, sweetie. Every well-stocked kitchen has a little brown sugar in it."

Christine's improvisation was quick and natural. "I don't know, Estelle. You're kind of the total package. I'm feeling a little threatened."

Having squeezed most of the oxygen out of me, Estelle finally let go and took a step back. She lifted her head in a rather queenly fashion and spoke airily, as if making a closing soliloquy. "I know, I know. But don't worry, dear. For you, I'll keep my irrefutable charms in check and just play catch and release. There're always more fish in the sea."

This brought no small amount of laughter from the three women, who were clearly having a good chuckle at my expense. I smiled, shrugged, and put my hand lightly on Christine's back, ushering her toward the door.

Estelle continued laughing, quite pleased with herself. "You two have fun."

As we exited, I noticed that two doors down, Trina Hamilton, the owner of the Tilted Tulip, was locking up for the day. I asked Christine to give me a minute, and I walked toward Trina. Curiosity had gotten the better of me.

"Hey, Trina, mind if I ask you a question?"

"Oh, hi, Dr. Bradford." Trina was a small but pert and engaging woman. She dressed smartly and had short blond hair with bangs that wonderfully accentuated her lively brown eyes. She had a degree in marketing and had been an account manager with IBM before moving to Watervalley. Her outgoing and winning personality had a professional polish a notch above the norm. She had both a love and a gift for flower arranging and had owned the shop for almost a decade.

Trina peered around me, noticing Christine standing next to the Austin-Healey parked down the street. "I can open back up if you want to buy some flowers, Dr. Bradford. But I think you've lost the element of surprise."

"Thanks. Actually, I just have a question."

"Sure."

"Was that Luther Whitmore I saw coming out of here a little while ago?"

Her puzzled face relaxed into an amused smile. "It sure was."

"Any idea what that's all about?"

She nodded her understanding. "Does seem odd, doesn't it? Every year on May twenty-seventh, Luther comes in and buys a bouquet of daisies. It's always the same. He calls ahead and places the order, comes in and complains about the price, then buys them and leaves. It's just speculation, but I figure it's his mother's birthday and he puts them on her gravesite."

"Well, I guess that makes sense. Even Luther had a mother." I paused and smiled. "Sorry to be so nosy. It just struck me as strange."

Trina smiled warmly. "Tell me about it."

"So, daisies, huh?"

"Yeah, same every year. Kind of an odd choice."

"Why is that?"

"Plenty of daisies grow wild in the countryside. Luther can pick them just about anywhere."

"I suspect he would rather wear a tutu than be seen picking flowers."

"Sounds about right." She tilted her head and glanced around me, once again observing Christine waiting at the car. "Anyway, you should surprise that pretty girl with a dozen roses sometime. Rumor has it that women like that kind of thing."

"So noted," I responded heartily.

"We do weddings too, you know, Dr. Bradford."

I swallowed hard and spoke with a discerning smile. "Let me try the dozen roses sometime and we'll see what happens."

Trina's eyes twinkled. "Funny thing, I haven't met a woman yet who thought later was better than sooner."

I smiled obligingly and held up my hand in a gesture of departure. "Thanks, Trina. I'll get back with you . . . sooner."

I returned to the car, and to Christine's amused scrutiny.

"Hey, sorry to keep you waiting. I just needed to ask Trina a quick question."

As we buckled ourselves in, Christine looked over at me and said a single word. "Yellow."

"Excuse me?"

Christine nodded with casual assurance. "Umm-hmm. Yellow."

"Yellow as in what?"

"Yellow roses. They're my favorite."

"Okay, do you have ears like a wolf and forgot to mention it?"

"No. It's just that Trina has a standard policy of telling every man she talks to that he should buy his sweetheart a dozen roses. She's done that for years. I'm sure she didn't miss that opportunity with you, so I thought I'd help you out. Yellow." Having confidently reiterated that, she smiled shrewdly.

I slowly realized that I was once again falling into the trap of small-town life. I responded obediently. "I'll see what I can do."

Christine stared straight ahead, all the while wearing an irrepressible smirk.

We stopped by the house to eat our wraps and take care of Rhett, my golden retriever. Something about Christine's presence always perked him up. As we entered the kitchen, he constantly wagged his tail at her and on more than one occasion tried to leap up and give her a dog hug.

"Hey, Casanova," I said teasingly. "Go find your own girlfriend." He ignored my admonishment.

"So, this will be your first visit to a Mennonite community?" Christine inquired.

"Yup. Truth is, I just want to see what their world looks like. I mean, how much fun can they be having without, you know, the benefit of duct tape and chili dogs?"

"When I was young, Momma would drive out to the Mennonites to buy their canned fruits and preserves. Best blackberry jam imaginable."

"So, did you know any of them growing up?"

"Not really. They keep to themselves pretty much. They were always nice, but not real chatty."

"Well, I don't know beans about them. They didn't exactly hang out at the Galleria when I was growing up in Atlanta. The first one I ever met was Jacob Yoder when he first came by the clinic a couple of months ago."

"Two or three hundred Mennonites live in the area. I know the Yoders are one of the larger families, but I don't think I've ever met Jacob."

"He's in his mid-forties. I got the impression he's a person of authority in their community, sort of an unofficial mayor."

"Why won't his dad come to the clinic?"

"Don't know. I read up on the Mennonites earlier today. They don't oppose modern medicine. I think his dad's just stubborn."

"If you're not too late, drop by the farm later." Christine lowered her voice, speaking mirthfully. "Maybe I'll read you something from my old journal, make a few comparisons."

"Nice. Put me in a lineup with some old boyfriends, huh? Won't that be fun?"

"Bradford, sarcasm is definitely not your long suit. Besides, I didn't write about old boyfriends."

"Seriously? I thought that's why teenage girls keep journals in the first place."

Christine's words seemed guarded. "Oh, I wrote about a boy from time to time."

"Really? And what was he like?"

"He was wonderful."

"Wonderful, huh? Well, hey . . . I bathe often and I'm lice free. Where does that put me in the ranking?"

"I think Rhett just moved in front of you."

"Who was this guy anyway?"

Christine smiled and regarded me shrewdly. "Wouldn't you like to know, Bradford? Wouldn't you like to know?"

CHAPTER 6
The Mennonites

I had grown to love Watervalley. Tucked away in the rural landscape of Tennessee, the town stood in the middle of a wide, fertile plain surrounded in all directions by farms and rolling pastures. Soaring hills rose in the distance, encircling the entire valley. It seemed a fortunate destiny rested upon this modest community, an innate sense that life here was permeated with richly satisfying possibilities. Combined with the immense beauty of this late-spring day, my journey had a feeling of impending discovery.

With the top down on the Austin-Healey, I passed the shaded lawns and picket fences along Fleming Street. Life in this quiet small town had all the trappings of a carefree lemonade summer. The air was rich with the smells of honeysuckle, lilac, and freshly mowed grass. Neighborhood kids were riding bikes or playing in their yards, squealing and laughing and slamming screen doors.

Soon I was in the open countryside, passing great fields of corn and soybeans before turning onto the road known as Gallivant's Crossing. Following the penciled map Jacob Yoder had drawn for me, I drove deep into the hills until I came upon a chert lane called

Mercy Creek Road. Dense trees lined both sides of the narrow passage, leaving it completely shaded with a thick canopy of leaves. After about half a mile, the woods on the left ended abruptly, opening up to a broad meadow, a scene so captivating that I brought the car to a stop.

The view before me was a still life painting framed on three sides by tall hills that rose sharply. High above, light summer clouds hung in the panorama of soft blue sky, made all the more brilliant by its contrast with the lush and vibrant green of the pasture below. In the foreground of this splendid canvas were several massive trees that marked the humble corners of a remnant foundation anchored by a stout fireplace and tall chimney, the remaining bones of a long-ago cottage, its stones now starched white from years of rain and sun. Just beyond the foundation stood a small enclosure outlined by the last vestiges of a stone fence and rusted iron gate, the once-proud citadel of a modest vegetable garden. Farther back, a pond surrounded by thick tussocks of wild grass lay in the shadow of a large, dilapidated barn.

Under the warm, hazy light of afternoon, I could easily imagine a quaint farmhouse that years ago completed this idyllic setting. The scene was so enchanting, so entrancing that I wanted to pull down the grassy drive to take a closer look. Yet that would have to wait. First, I needed to find the home of Jacob Yoder.

I continued on through more tangled woods, thinking I had lost my way. But after crossing over a modest ridge, I entered a different world. Before me was a wide expanse of low rolling fields, neat crops, and well-manicured fences. Years of sweat and toil had transformed the land into orderly farming operations.

I passed by simple white frame houses bordered by large gardens and dominated by great, boxy barns. Laundry lines were strung with black broadfall pants that billowed in the late-afternoon breeze.

I found the address and drove the short lane to Jacob's house, parking on the edge of the yard. Now that I was here, I felt awkward, an intruder. I grabbed my medical bag and had the sudden nagging wish that I had brought my lab coat, to give a more professional appearance.

My arrival in the shiny, top-down Austin-Healey hadn't gone unnoticed. Two women in long plain dresses topped by aprons were sitting in the shade of the front porch, and several children, three barefoot boys it appeared, were playing in the lush grass next to the house.

As I approached, the boys gathered in a row on the side of the high porch, partially out of sight and peering above the wooden floor, eyeing me with great curiosity. The two women stopped whatever handwork they were doing and stood. The younger of the two, a small but firmly built woman, probably in her early forties, turned and spoke to one of the children. Immediately, the largest of them, a boy of about twelve, took off in a blistering run toward the nearby barn.

I stopped a few feet from the porch and spoke cautiously. "Hello, I'm Dr. Bradford. I'm looking for Jacob Yoder. He asked me to come by this afternoon. Am I at the right house?"

Saying nothing, the two women looked at each other uneasily. Their eyes seemed to be communicating an array of well-understood thoughts from which I was completely excluded. The children continued to shyly conceal themselves, their gazes riveted on my face with total fascination.

I sensed the two women's discomfort and was uncertain as to their custom regarding talking to a stranger. "Perhaps I should come back at another time?"

Again there was silence. The older one, who was rather rounded and didn't seem to have a happy temperament, gave a subtle but tight-lipped nod to the younger woman. She turned to me.

"Jacob is my husband. He is at the barn. John has gone to get him." She spoke plainly and kindly. Now that the decision to speak had been made, she seemed more relaxed. And while she didn't actually smile, her eyes shone warmly.

Jacob arrived a few moments later. He was a man of modest height, his lean shape disguised under his loose clothing. His dark hair and beard were peppered with gray. And despite his generally serious demeanor, Jacob had a relaxed manner about him along with thoughtful eyes that spoke of a generous and considerate nature. I suspected that around his own kind he probably laughed easily and often. He shook my hand firmly and spoke in an English laced with a German inflection.

"Thank you for coming, Doctor. This is my wife, Hannah, and my mother, Letta."

I smiled and nodded. An awkward silence ensued. Jacob sensed my uneasiness and spoke accommodatingly.

"Come with me, Dr. Bradford. I will show you to the patient." As Jacob and I walked, he spoke with an affable confidence. "Father can be a little headstrong, so I appreciate your patience with him."

We entered the barn through a side door into a large open workshop with a wide plank floor. Seemingly dozens of woodworking tools hung in orderly rows above several workbenches. The room had the rich, earthy smell of stacked hardwood, mellowed and seasoned over years. There were bins of similarly cut wood pieces, small components that seemed part of a larger production.

"We make chairs and furniture here, mostly during the winter months when we are not farming." Jacob explained. "But my father's age is catching up with him, so he spends less time in the fields and more time in here." He nodded toward a man in the far corner of the room with his back turned to us. He was molding a piece of wood on a lathe that was powered by pumping a foot pedal connected to a series of wheels and belts.

Jacob tapped him on the shoulder, but it seemed he was already keenly aware of our presence. He turned slowly and regarded Jacob with a hard frown. Then he looked sternly at me. I could almost feel the weight of his heavy gaze.

"Father, this is Dr. Bradford. He has come to check your eyes. Dr. Bradford, this is my father, Eli Yoder."

The man facing me was an older version of Jacob, except he lacked his son's accommodating countenance. Instead, he regarded me grimly with a glare of withering intensity. He had a thin mouth absent of humor. Saying nothing, he lifted his arm to run his sleeve across his red and sweating face. His resentment of me seemed instinctive, and soon enough he turned his sullen glare on Jacob. Just that quickly the heat seemed to be thickening in the room's corners.

But Jacob was unfazed. "Father, you agreed to do this."

Again Eli looked at me with haughty suspicion before grunting a low sound of acknowledgment.

"What do you need him to do, Doctor?"

I retrieved an eye chart from my bag, hung it on a nail on a nearby wall, and stepped off twenty feet toward the center of the room. I grabbed a ladder-back chair and placed it at that point. Eli made no expression but seemed to understand. He walked over and sat in the chair, moving with a brooding reluctance. I asked him to read the letters above the red line. Before he could respond, Jacob interrupted.

"Father can't do that."

"He can't read?"

"No, he reads fine. He cannot see certain colors."

"Oh." I nodded in understanding, walked to the chart, and

pointed to the line I wanted him to read. He did so, but with difficulty. I retrieved my ophthalmoscope to look directly into his eyes. The clouding over his lens was readily apparent.

I spoke directly to Jacob. "Your father has the onset of cataracts. It's blurring his vision. I need him to come to the clinic for a thorough eye exam."

"Is there a treatment?"

"Sure. Surgery. It would have to be done over at Regional Hospital, but it's pretty routine."

Jacob nodded thoughtfully. His father heard my words as well. Aware that the exam was over, he stood and grabbed the chair, returning it to its place. He squared his shoulders and regarded me solemnly for a final time.

Jacob and I walked back to the house. Along the way, I asked if he wanted to go ahead and set up a time for his dad's appointment. I knew that this group of Mennonites didn't use telephones, and if the appointment wasn't made now, doing so would require a trip to town.

"Thank you, but not today, Dr. Bradford. Father harbors some old resentment and hasn't been to town in many years. His eyes may have to get a little worse before he's willing to go there."

I nodded, and as we walked back to his house, I surveyed the well-manicured farmland around us. "If I'm not mistaken, Moon Lake is not far from here. Is that correct?"

"Yes. It is just beyond that ridge," Jacob responded, pointing to a low rise in the near distance. "Father used to play there when he was a child."

"I understand it has been fenced up for years," I said casually, not wanting to reveal that I had a key.

"I believe that is correct." Jacob added nothing more. We returned to the porch to find Hannah and her mother-in-law gathering their handwork and carrying it into the house. "So, Dr. Bradford, thank you for coming. What do we owe you for your services?"

"Not a thing. Glad to make the trip out. Besides, I don't think I helped your dad much."

Jacob spoke with warm assurance. "For now, Father is unwilling to help himself. And I wouldn't think of letting your kindness go uncompensated." He turned and said something in German to his mother, Letta, who nodded and spoke to the oldest boy.

"John, get the red and green one from the basket in the kitchen."

The boy returned a moment later with a neatly folded quilt that he held out to me. I turned to Jacob.

"Look, I really appreciate the gesture, but this is completely unnecessary. A lot more time went into making this quilt than it took me to make the drive out here."

Jacob took the quilt from the boy and put it in my arms. "And you spent a lot more time studying to be a doctor than was put into making this quilt. Please, take it along with my thanks."

Refusal at this point would have been rude. "We'll consider this payment in full for when your dad does come to the clinic." I shook Jacob's hand once more, thanked him, and walked the short distance to the Austin-Healey. But as I dropped the quilt onto the passenger seat, something fell from the folds. It was a bonnet that must have found its way there by accident.

I took it and walked back to the house. By then Jacob had returned to the barn, and Hannah and Letta had gone inside. I rapped on the front door and waited. Moments passed and my mind drifted, leaving me unprepared for the person standing there when the door opened.

She was seventeen or eighteen, notably tall and straight shouldered with a slender figure that narrowed gracefully at the waist, accentuating the fluid, maidenly curve of her hips. I was immediately taken by the symmetrical prettiness of her face, which had a fragile, translucent delicacy. Her raven hair had a prominent widow's peak that protruded from under the rim of her kapp. And while everything about her manner and mode of dress was fashioned toward plainness, she was blessed with extraordinary dark eyes that were round and deep and framed by thick, luxurious lashes.

She gasped lightly upon seeing me, making it clear that it was someone else's knock she had been expecting. The other Mennonites I had seen that afternoon—Hannah, Jacob, and his parents—had something of a rumpled sweatiness about them brought on by the physical labor of their day. But this young woman and her clothes were fresh and clean.

"Hi. I'm Dr. Bradford. I wanted to return this. I think it mistakenly found its way into the quilt that was given to me." I held the bonnet out to her.

She stood frozen, her face absent of emotion save for the intensity of her expressive eyes. In any other setting, a face such as hers, with its haunting and vulnerable beauty, would be on a magazine cover or in one of those cryptic perfume commercials that advertise by whispering incomplete sentences. Hannah's voice broke the silence.

"Rebecca, you are being rude." The tone was more comment than reprimand. Hannah had entered the room and politely took the bonnet from my outstretched hand. "Dr. Bradford, this is Rebecca, our only daughter."

I smiled. With her perfect posture and willowy figure, she stood four or five inches taller than her mother. "Rebecca, good to meet you."

She nodded, the corners of her mouth touched by a thoughtful and gentle smile. Hannah explained, "We are expecting company for dinner tonight, a young man from the neighboring farm who has been away for some time."

I nodded in understanding. "I'm surprised you don't have a line of young men waiting at the door. Your daughter is very pretty."

The two women exchanged reserved glances. Rebecca looked down, clearly not accustomed to receiving compliments, her modest nature making her all the more appealing. Silence ensued, and I feared that perhaps my praise had overstepped. It was time to leave. I smiled, bid them good-bye, and returned to the car.

CHAPTER 7
Songs and Summer Nights

I drove back through the thick woods of Mercy Creek Road and once again came upon the meadow opening to the old ruins. Slowly I edged the car down the gravel drive that was nothing more than two stony paths separated by thick weeds. I parked under a large maple and cut the engine. Except for a lonely breeze that gently fluttered the leaves of the great tree, I was surrounded by a swallowing silence, a uniform tranquillity. This small lap of land, this perfect meadow, was strangely and woefully beautiful. The moment held me still.

I stepped through the tall grass, walking around the old foundation, and past the rock wall of the garden plot to take in the small pond. In time I circled back, standing on the outside of the cottage ruins. As much as a century ago someone had placed these rocks one upon the other to build a hearth for meals and warmth. Now the abandonment and desolation of this perfect place seemed such a waste. I couldn't help but think that some wretched story was buried in its past, that these remnant stones were a boneyard of tragic memories. Once, this small cottage lay at the center of someone's life, some obscure soul whose light was spent molding this small valley into his own Eden.

And it seemed in that moment, standing just outside the old foundation, I was touched by something strange and fleeting, a warm and uplifting revelation.

That was when I heard the singing.

At first, I ignored it, believing it to be nothing more than a peculiar noise floating on the wind. But in time the mellow notes echoed unmistakably across the small amphitheater of the grassy meadow. It was the melodious voice of a man. The words were not discernible, and yet the tune was strangely familiar, existing just beyond the gateway of memory. I slowly turned full circle, listening, looking, and straining into the distance to determine the source of the lilting and sweetly melancholy song. But it seemed to have no origin. It simply drifted on the air.

I breathed a muffled laugh. My mind refused to accept what my ears were hearing, and yet, the pleasing, silvery tune continued. I spoke aloud to no one. "Okay, fine. Nice voice. Why are you singing?"

I felt a little foolish and shook my head, again exhaling a short laugh. During my brief time in Watervalley I had occasionally heard stories of voices singing in the distance. Whether lore or fable, it was said that the delicate tones of ancient hymns could be briefly heard, coming from beyond the brow of the next hill or above the gliding flow of a nearby brook. I had accepted these tales with a respectful silence, relegating such experiences to the charm and superstition of the rural mind-set.

But there was no superstition here. This time, I was the one hearing the singing.

In time, the sound ebbed and finally disappeared, returning

the ruins once again to silence. Even for me and even in that moment, the incident was difficult to take seriously. It seemed that I was inclined to cast anything supernatural or miraculous into the realm of false notion, ignorance, or happenchance. I could make no sense of it and shook my head.

"Only in Watervalley."

I walked toward the low stone foundation, then stepped over it and into the enclosure of the original cottage. Once I was there, my eyes were drawn to a flash of color on the ancient hearth. I walked over and stared in disbelief. Carefully laid in the center of the elevated stones was a fresh bouquet of flowers.

They were daisies.

I bent and touched them. Given the surreal nature of the last several minutes, I found myself doubting my senses. There was no wrapping or tag, just two dozen or more delicate long-stemmed flowers. I stood abruptly and looked around to see if anyone was nearby, my mind immediately suspecting Luther Whitmore. But I saw no one. Still, it had been two hours since I had seen Luther downtown—plenty of time for him to have left these here.

And yet, I couldn't be sure. I had passed plenty of small patches of daisies growing wild along the road. Perhaps it was just an odd coincidence. Nevertheless, someone had been here not long before my arrival and, more than the voice I had heard in the wind, that thought gave me an eerie feeling. It was time to leave.

I drove back to Gallivant's Crossing and made my way out to Christine's. She met me on the shaded front porch of her family's large farmhouse with a glass of iced tea and an endearing smile.

"So, how was it?"

I plopped into one of the wicker chairs. "Quite interesting, actually. I met Jacob's wife and mother. They were pleasant but reserved. I did the exam on his dad. Boy, was he ever a stern one. Oh, and I met Jacob's daughter. Probably about eighteen. Really pretty and really tall."

Christine nodded. "So, what was the area like? You know, the houses and the barns?"

"Well kept and plain."

"Gee. Didn't see that coming."

"Anyway, apparently the daughter I met was expecting an admirer. One of the neighborhood farm boys was coming over for dinner. I'd love to see what that looks like."

"It's probably very sweet."

"It's probably very stifling."

"Oh, so is it stifling when you eat a meal with my family?"

"They're not exactly Mennonites." I sipped the iced tea and settled comfortably into the deep cushions. "Besides, I'm just spitballing here, but I'm guessing Mennonite courtships are kind of a negotiation. Like, you know, I'll give you my daughter along with two cows and four chickens."

"I guess if word gets around that my family owns a dairy herd, those Mennonite guys will be beating a path to my door."

I winced. "Hmm, I don't know, Chambers. You're kinda on the homely side."

She lowered her chin in feigned offense, repeating my words slowly. "Homely side? Tread carefully here, Bradford."

I rubbed my chin reflectively. "Yeah, I mean, look, you might be able to get a date at a lumber camp . . . but short of that, it's kinda iffy. You may have to throw in a couple of horses and a bushel of rutabaga to get any serious takers. These Mennonite guys are different. They want a woman with skills."

Christine laughed at my teasing, yet continued to play along, speaking reproachfully. "I have skills."

"I'm talking about domestic skills. I don't think a great jump shot is high on the list." Christine had been an All-State basketball player.

"I'll have you know, Luke Bradford, that I have a thorough understanding of sewing and cooking and cleaning." She paused and added in a low, mirthful voice, "Granted, understanding them is pretty much where my interest stops."

"And there's the girl I love. I knew she'd show up soon."

Through her own laughter, Christine spoke with renewed authority. "For your information, Bradford, Mennonite courtship has traditionally had some pretty interesting practices."

"You mean besides holding hands and sharing a zesty cup of hot chocolate?"

"I don't know if the Watervalley Mennonites still do this, but they used to have a courtship practice called bundling."

"Okay, you got me on that one. What's bundling?"

"It's where the boy and the girl are each fully clothed, wrapped in individual blankets, and lie in bed together. They are expected to talk to each other all night."

"What if talking leads to show-and-tell?"

"They put a board in the middle of the bed, just in case."

"And if someone goes overboard?"

She stared at me blankly. "Why do I talk to you?"

I took another swallow of tea while Christine did her best to muster a look of admonishment. "I have to tell you, though," I said. "On the way there, I came across the most interesting place. It was the ruins of an old farmhouse that sat in the middle of this absolutely beautiful meadow surrounded by high hills. The place looks to have burned down decades ago and been left abandoned. I stopped on the way back and looked around. It was both enchanting and haunting."

"You actually stopped and walked around it?"

"Sure. Why not? There seems to be a story there."

Christine laughed at me and shook her head.

"What?" I responded in mock offense.

She smiled through her words. "You, that's what."

"Meaning?"

"You can take the doctor out of research, but you can't take the researcher out of the doctor." She was referring to my well-known desire to do medical research instead of working as a small-town doctor.

"Okay. So I have a natural curiosity. Anyway, laugh all you want. There was something really fascinating about the place."

"Where was it, anyway?"

"On Mercy Creek Road."

"Hold it. Mercy Creek Road?"

"Yeah, why?"

"Okay, this is wild. I saw a newspaper headline about that place earlier today."

"How?"

"Up in the attic when we were unpacking my grandmother's china this morning. The first piece I pulled out was wrapped in a newspaper from 1968. I remember looking at it because I was curious as to when the box was packed. It was on the front page from July of that year, something about the volunteer fire department getting called out in the middle of the night to a fire on Mercy Creek Road. But when they got there, they realized it belonged to the Mennonites and were told their help wasn't needed."

"Looks like someone made a poor judgment call on that one. There was nothing left but the stone foundation and the old chimney."

"I think the article said that the house was unoccupied and that the Mennonites were just letting it burn."

"Well, that doesn't make any sense. If the house was in bad shape, you'd think they would have torn it down rather than burn it down, especially in the middle of the night."

"Beats me."

"Do you still have that newspaper?"

"Yeah. I'm pretty sure I know where it is."

"I'd like to read it. Maybe you can find it before I leave."

Christine nodded. For some reason, I wasn't sure why, I decided not to mention the singing or the daisies.

"So, anything else interesting?" she inquired.

"Yeah. Apparently the Mennonite community is really close to the back side of Moon Lake." I paused a moment. "You know, if you had come along with me, we could have gone for a swim and cooled off."

"I wouldn't have had my swimsuit."

"I wouldn't have had mine either. Sounds like we would have been even."

Christine spoke with amused resignation. "Bradford, you're the king of wishful thinking."

"I'm not reaching for that scepter just yet, brown eyes. It's not an altogether out-of-the-question idea."

Christine responded with only a blushing, secretive grin. Moments passed. When she finally did speak, there was a noted change of subject.

"So, you want to watch a movie or something?"

I stretched my arms above my head. "You know, I'm pretty good right here. I've got a comfy chair, a glass of tea, a pretty girl . . . living the dream."

Twilight was approaching. Christine put ice cream into a couple of bowls, and we continued to sit in the cool of the front porch. From there we watched the sunset spread across the open fields, our voices soft and singular against the approaching darkness.

I had to laugh at myself. It was a life far from the one I had known while living in Atlanta and Nashville. In the city, the onset of the night brought about an excitement, an anticipation associated with the noise and revelry of sharing a few beers with friends and the potential for laughter, furtive glances, new attachments.

Here in Watervalley, the slow ebb of sundown brought about a tranquil, reflective close to the day. Cooler, moister air tumbled in, enveloping us in the delicate, sensuous smell of freshly cut hay. The solemn moon illuminated the countryside, casting a low white luster that vanished into the black, shadowy tucks of the distant hills. The dusty confusions of the day faded, and our world slowly lapsed into an immortal stillness, a soft, brooding hush brought on by the fading twilight.

Evenings on the summer porch had become our nightly ritual. Often I would lie on the long wicker sofa, sometimes with my head in Christine's lap, and we would talk and laugh and giggle . . . our voices echoing into the lonely distance. The hours would pass. Eventually our eyes would grow tired and we would fall silent, listening to the vast orchestral music of the night. Crickets would chirp nearby, or occasionally there was an elusive humming in the evening breeze. The low groan of a car could be heard distantly, winding its way around the far curves of Summerfield Road until the solitary headlights would fade into the black. Despite the delight and the rich comfort of being together, sagging weariness would overtake us, telling us it was time for me to go home.

But not before we passed several moments in the delightful euphoria of some long and passionate kisses. With the moonlight on her face, Christine would appear luminous. The warm, fragrant smell of her skin was intoxicating, and I would gather her in, embracing her wholly with eagerness and longing.

And in those parting moments, even against the drowning fog

of fatigue, a quiet yearning would steal through us, a desire to physically express our consuming emotions. Holding her so delightfully close left me drunk with passion. In time we would separate, whisper awkward good-byes, and I would walk to the car in the shadowy moonlight, all the while feeling the contemplative, wishful glow of her eyes upon me.

Despite the affection, the great intimacy and honesty we shared, it seemed we could not find words to discuss our arrested desire any more than we could refute its unspoken presence. We had been caught in our own trap since our first date. Perhaps from the very beginning, the vast weight of the potential each of us saw in the relationship had made us cautious, careful, respectful, apprehensive about boldly pursuing sexual intimacy. In these days of promiscuity and permissiveness, our puritanical practices seemed almost laughable, but they had become our uncanny norm.

Now, despite our abiding love and aching hearts, we stood on uncertain ground. Neither of us wanted to confirm or deny the possibility of our greater intimacy. It was a language we had not found and yet, I was certain, one we both desperately wanted to express. Perhaps we weren't so unlike the Mennonites, struggling to find harmony between the eager desires we felt and the ideals we held.

I waved good-bye and headed into the darkness.

After arriving at Fleming Street, I took care of Rhett. I didn't know it at the time, but the night would be a short one.

CHAPTER 8
The Storm

There was a stagnation in the air as I stood in the backyard waiting for Rhett to accommodate his finicky bladder. The night had a brooding and strangely malevolent feel: a grave silence save for the low droning hum of the AC unit. Rhett was painfully slow in taking care of business, seemingly more occupied with sniffing the air in a curious and cautious manner, as if sensing an imminent change.

"Come on, buddy. Some of us need to get some sleep," I said in encouragement, fully confident that he, as well as most dogs, had a thorough command of the English language. Yet his ponderous investigation continued as he paused often and peered sharply into the gloom of the great trees that surrounded the yard. A few more of my encouraging comments finally did the trick, and I made my weary way toward the back porch, up the stairs, and into bed. But the telltale signs were there. Just beyond the far hills, a storm was plummeting toward the valley, preparing to sweep down the high slopes with a savage indifference.

Sometime after midnight, a series of strobing flashes illuminated the distant horizon. Within the mystery of deep sleep, behind my closed eyes, my subconscious was blindly registering this magnificent light show. A minute later, a singular brilliant flare, infinitely more powerful than the previous distant flickers, transformed the world outside my window into daylight. Somehow, in the slumber of half sleep, I held my breath, awaiting the inevitable crushing explosion. When it came a millisecond later, I woke with a start, clutching at my dream even as it dissolved.

The lightning strike had landed downtown scant blocks from my home. It was an early vanguard of the coming fury. For the moment, the drowsy and dispirited world outside was still strangely calm, an empty stage of lifeless shadows. The hot, stealthy breath of the southern wind was just about to make its volatile presence known.

In the dark of my room, I moved to the window and gazed at the incredible blazing night sky. There was a phantasmal eeriness and yet a magnificence that captivated me in a cataleptic trance, rendering me able to do little more than stare with rapt fascination. The far horizon was flashing brilliantly, an awe-inspiring spectacle that was raw, powerful, and yet oddly transcendent.

In time, the great spectral moan of the wind increased. It howled down from the hills and hit the smooth plane of the valley floor in a roaring swell. No longer content with its serpentine glide around the trees, it now lashed bluntly against them with a ferocity and a madness. As if in a grand coordinated assault, the wind, the lightning, and the thunder exploded upon the landscape. The rain fell in sweeping sheets, and constant booms and flashes filled the night, providing fleeting snapshots of the relentless thrashing being given to the outside world.

The worst of the storm lasted twenty minutes. After that, it settled into a steady, pounding rain that eventually softened to a quiet dripping from the eaves and boughs. I had stood in the dark the entire time and now crawled back into my bed, only to find that I had company. Rhett, who normally slept on the floor, was cowered into a tight ball on the far corner. The big baby.

Exhaustion had overtaken me again, and there was an accommodating drowsiness brought about by the muffled sound of the rain on the roof above me. Still, I slept fitfully.

Shortly after four in the morning, my cell phone rang, waking me from a fragile sleep. It was Clarence, one of the Watervalley EMTs.

"Doc, need you to meet us at the clinic. We're coming in from a fire out on Covey Hollow Road. Got three firefighters with us; two with smoke inhalation, one with a severe burn on his right arm. ETA is about fifteen minutes."

I asked Clarence to have dispatch activate the clinic staff for an emergency callout and told him I would head to the clinic immediately.

I switched on the light and rubbed my face. After the initial jolt of adrenaline that accompanied such conversations in the small hours, I always felt a certain residue of confusion. I opened my eyes wide, shook my head briskly in an effort to wake up, and refocused quickly. A few minutes later, I was out the door.

The rain had moved on, leaving the night air thick and muggy. The EMT van pulled into the clinic parking lot soon after my arrival.

We hastily helped the three injured men inside. During this hurried process, Clarence and Leonard gave me a brief report on the men's condition and what had happened. The volunteer firemen had been called out to a barn fire that was dangerously close to the adjacent farmhouse. The two men suffering from smoke inhalation were Chick McKissick, the local mechanic, and Maylen

Cook, the local barber. The burn victim, unfamiliar to me, was a fellow in his mid-twenties named Clayton Ross.

I spoke decisively. "Leonard, put the burn victim in room one. Is he having respiratory issues?"

"Don't think so, Doc."

"All right. Get him settled and stay with him." I turned to the other EMT. "Clarence, go with Maylen to room three. I'll take Chick to room two. He seems to have gotten the worst of it."

My mind was racing, endeavoring to make orderly, methodic decisions. But it was a surreal moment. Seeing the exhausted, soot-smudged faces of Chick and Maylen and witnessing their violent coughing and gasping brought front and center to me the hard reality of being a small-town doctor.

These were not strangers in a metropolitan ER whom I would treat with earnest but detached professionalism. These men were *my* mechanic and *my* barber. They were friends; good, honest, uncomplicated men who lived modest lives, men who had willingly left their homes and gone into the grim misery of the storm to safeguard one of their neighbors.

After getting Chick settled, I pulled an oxygen tank to his room. He was short of breath, wheezing and hacking. His panicked face was a far cry from the normally lively and spontaneously happy fellow I knew. He was also experiencing confusion and nausea, both classic symptoms of smoke inhalation. Fortunately, my staff nurse, Ann Patterson, arrived just as Chick was inhaling two deep breaths of a bronchodilator. She helped me place a non-rebreather mask and an O_2 saturation monitor on him. I instructed her to do the same for Maylen and to let me know the results.

Like a man who had just surfaced from almost drowning, Chick gasped deeply of the oxygen-rich air. He was dirty, wet, and trembling uncontrollably as he held the oxygen mask with one hand. His other hand was drawn tightly to his chest in a twisted and unnatural way, shaking violently. I reached out and held it. "It's going to be all right, Chick."

He looked at me through frightened eyes and responded with short, jerky nods, gripping my hand ever tighter. For me, it was a heartrending, sobering moment.

"Long, slow breaths, Chick. Long, slow breaths."

Soon his oxygen saturation climbed to a safe level. By now, the rest of the staff, Cindy and Camilla, the two middle-aged sisters who were the lab tech and the phlebotomist, had arrived.

"I want you to draw an ABG and CBC on each patient." They nodded and set about the business of drawing blood for an arterial blood gas and a complete blood count, critical information that would help determine hemoglobin levels and lung functionality.

Ann reported that Maylen's oxygen levels were fine. I instructed her to collect vital signs on Maylen and Clayton while I took care of Chick. Slowly his respirations returned to normal and he sat calmly, but with a drained and anxious face. I examined him, thankfully noting that all his numbers were normal.

"Chick, you're going to be okay. I need to check on the other two, but I want to keep you here for observation."

He responded in a hoarse whisper and with a grateful nod, his body still occasionally shuddering. "Thanks, Dr. B. If you think I'll be okay, that's good." There were remnants of tears in his eyes, and he spoke with a tinge of apology. "It just . . . It just shook me up, that's all. Not being able to breathe and everything. Clayton gonna be okay?"

"I'm about to find out. Sit tight."

I checked on Maylen, who was now showing no distress and expressing a desire to go home. His wife, Alice, had arrived and was in the room with him. I examined him and asked a few questions.

Other than an occasional cough, he seemed fine. I asked him to wait for the blood test results. In his deadpan way, Maylen offered a low sound of acknowledgment.

I headed to Clayton's exam room.

From the report the EMTs had given me, part of the barn had collapsed in Clayton's direction. While turning to retreat from it, he had tripped and fallen, leaving his arm pinned momentarily under a burning pole. Before he could be pulled free, he had suffered second-degree and nearly third-degree burns on his right forearm and hand. The EMTs had triaged him with a simple sterile bandage.

By now, some of his family had arrived and were standing in the waiting room with hard, worried faces. They were talking in low voices and casting uneasy, troubled looks at one another. I nodded to them as I crossed to the exam room.

Clayton looked to be about twenty-five. He was of modest height with a tough, boxy build and strong shoulders. His eyes were bloodshot from the smoke and lack of sleep. As I entered, he stiffened in straight-backed attention and nodded with a measure of respect and reserve. Per my instructions, Ann had placed his arm on an elevated mayo table covered with a sterile drape. I introduced myself.

"Any trouble moving your fingers, Clayton?"

His answer was polite and crisp. "No, sir, don't think so."

"Feeling much pain?"

"Not too bad, sir."

His posture, manner, and frequent use of "sir" made his recent history all too obvious. "So, which branch of the service were you in?"

He smiled and seemed to relax. "Army, sir. Hundred and First Airborne. Fort Campbell. Discharged out a month ago."

I nodded thoughtfully. "Any overseas duty?"

"Afghanistan, sir. Two tours."

I pursed my lips and nodded respectfully. "Wow. That's impressive. Ever wounded?"

"Nothing except for a heart broken by a barmaid in Ramstein."

I smiled lightly. "Well, isn't that the way of things? Two tours and not a scratch. One month back in Watervalley and here we are."

"It happens, sir."

"Okay, Clayton. Here's what I need to do. I'm going to remove this bandage, see what we've got, wash and clean up the wound, and then put a new dressing on. It's probably going to hurt. I can give you a local anesthetic or a bullet to bite. Your choice."

He grinned. "Go, ahead, Doc. If it gets too bad, I'll let you know."

Fortunately, the injury was not so severe as to need a skin graft. Clayton winced a few times, and I could tell that the pain was sharp, but he gritted his way through it.

"What kind of work are you doing now, Clayton?"

"Just helping my dad on the farm. I've put in several applications around town."

"Well, you may need to do light duty to let this thing heal some. The biggest problem with burns is infection. If this gets infected, it'll upset my whole day, and no telling what it will do to yours. So, here's the plan. I want you to come back each day for me or Ann to put a new dressing on this until I say uncle."

Clayton nodded in understanding, but I could tell that this plan didn't appeal to him. His shoulders and posture slumped. Camilla had stepped into the room to give me his lab results. They looked fine, but something was bothering me. I took out my pad and wrote a note for her.

"Camilla, if you've got enough blood left from the sample, have Cindy run this test for me too." She looked at the paper and then at me before quietly leaving.

As I stepped into the hall, the slowly opening door of morning was beginning to show through the large waiting room windows. I grabbed the charts of both Maylen and Chick to review their lab tests. Fortunately, the results were good. I found both of them in Chick's exam room along with Clarence and Leonard.

To my delight, Chick seemed to be doing much better, the company of friends proving to be the best medicine. His wife, Delilah, had arrived as well. The men were engaged in a friendly banter about the events of the previous hours, replaying tense moments through a filter of wit and humor. Alice and Delilah stood by with tolerant grins that only thinly masked the mixture of relief and pride that they were no doubt feeling for their husbands. The tension of the last hour had vanished, and the lighthearted mood was a welcome relief.

Leonard was in the middle of a protracted story as I entered, and I motioned for him to continue. But within seconds, from behind the exam room door came heated voices in the hallway, followed by a yell that pierced the clinic walls.

"It shouldn't have happened, dammit. It's all their fault."

The angry announcement served as a vacuum, draining away all the laughter and merriment. A hush fell over the small gathering. I immediately stepped into the hallway, where I found Clayton and an older man. He was slightly taller than his son, thickly built with a heavy jaw and a red face. Clayton was trying to leave, but the other man seemed bent on venting his temper. Upon seeing me, he turned, speaking sharply.

"How long will it take this to heal?"

I responded coolly. "Who are you, sir?"

"I'm his father, that's who. You didn't answer my question."

I looked to Clayton for confirmation. He offered a low nod. I spoke calmly.

"It's a significant second-degree burn, so it will likely take several weeks. It could have been a lot worse."

My words seemed only to fuel the man's anger. "Well, pardon me, Doc, while I go whistle a damn happy tune."

That was enough. This fellow wanted a shouting match, not a discussion. Clayton saw the look on my face and spoke first. "Let's go, Dad. We'll talk at home." He placed his unhurt hand on his father's chest to push him away. The man yielded reluctantly, taking several steps backward under the pressing guidance of his son. There was no waver in his furious glare. Before turning to exit, he pointed his finger at me and spoke a last venomous declaration.

"It's those damn Mennonites. It's their fault, and they're gonna pay."

CHAPTER 9

EMTs, DOA, and DRT

I had no idea what Clayton's father was talking about. The incident had cast a pall over everyone's mood. Faces were now brooding, preoccupied. The headache and exhaustion from a long night remained. I did a final exam on Chick and allowed him to go home with a long list of instructions and an insistence on follow-up.

I did the same with Maylen. But as he was readying to leave, I stopped him. "Maylen, you know everybody in town. Who was that Ross fellow, and what was that all about with his father?"

As was his way, at first Maylen simply stared at me with a wooden face and doleful eyes, thinking before responding. "That's Cal Ross. He's not intentionally mean, Doc, just not inclined to show any restraint. He'll cool off."

"What was that about the Mennonites?"

"The first call we got last night was about a barn fire out Gallivant's Crossing. Turned out to be in the Mennonite community."

"Who made the call? I didn't think the Mennonites had phones."

"We don't know. It was a woman on a cell phone. Dispatch tried calling back, but nobody answered. Still, we had to respond.

There was a fire, but it was just an outbuilding at the Yoder place, under control long before we got there. Meanwhile, a second call came in regarding the fire at Dora Mae Taylor's place, clear across the county. By the time we arrived, the barn was mostly gone. It all happened pretty fast. Every fire seems to have a tipping point. Clayton was too close when the barn collapsed. If we'd gotten there sooner, it might not have happened. Maybe Clayton wouldn't have been hurt. So I'm betting that's what Cal was mad about."

"Thanks, Maylen. I'll call you later to check in. Get some rest."

I went to the lavatory to wash my face, now feeling the fog and headache that accompanied too little sleep. When I arrived at the break room, Clarence and Leonard were engaged in a robust conversation. Nothing seemed to faze these two. The paramedics had a private language of their own, stand-ins, acronyms, and subtleties about things that only they understood. Clarence was in rare form, chiding his partner.

"Preacher, I think if you had given Mr. Calli mouth-to-mouth, you might have saved him from being DOA."

Preacher was Leonard's nickname. Leonard Lee Lineberry was tall and lanky with a perpetual toothpick dangling from the corner of his mouth. He used to be called Triple L, which I'd assumed was derived from his name, but I'd learned more recently that it stood for Lounge Lizard Leonard. In his younger days, he had been a low-end honky-tonk crooner, fashioning himself as a Porter Wagoner wannabe. It was also rumored that he had been something of a ladies' man, although to look at Leonard now, I was certain that the ladies must have been under the influence to have earned him that moniker.

Somewhere along the way Leonard had had a road-to-Damascus conversion and started his own church called the Whosoever

Will, Full Gospel, Praise Band Church. A couple of years ago the church had changed its name to the Love From Above Chapel and become a small independent congregation on the outskirts of town.

Leonard spent a lot of time studying the Bible. He believed there were secret messages hidden in the text and symbolic meanings to the numbers found in scripture, even the ones at the bottom of the page. Still, something of the oily lothario lingered in his demeanor. I got the sense that he was a man for whom hair care was still an important priority.

"Oh Lordy be," responded Leonard in his amiable, drawling voice. "I thought Dora Mae was having a conniption. I walked up and there was Mr. Calli, stiff as a flagpole. Dora Mae was moaning and wailing and a-LJ-ing, wanting me to do something for him. But I'm tell you right now, it wasn't no resuscitation situation. Mr. Calli wasn't DOA. He was DRT. They wasn't a thing I could'a done to save him."

This set off some minor alarm bells. "Leonard, whoa. Explain what you just said. What are LJ-ing and DRT? And who's Mr. Calli?"

Clarence intervened. "LJ-ing is yelling 'Lord Jesus,' Doc. Preacher don't like to use the Lord's name in vain." The two men shared rather pious, confirming nods. Clarence continued. "DRT means 'dead right there.' And Mr. Calli is Dora Mae's calico cat."

"Oh," I responded in relief. "A cat. Well, that's too bad." I walked to the counter to pour a cup of coffee. Leonard spoke reflectively.

"Dora Mae thinks the lightning got him, but there wasn't a singed hair on him. He was nigh on to fifteen years old anyway."

"Leonard, how do you know so much about Dora Mae's cat?" I inquired.

"My cousin, Tommy Dean Lineberry, lives in a trailer down

the way from Dora Mae and does odd jobs for her. She's in her seventies and lives out there alone. She puts up with him despite his drinking."

"Leonard, I don't think I know Tommy Dean."

He leaned back and rubbed his chin. "Oh, I'd say Tommy Dean's in his early fifties now. He never quite found his depth, you might say."

Clarence took a sip of coffee. "There's quite a few Lineberrys out in that part of the county, ain't there, Leonard?"

"Yeah, but I'll tell you," he responded, "Tommy Dean's a true-blue Lineberry."

I was only half listening to the conversation, but Leonard's comment piqued my curiosity. "What do you mean by 'true-blue Lineberry'?"

"Well," said Leonard, pausing for effect, "it's like this, Doc. Before they was married, Tommy Dean's daddy was a Lineberry and Tommy Dean's momma was a Lineberry. So Tommy Dean, he's a true-blue Lineberry. He's Lineberry all the way to the bone."

I nodded, doing my best to feign an innocent and nonjudgmental face.

"Now, don't be getting the wrong idea, Doc. It was just a coincidence. They wasn't even second or third cousins. 'Course, you wouldn't know it by looking at Tommy Dean."

"Leonard, I think I already know more than I want to."

They finished their coffee and departed. It was only six thirty; the clinic didn't officially open for another hour and a half. The rest of the staff had already left, so I locked the doors and returned home to clean up before starting the day.

When I pulled into my driveway, my thirteen-year-old neighbor, Will Fox, was holding Rhett on a leash, and I was at a loss as to how my crafty dog had gotten out. It was only after I stared for a moment that I realized my mistake. The dog Will was holding was definitely a golden retriever of similar size and shape, but it wasn't Rhett.

"Hi there, Willster. Who's your new friend?"

"This is Mattie," Will responded, pleased and proud. "We just got her yesterday."

"Fine-looking gal. Where did she come from?"

"Lawrenceburg. There was an ad in the paper. The family was moving to Nashville and giving her away to a good home. I've been wanting a dog, so Mom agreed."

Will was a bright and clever, albeit peculiar, boy. I liked him. We shared a quirky friendship. He had lost his father to an accident more than a year ago, just as I had lost my parents when I was twelve. An unspoken bond of understanding existed between us.

"Well, I'm sure Rhett will be ecstatic to have a play friend."

"That's why I told Mom I wanted a golden." Will paused a moment and then added confidentially, "Don't worry, Dr. Bradford. She's been fixed." He made a gesture of quotation marks with his fingers.

Somehow the idea of discussing sex with a thirteen-year-old, even sex among pets, felt awkward. I answered stiffly. "Well, I'm sure they can, um, enjoy a kind of austere and cerebral relationship."

"I think the word you're looking for is 'platonic.'"

"Shut up and take your dog inside." I winked at him and smiled as I turned toward my front door.

"See ya later, Dr. B."

"You too, Willster. I'll let Rhett know the good news."

Rhett greeted me at the front door with a wagging tail and his tennis ball in his mouth, something he never did first thing in the morning.

"Well, hello, Mr. Perky. Looks like somebody saw the new

neighbor out the window and wants to show off a little." I reached down and rubbed his ears and, for the first time, noticed that his right eye was cloudy. I took the ball, along with a little associated slobber, out of his mouth and waved it from side to side to watch his eye movements. He followed it with rapt attention, but admittedly it was a poor test. I shrugged, unable to tell anything more, and set the ball aside.

Luther Whitmore, Eli Yoder, and now my own dog. Everyone around me was going blind, and the day was just getting started.

CHAPTER 10
Patients

I was late getting to work that morning because I decided to walk the six blocks to the clinic. The day had a pristine, well-scrubbed feel that comes after a rain. Walking gave me time to think.

While I enjoyed my life in Watervalley, some days I saw myself as a stranger in a strange land, more of a curious and amused observer than a participant in the life of the town. The clinic had proven to be a small stage with an ever-changing cast of players as patients came and went. All the emotions of the human experience—courage, joy, fear, sorrow, hope, depression, heartbreak, and of course humor—were part of the daily theater. And admittedly, I loved my work . . . at least for the time being.

Privately, I still held tight to my dream of doing medical research. And despite my long-standing habit of emotional detachment, my life here had taught me that I inevitably cared deeply for those around me. Today would be one in which comedy and tragedy would be deceptively entwined.

I entered the back door of the clinic and slipped into my office before suiting up in my white coat and working my way through the already full exam rooms. Nancy had placed a stack of notes on my desk regarding phone calls and a list of the day's appointments. I glanced at these quickly, taking particular interest in the findings from the final lab test on Clayton Ross. It was for a blood alcohol level, and the result was difficult to believe. I thought about this for a moment and then mentally filed it away.

My first patient of the day was Beatrice McClanahan, a pert and lively little woman with a cheery, grandmotherly disposition. Beatrice drove an old Country Squire station wagon, wore brightly colored cotton dresses, and, I was certain, lied with impunity about her age. Beatrice said she was pushing seventy. I was certain she was pulling eighty. I glanced at her chart and shook my head. She had come to the clinic for an eye exam.

Watervalley had an optometrist named Gordon Kelly who came in one day a week, if that. Gordon was in his early seventies and liked to fish. I began to secretly wish that Karen Davidson would forgo being a veterinarian and practice optometry instead. How much difference could there be between the two professions?

I quickly learned that Beatrice wasn't there voluntarily. Apparently the sheriff, Warren Thurman, had found her driving on both sides of the road a little too often and was holding her license until she had her eyes checked. As I entered the exam room, Beatrice was sitting primly in the chair with her hands in her lap. She was wearing a bright red cloche hat, and her eyes sparkled behind her emerald green cat-eye glasses. She smiled sweetly at me with all the polite innocence that a crafty octogenarian could muster.

"Good morning, Beatrice. How are you?"

"Oh my, Dr. Bradford. It's so nice to see you." She conspicuously placed a strong inflection on the word "see." Beatrice thought she was working her magic. I smiled pleasantly.

"What seems to be the problem today?"

"Oh," she said with wide-eyed naïveté. "I just have a little piece of paper I need you to sign." She handed me the documents from the sheriff, which included a police report. I knew what the sheriff was up to. Anyone who had seen Beatrice out driving with her hands locked at the ten and two positions and her nose barely level with the steering wheel would be at a loss as to how she stayed out of the ditch. Whenever anybody in Watervalley saw the old Country Squire coming, they automatically gave her a wide berth and sometimes even pulled off the road altogether. Warren was trying to find a polite way to keep Beatrice from driving.

I rubbed my chin and feigned ignorance. "Beatrice, tell me what brought this about?"

"Well, I'm not really sure. Warren seems to be concerned about my driving. He pulled me over Thursday afternoon, and for the life of me I don't understand all the fuss. He even had a deputy drive my car while he drove me home, entirely against my will."

"It says here, Beatrice, that you were swerving all over the road."

"Why, that's just silly. I veered out of my lane for only a second," she declared diplomatically. "Besides, there was a bee in my car. I tried to explain that to Warren, but he just had a bee in his bonnet." She finished with an authoritative nod.

"I see. Beatrice, it also says here that Warren suspected the presence of alcohol."

She flipped her hand at me. "Oh piddle. That was just Listerine."

I was doing my best to keep from laughing outright. I knew that the sheriff was too nice a fellow to administer a sobriety test to a kindly eighty-year-old woman on the side of the road. "And the empty liquor bottle the deputy found under the seat?"

Beatrice looked away, speaking innocently. "Why, I have no idea how long that's been there. My late husband, Henry, must have left it."

"Hmm. So, Beatrice, you don't drink?"

She hesitated and stared at me for a moment before speaking in a voice of polite contrition. "Well, Dr. Bradford. Don't misunderstand. I love Jesus, but I do drink a little from time to time. It helps keep me regular."

I nodded, offering no response. Beatrice regained some of her pluck and continued. "Anyway, I think Warren is just overreacting, don't you? He even accused me of trying to bribe him."

"Bribe him?"

"All I did was offer him some chess pie and told him we should just forget the whole thing."

"Chess pie, huh?"

"Why, yes. Can you imagine? He acted like I was trying to slip him a roofie."

I wanted to laugh so hard, I could pop. I covered my mouth with my hand. I knew from Beatrice's chart that she was beyond passing any eye exam, despite corrective lenses. Still, I also knew that the inability to drive would mean the loss of freedom and independence. I would have Nancy work with her to coordinate community resources and relatives to help her with daily living. It was a tough choice, but the right one.

However, apparently Beatrice mistook my silence for agreement. She smiled winsomely, reached into her bag, and produced a small foil-covered plate.

"Oh, I almost forgot," she said. "I brought you some peanut brittle. It's homemade." She discreetly placed an ink pen on the top and handed the plate to me.

She wasn't very happy when she left the office. Maybe I shouldn't have kept the pen.

Thankfully, the rest of my appointments were routine. Except for Gene Alley, my last patient of the day.

Gene worked as a disc jockey at Watervalley's only radio station, WVLY, "the Voice of the Valley." Years ago, he had taken a piece of shrapnel to the head in Vietnam. As part of his treatment, the army had placed a small metal plate over his parietal bone, the upper rear part of the cranium. I had been told that Gene had always been a little goofy, even before the war, but in the intervening years his ascent into the world of wacky had become legend. Any conversation about him always ended with the statement, "That boy's just not right."

Including my residency at Vanderbilt and my time as the physician at the Watervalley Clinic, I had a few thousand exams under my belt. I had seen some rashes that bordered on outright icky, heard abdominal sounds that needed an exorcist, and even had a patient who wanted a pill for her allergy to squirrels. However, my discussion with Gene topped all of those.

Ann had already taken his vitals, which all seemed fine. However, beside the "reason for visit" section, she had written the words, "the storm." Ann was nowhere to be found, so I shrugged and proceeded into the exam room, where Gene's wife, Peggy, was with him, wearing a face of pallid worry. Conversely, Gene was relaxed with a bemused smile. My confused look was difficult to mask.

"Gene, Peggy, how are you doing today?"

Peggy responded immediately. "Only so-so, Dr. Bradford. It was the storm last night. It got him going."

"Going . . . as in how?"

"He started doing it again."

"Doing . . . what?"

Peggy pursed her lips and cast a worried glance toward Gene. She spoke with a mixture of fear and frustration. "He's talking in song titles again."

"Did I hear you correctly? Song titles?"

"Yes, song titles."

"Gene, is this right?"

He nodded sheepishly. "'True.'"

I paused, regarding both of them cautiously. "When did this start?"

"'In the Wee Small Hours of the Morning,'" he responded.

"And you think the cause is . . . what?"

Gene shrugged, a childlike smile still etched on his face. "'Thunder and Lightning.'"

I held up my hand and released a muted laugh. "Okay, hold it. I feel like I'm the setup man in a comedy routine."

Peggy responded flatly, "Tell me about it. I can't make him stop. Everything I say comes back with a Top Forty response. We just go . . ."

"'Round and Round,'" blurted Gene.

Peggy closed her eyes, and her head sank to her chest in resignation. "Dr. Bradford, do you think he's . . ."

"'Crazy,'" Gene finished. He sat there with a complacent, vacant stare.

Peggy was looking for an answer, and I had nothing to offer. I turned and grabbed one of the exam room chairs, pulled it in close, and took a seat. I was stumped. I wanted to think this was just a hoax, but that seemed unlikely. I knew of no mental disorder into which this symptom neatly fit, nor was I a psychiatrist by training. But Peggy was staring anxiously. I had to try something.

"Gene, I'm going to ask you some questions. Tell me what pops into your head."

He nodded in agreement.

"How are you feeling right now?"

"'Under Pressure.'"

"Okay, so when you heard all the thunder and explosions last night, what did it make you think about?"

"'It's the End of the World as We Know It.'"

"Right, so you were scared?"

Gene nodded. "'I Fall to Pieces.'"

This was getting nowhere. I began a different line of questions. "Gene, when you get scared like that, does it cause you to drink?"

"'One Thing Leads to Another.'"

I scratched my head, trying hard to appear serious. "And does the drinking help calm you down?"

"'Whatever Gets You Through the Night.'"

I exhaled a deep sigh. "Okay. Let's try something else. Gene, I want you to concentrate. What was the one thing the storm last night made you think about?"

"'Stayin' Alive.'"

It seemed hopeless. Gene was answering my questions, but only by channeling everyone from Patsy Cline and the Fixx to the Pointer Sisters and the Brothers Gibb. Sitting there with the face of an amused simpleton, he seemed to be enjoying the conversation immensely. I leaned back in my chair, dumbfounded.

"Unbelievable," I exhorted.

Peggy shot me a look of disbelief.

"Oh, sorry. I forgot. . . . That's a song title too, isn't it?"

I crossed my arms and studied both of them. Physically, Gene was fine; oddly, he seemed aware of his own malady, but unable to do anything about it. There could be no sure diagnosis. Nonetheless, I wanted to provide Peggy with some encouragement.

"Guys, I don't have a ready answer for you. It all points to some kind of post-traumatic stress event triggered by the flash and noise of the storm. I'm not well versed in treating that. My best advice is to take it easy for a couple of days. I can write you a prescription for a sedative if you think that will help. But if this . . ." I paused, unsure how to define Gene's ailment. "If this situation persists, I will need to refer you to a specialist. I wish I had a better answer. But that's my game plan for now."

They both nodded. Peggy responded with a weak thank-you. As they left, Gene winked at me. I'm not sure what he meant by it, whether it was a gesture of confidentiality or just easier than saying, "'Happy Trails to You.'" I stayed seated in the exam room chair, both fascinated and frustrated. Soon afterward, Nancy found me.

"Dr. Bradford, John Harris is waiting in your office."

CHAPTER 11
The Statue

I had met John Harris a year ago, soon after my arrival in Watervalley. I remembered the day well because he almost shot me. I had taken a hike into the hills and stumbled upon his apple orchard. John, a brooding recluse at the time, had thought I was trespassing. In all fairness, the rifle he was pointing at me was actually a BB gun. Ours was something short of a spontaneous friendship.

In time we had grown to like each other and shared a bantering camaraderie. John had a PhD, was a retired chemical engineer, and was quite wealthy. Tall, modestly handsome, and muscular for a man in his late fifties, he possessed a subtle yet powerful charisma. He had grown up in Watervalley and had been a tireless community leader until two years ago when his wife, Molly, died of cancer, sending John into a time of bitter isolation and alcohol abuse.

However, in recent months he had undergone a significant transformation. He had gradually reengaged in the life of the town, slowly put his anger and heavy drinking behind him, and kindled a romance with the clinic's staff nurse, Ann Patterson. Still, he was a man both loved and feared. While he was a strong individual capable of great generosity, he could also be tough and intolerant. On more than one occasion I had seen him use his commanding presence, brilliant mind, and acid tongue to lay waste to those foolish enough to cross him.

He was also Christine's uncle.

John was seated in one of the wingback chairs facing my desk and rose when he heard me enter. But after two steps I stopped in my tracks, not believing what I was seeing. John, who perpetually wore a farm shirt, jeans, and work boots, was dressed in paisley shorts and a polo shirt. This was a rift in the order of the universe.

"Hey, sawbones. Want to see something interesting?"

"I think those shorts have already accomplished that for me. It's like seeing John Wayne wearing flip-flops."

"Yeah, smart-ass. Get your giggles over with. I've got a photo I want to show you."

Ignoring his comment, I was still a little taken aback by his outfit. "I'm guessing you and Ann have plans for later?"

"It's five o'clock, sport. So actually we have plans for right now. She told me to give her a minute. Take a look at this."

John handed me his cell phone to show me a photo he had taken.

"Isn't that the courthouse square?"

"Yeah, and all those fragments you see are what's left of the statue of *The Grateful Farmer*."

Decades ago, a statue had been built on the courthouse lawn of a man in overalls holding a handful of vegetables. The statue commemorated one of Watervalley's own, who had been named State Farmer of the Year. I had never paid it any serious attention.

"What happened to it?" I asked.

"Lightning strike from the storm."

"You know, there was a huge flash that hit nearby last night. I bet that was it."

"Cracked it into more than thirty pieces."

"Wow. Well, that's a shame. Guess the farmer's not too grateful anymore."

"No, but everybody else is."

"Why is that?"

"The statue was well intended, but it's always been somewhat of a community embarrassment."

"How so?"

"You've never looked at it closely, have you?"

"Not really."

"You know how the guy is using both hands to hold a bunch of vegetables about waist high."

"Yeah."

"Well, if you ever viewed him from behind, the way both of his hands were together at that level, it looked like he was holding something else."

"Oh, so it looked like Watervalley's version of one of those Italian fountains?"

"Yeah, right there on the courthouse lawn too."

I handed the phone back to him, and he studied the picture, lost in thought.

"So, John. I guess I'm a little curious. As fascinating as this bit of trivia is, I'm not sure why it was significant enough to take a picture and show it to me."

John looked at me shrewdly. "I've got a really great idea."

"What? You going to suggest they put up a statue of you?"

In a show of easy manners, John didn't miss a beat. "Oh, it's a given that the town will put up a statue of me at some point. The only question is whether or not they'll spring for having it lit up at night."

"I expect nothing less."

"No, sawbones, I've got an idea that's been long overdue. I want the town to build a memorial to all the soldiers from the valley who have been killed in combat. You know, a war memorial."

"Hmm. Nothing wrong with that. But isn't the memorial building downtown a, well . . . memorial?"

"Sure. But the hall was built in the twenties as a dedication to all who served in the Great War. Nothing has been done since then. I'm just guessing, but I bet there are more than fifty men and women from the valley who have died in wars over the last century. Something, somewhere, should have their names on it."

I nodded in agreement. "Seems like a grand idea. What's your plan?"

"The town doesn't have much money for this kind of thing, so we'll have to solicit private donations, probably through some kind of fund-raising campaign."

"Sounds good. Except, was there a significance in your use of the word 'we'?"

John's face eased into a sly grin. "I want you to cochair the campaign with me."

I didn't immediately say yes. Perhaps I should have, but instead I hesitated. I couldn't think of a more worthy project, but in truth, I knew this effort would swallow a fair amount of my time and that was one thing I was pretty selfish about. The years in med school and the long hours during residency had put me on a treadmill that required every spare minute. Now, the demands of being Watervalley's only full-time doctor and my romance with Christine filled my days, making me reluctant to readily commit.

But there was a pleasant warmth in John's persuasive charm. He persisted, and I knew I had no choice. "Well . . . sure, okay. Put me in, coach."

Having attained my agreement, he was all business. "Good. We'll need to form a committee and get a consensus of what the memorial should look like, put together an estimate, and start to round up donors. I can connect with the mayor to streamline any city council issues. There are a limited number of deep pockets in the county, so we'll have to hit them all up to give till it hurts."

I grinned. "That includes you, I presume?"

John smiled. "Heck, sawbones, I may even give till I'm middle class."

Before I could respond, there was a knock at the door and Ann entered, smiling warmly at John. He grinned and winked at me before turning to Ann, "Thanks for stepping up, sport. I'll be in touch."

The two of them left, and soon afterward I locked up. I had been up since four a.m., and it had been a long day. But I smiled all the way home. Connie was making dinner.

CHAPTER 12
Life with Connie

Normally I would arrive home to find Connie with her apron on and in the kitchen, rattling pots and pans and cooking in high gear. Instead, she was in the living room watching a movie. Rhett was sitting in rapt attention, also focused on the TV screen.

"What gives, Connie T? Don't tell me all those millions I'm paying you are not enough?" This, of course, was said in jest. Connie Thompson was a wealthy woman, having made a fortune from investing her deceased husband's pension in the stock market and in the local bank. I did pay her a modest wage for her services as cook and housekeeper, but she helped out more as an act of kindness and friendship than out of any need for money.

Connie looked drily up at me and spoke in her usual breezy monotone. "Humph. You'd have to give me a raise just to get me to 'not enough.' Anyway, there's a chicken casserole in the oven if you're hungry."

"Sounds good. What are you watching?"

She held up her hand for me to be silent, focusing intently on the scene playing in the movie. After a moment, she reached over, grabbed the remote, and turned it off. "Mmm-mmm-mmm. That Denzel Washington. Now, that's a man who could make a girl lose her principles."

I feigned shock. "Why, Constance Grace Thompson. I cannot believe my ears. I'm shattered, just shattered. Should I call Pastor Dawson and activate the prayer chain?"

Connie regarded me coolly above her gold-inlay glasses. "Keep your shirt on, Doctor. It's not like Denzel's gonna be dropping by the house."

I laughed and followed her to the kitchen. "So, are you telling me there's a man who could use sex to get what he wants?"

She responded flatly. "No. I'm not saying that at all."

As she carried the casserole to the table, she spoke again, this time with blunt authority. "Besides, men don't use sex to get what they want. Sex *is* what they want." With that, she grabbed a plate and began to serve, her chin judiciously elevated.

I grabbed a pitcher of iced tea from the fridge, and we sat down to dinner.

"Go ahead and eat, Doctor. I've already blessed it."

I nodded obediently.

"So, how's everybody at the clinic today?"

"Tired and not very motivated after being up part of the night."

"Speaking of not being motivated," Connie said in a decidedly lecturing tone, "I noticed you didn't make your bed this morning. Now, I'm not your momma, but it seems to me you're getting a little sloppy in your bachelor ways, don't you think?"

I rolled my eyes and mumbled under my breath, "Not my momma, huh? Walks like a duck, talks like a duck."

"I heard what you just said," Connie declared sharply.

"Me? I didn't say anything."

"Humph. Keep it up, Doctor. When I'm done here, I might just reach over there and smack you."

"I look forward to that."

"Humph," Connie grunted again. "The point is, this house needs a woman's touch. I've taken you to raise as long as I can. It's time for a handoff. You need a woman around here to keep you straight. I'm thinking Christine Ann Chambers could do the job just fine."

"I'll ask her to fill out an application."

"Don't start with me, Luke Bradford. You know what I'm talking about."

Even though I tended to keep my feelings private, I was amused by Connie's bluntness. I chose to disregard her inference of matrimony. "Connie, I'm not sure I get the logic of making my bed. I mean, after I take my shoes off, I don't retie the laces."

Connie stared at me deadpan, shaking her head. "You know, sooner or later we all have to be grown-ups. Don't you think it's time you took a turn?"

Ignoring her question, I told her about the destruction of the statue and John's plan for the new memorial.

"Umm-hmm," Connie mused. "I heard that lightning got it."

"Yeah, he wants me to cochair the drive to raise money for the new monument."

"Sounds like a good character builder."

"I'm sure you're right. It's just that every time I've done something that's supposed to build character, I've regretted it."

Connie offered no response.

"Hey, why don't you cochair it instead of me? You and John would make a great team."

"Why, Doctor, I wouldn't know where to begin to fill those big floppy shoes of yours."

"It's just that it's a busy time, and I'm, well . . . I'm kind of at an awkward stage."

"And what awkward stage is that, the one between birth and death?"

"Very funny."

Continued complaint seemed pointless. "Anyway, it is what it is, and it's the right thing to do," I said with resignation.

"That statue was dedicated to Wicky Willoughby," Connie added. "He was the State Farmer of the Year in 1955."

"Wicky, huh? Weally?"

Connie scowled. "Just keep it up. I'm fixing to grab the broom and come at you piñata style." She took a bite of casserole, quite pleased with herself.

"Pretty lofty talk for a woman who not ten minutes ago expressed a willingness to acquire a little carnal knowledge with a certain movie star."

Connie stopped in midchew and shot me a withering stare. "Denzel, Dr. Bradford, is off-limits. You need to leave him out of this."

I smiled, and we both ate in amused silence.

"I heard about Chick and Maylen and the Ross boy getting burned. Are they going to be all right?" Connie inquired.

"Yeah, I think so. What a strange night, though."

"How so?"

"That whole business about the fire truck going out to the

Mennonite community. You always seem to have the skinny on everything, Connie. Have you heard anything more about who made the phone call?"

"Just that it was a young woman. There hasn't been a fire call out to the Mennonite community in decades."

"You know, speaking of which, I passed an old burned-out house on Mercy Creek Road on the way to see Jacob Yoder yesterday. The place sits in the middle of a beautiful meadow. It was sad, such a beautiful homesite, but it's been abandoned."

"Mercy Creek Road, hmm. I think I know the place. It burned back in the sixties, and if I'm not mistaken, the volunteer fire department was called out on that one too. It's on the fringe of the Mennonite community, and one of the nearby farmers called it in."

"I think that's right. While unwrapping her grandmother's china, Christine found an old newspaper article about the fire that she gave to me. I wonder who owns that place now?"

"Probably one of the Mennonite families."

"Really? Seems strange to leave it abandoned."

"Don't have an answer on that one. The Mennonites are pretty frugal, and they buy up property for their children to live on later. I guess that place hasn't been needed yet."

I shrugged. "Guess not."

"Anyway," responded Connie, "that storm seemed to wreak havoc on a lot of folks' lives. There were power outages and trees down everywhere."

"Yeah," I chortled. "I had a pretty strange case today that was storm related."

Even though it was stretching doctor-patient confidentiality, I went on to tell Connie about Gene Alley's visit.

"Mmm-mmm," she said. "So Gene's back to talking in song titles again, huh? That boy needs a genetic do-over. He should have orange cones placed around him."

"So he's done this before?"

"Oh, yeah."

"Well, even so. I feel kind of bad about it. Part of me wanted to keep talking to him to see what he would say. But he and his wife came to me for help, and it's just not my field of expertise. I don't think I did him much good."

"Don't beat yourself up, Luke. Gene has a bout of this malady every six months whenever he takes a notion to irritate Peggy. For years she talked about divorcing him, thinking she could trade up. I think that ship has sailed. She'll complain as long as she has anything resembling a puppet of an audience. You're just a new set of ears. It'll pass in a few days, and he'll be back to his slightly wacky self."

We finished dinner. I helped Connie clean up, and she left shortly before seven.

Afterward, I took Rhett out to the backyard to survey the garden that I had planted a few weeks earlier. It was my first foray into growing vegetables, and I was quickly learning that gardening was twenty percent inspiration and eighty percent perspiration. Weeds were everywhere. I pulled a few but soon quit, taking on a stoic attitude of survival of the fittest, tomatoes versus dandelions. Rhett gave me a disapproving look.

"What are you staring at?" I said. He continued to regard me with a droopy and dour disdain. The cloudiness in his right eye seemed more pronounced. I would need to get Karen Davidson to check it out.

By eight thirty, I was showered and ready to hit the sack. Maybe it was because of the unusually early hour, but as I lay in bed that night, the sounds of the street took on an unfamiliar restlessness, an almost brooding malevolence.

In the watches of the night, when my body was drinking deeply of much-needed sleep, the press wheels of the Watervalley newspaper were roaring in high gear. The buried anger of events from long ago was preparing to find a voice.

CHAPTER 13
Headlines

I awoke early the next morning and decided to take a short run. Normally, Rhett would enthusiastically wag his tail in anticipation when he saw me lacing up my running shoes. But this morning, he was awash in lethargy, doing little more than lie on his side and strain his neck slightly to follow my movements. I fully expected him to be drinking coffee and watching cartoons upon my return.

We were in the thick green of June, and the cooler morning air provided only a slight reprieve from the consuming humidity. I jogged toward Watervalley Lake and its newly renovated bandstand, built out over the water. The historic structure's renovation had been largely underwritten by John Harris. In completing the project, John had fulfilled the last dream of his departed wife, Molly. Built in an elaborate Victorian design, with detailed embellishments, it had been an iconic landmark of Watervalley for nearly a hundred years.

Upon my return home, I found Will in his front yard, throwing a ball to his new dog friend, Mattie. But instead of his usual mischievous and witty air, Will was the definition of glum.

"Morning, Willster. Why the long face?"

He spoke sheepishly. "Girl problems."

"Oh," I said thoughtfully. "I see." I knew that Will harbored a small crush on Wendy Wilson, the cherub-pretty daughter of a local dairy farmer, Hoot Wilson. "So, what happened? Ugly breakup?"

"Uh-huh. She says she wants to just be *friends*." Will's emphasis on the last word indicated what he thought of that idea. "It's all because of Tommy Short. She thinks he's so great because he made the Little League All-Star team."

I nodded. "Hmm, jocks. Well, what can I say? Girls can be like that."

"Yeah, I just never figured her for a cleat chaser."

"Give it time. She may come back around. Meanwhile, looks like you still have Mattie's undying affection."

Will's mood lightened, and he reached over to rub her head. "Mom says we're going to build a picket fence around the backyard so Mattie can be outside more. Maybe Rhett can come over and play."

"He would love that, I'm sure. Meanwhile, chin up, big guy. All-Star season doesn't last forever."

"Yeah. I'll be all right. I'm thinking I should pour my feelings into poetry."

"Wow. Poetry, huh. Okay, that's interesting and, well, different."

"Too nerdy?"

"No, no. Not at all. Sounds like, um . . . like a good way to think outside the Xbox. Let me know how that works out."

I said good-bye and walked to my house, all the while thinking that Will Fox might be the most peculiar kid I could ever imagine.

I was showered and ready shortly after seven, enough time to stop by the Depot Diner and grab some breakfast. The diner, owned by saintly and spunky Lida Wilkins, invariably served as the morning source of lively gossip and interesting news. It was normally a cacophony of loud chatter and clanking dishes, but today it had taken on a subdued air, a place of huddled conversations and sullen exchanges.

I took my usual seat at the counter, where Lida met me with the coffeepot. "Lida, is it just me, or am I missing something? This place seems all whispery and secretive."

Lida slapped a copy of the *Village Voice* on the counter in front of me.

"There's your answer, Doc."

The headline read, "Mennonite Hoax Contributes to Veteran's Injury." The story was an inflammatory account that linked the injuries sustained by Chick, Maylen, and Clayton Ross to the fire truck's unnecessary trip to the Mennonite community. The language was full of rancor and invective, written more like an editorial than an unbiased news report. There was a naked bluntness to Luther's attacking words.

> The Mennonites, who shamefully make no voluntary contribution to protect the very freedoms they enjoy, are now maliciously responsible for the injuries of three Watervalley veterans.

Despite their unsophisticated ways, the people of Watervalley were not gullible. But it was clear that the article had cast a pall over the mood of those around me.

The piece did little to inform and much to inflame. Perhaps everywhere, and especially in small towns, devotion to those who serve our country runs deep. A respect for the sacrifice of servicemen and -women permeated the people I knew here, and they would not be happy with the suggestion that our local veterans had been made to suffer needlessly. But the greatest aggravation for me was that another factor had contributed to Clayton's injury, one that I could not reveal.

"Pretty sour situation, huh, Doc?" Lida's voice brought me back.

"Yeah, I think this is the work of Clayton's dad. I didn't get the impression Clayton was that upset, and I'm quite certain Chick and Maylen would not be expressing these sentiments."

"Sticking up for his boy, I guess."

I shrugged. "Doesn't mean he's right."

"Well, parents get that way. They get convicted and righteous in their opinions when it comes to their kids. And I have to say, if it had been my boy . . . who risked his life in Afghanistan only to be hurt because of some foolish Mennonite, I'd be a little hacked, too."

"I suppose you're right. Still, I'm surprised Luther would print such a biased rant. There's no proof that a Mennonite even made the call. They don't carry phones as I understand it."

"I get your point, Doc, but we're talking about veterans here. I don't think speaking on behalf of the Mennonites is going to win you sustained applause from this crowd."

I said nothing and sat there, silent and disgusted. Lida poured me more coffee. "Besides, you know how Luther is. He's got a soul the size of a peanut. He can be pretty obnoxious sometimes, and when those sometimes happen, he sells a lot more newspapers."

There seemed little else to say on the matter, and I wanted a change of subject. The talk of veterans brought Karen Davidson to mind. Since Lida owned Society Hill B and B, I knew they had met. "Hey, what do you think about our new veterinarian?"

"Dr. Davidson? I like her. Keeps her room as neat as a pin and is as quiet as a mouse. Trooper loves her, too." Trooper was Lida's corgi. "I think he's ready to propose marriage. Get this—he sleeps outside her door every night, the little traitor."

"Did you know she's a veteran? Fifteen years in the army."

"She hadn't said, although I guessed as much," responded Lida. "She's a bit on the plain-Jane side and a little shy, but plenty likable."

"Well, I wish the best for her. I hope the local farmers will give her a chance."

Lida puckered her lips in an expression of doubt. "Hmm, hard to say on that one. I heard several of the boys express concern about her getting hurt, you know . . . her being so little and cows being so big. Of course, if Trooper is any indication, all she'll have to do is walk down the street playing a pipe. Every dog and cat in town will come running."

"I think that only works on rats."

Lida thumped her finger on the newspaper and winked at me, speaking with unvarnished tact. "Well, if that's the case, the *Village Voice* will need a new editor."

I nodded in agreement.

"So, Doc, what'll it be this morning?"

I ate pancakes and reread the newspaper article. The words set a discordant tone to the day. I finished, paid my bill, and drove over to the clinic.

The morning was filled with mostly routine patients, but I felt ill-tempered. All of them wanted to talk about the Clayton Ross incident. The story had roared across Watervalley. It seemed that scandalous news had longer legs than the other kind.

I ate lunch in my office and was finished with appointments by three that afternoon. Near that time, Joe Dawson, the new pastor at Watervalley First Presbyterian, dropped by.

Although he had a wife and two children, Joe and I were about the same age and friendly acquaintances. He was a lively, slim fellow with dark hair, a big smile, and an easygoing manner. Perhaps his greatest attribute as a pastor was that he came off as just a regular guy. He invariably wore the robe and vestments on Sunday, but was in blue jeans most any other day of the week. He loved to cut up, laughed easily, and had nothing of the serious, sanctimonious air assumed by many in his profession.

We shook hands as he entered my office, and I invited him to have a seat.

"No need, Luke. I just have a quick question for you. Earlier this morning, I was working through the old church rolls and came across a name I didn't recognize. Normally, Alice knows who everybody is, but she's off today. So, I was walking by and thought I would ask you."

"Sure."

"Does the name Leyland Carter ring a bell?"

"Can't say it does. Should it?"

"Not necessarily. Apparently he's an older fellow who has been on the church rolls for years. I can't determine his exact age. He doesn't have a phone, so I can't get in touch with him, and he hasn't been to church in a while. Just wondering if you had seen or treated him."

"No, don't think so. Where does he live?"

"On Beacon Road out in the eastern edge of the county."

I looked at Joe and folded my arms. An idea struck me. "I'll tell you what. I've seen my last patient and could use some fresh air. It's been something of a troublesome day here. Give me the address, and I'll drive out there this afternoon and check on the old fellow."

"You sure?"

"Yeah, no problem," I responded pleasantly, hiding my real

thoughts. I was in a brooding, sour mood and wasn't even completely sure why.

Joe smiled cautiously, perhaps sensing my buried aggravation, but was too polite to press me further. "Let me know what you find."

Ten minutes later, I was in the Austin-Healey and heading out. Along the downtown streets, men and women huddled in small groups with sober faces of concern and resentment. Invariably, one of them was holding a newspaper. Luther had used Clayton's injury to turn the normally kind and tolerant townspeople against their better selves. Despite the sweltering sun of the June afternoon, it seemed that Watervalley lay in shadow.

I drove out of town on the east highway, away from the noise and gossip. The passing wind, the dull drone of the engine, and the rippling haze off the shimmering hot pavement lulled me into a trance. The empty road stretched into the distance and was bordered by a few scattered farms and pastures that soon gave way to miles of jumbled hills. Long stretches of thick woods lay beyond.

Decades earlier, this part of the county had been strip-mined for phosphate. The mining had long since played out and the land had been reclaimed, but a coarseness remained. This was a poorer part of the valley, populated only by the occasional trailer or shabby house with tall weeds, ratty fences, and yards cluttered with the broken refuse of accumulated years. The farther I drove into these desolate reaches, the more it seemed that an immense and lonely sky pressed down on me.

Watervalley had provided me with a few dear friends and perhaps the love of my life. But recent events and acrimonious tongues had robbed it of its larger charm, and I felt a need to distance myself. The day had exposed the unvarnished contrast between my life and theirs. Despite the gratifying bonds of community that I shared with them, I held larger dreams, higher goals. My dispirited mood cast a veil over everything. Even the passing countryside now felt raw, neglected, ugly.

Soon, I entered deep woods, making numerous turns before I found the dusty sign indicating Beacon Road. I traveled for another mile until I came upon an unkempt driveway with a rusted mailbox. The faded numbers on its side were barely legible, leaving me uncertain that this was the correct address. Thick trees hovered above the overgrown and sparsely graveled drive. I drove slowly. At the end of this long, winding lane was a small house surrounded by woods with a small clearing in front. I pulled up and killed the engine.

It was a rude shack of unpainted pine boards with a weathered and rather shaky-looking front porch. Tall oaks sheltered it, and I sensed that once upon a time it had been an orderly cottage of white boards, fresh sunlight, and tidy flower beds. Now it had all the markings of desertion, save for a front porch rocking chair that creaked softly with the occasional breeze.

I grabbed my bag, carefully picked my way up the rickety steps, and knocked on the front door. There was no sound or answer. Heavy drapes covered the windows, restricting any view of the inside. Given the general neglect of the place, I was quickly certain no one was here. I had made the trip in vain, adding yet another frustration to my day. I took out my cell phone to call Joe, but it was out of range with no service available. I was alone, isolated in this forgotten place.

My mind was filled with a tangle of broken thoughts as I tried to reconcile events, issues, and emotions. The previous harmony of my small world seemed gone, and all that remained were fragments of worry and anxiety over everything and nothing. I walked back down the steps and sat on the lowest one, leaning my shoulder against the rail post. The surrounding woods seemed deep, still, mysterious. Dappling sunlight played through the fluttering leaves. The lulling effect of the thick shade and soft breeze was forcing my eyes to shut, leaving me with a drowsy lethargy.

Perhaps somewhere in my subconscious I had known that I would find no one here. Perhaps I was doing what I had always done—disassociate, move away from the noise and ignorance. I sat for the longest time, staring in a half daze at the slumberous shade and patchy sunlight, my thoughts floating unfinished into the air.

When I heard the voice behind me, I almost jumped out of my skin.

CHAPTER 14
Leyland Carter

"It's a dangerous thing, you know."

Startled, I stood and turned abruptly. An old man in overalls was sitting in the rocking chair.

"Hello. Sorry. I didn't hear you come out. I'm Luke Bradford, the town doctor. Are you Mr. Carter?"

He smiled and gave a crisp nod of his chin. He looked to be in his eighties, thin, with soft eyes and a full head of neatly cut white hair. His mouth was shaped into a vague yet welcoming smile. There was an observant and shrewd manner about him, and he seemed to see the world with a quiet and contented humor.

"Good to meet you, Mr. Carter. Um, I'm sorry, I'm not sure I caught what you said."

"I said it's a dangerous thing, you know."

"What would that be?"

"It's dangerous to be lost inside one's own head, to be looking for all the answers there."

"I'm uh . . . I'm sure you're right." My initial surprise having passed, I folded my arms and leaned against the porch post, endeavoring to speak lightly. "I thought I was alone. Looks like you caught me daydreaming."

He responded with polite scrutiny. "Hmm, daydreaming, you say? Looked to me like you had some weighty thoughts on your mind."

His penetrating smile made me feel transparent, vulnerable. I answered evasively. "Oh, nothing really."

The corners of Leyland's eyes tightened. His piercing stare was without menace, but something artful bloomed darkly on his face, revealing his knowledge of my half-truth.

"Hmm, don't think so." He had an elfin smile. "A man who's daydreaming doesn't wear such a puckered brow."

I chuckled and looked away, nodding in a gesture of resignation. "Okay, fair enough. I didn't realize I appeared so intense."

"You don't happen to have any peppermint on you, do you?"

"Um, no. I'm afraid I don't."

"Hmm, shame. I love peppermint. Been my favorite since I was a boy. I don't get to the store much."

I paused, scrutinizing him. "So, Mr. Carter, as I mentioned, I'm the town doctor. How are you feeling these days?"

"Better than you, I think."

I chose not to respond despite his amiable and hearty manner. He spoke again.

"So, what does a fair-looking, well-educated young man such as yourself have to worry about? Seems you should own the world."

His question caught me off guard. During my short tenure in Watervalley, I had met a few men like Leyland Carter, older gentlemen with a penchant for blunt speaking and sharp inquiry who slid easily into philosophic commentary. And while it had never been my nature to unburden my thoughts to strangers, there was a pervasive atmosphere of ease and privacy in this remote woodland setting. I spoke openly.

"I guess on the surface it would seem that way. But it's been an unsettling day, and I'm far from owning the world, as you say."

He saw right through my thinly veiled frustration and spoke with impunity. "You're a young man, Dr. Bradford. And when we're young, we are intoxicated with the world, with the freshness of our ideas, with the possibilities for our future. Ambition, acclaim, passion, fortune; these things are everything. I'm guessing being a doctor in Watervalley has put such dreams on hold for you. Something has triggered your interest in revisiting them."

His razor-sharp insight baffled me. And there was something about his contented smile and tempered manner that, despite his impoverished surroundings, cast him as a man with whom life had not dealt harshly. With each passing minute, Leyland Carter was capturing my curiosity.

"You, uh . . . You seem to have a perspective that comes from experiences larger than living in these woods. Tell me about yourself, Mr. Carter."

He offered a short and rather vague narrative of his life, noting that he was born several counties away and that his family moved here when he was young. His people had been farmers and outdoorsmen. He had fought in the war, had once been engaged but never married, and along the way he had attained an education, earning a degree in classical studies from Vanderbilt. I watched him as he talked, and it seemed a legend of great distances was written on his face. After this brief summary, he turned and spoke pointedly, returning to his previous inquiry.

"So, which is it, Doctor, that has you in such a brooding mood? Ambition?"

I was amused by his persistence. "Yeah, in part. Being in Watervalley has been fine. But try as I might, I'm not one of these people. For the most part I respect and admire them, but some days I'm reminded pretty sharply of our differences."

He listened thoughtfully and answered in a low voice, "'One man in his time plays many parts.'" He was quoting from *As You Like It*.

"Okay, what is it about the people around here that they so readily cite Shakespeare?" Both Connie Thompson and John Harris had done this in the past.

"Living near the soil doesn't make you allergic to literature."

"Fair enough. It's just that sometimes it's hard to know what role to play." I went on to tell him about the newspaper article and how Clayton Ross's injuries were, in my thinking, being wrongly pinned on the Mennonite community.

"And why do you think that?"

"Because I suspected something and had a blood test run. Clayton's blood alcohol level was point nine. He was legally intoxicated although he didn't show many signs of it. That means he's probably a heavy drinker with a really high tolerance, especially given that the test was run hours after the accident occurred. In all the confusion and darkness of fighting the fire, nobody noticed his inebriation, but that's why he stumbled and fell. That's why he got hurt. And yet Luther Whitmore is using the story to stir everybody up against the Mennonites. Why, I don't know."

"Ah, Luther Whitmore," Leyland said ponderously. "I know of that fellow."

I picked up a rock and threw it at a nearby tree, missing my target. "Yeah, well, unfortunately he spreads his misery around, and there's nothing anyone can do about it."

Leyland focused hard on the nearby woods before speaking

his next words. "'This is the foppery of the world: that when we are sick in fortune . . . we make guilty of our disasters the sun, the moon, and stars.'"

I chuckled and threw another rock. *"King Lear."*

He waited for me to absorb his deeper meaning. After a few moments, I politely played along. "So, what are you telling me?"

"You can't blame the stars for what you don't want to do."

"You think I need to confront Luther about the article, don't you?"

"It would seem."

I picked up another piece of gravel and rolled it loosely in my hand. "I have a better idea. Why don't I just say screw it and leave the matter alone?"

A lengthy silence passed between us. Leyland lifted his chin and for the longest time, he rubbed the back of his fingers against the stubble of his whiskered face. He spoke slowly, reflectively.

"You could. But it wouldn't leave you alone. It would leave you disillusioned. And over time, disillusionment takes the light out of men, gives them a dry soul."

"Maybe. That seems a little dramatic, though, don't you think?" I turned to find his face framed in a gentle regard.

"It's always by a thousand cuts. A half-truth, an unspoken word, an overlooked injustice; they float by us like falling leaves. We ignore them, become blind to them. But we don't forget them, and as the years pass, we lose sight of the splendor of ordinary days."

The earnestness of his response kept me from further comment. I turned back to the woods and threw the rock at the tree, this time hitting it squarely.

Eventually Leyland began to tell about memories from his past. It was the idle talk of the lonely aged, but his voice was soft and melodious and pleasing, and I was content to listen. He talked about being a boy and the pungent smell of fermenting apples from the cellar, about burying best-loved pets, about the joy of walking down a lonely road at night in winter and seeing a light in the distance and knowing that it was his home. He spoke with wit and charm, and I found myself captivated by his small stories and reflections from decades past.

He also began to talk about going off to war, but he hesitated, as if touched by something odd and transitory, a momentary lapse of memory. In time, the somber glow of fading daylight began to cast deeper shadows on us.

It was time to go.

I stood, but he remained seated in the rocking chair, his hands gripping the armrests. I wanted to step closer and shake his hand, but something arrested the impulse. We exchanged confirming nods, as if we recognized in each other a sort of quiet understanding.

"Come back anytime you've got something on your mind, Dr. Bradford. Or even when you don't. I'll be here."

I bid him good-bye and walked back to my car. I liked Leyland Carter. He had a wisdom gained from long, solitary hours spent in the woods and with the soil.

I started the engine and carefully began the arduous process of pulling the car forward and backward in order to turn it around in the narrow space available. When I was finally able to head out the grassy driveway, I turned back to wave at him one last time, but he had already gone inside the house.

I drove toward the distant lights of Watervalley, consumed with a simple resolve. Ahead of me was a wholly disagreeable yet necessary task.

CHAPTER 15
A Talk with Luther

The last light of evening was fading as I made my way into town, leaving a lonely half-moon in the large bowl of night sky. I eased my car under the streetlights and shadows toward Luther's house. He lived on High Street in an old Victorian-style home with ornate porches, overgrown hedges, and ancient trees, all in desperate need of attention. The deterioration was not so bad as to warrant an official complaint, but cheerless enough to cast a dreariness on the otherwise well-manicured street.

I was filled with dread. Perhaps at the heart of my trepidation was the reality that I had nothing more to argue with than the weight of my opinion, since telling Luther about the sobriety test was off-limits.

I parked the car in his driveway and ascended the steps to the dark front porch, guided only by the lights from the street. A sign was tacked to his front door, and I used the light of my cell phone to read it. The large print read as follows:

NO SOLICITING.

FOR THOSE OF YOU WHO ARE STUBBORN,
STUPID, VOCABULARY IMPAIRED, OR JUST WANT
TO PISS ME OFF . . . ALLOW ME TO CLARIFY.

GO THE HELL AWAY.

1. I DON'T WANT ANY MORE MAGAZINES.
2. I HATE COOKIES.
3. I DON'T CARE ABOUT YOUR SOCCER TEAM.
4. I ALREADY KNOW JESUS.

My stomach churned, pulling nauseously on my throat. The massive front door stood sentinel in the gloomy dark. I took a deep breath and knocked.

For the longest time there was no sound, no movement, only me standing, listening, watching the eerie shadows upon the lifeless house. Something was foul about the whole business, and I felt a stifling uneasiness.

"Anybody home?" I yelled.

Soon, noises could be heard from within, and the porch lights came on, nearly blinding me. The large door creaked open, and Luther stood before me, regarding me stiffly. His face was dark and insolent, momentarily rendering me speechless.

"Well, Bradford, what do you want? You look like you're waiting for your voice to change."

My words were half-choked. "Hello, Luther. Sorry for the intrusion. I, um . . . I was wondering if I might talk with you for a few minutes."

At first he merely leered at me suspiciously. Then he grinned with a thin, rude coating of mirth. "Walk around back. I'll meet you in the garage." He slammed the door shut, and immediately the lights went out, leaving me fumbling in the dark. As my eyes adjusted, I descended from the porch and followed his instructions, making my way around the side of the house toward an attached garage in the rear that appeared to have been added in recent years. With its large wooden doors standing wide open, it was well lit.

I soon discovered, so was Luther.

He stood holding a half-empty bottle of Jim Beam by its neck. The walls and shelves were cluttered with beer cans and whiskey bottles. There was a thick smell of stale nicotine, and the dusty room had a cluttered, burly male quality.

"Bradford, I'd offer you a drink, but candidly, I really don't give a damn about sharing." There was a telling slur in his speech.

For some reason Luther's drunken state eased my intimidation. "I can see that you and whiskey are still on good terms."

"Yeah, well, my original plan for the evening was to take up needlepoint. But getting drunk seemed like a better idea."

"Clearly your life's a banquet, Luther."

He ignored my jab and took a long draw from the whiskey bottle before walking over to a folding chair and plopping awkwardly into it. "So, Doctor. My keen grasp of the obvious tells me you're here with an agenda. But first, I've got a question for you."

I grabbed another folding chair and placed it a few feet away from him. As I sat down, I couldn't help but notice his smug glare. He had the harsh face of one who took pleasure in other people's misery.

Luther's mind was probing, temporarily unconcerned with learning the purpose of my visit. His words were cynical and unenthused. "You were wanting to do research, weren't you, instead of coming to this backwater hick town?"

Luther was going for the jugular, attempting to gouge a

suspected vulnerability. I spoke cautiously. "There is some truth to that statement."

"Well, why don't you see if your ass can come up with a cure for brain freeze? That way I could just eat donuts and ice cream for dinner."

I spoke impassively. "Kind of a limited menu, don't you think?"

"Oh, what the hell," he said callously. "It'll give my cholesterol medicine something to do."

From within their cavernous sockets, his adder eyes gauged me. I got the impression that Luther saw himself maliciously toying with me, not unlike what a cat does with a wounded mouse. He knew I would eventually get to the purpose of my visit, but meanwhile I was something to trifle with, an unthreatening diversion.

"So, did you come to tell me you're going to pay for bush hogging the lake property?"

I grinned. "Not even close." But his question opened the door to my burning curiosity about Moon Lake. "Tell me something, Luther. Why did you enclose the place with the tall razor-wire fence like you did? Kind of overkill, isn't it?"

His face held unmasked contempt, as if he were weighing out the need to answer me. "Seems obvious, doesn't it? Keeps people out of there."

"A simple sign and a pasture fence would keep people out. That six-foot fence makes it a fortress. How come you never built a home out there anyway?"

His eyes were open, but he seemed to be looking far away into some lost abyss, haunted by some deep preoccupation. "Because when I came back from Vietnam, everything had changed."

"How so?"

"That's none of your damn business," Luther exclaimed with great delight.

I changed tactics. "Did your ex-wife not want to live out there?"

"No, it was never her choice anyway. It was never meant for her to live out there."

It seemed an odd thing to say, as if in Luther's mind Moon Lake were something private to which Claire was not allowed membership.

"I don't understand what you mean by that, Luther."

He took another long drink, ignoring my question. He looked out the large doors into the darkness and spoke distantly, again waving his bottle in a grand soliloquy. "Moon Lake, the promised land. 'And I saw the holy city, coming down out of heaven from God, prepared as a bride adorned for her husband.'"

Luther may have been drunk, but he was still clever. I didn't understand why he chose this passage of scripture, but I was certain it held some buried significance.

"Luther, how is it you so easily quote the Bible?"

He responded with sanctimonious pride. "There was a time when I thought about going into the ministry."

I lowered my head in disbelief. "Seriously? What happened?"

"My hormones kicked in." He wiped his mouth and glared at me. "Bradford, why do you care that I put a fence around Eden?"

"I'm just curious what you're trying to keep out."

Slowly he rolled his doleful, drunken eyes toward me. "The past."

I offered no response. I was searching, thinking, trying to frame a question. Before I could, he spoke again.

"So, what's the house call all about?" Luther had finally grown weary of our sparring.

I took a deep breath, speaking firmly. "I think it was a bad decision to print that article about Clayton Ross and the other veterans."

"Bad decisions make good stories."

"Your facts were laced with a lot of fiction."

"Are you saying there are some facts I'm missing?"

"A few."

"Like what?"

I sighed. "I'm not allowed to say."

Luther grunted, making a low scoffing noise. "Why? Did you pinkie swear you wouldn't tell anybody?"

"It's just not something I can disclose." I refrained from mentioning that it was medically related, although Luther would probably figure that out.

"Humph. So, what do you want me to do about it?"

"Retract your story."

"Bradford, you might want to consider pursuing more attainable goals."

"It's the right thing to do."

"Says who, you? On what basis?"

"Because it's inflammatory, it makes false assumptions, and it's cast a cloud of resentment and suspicion on the Mennonites. People get pretty emotional when they think a military veteran has been done an injustice."

"Oh, cry me a river, Doc. You're just one dead dog away from a good country song."

"The article put words in Clayton's mouth that he never said. It all came from his father, didn't it?"

A cunning grin spread across Luther's face, telling me that I had hit my target. He spoke in a voice absent contrition. "It doesn't matter."

"And why not?"

"Because I know what it's like. I used to be on the volunteer fire service. Years ago we made a wasted trip out to the buggy boys."

"Are you talking about the fire on Mercy Creek Road?"

Luther's eyes tightened with suspicion. It seemed he wanted to ask what I knew about the ruins, but for some reason, he chose to ignore the question and spoke evasively. "That doesn't matter. It's about the Mennonites. They're a damn nuisance."

"Why do you dislike them so much?"

"News flash, Bradford. I don't like anybody."

"Yeah, I get that. But you have a special loathing for the Mennonites, don't you?"

Luther's countenance grew hard and cool, as if somehow the mouse had landed a right uppercut and the fun had left the game. "What of it?"

"Why? Because they're pacifists?"

Luther grunted a low noise of contempt. "Look at you. Aren't you just bathed in stupidity? You have a soft spot for them, don't you? You think that because they're all meek and humble, I should cut them some slack."

I was unfazed, clearly aware of his attempt at redirection. "Why, Luther? Why do you hate them?"

"Because they think they stand on some theological high ground, that's why."

"So, you don't like them because they never served their country like you did?"

His voice was now loaded with a full measure of condescension. "No, I don't like them because I don't like them." His words hung fat in the air. Then with a superior tone he added, "Besides, you're wrong. Some of them did serve. They did their time during the war, so to speak."

This comment attained its intended effect, leaving me dumbfounded. "You're telling me that some of the Mennonites served in the military?"

"Hell no. What kind of dumbass question is that?" Luther shot me a look of complete disgust. He lumbered to his feet. "Go do your homework, Bradford. And leave me alone. I'm through talking."

He shuffled to the house's back entry and disappeared inside, slamming the door. I walked back to the car, knowing I had accomplished nothing. Talking with Luther left me uneasy and confused. There was a blackness in him I could not fathom.

As I drove down the dark and dispirited streets, the town now seemed smaller, more callous, and more tattered than before. Luther was only one voice, but it was a loud one that rippled through the public mind. I tried to put him out of my thoughts, but it was little use. Meanwhile, I was determined to find out what he'd meant about the Mennonites who had served.

It had been a long, difficult day, and I was exhausted. But as I pulled into my driveway, one good thought came to mind: Christine.

FROM THE JOURNAL OF
CHRISTINE CHAMBERS, AGE 14

June 23, 1999

Dear Mr. Wonderful:
You have a stupid name!

There is no way you can be wonderful. Because wherever you are right now, you're just a boy. And boys are stupid.

I wear a new swimsuit and all they do is stare.

They run around the pool and do nothing but scream and laugh like idiots. They want to play Marco Polo so they can pretend to bump against me and then laugh and whisper. But they don't laugh so big when I hold them underwater. They just get mad.

Then ten minutes later, they want to play Marco Polo again, so they can pretend to bump me, again. *They're just stupid.*

I hope you are not like the boys around here, Mr. Wonderful, because if you are, you need to change. You need to get all of the stupid out of you before you show up.

Otherwise, you better be a really good swimmer.

CAC

CHAPTER 16
Moonlight

Thursday at the clinic was uneventful, a welcome change from earlier in the week. I had gone online and learned that draft-age Mennonite men had, in fact, served in civil service jobs during the Vietnam era, rather than join the active military. Still, I was left with little insight regarding who and what Luther had been referring to.

As I had instructed, Clayton Ross came in each day to get his dressing changed. While Ann was doing this, I stepped into the exam room briefly to check the wound's progress. Clayton was silent and ill at ease. For now, I chose to say nothing to him about the newspaper article.

When I arrived home that afternoon, the Blind Boys Mowing Service had just finished trimming the lawn. Kenny and Kevin Blind had been cutting yards for nearly twenty years, but every time I saw the company name on the side of their truck, I had to laugh.

I took Rhett out to the backyard. The ragged state of my garden was absolutely shameful. The weeds were so large, I could almost hear them trash-talking me. So after feeding Rhett, I changed into some shorts, and armed with a hoe, I proceeded to declare war on the invaders. I quickly learned they weren't giving up without a fight.

With his head on his paws, Rhett watched lazily from the shade. The six o'clock sun still had plenty of muscle, and I was promptly drenched in sweat. I took off my shirt, used it to wipe my face, and tossed it on the nearby grass. For the better part of an hour I chopped, pulled, tugged, and swore at everything that didn't look like a vegetable. And I had to laugh at myself. I was a summa cum laude graduate from one of the best medical schools in the country and completely loved being a doctor. But weeding a garden surprised me with an odd satisfaction, a gratifying sense of accomplishment as I methodically brought order to this small patch of earth filled with plants that I had started from seed.

I was almost finished when Christine's car pulled into the driveway beside the house.

"Hey, I'm back here."

She looked radiant even in shorts and sandals. As she approached, I leaned on my hoe and blew away the sweat dripping from my nose. Her smile was full of warmth and humor. And in those brief seconds as she walked toward me, the sensuous movement of her long legs and lovely figure melted me far more than the blistering June sun had.

Suddenly galvanized, Rhett trotted briskly over to meet her. Christine dropped to one knee and rubbed his ears. "Hello, Rhett! Have you had a nice day?"

Rhett was doing his best to play the sympathy card, using his big brown eyes to look like a despondent and lonely puppy, prolonging Christine's adoration. I leaned casually on my hoe. "It's good to see you too, Miss Chambers."

She rolled her eyes and stepped toward me, taking in my grubby appearance. "I'd like to get a picture of this."

"Gee, hate that. *GQ* should be here in about ten minutes to do a photo shoot. Sorry, they got dibs."

"I see. *GQ*, huh? What's the article?"

I thought for a second. "Which doctor is best: The specialist or the garden variety."

"Cuuute," Christine chided. However, she was staring at me rather intently, her eyes walking up and down my six-foot-two frame. "You know, I'm kind of impressed. You're pretty cut. I can't think of when I've seen you with your shirt off."

Something in Christine's tone and eyes spoke beyond her jovial response. Admittedly, ever since I had been a college athlete, playing undergraduate basketball for Mercer, I had kept myself in good shape.

"For the last hour I've been doing mortal combat with weeds so gargantuan they're worthy of a Japanese horror movie."

"Seems to have done the trick. You look like the cover of one of those muscle magazines, all taut and shimmering."

"Actually, I was thinking more like wrenched out and sweaty, but I like your version better."

I walked over and grabbed my shirt from the grass, and we headed back toward the house.

"Have you had dinner?" I asked.

"Had a salad earlier. What about you?"

"Ate a late lunch. So I'm good." I stopped for a moment to stretch my back, hoping to work out a minor ache or two from the past hour's labor.

Curiously, Christine's adoring gaze remained unrelenting. She spoke playfully. "Yeah, Bradford, I have to say . . . this no-shirt thing is a good look for you."

"Good to know. Thanks for noticing." I again rested the hoe on my shoulder and stared at her for a moment.

"What?" she asked.

"Well, in the interest of fair play, I was just wondering how the no-shirt thing would look on you."

I was awaiting the usual rebuttal, but to my surprise, Christine responded with a cunning grin. "I have a better idea."

"Okay, you've clearly gotten my attention."

"I brought my bathing suit. Why don't we go out to Moon Lake for a swim?"

"Sure," I said in a mix of eagerness and delight. "I'll take a quick shower and we'll head out."

"I'll get my suit from the car and change."

Ten minutes later, we were in the Austin-Healey loaded with beach towels, a blanket, and some drinks. Christine had slipped her suit on beneath her T-shirt and shorts. Much to his dismay, Rhett had to stay home.

We chatted along the way, but our words were short, buoyant, filled with smiles and a dancing sense of expectation. It was past seven thirty when I pulled up to the gate outside of Moon Lake. I unlocked it and drove the car through. Normally I would leave the gate open, but this time I stopped and locked it behind us. Christine waited in the car, making no inquiry of me when I returned. By an unspoken understanding, we both wanted the evening to be ours alone.

I pulled along the water's edge and parked. The grass, to my surprise, had recently been mowed. After spreading the blanket out in the small area in front of the car, I folded my arms and leaned against the hood, taking in the view of the lake. Christine dropped her beach towel on the blanket. Then, before she began to unbutton her shorts, she paused and glanced at me.

As she had suspected, I was watching her, bewitched with anticipation. A slow, confident smile eased across her face, and for a second I thought she almost winked at me. She pushed her shorts down her long legs and stepped out of them. Then in a fluid, sensuous movement, she lifted her shirt above her head and tossed it to the side.

There she was, at long last. Silhouetted against the orange glow of the setting sun, her tanned skin, ripe curves, and tall, beautiful body made my heart jump. She literally took my breath away.

"Christine Ann Chambers. I think now I'm the one who'd like to take a picture."

As she walked toward me, I took off my shirt and sunglasses, laying them on the car. Smiling richly, she draped her arms around my neck.

"So, are you saying you like my suit?"

"I definitely like what's in it."

I drew her close for a brief kiss. The warm press of her skin, and so much of it, was absolutely intoxicating. She leaned backward, my arms still hanging loosely around her waist. We were both wearing irrepressible, almost giddy smiles that spontaneously erupted into laughter.

"You are wicked, Christine Chambers. Positively and completely wicked."

"And why is that?" she asked mischievously.

"Oh right. Listen to you playing innocent here while I'm gawking like a schoolboy. You're gorgeous, Chambers."

She looked down. "I've had one or two guys tell me that."

"I see. And did this happen when you were wearing a bathing suit?"

"Especially then." She paused for emphasis.

"So, a guy ogling and telling you you're gorgeous is nothing new."

"No. But this is different."

"Hmm, different how?"

She searched my eyes and spoke in a low, sweet whisper, placing her finger on my chin. "Because this time it's this guy, and this bathing suit, and unlike with all those other guys, I don't mind the ogling."

"I'm pretty sure ogling isn't all I'm thinking about."

She cut her eyes at me. "Come on, Bradford. Let's go for a swim and cool off a little." She squeezed my hand before turning and running toward the lake.

I stood there for a moment, mumbling, "Unless this thing is fed by an arctic glacier, I don't think that's going to help."

We swam out a short distance to where our feet no longer touched bottom. The water was surprisingly cool, but tolerable, especially against the residual heat of the day. We swam and talked and laughed and splashed each other. Christine playfully tried to dunk me, but her efforts only served as opportunities to grab her and bring her down with me. And mixed within the fun and laughter was the occasional stolen kiss.

The sun set, casting the distant hills into silhouette and shooting an array of orange hues against the cloudless sky. We had moved closer toward the shore to shoulder-deep water. The warm evening air was perfectly still, and our voices echoed softly against the night, our bodies making delicate ripples in the mirrored surface. Soon a lilting moon appeared and our frolicsome conversation ebbed, gently passing into whispers that were sweet, tender, intimate.

A silence fell upon us. In the low luster of moonlight, I watched the glistening dance of the water on Christine's face and shoulders. I drew her near, looking into her dark eyes, so completely sincere, pure, magical. All that was strong and beautiful of my life in Watervalley was buried within them. She said nothing, only gazed at me with a face that was wistful and alluring. The left shoulder strap of her bathing suit had slid off and was hanging down her arm, availing an enticing exposure of bare skin. It was impossible to resist.

I lifted her slightly in the water, kissing her neck and shoulders. Slowly, she reached around and pulled away her long hair, her voice forming a pleasing hum. It was a small gesture, but a deeply inviting one that ignited in me a cascade of stirring emotion. I pulled her closer. She reached up and ran her fingers into my hair. My kisses grew more lavish, more consuming. Our breath quickened. Down in the water I ran my hands along Christine's back and around the curve of her hips. She drew closer, and I felt the soft brush of her leg around the back of mine. But this spontaneous movement left her slightly off balance, and she tried to steady herself in the shoulder-deep water.

Instinctively, and without thinking, I put both hands on her bottom in an effort to stabilize her.

Christine hesitated and then murmured in a playful, teasing voice, "Dr. Bradford, do you realize that both of your hands are on my behind?"

I smiled and kept them firmly in place. "Is that so?" Undaunted, I held her tightly, giving her backside a shameless and delightful squeeze. "I believe you're right, Miss Chambers. That is definitely your derriere."

She was smiling through her words. "Derriere, huh? Is that what you doctors call it when you hold a girl's bottom?"

"No, actually I call it a good start. What do you call it?"

She looked down and spoke in a shy, earnest voice. "I call it a first. I've never let a guy do that."

I blurted my response. "Seriously?"

My quick utterance held a tone of disbelief. Christine seemed suddenly self-conscious, and there was almost a hurt quality to her words. "Well, yeah, seriously."

"So no guy has ever had his hands on your backside?"

"Nope." Again she looked down, as if the answer embarrassed her.

I thought about her words for a moment. If this were true, it perhaps told a larger story about Christine, one that I had only suspected. An awkward silence fell between us. We separated slightly. Softly illuminated by the pale moonlight, she seemed uncertain, tense, searching.

I said nothing, but I understood.

Slowly, I reached forward and carefully slid my hands beside her face, lightly cradling the delicate curve of her head. I leaned toward her and pressed my lips to her forehead, gently keeping them there. She seemed to understand this tender gesture.

She reached up and wrapped her arms tightly around my neck and rested her head on my shoulder, yielding the full measure of her soft body against me. Her voice was sweet, fragile, vulnerable. "I love you, Luke Bradford."

I rested my chin on her head and wrapped my arms around her, securely, protectively, and whispered into the darkness, "I love you too, Christine Chambers."

Whatever thoughts I had had about the romantic potential of the night were now pushed aside. I truly did love Christine, and it seemed that there was much to think about. Then again, the nearness of her yielding body was maddening, and I couldn't resist the tempting thought burning in my head.

"Bradford, why are you squeezing my butt again?"

"If you must know, it's a doctor thing. I was just checking for any flaws."

Christine pushed back from my shoulder. "And?"

"Good news. Yours is absolutely perfect."

Even in the moonlight I could see the light shaking of her head. She kissed me and laughed softly. "Come on, Doctor. Let's get to dry land."

Once ashore, we wrapped towels around us and sat on the blanket, watching the brilliance of the moonlight shimmering off the lake. Christine settled between my legs and leaned back against me, resting her head against my chest.

"I love this place," she said quietly.

I looked up at the tender stars dotting the night sky. "Yeah, I like coming out here, especially when I get to take you along."

Christine had closed her eyes and spoke in a drowsy, dreamy voice. "Out here, you can take me anytime."

I was still gazing at the stars when her words registered. I pressed my chin against her head. "What did you say?"

Christine sat up abruptly. Her words were flustered. "I said, um, I meant to say that you can take me out here anytime. You know, I mean, bring me here."

I reached over and pressed my finger to her lips. "Hush, Chambers." I wrapped my arms around her and pulled her back toward me, kissing her wet hair. "Just look at the stars."

She settled back, her shoulders melting against me. We sat silently for the longest time, and I closed my eyes. It was a moment from a dream.

But a minute later, Christine leaned slightly forward and turned to me with a puzzled expression. "Luke, do you hear singing?"

CHAPTER 17

Intruders

We both stiffened, endeavoring to be deathly still and listen. Christine was right. In the nearby darkness, the delicate tones of a woman's voice were drifting up from the grassy descent some hundred or so yards away. It wasn't like the man's voice that I had heard at the ruins. That one seemed to echo on the wind. This one had a lilting, earthy quality that cut through the still night air. We couldn't make out the words, but the tune was a simple and repetitive folk song. And it was growing louder, the singer coming closer.

We sat frozen, both of us momentarily unnerved at the thought that we were not alone. Admittedly, though, there was nothing threatening in the mellow notes. It occurred to me that whoever it was had no idea we were there. I pressed a finger to my lips and gestured for Christine to move around the side of the car with me. We crouched low near the door and listened. The woman's voice moved ever closer and was coming from directly in front of the Austin-Healey. Suddenly it stopped and was followed by giggling laughter. A second voice, that of a man, joined the first.

I had heard enough. I stood up, reached across the dashboard, and pulled out the knob for the headlights. Illuminated some fifty yards away were the outlines of a man and a woman. The man held up his arm to shield his eyes, and the woman raised both hands to her mouth, muffling a gasping shriek.

"Who's there?" I called out in a firm, clear voice.

They stood still for only a split second before he grabbed her hand. They ran out of the path of the headlights and into the darkness.

"Hello," I called out again, but there was no answer. By now Christine was standing beside me.

"Where'd they go, Luke?"

"I don't know. They took off. I think I scared them half to death."

"Could you tell who they were?" Her voice still carried a slight tinge of worry.

"If my guess is correct, I think it was a couple of teenagers. They sure moved quickly. Did you not see them?"

"No, they were gone by the time I stood up."

"So I guess you didn't see the way they were dressed?"

"What about it?"

"From the looks of it, they were Mennonites."

We loaded up our things, and I drove the car slowly across the grass in the direction that they had fled. I was at a loss as to how the two of them had gotten inside the fence, thinking that the road gate was the only access. I soon had my answer.

The enclosed area including the lake encompassed eleven or more acres. I headed toward the encircling fence, some two hundred yards away. Once there, I drove along beside it. After a short distance, a small passage gate came into view of the headlights. I hadn't known there was a second way into the property.

I positioned the car's lights on it and got out to take a look. The chain-link gate was three feet wide and tightly padlocked. Upon closer inspection, I saw that the metal ties holding the chain mesh had been removed, allowing for easy entry by simply lifting it up. Unless you looked closely, it appeared perfectly secure. Beyond the gate lay a path that was quickly swallowed by thick woods. The two Mennonite teenagers were nowhere to be seen.

As I was heading back to the car, something on the ground caught my eye. I picked it up and walked over to look at it in the car's headlight. It was a white handkerchief.

I got in the car and handed it to Christine. "They're long gone, but I'm certain they were Mennonites."

"There are initials embroidered on this handkerchief," said Christine as she held it toward the dashboard lights. "ELY."

I shook my head. "No idea, except the 'Y' could possibly mean Yoder. I was thinking the girl could be Jacob's daughter, but her name is Rebecca. Anyway, it doesn't matter. Excitement over."

"What do you think they were doing here?"

I dropped my chin, giving Christine a disbelieving look. "Probably the same thing we were doing, sans the really cute two-piece bathing suit."

"So, you *did* like the bathing suit, huh?"

I thought about responding with some boyish, clever remark. But somehow, somewhere in the course of the evening, something had changed. Something in Christine's words, in her willingness, had placed an earnest solemnity upon me that I did not yet fully understand. Instead, I reached over, held her hand, and smiled warmly.

"Very much, Miss Chambers. Very, very much."

CHAPTER 18
A Well-Kept Secret

The next few days passed like a blur. A work crew showed up at the Fox house next door and in the course of two days installed a crisp white picket fence around the backyard. Rhett was now the ever-vigilant nosy neighbor, standing sentinel at the kitchen door and peering through the glass anytime Maggie was let out to play. I half expected to walk in on him holding a pair of binoculars, salaciously wagging his tongue, or tail, or both. He was apparently quite smitten.

Clayton Ross continued to come in daily for his dressing change. He was always polite and respectful, but quiet. And as the days passed, the fervor from Luther's article seemed to ebb, so I saw little point in bringing up the matter with Clayton. Still, sometimes at the diner I would overhear an occasional disparaging remark about the Mennonites.

Word was also getting around about John Harris's initiative to build a new war memorial, and the idea appeared to be enthusiastically and universally endorsed. Unfortunately, the memorial also provoked comparisons to those who had not fought in the last century's wars, the Mennonites, fostering a mind-set of resentment that seemed to creep into the daily discussion. The majority of the townsfolk had tolerant and accepting spirits, but it required only a few malcontents to keep the pot stirred.

On the last Tuesday night of June, Connie cooked dinner for me. What had once been a daily ritual was now an occasional event. Her time was consumed with Estelle and the bakery, and my time was devoted to spending every possible minute with Christine. My house continued to be magically spotless and the laundry clean, but our meals together occurred infrequently. In some ways, Connie was my closest confidant, my best friend. So all day Tuesday, I was greatly looking forward to seeing her.

That afternoon I arrived home to a surprise. Both sisters had come for a visit. I remembered Connie's remark that the two of them had a Tuesday evening ritual of dinner and an Elvis movie. It looked like I was in for a night of great food and *Viva Las Vegas.*

I found them in the kitchen engaged in an energetic conversation about their upcoming family reunion.

"Estelle, honey, what is wrong with you? What kind of woman goes looking for a man at a family reunion?"

"I didn't say anything about looking for a man. I just said I hope Cousin Flora brings her brother, Tyrell. She's related by marriage, so I think he's fair game. He's such a sharp dresser, and so polite."

"Sweetie, I hate to break it to you, but Tyrell is not just a sharp dresser. He's also a hairdresser. Far be it from me to judge, but I don't think he's interested in female companionship."

"Well now, that's where you're wrong. He was awful keen on me last year till that little accident."

Although I had been standing in the kitchen during this conversation, neither of them acknowledged my presence. No greetings, no salutations, no change of subject. Yet, there was something wonderful in this treatment. It seemed that I was a family member whose arrival was not worthy of formal gestures.

Meanwhile, Connie continued to lecture her sister. "Sweetie, that was your own fault. If you hadn't been acting like the goofy fairy had just visited you, that accident, as you call it, wouldn't have happened." Finally, Connie turned to me. "Luke, it's almost ready. Go upstairs and get yourself washed up."

"Are you kidding? I want to hear the rest of this. What accident are you talking about?"

Connie gave her sister an admonishing glance and uttered a superior "Humph."

Estelle explained, "It was just a little allergic reaction. I accidentally ate the wrong food."

"Umm-hmm. Little, my foot. Your lips swelled up so bad, it looked like you had two hot dogs glued to your face." Connie was erupting in laughter . . . so much so that she put one hand to her chest and the other on the kitchen counter to steady herself. "Sweetie, you know I love you, but for the life of me, your lips looked like a baboon's butt."

"That's all in the past," Estelle responded indignantly, clearly not sharing Connie's amusement. "Besides, I don't care what you have to say about it. I'm going to Nashville the weekend before the reunion and get me a mani, a pedi, and some new shoes."

"What kind of new shoes?" inquired Connie.

"Some athletic shoes. I need to get some with lavender to match my outfit so I can play in the reunion volleyball tournament."

Connie was aghast. "Volleyball! Girl, what are you thinking? You've got no business playing volleyball with your heart condition. Besides, I've seen chess players with better reflexes than you have."

Estelle was not amused. "Talk all you want, big sister. Tyrell played last year, so this year, I'm playing too."

Connie closed her eyes, shaking her head. The two were such an odd and entertaining pair. It was as though matter and antimatter had been born into the same family. Still, there was a secret warmth between them.

I washed up at the kitchen sink, and we sat down to dinner. Connie, who was the arbiter of all religious matters, said a lengthy prayer that included references to the Ecclesiastes passage regarding a time for everything. I half expected her to say something about there being a time to play volleyball and a time to refrain from playing volleyball. But thankfully, she fell short of that. Amen was said, and I grabbed my fork.

"So," Connie began, "how are things at the clinic these days?"

"Mostly routine," I responded.

"By the way, I heard Gene Alley on the radio today, talking like a magpie. Looks like he decided he had tortured Peggy long enough."

"Really? So you think all that talking in song titles was some prank of his?"

Connie shrugged. "With Gene it's hard to say. That war wound to his head knocked out the last marbles he had."

"Speaking of which," I interjected, "John Harris came by today with a bunch of sketches for the design of the new memorial. He asked the art teacher at the high school to make it an assignment for her summer art class. One of them is really good. We'll probably use it."

"What will it look like?" Connie asked.

"It's a statue of a young man returning home from war. He has an elated expression on his face and is holding a large military duffel bag. Since the memorial covers numerous wars and conflicts, he's dressed in civilian clothes because no one uniform would be accurate. The statue will be on a large square base where the names of those killed in action will be engraved."

"That sounds wonderful," said Connie.

"Yeah, John is getting some estimates out of Nashville on the cost of doing the statue in bronze. Then the real fun begins."

"How so?" inquired Estelle.

"Raising the money. I kind of dread that part."

Estelle flipped her hand at me. "Oh, honey, you'll do fine at that. Just go chat 'em up a little. Take a few cupcakes along. That'll help loosen up their checkbooks."

I didn't share Estelle's confidence. "Luther Whitmore's on my list. I don't think a cupcake will do much to persuade him."

"I think you're going to have to try and overlook Luther's shortcomings," Connie said in earnest.

"I don't think they make a ladder tall enough."

Connie ignored my slight. "We're all God's children, Doctor, including Luther."

"Yeah, well. Luther must be thinking God grades on a curve."

Connie tilted her head and gazed at me above her gold-inlay glasses. It was a familiar look of reproach.

"Okay, Constance Grace, what am I missing here?" I asked.

She took a drink of her tea before speaking. "People don't know it, but Luther is probably Watervalley's most decorated veteran. He served three tours in Vietnam and was wounded multiple times. Apparently, Luther did some pretty courageous things. Claire never told me what. Luther didn't want it known."

"But why?"

"No idea." Connie paused briefly. "There's something else. Claire told me that one of Luther's injuries . . . Well, how do I say it? One of his injuries left him unable to have children. Claire knew it and didn't care. She just wanted to be married and happy. Unfortunately, she had to choose between one or the other."

I nodded, absorbing all that Connie had said. "I wonder why he hates the Mennonites so much."

"No idea on that one either. Like we've talked about, Luther and his family used to live out there near the Mennonite community. I got the impression from Claire that Luther played with them when he was a kid. He practically grew up with them."

I listened intently. There seemed little more to understand on the matter, and the conversation moved to other topics. Connie and Estelle left around eight, and I talked to Christine briefly on the phone. Around ten that night, I took Rhett out back for a final chance to do his business before bedtime.

As was my habit, I stared up at the stars and thought about the day, unable to get Luther out of my head. He seemed to have an insatiable appetite for self-destruction, and I wondered if this fatal mind-set had contributed to his valor in Vietnam. It seemed that somewhere along the way, something had happened to Luther to convince him that being alive was a punishment.

Satisfying my curiosity would have to wait.

CHAPTER 19

Every Dog Has His Day

Friday I was up at sunrise and went for a run, putting Rhett on his leash to make him trot along.

"Come on, fellow. We need to get you trimmed up for your big introduction to the new neighbor. Girls want a guy to be a little buff. You can't get by on your charm alone."

I was confident he understood every word of my advice by the way he eagerly wagged his tail. But as soon as we passed the Fox house and headed down Fleming Street, he was straining at the leash to go back. I mildly admonished him about getting in shape, injecting as much guilt into the conversation as possible. He responded by turning his back toward me and sitting down. A few tugs on the leash brought him around to my way of thinking.

Reluctantly, he consented, and we began the mile run out to Watervalley Lake. We soon passed the last of the tree-shaded streets and moved into the open countryside. A warm, drowsy breeze ruffled the blades of corn in the adjacent fields, and the morning air was filled with the fragrant aroma of late honeysuckle.

Given the discord that had overshadowed the town the past

couple of weeks, it was good to be reminded of the pervading tranquillity and lulling tempo of rural life. A light dew covered the nearby field grass, birds chirped in the tall trees, and a soft, misty fog hung motionless over distant pastures. It seemed that by small degrees I was beginning to understand Christine's love of this wide valley.

Normally, Rhett and I would have the lake to ourselves at such an early hour, but this morning as we neared the bandstand, I saw Karen Davidson standing in the grass by the water's edge, dressed in running gear.

I called out as we approached. "Hey, Karen. Good morning."

She waved and headed in our direction. "Hi, Luke. Good to see you again. Who is this fellow?"

I had been practically dragging Rhett the last hundred yards and saw no danger in letting go of his leash, thinking he would immediately faint into a big ball of panting fur. Instead, he shot up from his near collapse and bolted toward Karen, leaping into the air and knocking her to the grass, treating her like a giant lollipop.

Karen exploded with laughter and was immediately on her knees, affectionately rubbing behind his ears. She had to hold him at bay to prevent him from crawling all over her.

"Rhett! Rhett! Back off now! Karen, I am so sorry!"

Still bursting with laughter, she held up her hand. "It's okay, Luke. He's fine. He's fine."

"I don't know what got into him. Again, I am so sorry."

Karen continued to briskly rub Rhett's head and talk to him entreatingly, regarding him with a face of irreproachable devotion, as if he glowed. Eventually she stood and held her hand flat toward him, speaking in a low, instructive voice. "Stay. Now stay."

Rhett immediately assumed an obedient seated position and

stared at her with spellbound attention, rocking lightly in rhythm with his incessant panting.

"Okay," I said, "that was just amazing. I'd have to promise him a T-bone to do that for me."

Karen was practically jubilant, and her mood was contagious. She shrugged and spoke modestly. "I can't explain it really. It's always been that way with dogs and me. They just go nuts when they see me. It's, I don't know, a weird kind of gift."

"So you are used to this kind of reaction?"

"Yeah, with cats too sometimes."

"Well, for your sake, I hope the gift doesn't extend to cows and horses."

She half grinned, giving me a wide-eyed expression. "Fortunately, they're not quite so exuberant. But they do respond to me pretty uniquely."

"How so?"

"Hard to say, honestly. Animals are just really calm around me. Somehow I can tell what they're thinking. And sometimes I sense that they can read my mind too."

I stood dumbfounded, thoroughly intrigued. "That's just fascinating. Half the time I can't read my own mind."

She laughed and added rather shyly, "Yeah. It's just not the kind of thing you can put on your business card." She held up her hands with her thumbs extended, much like a movie director would do to frame a scene. "Karen Davidson, Psychic Vet."

"Right. I see. Not the kind of thing the boys at the Co-op are going to readily warm up to."

She scrunched her mouth into a tight grimace and nodded. I was beginning to understand her dilemma.

"Well, you've certainly made a believer out of me," I said.

"Yeah, one person down. One whole town to go."

"So, is that why you didn't want to give Luther an interview? Thought you might say something he'd take the wrong way?"

Karen smirked. "I didn't give Luther an interview because, quite frankly, he's creepy. And yeah, I have a bad habit of saying things the wrong way." She paused and looked down, her voice tinged with embarrassment. "But I guess you already figured that out after that fiasco in your office. I hope that didn't cause a problem?"

"None whatsoever."

She patted Rhett on the head and spoke with resolve. "But I'm good with animals, really good. If the farmers just give me a chance, I think I'll be okay."

"So, the grand opening of the new and improved clinic is in a couple of Saturdays, right? July fifth?"

"Yeah, the Sweetlife Bakery is going to cater a bunch of treats for both people and pets. Hopefully, we'll get a good crowd."

"Ah, so you've met the two sisters?"

"Sure have. They're certainly a pair."

"Know them well," I responded. "Anyway, I hope the grand opening is a big success."

"Thanks. Me too."

I detected genuine worry in her voice. She spoke again, noticeably changing the subject.

"So, are you trying to get Rhett in leaner shape?" All during our conversation, Rhett had remained frozen like a statue from the Jedi mind trick Karen had performed on him.

"Yeah, I told him if he didn't slim down some, I'd have to cut off his cigarette money."

She rubbed his ears playfully, then stopped abruptly. She was looking closely at Rhett's face. "Is there something going on with his right eye?"

"I'm glad you asked," I said. "I've noticed lately that it seems cloudy."

She bent down and held Rhett's head, gently pulling back the skin around his eye. "Hmm," she whispered softly. "I might need to take a look at this back at the clinic."

"What do you think it could be?"

"Hard to know for sure without a scope. Might be as simple as cataracts or as serious as a tumor."

"Treatment?"

"Depends. If it is tumor related, sometimes it's just best to take the eye out, before it metastasizes." She looked around toward Rhett's male parts, noting that everything was present and accounted for. "Might not be a bad idea to get him neutered too."

I winced at this thought. Rhett made no reaction whatsoever, proving that Karen truly had him under a spell. His perfect understanding of English would normally have him snarling at such a suggestion.

Karen read the look on my face. "It's actually healthier for them," she added.

"Karen, I'm sure you're right. But I don't know. For some reason, whenever I picture Rhett, I see him with testicles. So we'll leave the accessories alone for now."

"Sure. Just a thought."

It was time to head back. I reached over, grabbed his leash off the ground, and whispered to Rhett, "You owe me big-time."

We walked together to the road.

"Heading back toward town?" I inquired.

"No, I'm going farther out. I like to get in eight or nine miles each morning. But I usually stop and look at the lake for a few minutes. There's something about staring at water that's kind of transcendent."

I nodded politely, all the while thinking to myself, *Eight or nine miles, jeez Louise*. It was yet another reason to be impressed with the otherwise plain and oddly gifted Karen Davidson. "Eight or nine miles, huh. That's not bad. Normally, you know, I do a half marathon before breakfast, but hey." I paused and made a long-suffering gesture toward Rhett. "We're a team, and you can only go as fast as the slowest member."

Karen laughed at my teasing bravado. "Thanks, Luke. It was good talking to you this morning. Bring Rhett by the clinic anytime."

She trotted off toward the open countryside, and Rhett and I started toward town, although he kept looking back to catch a glimpse of her.

I liked Karen. She was kind and unassuming. But I also feared that her shy manner might make it difficult for her to find a foothold in Watervalley, especially given that she was a female in a profession that for generations the local farmers had known as a male occupation. It wasn't that the people here were ungenerous or mean. They were actually quite the opposite. But I also knew they had a tendency to give newcomers a respectful distance, and age-old frames of reference were sometimes slow to change. It was not a mind-set born out of chauvinism or bigotry, but rather one that was historically cautious toward the new and different. By word of mouth she had won some favorable acclaim for what she had done for Toy McAnders at the ballpark. I hoped that would be a springboard for a broader acceptance. But there were no guarantees.

After arriving home, and I showered, dressed, and got ready for the day. I fed Rhett, took him outside for one last bathroom break, and brought him back in, closing the rear porch door behind me.

Or so I thought.

Shortly after eleven, I received a phone call from Louise Fox, my next-door neighbor.

"Dr. Bradford, can you by chance break away and come home for a few minutes? We have . . ." She paused for a second. "Well, we have something of a situation here."

"Louise, is everything okay? Is Will hurt?"

"No, Will's fine. He's with some friends at the library."

"What is it, then?"

"Well, it's Rhett. He seems to have gotten out, and . . . I think I could explain it better if you were here. Can you come?"

"Um, sure. I'll be there in five minutes." I had no idea what Louise could be referring to, but it didn't matter. If Rhett had gotten out, I needed to go and put him back in the house. I told Nancy I would return shortly and drove quickly to Fleming Street, thinking I would find Louise's garbage cans tumbled over and Rhett wallowing in scattered trash. When I arrived, she was waiting for me in my driveway.

Louise normally had a sweet and pleasant face framed in a frail, accommodating smile. But this morning, her outlook was clearly laced with worry. I parked the car and approached her.

"Hey, Louise. Is everything okay? Which direction did Rhett go?"

"Everything's fine. At least now it is. Rhett's in my backyard, inside the fence."

"Oh, well, thanks for penning him up till I could get here. No telling where that rascal would have run off to. I must not have properly closed the back door this morning."

"Well, um, actually, I didn't put him in there."

"You didn't?"

"No, he got in there himself. Apparently, he jumped the picket fence."

"He did? Seriously? That's amazing. Rhett has trouble stepping over my shoes. Was Maggie back there?"

"Yes, she was," Louise said pointedly, her voice assuming a sterner tone.

"Hmm, I guess he was looking for a little company."

"Well, I can tell you, he found something more than a little company."

"Louise, I don't understand."

She exhaled and spoke with both apology and exasperation. "It's like this. Before I left this morning, I put Maggie outside so she could get some exercise. I got here about fifteen minutes ago because I needed to run home from the bakery for something I forgot. When I passed through the kitchen, I saw the two of them in the backyard, all locked up, doing, you know, it."

I was dumbfounded. "It?"

She looked down, apparently too embarrassed to make eye contact. "Yes, it!"

"You mean, as in it, it?"

After a quick glance, Louise again averted her eyes. "Yes, it, it."

I stood in openmouthed astonishment. "But how can that be? Will said that Maggie had been fixed."

"That's what we were told, so I don't understand it either." Louise nodded. She was openly upset and struggling with a mixture of concern and aggravation.

"Louise, I'm—I'm so sorry. I don't know what to say. I'm totally embarrassed by the whole affair."

Louise dropped her chin and glared at me.

"Oh, sorry. Maybe 'affair' wasn't the best choice of words."

She looked at me silently for another moment. Then her severe expression suddenly erupted into a muted laugh. She flipped her hand in an air of resignation. "Oh good heavens, Dr. Bradford, this isn't your fault. If Maggie's not really fixed, I can't blame Rhett for wanting to make her acquaintance."

"Listen, I'll be glad to pay for Dr. Davidson to check her out."

"Oh, don't be silly. I can take care of that. Besides, I had no idea Maggie was a woman of such easy virtue."

"I had no idea Rhett was such a Romeo."

Louise laughed again, shaking her head. "Truth be told, if it had to happen, I'm glad it was Rhett and not some four-legged traveling man."

"Louise, this is kind of new territory for me. If something does come of all this, I'd be more than willing to help pay child support. Or, well, puppy support, such as it is."

Louise placed her hand over her mouth and giggled. "We'll cross that bridge when we get there. I'm sorry. I probably overreacted." She closed her eyes and made a quick shuddering movement with her head, as if trying to erase the picture of the two lovebirds from her memory. "It was just kind of a shock."

"Well, let me go gather Rhett up and put him back inside. He'll definitely be in time-out for the next decade."

We walked around back where the two dogs were lying in the sun. Maggie sat up and watched our approach, looking innocent and unassuming. Rhett, on the other hand, had an expression I would be hard-pressed to describe. He wore a contrite and downcast demeanor, knowing full well that his behavior had been scandalous. But there was also a certain triumphant glint in his eyes that seemed to ask, *How do you like me now?*

I assumed an air of reproach, grabbed him by his collar, and walked him back through the side gate to the house. After plopping down in his usual spot on the kitchen floor, he rested his chin on his paws and looked up at me, his brown eyes full of penitence.

"Okay, big fellow, you've gotten yourself in the soup now.

When I get home tonight, we're going to have a serious discussion about things like commitment, getting a job, saving for college . . . the whole bit." He responded to my stern lecture by rolling over on his side and flapping his tail against the kitchen floor. I towered above him with folded arms and an admonishing glare, fully confident my sharp words had gotten through to him.

Satisfied that he would rise, go, and sin no more, I quickly made a sandwich and headed back to work.

CHAPTER 20
At the Movies

I slept in till eight o'clock Saturday morning, a rare luxury. An exciting day spread before me, filled with grocery shopping, pulling weeds, and bathing a dog. I tumbled downstairs and made coffee. I thought about cooking some breakfast as well, but decided to go over to the Sweetlife Bakery to snag some of Estelle's fabulous sausage rolls and maybe even a bear claw or two before continuing to the grocery store. Within fifteen minutes I was in the Austin-Healey and headed downtown.

After turning onto Chestnut Street, I suddenly came upon a line of traffic moving so slowly at first I thought there had been a wreck. I was the eighth or ninth car back and inching forward at a snail's pace. I had no choice but to chug along.

One by one the cars in front of me turned off, and when the last one did, I found myself creeping along behind the source of the problem. It was Beatrice McClanahan driving her riding mower down the center of Chestnut Street. Instead of being befuddled or mortified about it, Beatrice was having the time of her life, waving gaily at passersby and smiling like she was in a one-float parade.

Apparently, to her thinking, the loss of her driver's license didn't extend to lawn equipment.

I followed her to Courthouse Square, where she pulled into a parking space in front of the Sweetlife Bakery. I parked next to her, got out, and leaned against the car. She was digging through her purse, which was large enough to qualify as carry-on luggage.

"Good morning, Beatrice."

"Oh, Dr. Bradford! It's so good to see you!"

"And you as well. Interesting mode of transportation you have there."

Beatrice took on a pleasant, unassuming countenance. "Oh, thank you for noticing." With feigned politeness, she spoke in a mildly lecturing tone. "Since you and the sheriff won't let me drive my car anymore, I thought this would be a suitable alternative. It gets wonderful gas mileage."

"Well, that's um, that's rather creative of you." I paused, studying her for a moment. "So, Beatrice, did Nancy Orman give you the list of the local organizations that cater to folks like you who no longer drive?"

"Oh piddle, Dr. Bradford. I don't need those silly people. As you can see, I'm getting around just fine."

"Yes, I can see that. But it might be nice to get a little help. You can have groceries delivered right to your door." I was doing my best to be politely instructive. Beatrice wasn't biting.

"I'm sure they're nice people, Dr. Bradford, but I'm actually on my way to visit my friend Dorothy Benefield over on Terrace Street. While I'm there, I might mow her lawn."

"Beatrice, I admire your positive attitude. But I'm not sure that Sheriff Thurman will agree to your driving your lawn mower all over town."

Her indignant air was thinly veiled with an ingratiating smile. "Well, I guess if need be, I can mow Warren Thurman's yard too."

I shrugged. "Enjoy your Saturday, Beatrice."

I did admire her. She was determined not to live life limited by the frailties of age. And I highly expected that given her exuberant personality, loneliness was likely her greatest enemy. Driving her mower around town was not a viable option, but thankfully and perhaps selfishly, it would be Sheriff Thurman's problem to deal with. Still, my heart went out to her.

I grabbed some treats from the bakery and made my departure, but only after Estelle gave me a hug with a force equal to a Heimlich maneuver. The balance of my morning was spent grocery shopping, giving Rhett a much-needed bath, and working in the garden. Tomatoes and squash were starting to ripen in such abundance that if the 82nd Airborne were to stop by, I could probably provide lunch. I began to understand the need to inundate one's neighbors with the surplus, yet another blessing of getting one's hands in the soil. The innate value of not letting something good go to waste inspired an attitude of spontaneous charity.

Around midafternoon, I called Christine to make plans for the evening. She was way ahead of me.

"Let's go to the movie at Watervalley Lake tonight."

"There's a movie at the lake?"

"Yes. The Watervalley Parks Department puts on two or three of them each summer. Tonight they're playing *Frozen*."

"Isn't that an animated film?"

"Well, yeah. Bradford, where have you been lately?"

"Apparently not in junior high."

"Funny. All right, going or not?"

"Okay, sure, sounds like fun. I think."

"Oh, it'll be great. It's actually a sing-along."

"You do know that people have committed felonies after hearing me sing?"

"The singing is optional. Besides, if you haven't seen it, you won't know the songs anyway."

"Tonight just keeps getting better and better."

"I'll make us something to eat. Pick me up at seven."

"Do I have a choice in the matter?"

"Not really."

"Seven, it is."

We arrived at the lake that evening and found a place to pitch our blanket in the midst of an already burgeoning crowd. The Parks Department had erected a large temporary canvas screen in the short grass near the lake and set up part of the bandstand to serve concessions. Like so many events of this kind in Watervalley, the age groups ranged from young to ancient. The evening was filled with cacophonous laughter, a rainbow of lawn chairs, and acres of smiles.

I made my way to the concession stand to grab some drinks. While I was waiting in line, a huge set of hands grabbed my shoulders from behind and gave me a rattling shake. It was Hoot Wilson.

A third-generation dairy farmer, Hoot was large, loud, and immeasurably likable. He had a booming voice and a steady low chuckle that accompanied every conversation. It seemed that with Hoot, laughter was never far away. He was a single parent and devoted dad of Wendy, the thirteen-year-old who had been Will's secret heartthrob.

Hoot was dressed in overalls and flip-flops, unabashedly exposing a pair of very white ankles. Were it not for his tremendous smile, Hoots's massive size, scraggly beard, and mono-brow would strike fear in most mortals. But I knew that a good, hearty shoulder shake was just his way of saying hello.

"Hoot, how you doing, fellow?"

"Doc," he said robustly, "I'm just proud to be here."

"You and Wendy looking forward to the movie?"

Hoot glanced to the side, an indication that he was about to speak confidentially. "Actually, I'm under strict orders to keep my distance. I've got a teenager in the house now, and it looks like some of the young bucks are taking an interest." Hoot squinted his eyes and gave me a conspiratorial nod. "That's okay. I'll keep my distance, all right. But ol' Hoot, he's like the Eye of Sauron. He sees everything."

"Good to know, Hoot. I'll call you next time I can't find my car keys." He looked at me oddly, my attempt at humor lost on him. I let this pass.

"Hey, Hoot. Have you heard we have a new veterinarian in town?"

Hoot's smile collapsed slightly, and he assumed a withdrawn demeanor. "Yeah, I heard tell of that. I wish her the best, but I'm not sure she'll be able to do me much good."

"Why not, Hoot? You've got cows. She's a vet."

"Oh, I know, Doc. But the way I understand it, she's no bigger than a field mouse. I don't think her and a fifteen-hundred-pound Holstein make for a good combination. It ain't worth somebody getting hurt, Doc."

I nodded thoughtfully and found myself caught in Karen's dilemma. I believed what she had told me about her uncanny ability with animals, but I found her gift difficult to explain to others. Perhaps even I had my doubts.

"Well, try to keep an open mind about her, Hoot. She might surprise you."

He offered an accommodating nod. "We'll see, Doc. We'll see."

"Meanwhile, I'll put the word out to all the teenage boys I know to be on their best behavior."

"Ah, don't worry, Doc. I got that one covered. I snitched Wendy's cell phone and copied her contacts. I sent a little text message to all the likely offenders and told them ol' Hoot will be watching. I also let them know that my mode of observation was through the scope of my deer rifle. I think that did the trick."

He was joking, but I went along for the fun of it. "What makes you so sure they got the message?"

"Because I told them to send me a confirmation text."

I paused and stared blankly at Hoot. "And did they?"

Hoot ran his thumbs under the straps to his overalls, rocking lightly from heel to toe. "One hundred percent compliance, Doc."

After a moment of glazed disbelief, I leaned toward him, speaking in a modest and cautious voice. "Hoot, you're not, by chance, related to Christine Chambers in any way, are you?"

From the look on his face, I didn't think Hoot understood the purpose of the question. "Nope, Doc. Can't say I am."

"Good."

I bought some soft drinks and returned to where Christine and I had cast our blanket, only to find her surrounded by a swarm of adolescent girls. They all appeared to be between twelve and fourteen, awash in braces and the first attempts at makeup, poised near the boundary of an adult world they were anxious to join. Their faces glowed with the limitless possibilities of youth. As I approached, their eyes eagerly followed me, and they all spoke in unison.

"Hello, Dr. Bradford." An explosion of giggles followed. Apparently, I had been the topic of conversation. No doubt, Christine's and my relationship was seen through the idyllic lens of youthful imagination.

Christine and I exchanged a knowing glance.

"You know," I said, "I just can't figure it out. There has got to be some reason why all the girls in Watervalley are *so* beautiful." Another round of giggles ensued.

"No, seriously. I've never seen so many pretty girls." I paused and spoke in a more detached, confidential manner. "Of course, the big one in the middle is kind of pulling down the average. But it's still a very impressive bunch."

Wide-eyed "Ooohs" echoed from the small troupe. Many of them shot alarmed glances at Christine, who was now eyeing me sharply with a calculated and cunning smile. It was fun theater, and the girls loved it.

Suddenly the big screen came alive as the film started. About the same time, I noticed a black Mercedes pulling into the nearby parking lot. I knew of only one such car in the entire valley. It belonged to John Harris, and I was struck with curiosity as to what he was doing at a sing-along. I bent down to Christine.

"I've got someone I need to go talk to. Are you okay for a while?"

She smiled buoyantly, wrapped her arms around the two girls sitting nearest to her, and declared, "We are grand, Dr. Bradford! It's sing-along time!"

I grabbed a sandwich from the picnic basket and headed back toward the bandstand, where I found John in the concession line. He was smartly dressed in khakis and a polo shirt.

"Well, Professor, I didn't take you for the little-girl-movie type," I said.

"Bradford, you do realize that you're here too, don't you?"

I laughed. "So noted. My date dragged me here."

"You say that like there was a more exciting Watervalley venue to choose from tonight."

"Valid point. So, seriously, what brings you out tonight?"

"Let me grab an iced tea, and I'll meet you at the rail over there."

A minute later, we were leaning over the bandstand railing and taking in all the life and sound and singing of the marvelous Saturday night.

John seemed pleasantly lost to another world. He spoke thoughtfully. "Molly would have loved this."

I understood. Since the renovation of the bandstand had been his deceased wife Molly's last wish, it was fully appropriate that John would have wanted to experience the delight and celebration of the event. He seemed pleased, as if the last, satisfying page were turned on an important chapter of his life. As with many of our conversations, I made no comment. There simply existed between us a mutual awareness of the larger point.

He gazed out over the crowd and saw Christine delightedly singing along with her adoring entourage. "Looks like your date is having a grand time."

"Yes, and I'm standing here with you. Lucky me."

"I have to hand it to you, Luke. I thought she would throw you on the scrap heap along with all the other broken hearts. It's ironic, really. I'd say this movie is symbolically appropriate."

"Why is that?"

John gave me a studied look. "I guess she didn't tell you her nickname in high school?"

"No. No idea."

I was expecting a response, but instead John retreated into a puckered silence.

"Well, Professor Harris. Is there something you'd like to share with the class?"

He grunted a low noise of resignation. "The Ice Queen."

"Huh, really?"

John nodded, cutting his eyes at me. "Yeah . . . small-town stuff. You hear things through the grapevine. I remember at first thinking it was about the way she played basketball . . . always cool as a cucumber in clutch situations. But evidently she had a reputation. Apparently you couldn't get a kiss off her even if you needed CPR."

Amused, I folded my arms. "Seriously?"

"Yup."

"So I guess that's why you gave me that little speech about her last winter . . . that she'd have me crying like a little girl."

"Yeah, sport. But I have to admit, you seem to have broken the spell."

"Well, that may be. She told me that in another month we can start holding hands."

John cut his eyes at me again. "Yeah, right. And aren't you just full of crap?"

We exchanged wry grins, and an amused silence fell between us. The sing-along was not our cup of tea, but we were having a great time watching from the sidelines. There was something contagious in the exuberance of all the young and radiant faces. And in the center of them was Christine.

"So," I said, "what was she like when she was young?"

John spoke without the slightest change in his expression. "She was very focused, totally driven. She always had a kind of maturity, a wisdom if you will, beyond her years."

He paused briefly. "But it wouldn't be accurate to say she was always serious. She also seemed to live in a whimsical world of her own creation. She played out in the fields and along the creek when she was a little girl. Albert, her father, used to tell me that she would spend every waking minute playing on a small grassy rise at the back of the farm called Bracken's Knoll. Sometimes he'd have to go looking for her there. He said that as he approached he could hear her having dramatic conversations."

"Hmm. Who was she talking to?"

"You'll have to ask her that one yourself, sport."

"Fair enough."

John turned around and leaned against the railing, admiring the new and elaborately detailed bandstand. "A lot of great dances happened here over the years. Some really good times."

"Maybe there will be a few more."

John pressed his lips together. "Actually, that's not a bad idea, sawbones."

"Oh, yeah? How so?"

"We should have a big dance here as a fund-raiser for the statue. Get a good band out of Nashville and a few corporate sponsors. Make a really big splash."

"Sounds good to me."

"Yeah, I like the thought of it."

"Of course you do. It was your idea."

John winked at me. "Good point."

We stood a moment longer. Eventually John turned to me with his hand extended, and we shook firmly. "Good seeing you, Luke. I need to go work the crowd a little, see if I can turn some of this evening's spirited mood into a few donation dollars."

"Go get 'em, chief."

I stayed at the bandstand railing for the longest time, watching Christine, who was caught up in the shared laughter, the animated smiles, and the giggling foolishness of the moment. It seemed that a small part of her was still that innocent girl, seeing the world through eyes of wonder and expectation.

Yet by all measures, she was a woman, fully bloomed, graceful, sensuous, beautiful. She had such a compassionate heart. And much as John had described, she had an intuitive wisdom beyond her years. I loved her, completely. Standing there under the summer stars and surrounded by all that was Watervalley, I knew that I could never imagine my world without her.

Months earlier, I had been foolishly slow to tell her that I loved her, a reluctance that had almost ended our relationship. I wouldn't make the same mistake with my heart's intentions now.

CHAPTER 21
Fireworks

July arrived with record temperatures. The long days of hot sun and no rain were beginning to bleach the world of vitality. Just walking to the mailbox felt like a death march. Patches of muted brown could be seen on neighborhood lawns, the trees looked wilted, and the garden seemed in constant need of watering.

Nevertheless, the Public Works Department labored through the dog days, and little by little, colorful red, white, and blue banners began to appear on the streets and around Courthouse Square. By small measures the town was awakening from its listlessness in anticipation of the Fourth of July holiday. Local merchants advertised big Independence Day sales. Flags were hung in all the storefronts and from many of the porches up and down Fleming Street.

The Fourth fell on a Friday. The day started hot and continued up the thermometer. Shortly after four o'clock, families and church groups began to show up at the lake to set up their cookouts in anticipation of the town's annual fireworks display.

The Presbyterians were the first to arrive, partly to take advantage of the closest parking spaces, but also due to their general affinity for having a good time. For them, church gatherings and private gatherings followed the same rules, especially when it came to their beverage of choice. Thus, they approached such events with much less timidity than other church groups. They hiked to the far point of the lake and proudly hoisted the Presbyterian standard. Other groups soon followed.

The bandstand was alive with color, draped full circle in patriotic banners. At five o'clock, the local Boy Scout troop performed a ceremonial raising of the flag under the watchful eye of scoutmaster Neil Holloway. As two of the older boys carefully unfolded and hoisted the flag, Neil and the rest of the troop stood nearby, saluting while standing stiffly at attention.

With great pomp, Neil called out the orders for each phase of the ceremony. The boys, all of whom had forgotten at least one or more articles of their Scout uniform, shifted their weight from foot to foot and tried to look serious, a difficult thing to do at age thirteen or fourteen. Once the flag was successfully raised, the troop led the crowd in the Pledge of Allegiance.

Shortly afterward, a small, makeshift marching band that included a few teachers from the high school, the town librarian, and one or two other stragglers made its grand entrance. The group included a tuba, a flute, a trombone, a clarinet, a drummer, a tambourine, and an old guy with a ponytail who played bongos. Marching as they played, they started at the far end of the lake parking lot and moved along in a more or less organized clump until they made their way ceremoniously to the bandstand, a full one-hundred-yard journey.

They played tunes for the next half hour with a repertoire that included "You're a Grand Old Flag," "Battle Hymn of the Republic," "The Caisson Song," "America the Beautiful," and "Rocky Top." "The Star-Spangled Banner" was their big finale, which included a rather odd and lengthy improvisation by the bongo player right after "land of the free." Apparently the embrasures of the trombone and tuba players were on the verge of blowout, because they hit the final C with a discordant B. Nevertheless, the crowd applauded enthusiastically.

The fireworks display was set up on two stripped-down pontoon boats that were tethered together and floated out in the middle of Watervalley Lake. In charge was Ed Caswell, the fire chief, who had taken a special online course on sequenced fireworks ignition. The certificate hung proudly in his office.

Soon enough, the whole place was a cacophony of laughter and fellowship with children running, tumbling, giggling, and throwing sticks into the lake. The good, thick smell of charcoal and smoke permeated the warm evening air. The sense of celebration was contagious, and everyone seemed to be having a great time, especially the Presbyterians and Episcopalians. This likely had something to do with the presence of so many red Solo cups and frequent visits to the coolers hidden toward the back of their serving areas.

I floated among the various groups, making small talk and trying to guide the conversation toward donations to the memorial project. I managed to obtain a few commitments. But largely I was scraping the low ceiling of my fund-raising ability.

Along the way I saw Joe Dawson, the Presbyterian pastor.

"Hey, Joe. Wait up." He was wearing a Hawaiian shirt, shorts, sandals, and a huge smile. We shook hands, and after a quick exchange, he had a question for me.

"Hey, remember that Carter fellow? Were you able to find him?"

"Yeah, sure did. Interesting old guy. Lives very off the beaten path. We talked for a while, and I asked him how he was doing. Didn't seem to have any physical ailments that I could tell. But I don't think he gets out much."

"Is he a shut-in?"

"No, he seemed to get around okay. We talked on his front porch. The place was pretty run-down, though, almost deserted looking really. But he seemed to be doing fine."

Joe nodded. "Sounds like I need to pay him a visit."

"He'd probably appreciate the company. You'll get a kick out of him. Incredibly sharp mind for his age, whatever that is."

For whatever reason, I hadn't thought about Leyland for several weeks and now felt guilty for having so easily pushed him out of my mind. Something about his insightful words, or maybe it was just the tranquillity of the remote woodland setting, inspired a desire to go see him again, and soon.

Around nine o'clock, Ed Caswell came puttering down the length of the lake, towing the fireworks-laden pontoons with his small flat-bottom fishing boat. Mustering as much ceremony and dignity as he could, he threw off a couple of concrete blocks to serve as anchors. Then he announced over a bullhorn that the show would start in ten minutes.

I walked around the lake to find Christine so we could watch the fireworks together. Along the way, I noticed a small group of Mennonites gathered on the fringe of the woods some two hundred yards away. It seemed that even they enjoyed a good fireworks show.

It turned out to be a grand display, even for tiny Watervalley. At the end, everyone sang "The Star-Spangled Banner," this time without the help of the band.

At six o'clock the next morning I was already downtown on the square, setting up tables for the community charity yard sale. This wasn't by choice; Christine had volunteered me for the duty. During the fireworks display, she had placed her chin on my shoulder and made her request in a soft, pleading voice.

"You don't mind, do you, Luke? It would be such a big help."

"Six o'clock. Seriously?"

"Pleeeease."

"You're evil and should be destroyed," I said, borrowing a line from *Steel Magnolias*.

By seven that morning, I was soaked in sweat. By nine, the oppressive, muggy air was having a subtly agitating effect on everyone, casting a faint pallor of intolerance on the day. Nevertheless, the charity yard sale had a huge turnout, and the downtown square was packed with people examining table after table of clothes, furniture, electronic items, and various other things that most observers would call junk. It seemed that all of Watervalley was there en masse, including a large contingent of the Mennonite community.

Midmorning I went home and showered. Shortly after twelve, I drove over to the grand opening of Karen Davidson's office, located about two blocks off the square. I was anticipating a huge crowd and a robust Watervalley welcome for her new practice.

But the small parking lot adjacent to her building was virtually empty. Inside, I found Karen talking to Connie Thompson; both were preparing to lock up and leave.

"Hey, what gives?" I asked. "Did I come at the wrong time?"

The two women exchanged glances, and the room had the stiff air of a funeral home. On a nearby table sat full trays of cupcakes and other bakery treats. Karen spoke in good-natured defeat. "No, actually you are right on time."

"I don't get it. The open house was from ten to one, wasn't it? Did the crowd come early?"

Karen exhaled. "Not exactly. Except for the two of us, my

receptionist, and Toy McAnders and his wife, you are the only other person to set foot in here today."

I stood there stunned and glanced at Connie, whose somber face confirmed the news. "Wow, Karen, I am really sorry. I know this is disappointing."

"Well, it probably isn't the best timing with the big yard sale going on downtown." She was doing her best to put a good face on the situation, but she was clearly crushed.

Connie spoke in a kind, instructive voice. "Don't you worry about paying for all the bakery goods. I'll just take them back, and we'll sell them at the shop."

"Connie, that's really sweet, but you don't have to do that." Karen paused briefly. "Actually, I'm thinking about binging on them. Maybe a sugar rush will pick this day up a little." She produced a forced smile, doing her best to appear courageous. "Thanks for coming by, Luke."

"Not so fast, sister." I said. "I'm looking for the full tour here. Rhett insisted I check everything out."

Karen shrugged. "Sure, why not?"

"I'm going to grab this tray and head on back," Connie interjected. "I'll leave you two doctors to talk shop."

Karen and I spent the next half hour together, and she proudly showed me her exam rooms, the surgery, and the small kennel area. I did my best to assure her that the low turnout was just an anomaly, but it seemed I could do little to change her wilted outlook. And privately, I wondered if I was perpetuating a false hope. Karen's painfully reserved nature wasn't allowing her to make headway in Watervalley. I had thought the need for veterinary services in this small community would generate a modest crowd, but apparently, that wasn't the case.

Still, she endeavored to make light of her situation. "Well, Luke, I guess the good news is that I have an excellent work-life balance."

"How so?"

"I have no work and no life."

"I have an idea. Let's walk up to the square and I'll introduce you around. I know you've met a lot of people, but it would be good to mingle."

She was about to answer, when the ring of my cell phone cut her off.

"Hello."

"Doc, Warren Thurman. Got a small emergency at the jailhouse. There's a fellow here that got into a fight downtown and needs to be stitched up."

"Sure, I'll be right there."

Karen read my troubled face. "That was the sheriff. He needs me at the jail. Mind if we take a rain check on the introductions?"

"Not at all."

It was lousy timing. I was abandoning Karen at the worst possible moment. I was determined to try to help her, but it would have to wait. Still, my concern over her situation combined with the scorching heat left me in a foul mood.

At the sheriff's office, I found Warren in the front room. "Thanks for coming, Doc. Two fellows got into a fight downtown, and one of them got a bad cut to his head."

I followed Warren down the cell block hallway to find Clayton Ross sitting in the first holding cell. He never looked up but sat with his face in his hands. In the cell next to him, holding a bloody towel to his head, was a young Mennonite man.

I looked at Warren in disbelief. "What's he doing here?"

"Fighting in public, Doc. He broke the law."

"Warren, you can't be serious. You and I both know the Mennonites are pacifists." My smoldering frustration poured through my words.

Warren seemed slightly taken aback by the fervor of my tone. "It's routine police work, Doc. When there's a fight, you bring both of them in."

I was incensed. This was absurd. I pointed toward the Mennonite. "And just how many punches did he throw, Warren?"

Warren didn't like the question and regarded me sternly. "He knocked Clayton down with a chair." His words were blunt. "You going to take a look at this fellow or not, Doc?" He unlocked the door and swung it open for me.

"What's his name?"

"He wouldn't say. And they don't exactly carry a driver's license."

I ignored Warren and stepped into the room. The young man was thin with brownish blond hair and couldn't have been more than nineteen or twenty. I introduced myself and told him I was a doctor. He regarded me impassively and nodded. He had a swollen left eye, and just above the back of his neck was a long laceration still oozing blood. His wounds told a simple story. Clearly he had been slugged brutally in the face and fallen back against something that had cut his head.

The injustice of the situation pushed me beyond any amiable restraint. My words were raw, determined. "I'm taking this man to the clinic."

Warren was standing in the cell doorway. He folded his arms and stayed firm. "Can't let you do that, Doc."

I calmly placed my things back into my bag, walked up to Warren, and stood six inches away, intentionally crowding him. We were the same height, but he had a good fifty pounds on me. It didn't matter. I spoke with conviction. "Yeah, Warren, you can. I don't have what I need to treat him here. He has both a cut and a likely concussion, so I'll need to observe him for a few hours." Looking Warren squarely in the eye, I said the next words with a hard confidence. "I'll be damned if I'm doing that here."

Warren maintained his grim countenance, but finally nodded. "Okay, fine, Doc. But I'm sending one of my deputies with you."

"No, you're not."

My terse response hit Warren like a whip, and he looked at me in openmouthed astonishment. "Why . . . hold it." He paused for a moment and held up both hands. "Look, Doc, I can see you're upset, but the man was fighting in public and resisted arrest."

"Resisted how?"

"He refused to get into the patrol car."

I closed my eyes, shaking my head in exasperation. "What did you expect? The man drives a horse and buggy. Doesn't exactly make him an intimidating flight risk, now does it?"

"But why no deputy?"

"Because I said so, Warren. Because I need this man to talk to me, and he's less likely to do that with a guy in a uniform standing over him."

I walked back to the Mennonite fellow, helped him to his feet, and told him to come with me. Reluctantly, Warren let us by. We passed Clayton Ross's cell. His face was still buried in his hands. I helped the young Mennonite man to the cell block door and asked him to wait for me there.

I walked back to Warren. "Did you administer a breathalyzer test on Clayton?"

"Why? I didn't smell any alcohol on him."

"You had him empty his pockets before going into the cell, right?"

"Yeah."

"Ten bucks says he had a pack of breath mints."

Warren's silence told me my guess had hit home. He nodded grimly. "I'll look into it."

I returned to the Mennonite, who was leaning weakly against the wall. When we stepped into the front entry room, Jacob Yoder was waiting on us.

"Jacob, you know this young man?"

His worried face was resolute. "Yes, our families are friends, and he is courting my daughter. He rode into town with us today."

"I need to get him to the clinic. He's got a bad cut on the back of his head."

Jacob nodded. "My wagon is outside. We can take him."

The wagon was parked in the shade on the side of the building. Jacob's wife, Hannah, and their daughter, Rebecca, sat there with anxious faces. I was preparing to help the young man onto the rear of the wagon, when an angry voice from behind me called out my name.

CHAPTER 22
Boiling Point

"Hold on, Bradford. Your boy there needs to answer a few damn questions."

It was Cal Ross standing three feet away from me, seething with irritation, his swarthy, thick-jowled face dark and contemptuous.

"I don't think that's going to happen right now," I told him.

He tried to move past me toward the Mennonite, but I stepped in front of him and spoke coolly. "Cal, if you're asking for trouble, you're going to get a quick reply."

He grinned brutally, seemingly hardened by the challenge. "What you got against my boy? I just talked to the sheriff, and he told me you think Clayton needs an alcohol test." Cal's own breath was rank with the smell of beer. "Why are you taking sides?"

"You know, in my experience it doesn't take a lot of guts to hit a man that you know won't hit you back."

"You calling my boy a coward?"

"No, I'm calling your son a bully."

"Oh, a bully, huh? Well, why don't I show you what a bully looks like?"

I looked to the side and smiled. "You could. But first you might want to think pretty hard about that."

"And why is that?" he snapped in return.

I stepped forward and stood squarely in front of him. "Because, unlike your son, you'd be picking a fight with someone who will definitely hit you back."

He was about to respond, when Warren's booming voice filled the air. "Is there a problem here, fellows?" He was standing on the sidewalk and had undoubtedly heard the exchange. Cal Ross immediately stepped away, recoiling under Warren's authority. I never moved.

After a few tense moments, I helped the injured Mennonite onto the wagon. Then I turned to Warren, expecting a stern admonition, but instead he regarded me with a slight nod of his chin. I grabbed my bag and as I walked toward my car, Cal Ross blurted out a rather odd declaration. "You should want to help my boy as much as you're helping that Mennonite kid."

At the clinic, Jacob and I assisted the young man inside. The poor fellow seemed wilted and ashamed. Hannah and Rebecca followed close behind.

I addressed him with polite reassurance. "Tell me your name."

He spoke with a slight German accent similar to Jacob's. "My name is Levi Beiler."

I showed him to an exam room. Jacob joined us while the two women stayed in the waiting area. I asked Levi several questions about dizziness, and checked his visual and motor responses. Aside from the laceration on his head, he had a headache and a throbbing pain around his black eye.

"Levi, you've got a pretty nasty cut and it needs stitches. To do that, I'm going to have to shave the hair around the wound." He nodded in understanding. There was a knock and simultaneous opening of the door. It was Ann Patterson.

"How we doing?" she asked. "I got here as quick as I could."

"Word travels fast. How did you know I was here?"

"I got a phone call. You want me to prep so you can scrub up?"

"Sure."

Minutes later, I was sewing in the stitches. Jacob stood patiently next to the boy.

"Levi, can you tell me what happened?" I asked.

He glanced at Jacob. The two of them exchanged uneasy looks. Jacob answered. "You will hear many versions of what happened, Dr. Bradford. I'm sure you will find one that will satisfy you."

"I think I'd like to hear Levi's version."

Jacob nodded to Levi, who spoke in a detached voice. "The man kept trying to talk to Rebecca, bothering her. She walked away from him a couple of times, but he wouldn't stop. He was loud and rude. We were standing beside some tables and chairs near where food was being served. He tried to approach her again, and I set a chair in his path, trying to shield her from him. For some reason, he walked right into it and partially fell. When he came up, he struck me."

"And you never hit him back?"

"No, of course not," he responded with an amused dryness. "I was too busy bleeding on the ground."

"So, what happened after that?"

"Almost immediately the sheriff's men were there, and the other man claimed I hit him with the chair. The next thing I knew, they were putting me in the police car." Again, he exhaled a muffled laugh. "I lived for two months in Nashville without a single incident and came back home to be thrown in jail."

"Levi, if you don't mind my asking, why were you in Nashville?"

"It was a time of testing before being baptized into my faith."

"You mean like . . . What's it called? Rumspringa?"

"We don't really practice rumspringa in the traditional sense, but my parents thought it would be a good idea for me to experience the larger world for a couple of months."

"I'm sorry this happened," I said quietly.

"Persecution is nothing new to us, Dr. Bradford," Jacob replied. "It has been our lot for centuries."

I nodded and let the matter drop. I continued stitching the wound and addressed Jacob on a different matter. "How is your father's vision these days?"

He smiled stoically. "It is much worse than he will let on."

"Why doesn't he come in for a thorough exam? Cataracts can be treated."

"I have no doubt you are correct, Dr. Bradford. But Father can be a hard man. Things have to be done his way and on his time."

It was an evasive response, one that left questions unanswered. As much as I liked Jacob and his affable, soft-spoken ways, I had come to learn that he was a cautious and very deliberate man.

"So, Jacob, I have a question. I recently heard that many Mennonites served during Vietnam. What can you tell me about that?"

His surprise was only faintly masked. "How did you know Father did that?"

I hadn't known, but this gave me an opportunity to inquire further. "Oh, I just heard it somewhere. What kind of work did he do to fulfill his service time?"

Jacob had been tight-lipped about today's incident, but apparently he considered events of almost fifty years ago idle talk to pass the time. "He milked cows at a research farm run by the University of Tennessee. It was considered government service."

"Where was this?"

"About ninety miles away, near Columbia, Tennessee. He had just married Momma, and they lived in a small house near the milk barn. I was born there."

I continued sewing the stitches. "Was having a baby away from your community difficult on your mom?"

"Perhaps. But it was a much harder time for my dad."

I paused momentarily and looked up. "Why was that?"

"Father didn't like being away from home, so my aunt came to live with them and help with the delivery of the baby. Unfortunately, my aunt became ill with a sudden fever that turned into pneumonia. She died not long after I was born."

"Sorry to hear that." I continued suturing Levi's wound but was struck with curiosity. "How old was she?"

"My aunt was nineteen, like my dad. They were twins."

"And she died of pneumonia?"

"Yes. Papa has never talked much about his service time. Momma had a difficult labor, and by the time my dad could take my aunt to the local hospital, her sickness was too advanced. I think he blames himself. Since you are a doctor, perhaps you understand these things."

As I finished the last of the sutures, I considered Jacob's words. Pneumonia was a top-ten killer, but usually in the very old or the very young . . . not in nineteen-year-olds. Then again, we were talking about events from almost fifty years ago. "What was your aunt's name?" I asked.

"Ellie, Ellie Louise Yoder."

Moments later, I had just asked Ann to put a dressing on the wound when my cell phone rang. It was Warren Thurman. I stepped into the hallway to answer it.

"Doc, you got that Mennonite boy patched up?"

"Yeah, Warren. I'm going to observe him for a while. We'll head back after that."

"No need. We're going to let the matter drop."

"Okay, good. Should I ask why?"

"Probably best if you didn't."

"Warren, did you run the breathalyzer test on Clayton?"

There was a noticeable pause. "Like I said, we're going to cut everybody a little slack here. I hope that's okay with you."

Warren was smart. He had the option of making both Levi Beiler and Clayton Ross toe a hard line, but he was trying to defuse an otherwise lose-lose situation. Still, I was certain Clayton was the aggressor, and the omission in Warren's response made it clear that alcohol was involved. I didn't like the injustice of it and let out a heavy sigh.

"Yeah." I paused. "Yeah, I get it, Warren. Thanks for the call."

Jacob had stepped into the hall and stood a short distance away.

I endeavored to put on a positive face. "Jacob, good news. That was the sheriff. He said Levi is free to go. The charges against him are being dropped."

Jacob nodded thoughtfully. "And the young man who hit Levi. He is going free as well?"

"The sheriff didn't exactly say, but my guess is yes. I think he believes the whole matter is best set aside."

Jacob said nothing, but his disappointment was clear. I was embarrassed at having to tell him. It was shameful. Levi had done nothing wrong, but he had received a black eye, a nasty cut, and a healthy dose of humiliation for his trouble. Clayton Ross was being given a free pass.

"Jacob, it is certainly Levi's option to press charges," I said.

Jacob seemed amused by my statement. "That, Dr. Bradford, is not our way."

He walked to the front waiting room to speak with his wife

and daughter. A moment later, Rebecca was timidly heading down the hall toward the exam room. I could tell that she had been crying, but still, she had a strikingly winsome and delicate prettiness about her. As she passed, I offered her a tight-lipped smile of encouragement and pointed toward the exam room door. Ann was coming out of the exam room just as Rebecca entered.

The two of us stood in the hallway, our mutual disgust of the situation easily communicated in our silence.

"Let's give them a moment," I finally suggested.

She nodded in agreement and headed toward the break room.

I went to my office, dropped into my chair, and spun around to gaze out the large windows. The handkerchief that had been dropped at Moon Lake was on my credenza. After studying it for a brief second, again noting its embroidered initials, ELY, I grabbed it, put it in my lab coat pocket, and walked back to Levi's exam room. Curiosity had gotten the better of me.

Levi and Rebecca were alone, talking softly to each other. She was touching the bruise around his eye. I reached into my pocket and held up the delicate piece of cloth. "Yours, I believe?"

Panicked glances shot between the two teens. I had the answer I needed. Rebecca stared at me behind a face seized with apprehension.

I brought my finger to my lips and shook my head lightly to communicate that I saw no reason to speak further on the matter. I held out the handkerchief, smiling warmly.

Cautiously, she took it from me, her shy face framed in embarrassed gratitude. "Thank you." Quickly, she slipped the cloth into her pocket.

I turned to Levi. "It's very important that you keep the wound clean. Let me know if you see any signs of infection. Come back in about ten days and we will take your sutures out."

"I will, Dr. Bradford."

We all gathered in the clinic lobby, and Jacob thanked me again. But before he left, I had a final question for him.

"Jacob, I understand there was a fire out your way recently. Was it anything serious?"

"No, just an outbuilding where we keep hardened corn ears to feed the livestock. It was near our main barn. The rain had stopped, and it looked like it might catch the large barn on fire as well. Fortunately, the rain started again and prevented that."

"Any idea what started it?"

"We presume a lightning strike."

"The volunteer fire department came out. Do you have any idea who called them?"

Jacob smiled. "That, Dr. Bradford, is a mystery even to us. As you might guess, we don't have telephones. It was an unfortunate waste of their time."

"Well, I'm glad the fire wasn't serious."

I bid him good-bye and they departed. But the mention of the fire and the phone call had sent a subtle bolt of panic to the faces of Levi and Rebecca, just like the one I had seen in the exam room. They had quickly exchanged a series of worried, nuanced glances. Levi had just returned from two months in Nashville, and a young woman on a burner phone had made the call to the fire department. It was the first piece in a larger puzzle.

CHAPTER 23
Aftermath

John Harris entered the waiting room of the clinic right after Jacob and his family left. "Hey, sawbones. You okay?"

Emotionally exhausted, I answered in a detached monotone. "Yeah, fine. Why?"

"I got a phone call from the sheriff. He's a little worried about you."

"Oh really? And why is that?"

John studied me for a moment, flashing the robust, infectious smile that was central to his persuasive personality. He stepped toward me, putting his hand on my shoulder. "Come on, Doc. My office is down the hall. What say you and I have a chat?"

I walked around my desk and fell into my leather chair while John eased lazily into one of the wingbacks across from me.

"Luke, is there something about you that you haven't told me?"

I thought for a moment. "Yeah, I once took a macramé class. It had to do with a girl."

John's mouth eased in a fleeting smirk. "I was thinking more along the lines of a boxing class. Ever taken one of those?"

"No, can't say that I have. Why do you ask?"

"Warren said you were ready to go to blows with Cal Ross. Heck, he also said that for a second there in the jail cell, he thought you were going to give him a punch."

I was amused. "Did he, now?"

"Yeah, he did. Is that true?"

I shrugged and stared out the window. "I don't know. Maybe I wanted to hit somebody. But as you are well aware, that didn't happen."

"I understand. We all get that way from time to time. I guess it just seemed a little out of character for you."

"And why is that? I mean, look at you, John. Half the people in this town are scared to death of you. Why do you get to have all the fun?"

His neck stiffened. He couldn't seem to decide if my comment was a compliment or an insult. "Gee, I'm a little crushed. I thought everyone saw me as one of those tortured, sensitive guys."

"John, based on that comment, I don't think you're getting enough fiber in your diet, if you catch my larger meaning."

He grinned, content to let me fill in the silence. I exhaled a heavy sigh. "So, you're saying I've established myself as one of Watervalley's tough guys."

John nodded. "Heck, sport. You took on Warren Thurman and Cal Ross both in the same day. That all by itself gives you a top-ten ranking based on strength of schedule alone."

"I'll have to add that to my résumé."

"Anyway, I think Warren was just doing his job."

"I think he was overdoing it." I paused, reflecting on John's previous comment. "Did Warren really think I was going to hit him?"

"Probably not. But he thought you and Cal were about to duke it out."

"It wouldn't have been much of a fight. Cal Ross was already well fermented. Any swing he might have taken would have been telegraphed an hour ahead."

"Maybe so," John added, "but it's never a good idea to get into a brawl with someone who's not afraid to go back to jail."

"So, Cal Ross has done some time in lockup?"

"Yeah, he does a little shift work out at the cabinet factory, but for the most part I think he's pretty shiftless. Getting drunk and into fights is nothing new for him."

"Well, the apple doesn't fall far from the tree."

"What makes you say that?"

"His son, Clayton. I think he's an alcoholic. He just does a better job of hiding it. I asked Warren to run a sobriety screen on him, and I'm pretty sure it came back positive. That Mennonite guy didn't do anything to him. Clayton tripped over a chair."

"Alcoholism seems like a pretty fast conclusion based on one incident."

"Trust me. I know what I'm talking about."

"What makes you so sure?"

"Because I'm a doctor with a degree from Vanderbilt. When I'm wrong, the world makes a little less sense."

John laughed and offered a nod of concession. "Fair enough, sawbones. I'll take your word for it."

Silence ensued and John sat patiently. I picked up a pencil and began to thump the rubber end against the arm of my chair while staring out the window.

"I'll let you in on a little secret," I finally said. "That article in the paper a few weeks back about the bogus trip by the volunteer firemen to the Mennonite community, the one where Clayton got hurt . . ."

"Yeah."

"When I treated him that night, I sensed something wasn't right. I had a blood alcohol test run, and he was three times the legal driving limit. I don't know how he was standing up. He must have an incredible tolerance. That was why he fell and got hurt that night. But Luther Whitmore twisted the truth, used it to stir everybody up against the Mennonites."

"Is that what has you all bent out of shape?"

"I don't know. Maybe. That's part of it, I guess. I think it's the way everybody reacted. It's like the whole town bought into Luther's viewpoint."

"Careful. You're starting to sound like you care about Watervalley."

I grinned. John knew that I had nearly left town six months ago. "Well, yeah. On a certain level it's my town too."

John shrugged. "I think the reaction says more about how the town reveres veterans than any issues it has with the Mennonites. Anyway, that's just Luther. He writes stories that everyone thinks are vulgar and offensive, so naturally they buy additional copies of his newspaper."

"Could be. But Luther, he just poisons the water for everyone."

"He does seem to be wrestling with some pretty dark demons. I've made it a practice to keep Luther as a minor character in my life story."

"The bias of the whole thing has just . . . I don't know. It really bugged me, and I couldn't let go of it. I went and talked to him."

"How did that go?"

"Peachy, of course."

John nodded. "So, I guess it's safe to say that Luther's not putting a selfie of you two on his Facebook page?"

"Strong insight as always, Professor."

Again, we sat in silence. I thumped the pencil rhythmically.

"Connie told me that Luther was highly decorated for combat valor in Vietnam."

"Didn't know that."

"Apparently few people do. He's kept it a secret. Speaking of which, John, what about you? You were around during the last of Vietnam. Did you serve in the military?"

"My draft number was three hundred fifty-eight. The Viet Cong would have to have taken Iowa before I got called up."

"Well, I'm pretty sure Luther will use this incident today to add more fodder to his anti-Mennonite rhetoric."

"Don't know what to tell you, sport. Luther usually reports a pretty clean accounting of the facts, but he does seem to have it in for the boys in black."

"Doesn't make it right."

"Doesn't make it a big deal either. Look, people get stirred up for a little while, but it passes."

"That may be so, but I wish I knew what's behind Luther's bitterness. It's got something to do with Moon Lake and something from his past."

"Why don't you ask him?"

"I did the other night. He didn't exactly say the words 'Go to hell,' but that's a pretty close approximation."

John grunted a short laugh. "Give it time. I'm sure you'll figure it out. Meanwhile, anything else troubling you while you still have my undivided attention?"

"Everything seems out of kilter lately. The new vet, Karen Davidson, had her open house today. Nobody showed up. She was crushed. It's just been one of those days."

John stood, signaling his departure. "Take a drive. Clear your head. Or, on the other hand, you could go slap Luther around to your way of thinking. That might make you feel better."

"A thoughtful recommendation. Thanks."

"Take care, sawbones."

He left and I sat brooding. Then I decided to take John's advice. Maybe I just needed to rethink my approach. After locking the clinic door, I made my way toward High Street.

CHAPTER 24
A Hidden Eloquence

Unlike my last visit to Luther's house, this one was not haunted by feelings of uncertainty or trepidation. I climbed the porch steps and pounded on his front door. After a short minute, it opened. Luther stood before me, wearing a face of shrewd curiosity and holding a glass of water.

"Bradford, you keep dropping by like this, people are going to think we're an item."

"I need a word with you, Luther."

My hard, clipped words told him I wouldn't back down. Still, he let a few awkward seconds pass before giving a slight nod and stepping aside.

The main hallway of the grand Victorian home was wide and stately. A large cased opening to the right led to a formal parlor with a pale marble fireplace, dark paneled walls, and towering windows. Luther motioned me in that direction. There was the musky odor of gathered time: air made stale from the smells of old rugs, aged leather books, and fireplace ash. Heavy window drapes had been pulled closed, leaving the room dimly lit. Only a few brilliant shafts of light shone through the slim openings along the edges. The ancient furniture was bulky and heavy, stiff, and inhospitable. Decades' worth of old black-and-white photographs were neatly framed and stood in tight clusters atop every surface. A layer of dust rested upon everything.

Nevertheless, the room spoke of earlier money, of staid wealth from the past. I suspected Luther was still a man of considerable fortune but had grown miserly in his later years. He looked much the same as the room. In spite of his weathered frame, he was clean-shaven and wore a crisply starched open-collared shirt tucked into neatly pressed slacks. He carried himself in a loose, almost regal manner. He was surprisingly relaxed and sober. I sat in one of the large chairs as he took the couch opposite me.

"Luther, you're looking rather stately and composed this afternoon," I said. "I don't think I've seen this version of you."

He took a sip of water and answered casually, "Must be the Pilates."

"No, really. You seem dressed for some special occasion and . . . drinking water, I notice."

Luther set his glass on the coffee table. He crossed his legs at the knee and tugged on the crease of his slacks, pulling it straight. He spoke calmly, plainly. "Today was my mother's birthday, Bradford. She abhorred drinking. So, in respect to her, I abstain for this one day." He regarded me disdainfully. "You may giggle now."

I lifted my hand in a gesture of accommodation. "Nope, nope, not at all. As good a reason as any. Sounds like you have fond memories of her."

He paused. "This day holds many memories for me. July fifth was the day I shipped off to Fort Polk." He let this thought sink in for a moment. "What's on your mind, Doctor?"

"Luther, I was wondering if you could tell me what Vietnam was like."

I expected some vile riposte from his acidic verbal arsenal, but instead he asked almost politely, "Why do you want to know?"

"I'm cochair of the fund-raiser to build the memorial statue for Watervalley's soldiers killed in action. I've never served in the military, I've never been shot at in a hostile conflict, and I've never aimed a gun at someone and pulled the trigger. So I guess I'm trying to get a better appreciation of what that experience is like." It was a thin excuse, but I was hoping it would be enough to get him to talk.

Luther drew in a long breath, his gaze studied, apprehensive, searching.

When he finally did speak, it was with surprising elegance and a careful choice of words. "I was born a child of the midcentury, a child of the victory years. So I grew up with the romance of stories about brave soldiers, and grand parades, and glorious purpose. My generation was consumed with the mystery of war. With the moral purity of childhood, we imagined ourselves heroes with our stick guns, fighting it out on the pretend battlefields of Bastogne, Monte Cassino, Iwo Jima. . . ."

He paused a moment. "At least, some of us did. Our fathers' reluctance to talk about the war only heightened our fascination. The footlocker in the attic, with its uniforms and medals, was practically a secret shrine to my friends and me. We were intoxicated with naïve ideas about country and service. North Vietnam was never a threat to us as a nation. We knew that. But war in the abstract can cast a strong allure. Yet all that grand intent, that sense of righteous mission, turned out to be vaporous. Our disillusionment was inevitable. Surely, Bradford, you don't need me to explain that."

"I heard that you received a number of medals for valor in combat. Is that true?"

"There may be some truth to that. But it's not a subject worth discussing."

I nodded and changed direction. "What was the day-to-day like?"

Luther sipped his water and reflected before speaking. "Early on, a lot of guys threw themselves recklessly into the fight, and they were pretty quickly massacred. And those first few times you see a man half-blown apart and lying in those awkward positions of death, it sobers you, teaches you to be cautious, careful. Your days are spent in the stretch and sag of nerves, riding the crest and fall of frayed emotions. Oftentimes, due to fatigue and lack of sleep, our thoughts bordered on madness. Death sat beside us constantly. In the dark at night, we talked about food and women, the things we missed. But it seemed that most of the time was spent in fear and waiting, always waiting."

Luther's words flowed seamlessly, creating what felt like a grandly surreal moment. It occurred to me that his normally acidic tongue had cruelly overshadowed his incredible gift of expression. I prompted him further. "What were you waiting for?"

"To come home, of course. To return to things the way they were. To summer evenings and people talking on their porches, to the sound of church bells on Sunday, to the faces we'd left behind. We thought about these things constantly, and we waited."

"How many tours of duty did you serve?"

"Three."

"So . . . you re-upped a couple of times?"

"That's right."

"Then I guess I'm confused. If you wanted to come home so badly, why did you keep going back?"

I did my best to pose the question innocently and could only hope he was not second-guessing me. He set his glass down again on the coffee table and rubbed his face. The game was up. I was about to catch the brunt of his venomous tongue. But instead, it seemed that memories, long ago relegated to the dark corners of his mind, began to slip through the cracks. He cocked his head to one side and spoke reflectively.

"Things change, Bradford. People change. The life I had before the war was never going to be the life I would have after the war. That life had died. The war changed everything. Lost youth and lost dreams—there was a whole generation of us from the sixties who were forever stained by the experience. So yeah, I stayed on till it finished. I met Claire in California, and after being gone for eight years, I finally decided it was time to come home."

There was a pause in the conversation, and I felt uncomfortably conspicuous, as if my naked intent in asking these questions were becoming all too obvious. Fortunately, Luther broke the silence.

"After returning here, Claire and I were happy for a short period. I had sealed up the past, blotted out the old voices, the old life. But they still haunted me. I couldn't sleep, and I began to take long walks at night. And slowly the old memories of my childhood simmered."

"Luther, if you don't mind my asking, what memories?"

He looked at me drily and snorted. "Actually, I do mind."

I nodded and held up a hand of dismissal, communicating that it was none of my business. This seemed to satisfy something in Luther, and in that moment an odd understanding came between us. Luther twisted his mouth to the side in a gesture of resignation.

"Oh, what the hell, Bradford. There were other influences, other ideas in my childhood that defined me."

"You mean living near the Mennonites?"

"Yes, living near the Mennonites."

"How so?"

"We were all just children out in the country, several of the Mennonite kids and me. We were young, innocent, foolish. . . . We played together every day."

"You're talking about Eli Yoder?"

"Yeah. Eli and I are the same age. We were best friends when we were very young. We were in a world of our own, playing in the fields, swimming in the lake, hiding in the woods. My parents knew, but I'm not sure his did. It doesn't matter now. All that ended."

"What happened?"

"My father sold the farm and we moved to town. We became teenagers and saw each other less and less. I got drafted. Things happened."

"I learned from Eli's son, Jacob, that Eli did government service during the war. Is that what you were talking about the other night?"

A sly grin spread across Luther's face. "So, Bradford, you did do your homework." He looked down and again pulled at the crease in his slacks. "Yeah, he served at a government agricultural research facility working in their dairy, I believe."

I thought for a moment about all that Jacob had told me. "So, I guess you knew his twin sister, Ellie?"

Luther looked at me sharply. He seemed to choose his words carefully. "Yes, we were all friends."

"I understand she died of pneumonia?"

"Yes, she did," Luther responded. "It was senseless. He didn't get her to a hospital, and she died needlessly."

"Yeah, I don't understand that either. It would seem the situation just fell apart."

Luther spoke with tired resignation. "Her death was quite tragic. It was a long time ago."

He ran his finger around the rim of the water glass, lost in reflection. Eventually, he spoke without looking up. "Like I said, we were all friends." Amusement spread across his face. "Ellie spent her entire time keeping Eli and me in line, declaring that she would need to spend half of her waking hours praying for us. She was the unblemished warden of all morality, as good and virtuous a person as I've ever known. That was why her death was so appalling."

"So why did you and Eli have a falling-out?" It was the linchpin question, the one that I hoped would explain Luther's bitterness.

"Because we finally realized we were different, Bradford. We saw things differently. The war. Everything."

I nodded. "And Moon Lake was a casualty of all that?"

Luther let a long silence fill the room, after which he spoke in a dispirited, reflective voice. "Moon Lake belonged to my childhood. It belonged to another time."

I wanted to probe deeper, but I knew that I had pushed Luther as far as I could. I changed subjects.

"So I guess you heard about the mishap this morning with Clayton Ross?"

"I did. What of it?"

"I'm wondering what you plan to do with the story."

He shrugged. "Two men had a misunderstanding. One of them got slugged. Ultimately, no charges were filed. So what?"

"And you're willing to let it go at that?"

"I leave something out?"

I was certain that Luther already knew the answer to this question. Despite Clayton's ability to mask it, he had been intoxicated. But Clayton was a veteran of two tours in Afghanistan, and

Warren was giving him a pass . . . this time. Luther seemed fine with that. And I guess, ultimately, I had to agree it was the right thing to do. It occurred to me that Clayton Ross had made sacrifices that I had not, had seen and done things that I had not. Perhaps he deserved some leeway.

"No, Luther. I don't think you did."

There was a tightening in his eyes that communicated our unspoken understanding. "So how bad was the Mennonite fellow hurt?"

"A few stitches and a black eye."

Luther nodded thoughtfully. "'The meek shall inherit the earth,' Doctor."

"Yeah . . . It doesn't exactly say when, though, does it?"

He stiffened, slightly amused. "Why, if I didn't know better, I'd think you just stole one of my lines."

"Your sparkling personality is contagious, Luther."

"By the way, Bradford. I found out some skinny on our new veterinarian."

"What do you mean?"

"She did a little time in an army mental hospital a few years back, Beaumont Medical Center, Fort Bliss, Texas."

"Luther, that's private patient information. How did you come across it?"

"Relax. I still have a few old friends in the military, and I made some inquiries. We both know it's not for publication. Just thought you might want to know."

Karen's past was neither Luther's business nor mine, but admittedly, it was an interesting revelation. I didn't pursue the matter further.

Luther rubbed his hands together and stood. "So I'm guessing we're finished here. I assume you got what you came for?"

There were layers of subtlety in Luther's remark. I couldn't be sure if he was referring to Clayton Ross or if he had known all along that I wanted to pry into his past.

"Actually, Luther . . . no, I haven't."

He regarded me with a discerning curiosity. "So, what do you want?"

"A check. Your donation to the statue fund."

A buried wit emerged and he nodded. "Well played, Bradford. Sit tight. I'll get my checkbook."

He disappeared down the central hallway. I stood and walked around the room, examining decades' worth of old black-and-white photographs. There were a few candid shots taken of fishing trips and mountain vacations, but most were formal in nature, including weddings, black-tie social events, and military portraits.

One photo in particular caught my eye. It was of a young woman, a teenager dressed in an evening gown. The style of the dress and the patina of the photograph gave me the impression that it was well over a half-century old, possibly from the forties. The girl in the picture had a compelling beauty, and I had the fleeting notion I had seen her before. I had just picked up the frame to study the photo closely, when Luther's voice broke the silence just behind me.

"That was my mother, Evangeline, at her debutante ball."

Somewhat startled and embarrassed, I set the frame down quickly, endeavoring to be careful to leave it standing properly. "She was an attractive woman."

"She was eighteen, I believe. She married my father shortly after that. I was born in 1950." Luther handed me the check. I put it in my pocket and thanked him, and he showed me to the door. Before exiting, I turned to him and extended my hand.

He looked at me and then at my outstretched arm. Then slowly, he extended his and we shook, exchanging solemn nods. I turned away, and he shut the door behind me.

The meeting with Luther had not been the confrontation I had expected. And while the conversation had shed some light on the origins of his dark nature, there remained unanswered questions as to what had soured his life. I understood how certain experiences could not be shared any more than they could be forgotten. But more than ever I was convinced that something in Luther's past had poisoned him.

From what Connie had told me, Luther's battle injuries had left him unable to have children of his own, and apparently adoption was never considered an option. The disillusionment of the war, the loss of one childhood friend, and the untimely death of another had been difficult chapters in his life. But collectively, these events seemed to fall short of explaining a lifetime of bitterness.

Although it wasn't outwardly visible, Luther had a disfigured spirit. Something dark in his past had left him unable to see any possibility of a happy ending. Somewhere in the rice paddies of Vietnam Luther's soul had died, leaving him consumed with some terrible regret.

I pulled into my driveway, trying to piece together everything Luther had told me. In time, I cut the engine and headed inside. On the porch steps I pulled out the check he'd given me, noting that it was for five hundred dollars.

It was a small victory, especially considering the mean-spirited sign on his front door. At least I had fared better than the Girl Scouts.

CHAPTER 25
Levi Beiler

The hot days of July came and went.

Daily life returned to its routine if mildly mundane tempo. The shared misery of the sweltering heat made for a ready topic of conversation, and most chose not to suffer in silence. Once or twice a week it would rain, providing a brief relief, but it was often followed by humidity tantamount to a steam room.

Gardens exploded, including mine. If it was left untended for more than two days, I had zucchini the size of a Wiffle ball bat. The surplus was so absurd that neighbors began to lock their doors and hide when they saw me coming with a loaded paper bag. I would walk out my front door in the morning, only to find a large sack of cucumbers, bell peppers, and tomatoes left by the vegetable fairy, some poor soul whose ingrained mind-set of waste-not-want-not had reduced him to such covert acts.

Beatrice McClanahan no longer trolled the streets on her lawn mower, having been given a kind but firm ultimatum by Warren Thurman. I decided to visit her one afternoon. It was a convenient excuse to find a new victim in my ever-widening search for recipients of the garden overflow. She seemed delighted to see me and grateful for the bag of veggies, but I couldn't help notice that some of the light had gone out of her eyes. She was lonely, and the heat kept her confined, unable to walk any great distance. I made a mental note to check in on her more often.

After a brief exam, Karen Davidson determined that Rhett did, in fact, have a small tumor behind his left eye. Her advice was to watch it for a while but that it might require surgery. She also confirmed that Maggie was expecting. Perhaps it was my imagination, but Rhett seemed to have a little more strut in his step after hearing the news. Louise Fox had graciously invited Rhett to spend his days in the fenced backyard so that the newlyweds could discuss favorite names and what color to paint the nursery. The two would frolic with each other for the first ten minutes and then settle down to a morning of lounging under the shade of the tall trees. The lucky dogs.

Meanwhile, Karen's practice limped along poorly. She had grown a modest cat and dog business, and a few of the horse owners in the valley who had engaged her services had been amazed by her talent and skill. But word of mouth was slow to take hold, and the large beef and dairy operations were not calling. It was tough going, and there seemed little I could do to help her.

The community charity yard sale had netted more than eight thousand dollars, which was being donated to the statue fund. So despite all the unrest and frustration that day had held for me, it had also produced a sizable donation to a worthy cause.

A company in Nashville that specialized in bronze work was awarded the contract for the memorial statue. The final quote turned out to be slightly over a hundred and eight thousand dollars. We had raised nearly two-thirds of that. Fortunately, the company agreed to begin the project with only half down and the balance due just prior to delivery.

John had recruited a group of volunteers, including Connie, to begin the arduous process of digging through the county, state, and national archives to come up with a list of veterans from the valley who had died in combat. The fund-raiser dance down at the lake had been scheduled for the Saturday of Labor Day weekend, with the intention of catching some cooler weather. We were all in great hopes that this event would go far to closing the gap on the needed funds.

As instructed, Levi Beiler returned to the clinic to have his stitches removed. He had driven his wagon to town alone, giving me an opportunity to talk to him individually. At first he had little to say, but he opened up when I asked him about his time in Nashville.

"It was quite an interesting city."

"How did you get around?"

"Buses and taxis. Sometimes I would catch a ride with strangers." He grunted an amused laugh. "Mostly women."

"So, what did you think of it all?"

His words were cautious. "What you are asking requires me to be critical of your way of life, Dr. Bradford. I'm not sure that's such a good idea."

I almost laughed. "I'm quite certain, Levi, that I could be much more critical about it than you would ever be."

He nodded his understanding. The succinctness of his answer convinced me that this was a question to which he had devoted considerable thought. "The city gives you a certain oblivion, an ability to re-create yourself. Perhaps for some that is a good thing. But for most of the people living there, life was so competitive. It makes them want things, things to replace their existing things that are perfectly fine. They want it all. There, the answer to 'How much is enough' was always 'Just a little bit more.' At home with my people, with the Mennonites, we just wanted to know what the temperature was going to be that day."

I smiled.

He continued. "Don't misunderstand, Dr. Bradford. It wasn't all bad. There were some enjoyable amusements. And a lot of the beer was really good."

This assertion left me curious. "Hold it, Levi. You're only twenty. How did you get beer?"

His face eased into a wry smile. "Fraternities."

I had to laugh. Wearing a T-shirt and jeans, Levi would look right at home on Twenty-fourth and Kensington, the intersection of Vanderbilt's Greek world.

"So I take it you found your way into a few parties?"

"More than a few, I'm afraid, Dr. Bradford."

"How did you pull that off?"

"By telling the truth. That I was Mennonite."

"And they bought that?"

He seemed surprised by my skepticism. "Sure. They had a thousand questions, and they always wanted to talk about theology."

"Interesting. How did that go?"

"It was sad, really. For me, speaking of God is an eloquent, rewarding thing. For them, he was little more than a short and ugly monosyllable. They treated religion as if it were constantly in need of mending. You see, Dr. Bradford, for the Mennonites, there are truth and untruth, belief and unbelief. We are at ease with extremes and inhabit them by choice. We sin and have our failings, as all men do. But we see our world in black and white, not the halftones and gray shades that the larger world accommodates."

I thought about Levi's words for a moment and couldn't help

but be impressed with the succinctness of his insights, with the clarity with which he so easily articulated the tenets of his faith. Admittedly, his sense of conviction was enviable.

"Well, Levi, that's rather impressively said. Did you win over any converts?"

He laughed lightly. "That was hardly my intention. I did meet a lot of rather interesting people, though." He paused, reflecting for a moment before speaking with a subdued smile. "Some of them were rather pretty."

"Hmm, I'm guessing you met a few coeds at the parties."

Levi looked confused.

"'Coeds' refers to girls."

His wry smile returned. "Yes, quite a few. Some of them saw me as a challenge. I'm quite certain a few of them wanted to take me to bed, like I was some kind of prize. One or two were almost winners. But ultimately, I could not let it happen. All I could see was the face of Rebecca."

Again, I nodded. "Well, that's certainly understandable. Rebecca seems quite fond of you."

His face glowed at the mention of her name. "Yes. I came back because of my faith. But my heart never left her. We have been in love for a long time. Mr. Yoder has consented for us to be wed."

"Congratulations! I have kind of a dumb question. For some reason I assumed that Mennonite marriages are arranged. I'm guessing that's not true?"

"It's a common misunderstanding, Dr. Bradford. But no, we date and fall in love like all people do. Courtship is more structured, and we are required to marry within the faith."

"So, a Mennonite would never marry an outsider?"

"Only if that person joined the faith."

"And that's allowed?"

"There are no rules prohibiting it, but it would be quite difficult."

"I see. Well, congratulations again. I'm happy for you."

"Yes. We are quite excited. We will be married in October."

"Levi, with both of you being so young, where will you live?"

He spoke with polite reserve. "Dr. Bradford, we are a frugal people, but that does not mean we are poor. Both of our families have set aside money and land for us to begin our life together. We will do the same for our children. For a brief time, we will live with my parents, but I am buying some land from the Yoders. It is on Mercy Creek Road. Next spring I will build a house there."

"Where on Mercy Creek Road?"

"It's a small farm surrounded by large hills. There used to be a house there, but it burned years ago. I will probably build on the old foundation."

"I know the place. I passed it a while back when I went out to examine Jacob's father. So the Yoders own that property?"

"Yes. Eli's father bought it when Eli and his sister, Ellie, were children. It was supposed to be a home for Ellie when she got married. But she died young of sickness, and the place has been left all these years. Now Rebecca and I are to have it."

I was fascinated. It had never occurred to me to ask Jacob who owned the property. Now I understood why the ruins had remained untouched for decades. Perhaps because of the unexplained singing in the wind I had heard there, the place held a peculiar enchantment for me.

I congratulated Levi once more, and soon after, he departed.

I was happy for him and his lovely bride to be. But what he'd told me also held up a light to a simple reality.

It was time to move forward with my own plans.

FROM THE JOURNAL OF CHRISTINE CHAMBERS, JUNE 10, 2000

Dear Mr. Wonderful:

I haven't written to you in a while, but I thought of you today. So I am writing this letter. I don't know who you are or where you live, so I can't mail it to you. But I'd like to think that when I dream about you, magically you can hear what I am saying and know what I am thinking.

I've been out on a couple of car dates. The boys were sweet, but they weren't you, Mr. Wonderful. I don't why I know this. I just do.

I spent a couple of hours over on Bracken's Knoll late this afternoon. I got a new CD player for my fifteenth birthday, so I took it with me and listened to songs. My favorite is "Breathe." It made me think of you and that day I heard your voice floating in the air.

Or did I just dream that?

Will we have a song, Mr. Wonderful? What will it be? Will you sing it to me?

I wonder where you are right now. Are you dating? What kind of girls are they? Are they pretty? I hope you'll think I'm pretty.

That's stupid, isn't it? You would never be Mr. Wonderful if you didn't think I was pretty. But I'm smart too, and athletic. I make good grades and play basketball.

I think I'm pretty. And it's nice when boys notice and say so and ask me out. But I don't think they care that I'm smart and a good athlete. You won't be that way, will you, Mr. Wonderful? You'll love everything about me, won't you?

I do hope we have a song. And it will be playing when we meet, or when we first kiss, or when you first tell me you love me. That's the way it should be. Our song should be playing when something important happens.

But you already know this because you can read my thoughts; you know what I'm thinking.

I hope we meet soon.

I love you, Mr. Wonderful.

CAC

P.S. I hope you can sing.

CHAPTER 26
Our Song

The first of August signaled Christine's return to work as a schoolteacher. Our evenings together on the farmhouse's broad porch became less frequent, and when they did occur, they included stacks of papers to grade and the preparation of lesson plans. When I wasn't reading a medical journal or a book, I was doing my best to distract her, using small acts of affection that were not as greatly appreciated as they might have been.

One Thursday evening in mid-August, I was lying on the wicker sofa absorbed in a mystery novel while Christine sat nearby grading a pile of tests. She looked up from her papers and asked, "Luke, do you think I'm smart?"

"You're dating me, aren't you?"

"That hardly qualifies."

I continued reading. "I love you too."

"Oh come on, Bradford. Answer the question."

I stayed hidden behind my book. "I think you are very smart. Why even ask such a question?"

"Oh, it's nothing." She returned to grading her papers.

But a minute later, she spoke again. "Luke."

"Hmm."

"We're a couple, right?"

I was at a critical, consuming point in the novel and left a long pause before my idle response. "Sure."

"I need you to look at my eyes when we talk." It was her schoolteacher voice.

I rested my book on my chest and peered over the top. "Okay, brown eyes, I'm missing something here. Why all the questions?"

"No big reason. The girls in my classroom were asking me about it today."

Returning to my book, I responded lethargically. "Well, I hope you didn't tell them we were going steady, because if that gets out, I'll never hear the end of it down at the Co-op."

"Gee, hate that. Looks like you're just going to have to man up."

I knew that tone only too well. There was something deeper, a cloaked desire in the question that my clownish answer had not accommodated. I sat up, put my book aside, and spoke with all the earnest affection I could muster. "What other kinds of questions were they asking, Christine?"

She remained focused on her schoolwork for a moment longer, requiring me to pay penance for my detached behavior of the last few minutes. But I could see her eyes soften with the change in my tone and posture.

"Oh, you know, the kind of things that twelve- and thirteen-year-olds are curious about. How did we meet? Where do we go on dates? What's our song?"

"Do we have a song?"

"No, don't think we do."

"Well, I think we should have a song. I'm pretty sure it's required for couple status."

"Well, what's your suggestion?"

"Absolutely no idea. I flunked the 'pick your song' class. You're going to have to do the heavy lifting here."

"It should be something from a special moment we shared."

"Define 'special moment'?"

"Hmm, I don't know. Maybe something to do with our first date, first kiss, first something."

I thought about this for a second and realized I was completely clueless. "Okay. It's official. This is definitely a girl thing."

"Oh come on, Bradford. Try to be the romantic for a whole five minutes."

"Ooooo-kaaaaay. Jeez." I exhaled and rubbed my chin. "How about the first time I told you I loved you?"

"Nah, not good. We were at the dairy barn, and you had just finished helping with milking. You smelled like a cow."

"Well, dang, I thought it was pretty romantic."

Christine noted my wounded tone. "Oh come on now. Yes, it was sweet and wonderful and everything, but it wasn't exactly song worthy."

I twisted my lips into a tight pucker. "Well, then, what about the moment I fell in love with you?"

Christine's face softened. "When was that?"

I breathed a small sigh of embarrassment. "You're probably not going to believe me. But looking back, it was the night of our first date when we went out to Moon Lake and built the fire. I mean, I can't say that even at the time I understood it or was even willing to admit it to myself. But I felt the same way about you after that night that I feel right now. So, Miss Chambers, I guess you stole my heart from the very beginning."

An adoring tenderness welled in her eyes. "Luke Bradford, I take it back. You are the romantic." She lowered her chin and regarded me with glowing affection. "Seriously? That first night at Moon Lake?"

"Yeah, that first night. You remember; we talked for hours. I never told you this, but I had looked you up on the Internet. You were valedictorian of your class, a five-star basketball recruit, everybody said you could sing like a bird, and yeah, you were also quite gorgeous. So sure, I was a little intimidated."

"You're telling me *you* were intimidated?"

"Well, sure, a little. Look, for months I only knew you from a distance. And then there we were—the lake, the fire, the stars, and I had you all to myself. I thought I would spend the whole evening just staring at you, trying to memorize you. But the more we talked, the more I was fascinated. You were smart, strong, funny, and yet, you were also sweet and vulnerable. I guess I fell in love with all of that."

In a fluid motion Christine left her chair and came to sit beside me, bending her legs across my lap and draping her arms around my neck.

"So, Mr. Luke Romantic-After-All Bradford, what do you think our song should be?"

Nothing was coming to mind. When an idea finally did hit, I spoke before thinking. "Well, since we built that fire, how about 'The Campfire Song' by SpongeBob SquarePants?"

Christine slumped and spoke in dry disbelief. "Bradford, how can you be so smart and so clueless at the same time?"

I answered sheepishly, "Practice?"

She shook her head, speechless.

We sat in silence for a moment, and I thought about that wonderful first date. I spoke softly, reflectively. "It was incredible, actually—the lake, the sunset, and just the two of us on that high hill looking over the valley."

Christine's eyes grew large. "That's it! That should be our song!"

"Okay, 'that' as in . . . what?"

"'Over the Valley.' It's a song by Pink Martini."

"I know of the group, but I can't say I know the song."

"Trust me. It's perfect."

Christine smiled and closed her eyes. She became lost to some distant land, some secret world that lent an air of enchantment to this one. She was incandescent with delight.

"Perfect, huh?" I whispered.

"Yes!" She closed her eyes again, pulled her shoulders up, inhaled deeply, and then dropped them in a gesture of great satisfaction. "Just perfect!"

In the days that followed, Christine's joy that evening reminded me that it was time to put my plans together. Ideally, a proposal of marriage was something I intended to do only once in this lifetime. Given my inclination to hide my feelings, asking Christine to marry me was the quintessential private, intimate moment between us. I knew that my capacity for romantic expression was dismal at best and considerable forethought was needed. In the closing days of August, I put my lofty scheme into play.

I still had grand intentions of going to my storage units in Atlanta, but I had a more pressing need of my free time. I took a half day off and traveled to Nashville, where I had arranged for a jewelry store to mount a two-and-a-half-carat diamond that had come into my possession sometime earlier. While there, I dropped in on some favorite professors from med school.

To no large surprise, none of them had ever heard of Watervalley. I had finished first in my class, and I could see in their eyes an unspoken disappointment at what they considered a squandering of my abilities. My major professor, Dr. Burns, casually suggested that several new grants were pending that could avail some research fellowships in the near future. I smiled and thanked him, politely avoiding a response.

Later that afternoon, after I had picked up the finished ring, I was nearly incandescent with excitement. All of my old regrets about doing medical research were temporarily forgotten. I made the two-hour drive back to Watervalley consumed in thought as to how, when, and where I would propose.

As I pulled into my drive, I noticed Will Fox sitting on his front porch steps with a pad of paper and a stack of books. Curious, I walked over to him. He was intensely absorbed in some faraway world.

"Hi, Willster. You seem pretty adrift. A fellow once told me it's a dangerous thing to be lost inside one's own head."

Will lifted his chin and stared at me for a long moment, his gaze completely absent of expression. He was in his pseudo-sophisticated mode, one of the many personas he occasionally chose to inhabit. He said, "That statement might have relevance if, in fact, I were actually lost."

"Oh," I replied thoughtfully. "Do tell." At first I feigned an expression of enlightened innocence. Then ever so slowly my eyes tightened, regarding him with a sly, furtive smile. The little smart-ass. I could see the corners of his mouth turning upward, betraying the bursting grin that he was hard-pressed to contain. But the moment was telling. He had read my unspoken affirmation of his cleverness, something I knew he yearned for. He returned to his book in an effort to mask his contentment. I reached over, tousled his hair, and took a seat beside him on the step.

"So, what are you reading? Homework?"

"No, I got a bunch of books on poetry from the library."

"Hmm, still trying to capture love's labor lost on paper?"

"Nah. I'm over Wendy Wilson. She's so June."

I wanted to laugh, but the seriousness of his remark held me in check. "Okay, good, glad to hear it."

"I've decided I'm pretty good at writing poetry. So I've been reading all the poems I can. I don't get some of them. But a lot of them I do."

This was wildly entertaining. I truly liked Will, but after he had told me a few months ago that his avatar name for an online Gladiator game was Geekus Maximus, I honestly didn't think he could get any more nerdy.

"Who have you been reading?"

"Wordsworth, Longfellow, Whitman, a little bit of Tennyson, and some unknowns like this one called *Poems to Sylvia*." He was holding a small, antiquated library book.

"What kind of poems do you like to write?"

"Poems about feelings . . . love, hope, despair, allergies, that sort of thing."

I looked at him quizzically. "Allergies?"

"Yeah, I wrote a poem about things I'm allergic to. You want to hear some of it?"

"Umm, sure."

He flipped open his notebook. "This one is called 'Allergic to You.'"

You saw me crying,
I said it's the flu.
But I was just lying
It was really about you.

I protected my heart,
With indifference and candor.
My nose only smarts,
From the pollen and dander.

There's no longer a "we,"
Most unequivocally.
But don't worry about me,
I'll be snivelly, civilly.

For a moment I sat speechless, struggling with what to say. "Okay then. Good. Pretty clever."

Will smugly closed his notebook. "Yeah, I think it's pretty good too." We shared a silent moment of head-nodding guy bravado. "You know, Dr. B., I could probably help you out if you needed to write a poem for Miss Chambers. Girls like that kind of stuff, you know."

"Will, that's a great offer. Let me, uh, let me think on that, and I may take you up on it in the near future."

"Sure. Anything I can do to help."

I tousled his hair again and headed back to the house, where Connie and Estelle were waiting with, I could only imagine, a delicious calorie-laden dinner. With the ring in my pocket, the first step of my master plan for the perfect evening, the perfect moment, and the perfect proposal was in place.

I was fairly certain that Will's poetry would not be included.

I found Connie and Estelle in the kitchen, talking nonstop above a clamor of banging pans and clattering dishes. We sat down to dinner, and after saying grace, Connie turned toward me.

"I hear Lida Wilkins has a buyer for the bed and breakfast."

"So I hear." I nodded in reply.

"Some fellow out of Charleston . . . a widower with two little children. Not exactly the normal profile of someone wanting to get into the lodging business. There's bound to be a story there."

"Well, Connie," I replied with good humor, "I have no doubt that in no time you'll get to the bottom of whatever deep, dark secrets are behind this mysterious fellow."

She stopped in midchew to eye me scornfully. "Watch yourself, Doctor. The rest of your dinner might just be a peanut butter and jelly sandwich."

I winked at her and continued eating. "Speaking of dads and children, Dr. Davidson says that Maggie should deliver sometime around Labor Day." I glanced over at Rhett, who was lying forlornly in the corner of the kitchen. "As you can see, Rhett is giddy with excitement."

"Humph," responded Connie as she eyed Rhett sharply. "I'm still not speaking to him, the little four-legged reprobate."

"Hate the sin, love the sinner, Mrs. Thompson," I said teasingly.

Connie ignored me. "I hear that Dr. Davidson's veterinary practice is still having a hard go of it. I like that gal. I wish there were something we could do to help."

"So do I," I said. "I've talked to several of the dairy and beef farmers, but it hasn't done much good."

"Is it because she's a woman?" inquired Estelle.

"No, that's not the impression I get," I said thoughtfully. "Nobody seems to doubt her ability. They're just concerned that she'll get hurt trying to handle big animals."

"Well," said Estelle shrewdly as she leaned back in her chair, "looks like I'm going to have to come up with a solution for Dr. Davidson's money woes."

Connie rolled her eyes. "And this from a woman who spent five hundred dollars on a pair of shoes."

Estelle sipped her iced tea. "Don't judge what you don't understand, Constance Grace."

"Well," I said, "I'm open to any ideas."

Estelle gazed into the middle distance. "Just let Estelle put a little thinking time on this situation. She'll come up with an answer!"

Connie snorted. "That assertion loses its gusto when it comes from a woman who talks about herself in the third person."

"Keep it up, Constance, and you won't be riding in my car on the way home. You'll just have to use your broom."

As entertaining as the two sisters were, it seemed a good time for a change of subject. "So, Estelle, the big family reunion was this past weekend. How did it go with Tyrell?"

The two sisters exchanged subtle glances.

Connie answered for her. "Luke, let's just say that my suspicions about Tyrell turned out to be correct."

Estelle straightened the cuff of her blouse. "It was something of a disappointment, but we did have some nice conversations."

"Who are you kidding, girl? You couldn't get away from him fast enough. You looked like Indiana Jones getting chased by that big ball."

"Umm-hmm," Estelle responded smugly. "Sort of like you and Cousin Maureen."

"Oh heavens," Connie replied. "Talk about running away . . . I got stuck sitting next to Cousin Maureen at the dinner Saturday night. That girl talked on and on about all her aches and pains and strange rashes. And all the while she was eating like a pig. She might have been in declining health, but she sure wasn't declining food."

We all laughed, and Estelle added, "Connie, you should tell Dr. Bradford your big news."

"Oh?" I inquired.

Connie beamed. "Theodus, my youngest son who teaches at Rhodes College, he and his wife, Elaine, are adopting a baby. Come October, I'm going to be a grandmother!"

"Congratulations, Connie. I'm very happy for you!"

The two sisters seemed radiant at this news and continued to talk about Connie's other three children, all of whom were single and pursuing professional careers. Estelle began to clear away the dishes but stopped and stood behind my chair. Placing both hands on my shoulders, she spoke teasingly.

"Connie, maybe you can give Theodus and Elaine some pointers since you've adopted a child of your own here." She squeezed me with her pudgy, fragrant hands.

"Thanks, Estelle. I'll be sure to give Connie a call whenever I go through that second-childhood phase."

Connie regarded me deadpan. "I was unaware you had left your first one."

I let this pass.

Connie reached over and patted my hand. "It's okay, sweetie. Your secret's safe with me."

"Well," I said, finishing my last bite, "one day when I have half a dozen kids, I'll introduce you as their grandmother. Boy, won't they be surprised."

Connie stiffened. "First of all, I would be proud to be grandmother to your children. Second, if memory serves, it's customary for a young man to get married first, although I realize these days it's hardly a requirement." She stared at me silently, awaiting an answer to her inferred question.

I cut my eyes at her and spoke with a sly grin. "Go fish."

Connie shook her head in disdain as she carried a handful of dishes to the sink. "Humph. Sometimes I wonder who ties your shoelaces for you."

"Some things in this life, Mrs. Thompson, are on a need-to-know basis," I responded smugly.

"Well," Connie said bluntly, "all I'm saying is this, Mr. Need To Know. You need to know that the clock is ticking. If you're having all those children, you might want to get a move on. Or do I need to pin a note to your sweater to remind you?"

I folded my hands behind my head. "Connie T., you may rest assured that if and when I decide to make a proposal of marriage to a certain young lady, not a soul in town will see it coming."

I made this declaration with all the self-confidence that God in heaven above could possibly allow a man to have. Apparently, I had forgotten I was living in Watervalley.

CHAPTER 27
Gene Alley

Tuesday morning I caught a quick breakfast at the diner. I was sitting at the counter, reading the paper, when there was a tap on my shoulder. It was Clayton Ross.

His words were hesitant. "Doc, I uh, I just wanted to thank you for taking care of my arm. It's healed up really good." He extended his hand to me.

I didn't have a high opinion of Clayton, especially after what he had done to Levi and what I privately knew about him. Nevertheless, I returned his handshake.

"You're welcome. Glad you're better." I thought that would be the end of the conversation, but Clayton remained. He seemed nervous, searching for words.

"I, uh, I have an interview at the cabinet factory later today. So uh, so maybe I'll be able to put the arm to good use."

I wondered why he was telling me this. A strained silence fell between us, and Clayton pressed his lips together and nodded, a sign of closure. With that he turned and left.

I went back to my breakfast and the paper. It was an odd

encounter, and I endeavored to put it out of my mind. But it nagged at me all day. More than once the mental picture of Clayton and his outstretched hand crept into my head. It occurred to me that perhaps he was reaching out for more than a handshake.

The morning passed quickly, filled with a full slate of annual physicals, some runny noses, and a few bad backs. Around lunch I slipped away to make a clandestine visit to Gene Alley out at the radio station.

I had called earlier to see if he could meet with me privately. Thankfully, he had responded in language other than song titles, albeit there was something in his tone that seemed off. It should have been my first clue.

The radio station WVLY, "the Voice of the Valley," was located on a modest hill a few miles out of town on Leipers's Creek Road. It was a small, windowless brick building set adjacent to a large radio tower. I was relieved to find only one car in the parking lot when I arrived . . . meaning that only Gene would hear my plans.

I entered the front door into a small, poorly lit reception area with a large plate glass window for viewing into the studio. That room was even darker, illuminated by the blue and red diodes of the electrical equipment and a low-wattage desk lamp. Gene sat with his chin resting in his hand, his eyes closed.

I tapped lightly on the window and woke him with a start. He had the shocked look of a fugitive who had just heard bloodhounds nearby. However, once he recognized me, his face lit with impish glee. Despite his fifty-nine years, he had the sprightly actions and perky manner of a younger man. He held up a finger to signal me to wait a moment and proceeded to make a short announcement into the microphone. Then, he removed his headphones and opened the locked steel door adjacent to the picture window. He seemed wrapped in a secretive but pleasant euphoria.

We shook hands robustly. "Greetings, Doc. Glad to see you." He peered over my shoulder, lowered his voice, and spoke in a confidential whisper. "Did anybody follow you?"

"Umm, no, Gene. I'm pretty sure I'm alone." He ushered me into the studio, shut the door quickly, and exhaled a sigh of relief.

"Good, Doc, good." His eyes had an energized, feral quality, comically bordering on a faint glint of madness. Still, there was an engaging, openly friendly air to his manner. He looked at me sharply. "Doc, you got any combat skills?"

I hesitated. "I'm not sure I follow you."

"Fighting skills, Doc, you know, martial arts. You by chance have a black belt in karate?"

"Gene, I don't think I have a black belt in my closet."

He twisted his mouth in a hard grimace of understanding. Then his eyes brightened with another question. "You packing any heat, Doc?"

I stared at him blankly. "Well, no, Gene. I'm not even packing a lunch."

Again he nodded his head in shrewd assessment, momentarily lost in a generous fog. "I think we need to fall back to a more secure area, Doc. Come with me."

In spite of his bizarre eccentricities, Gene had an amiable, completely harmless nature. His involvement was critical to my plans, so I went along. He walked over to the control panel, selected a disk, and popped it into the player, speaking with a conspiratorial assuredness. "That should buy us some time."

He grabbed a small flashlight and opened a door on the backside of the studio room. After pausing for a short survey, he stepped inside and motioned for me to follow. I did so and he shut the door behind me.

I now realized I was standing in a five-by-seven-foot storage closet with a man who clearly did not limit his madness to March. Holding the flashlight under his chin, he changed the intonation of his voice to that of a reserved business professional.

"So, Dr. Bradford, how can I help you?"

I swallowed hard, deciding not to question Gene's covert antics.

"I, um. I was wondering if I could get you to play a certain song for me at nine o'clock Friday night?"

"Sure," he answered readily. "You mean on the radio, right?"

"Well, yeah."

He nodded, telegraphing his understanding. "What's the song, Doc?"

I told Gene about the song "Over the Valley" by the group Pink Martini, and the name instantly registered with him. This offered small assurance in what had otherwise been a rather surreal encounter. His face melted into a scheming grin, and he waggled his index finger at me.

"I gotcha, Doc. I'm with you. Got a little something-something special planned, huh? Want to set the right mood, the right ambience." He floated his hands outward like a symphony conductor.

"Yeah, well, something like that."

Gene rubbed his chin. "Hmm, smart plan, Doc." He paused and winked. "You need any other ideas? 'Cause I know a thing or two about captivating the honeys."

"Um, no, Gene. I'm good. But thanks." I repeated all the details to him again and thanked him for his help. But by the time I finished, his expression was vacant, preoccupied, and he seemed miles away.

"Gene, do I need to write this down for you?"

He made a sign of dismissal. "I got it, Doc. It's all stored right up here." He tapped his finger several times to the side of his head. "I learned in 'Nam it's better not to write things down; otherwise people can figure out what you're up to." He leaned in closer and looked from side to side as if someone were in the closet with us. "Matter of fact, I got a theory that not writing things down is actually the eleventh commandment." He squinted his eyes and gave me an emphatic nod.

"Okay, interesting."

"Yep, pretty sure that's right. Of course, you know, it's not written down in the Bible for obvious reasons."

I just didn't know what to make of Gene. I couldn't help but think that a part of him had forgotten to show up for the conversation. His adaptive mind didn't seem troubled by the pitfalls of chance and daily nuisances that beset most of our lives. Then again, part of me wondered if, in fact, Gene was the quintessential practical joker; that long ago he had found life a little too dull and over the years had developed this kindly yet slightly deranged persona. I simply couldn't figure him out.

We stood for a moment in the dim illumination of the flashlight. Gene had begun to look around, clearly puzzled. After another moment of hesitation, he regarded me with an innocent, inquisitive face and asked a question that seemed to say it all.

"Doc, why are we standing in a closet?"

CHAPTER 28

Estelle to the Rescue

Friday morning I stopped by the Sweetshop Bakery for a lifesaving infusion of coffee and one of Estelle's elaborate pastries. Connie emerged from the kitchen, dusting flour from her hands.

"My, my, Doctor. Pray tell . . . where have you been all week?"

"Same old same old. Work, sleep, and eat. Oh, and practicing all my steps for the big dance tomorrow night."

"Umm-hmm. Well, you might want to modify your 'Gangnam Style' for a little fox-trot."

"Why is that?"

"I heard yesterday from John that the band canceled at the last minute . . . something to do with a DUI charge. The only group he could get to replace them is called Guy Dupree and the Night Owls. They play big-band music."

I was unaffected by this news, but knew that it would likely disappoint some Watervalley regulars. "Not exactly hoedown material."

"Oh, I think it will be fine," Connie responded. "People just want to have a good time."

"Hey, grab a coffee and join me."

We sat at one of the small tables. "So, you've been keeping a pretty low profile for the past week. Anything you need to confess?" Connie inquired.

I almost laughed at her bluntness. "No, Mrs. Thompson. My life has been just a fairy tale."

"Hmm, do tell. Speaking of which, how are things with the big bad wolf? Have his eyes gotten any worse?"

It should have been no surprise that word about Luther's macular degeneration had gotten out. "Luther's the same old sweetheart. He had an appointment last week, which, of course, made my day."

"Luther's pretty complicated. A lot of those guys from the war era are like that."

"Yeah, but with Luther, I get the sense that it's not just the war. It's something else."

"By the way, how has Gene Alley been? Any more bouts with the Top Forty countdown?"

I was suspicious that she knew more about my visit to Gene and my proposal plans for later that evening than she was letting on. I strove for nonchalance.

"Mmm, all right, I think. I talked to him briefly earlier in the week, and he seemed to be okay."

"I don't think the words 'Gene' and 'okay' belong in the same sentence."

As Connie finished, Estelle approached, sparkling with her larger-than-life self. "Morning, morning, morning, Dr. B. Did you come by to fill up my dance card for tomorrow night?" She held up her hands and swayed her hips from side to side.

"Estelle, it breaks my heart to tell you this, but I think Cinderella already has me booked up."

"Well, no matter. It's your loss, sweetie." She pulled up a chair and joined us. "Anyway, I'm glad I've got you two together for a moment. Speaking of Cinderella, we need to do something about our little ugly duckling."

"Who you talking about?" Connie asked.

"Dr. Davidson, that's who. She was in here yesterday and let it slip that if things don't change, she may be folding her tent in another month. That's just wrong."

I exhaled an exasperated sigh. "Look, I need to level with you two. Like I mentioned the other night, the beef and dairy farmers think she'll wind up hurting herself around big livestock. But Karen has this kind of magic power with animals, this amazing ability to calm them. I can't explain it, but I've seen it firsthand. We just need to get one or two of the farmers to give her a chance. I pitched her to several of them, but no one's biting."

"Well, sweetie," responded Estelle, "there's your problem. Your approach is all wrong."

"I'm not following you."

"You're trying to bring the honey to the bees. You need to let the bees come to the honey."

I glanced at Connie, who was nodding in agreement. "Estelle, I'm . . . I'm still in the dark here."

"We need to de-ugly that duckling," Estelle declared. "Bless her heart, that girl has the fashion awareness of an eggplant. There's a good-looking woman under all that plain G.I. Jane. You let Connie and me work our magic, and I guarantee the farmers will take notice."

"I'm not sure that's the kind of noticing Karen wants," I responded skeptically.

"Sweetie, men are like mules," Estelle added. "They'll do what you want, but sometimes you first have to pop them on the side of the head to get their attention."

"Gee. I don't know. You make us sound more like pigs."

Estelle pretended to admire her nails. "Your words, not mine."

"Even so, Estelle, I'm not sure Karen will go for this."

She flipped her hand at me. "Oh, honey, you're just blind with love. I admit she's a little on the skinny side and doesn't have an hourglass figure like me, but there's enough there to work with."

Connie turned to her sister. "Girl, did I just hear you say you had an hourglass figure?"

Estelle continued to admire her nails. "You certainly did."

"Humph," Connie responded coolly, taking a sip of her coffee. "Don't look now, but I think the sands of time have shifted on you."

Estelle spoke aloofly. "I've kept my shape."

"And you've certainly added to it."

Estelle ignored her. "So, what do you think, Doctor?"

I shrugged. "Okay by me. But how do you propose to get Karen on board with the idea?"

Estelle looked at her watch. "It's seven thirty-four. That opportunity is going to happen in three, two, one seconds." She looked up and pointed toward the door.

As if on cue, Karen Davidson walked in. Estelle waved her over. "Dr. Davidson, honey, we were just talking about you."

Karen pulled up a chair to join us, and we all exchanged greetings. She smiled cautiously. "So, guys . . . what's up?"

I glanced guardedly at Connie and Estelle before speaking. "Look, Karen. The three of us are aware that your veterinary practice has not been as robust as you'd like."

"There's an understatement."

"Well, we'd like to help."

"I'm not sure that's possible. But I'm open. What do you have in mind?"

Estelle leaned across the table toward Karen. "Dr. D., we were just curious. . . . Do you have a special somebody?"

Karen sat puzzled and threw a quick glance in my direction. "Um, Estelle, I'm not sure I understand the question."

Connie responded in a kind, motherly voice. "Dr. Davidson, my sister is wanting to know if you are seeing a man."

Karen laughed. "Only if I close my eyes and concentrate."

"Well, Dr. D.," Estelle said, "if that's right, it's just a crying shame. A good-looking woman like you ought to be swatting the men away like flies."

Karen shrugged. "I don't know about all that. I work around animals all day, so I spend most of my time swatting flies away like flies."

"Honey," Estelle said, "are you planning on going to the big dance tomorrow night?"

"I hadn't really decided. I could either go to the dance or stay home. But I'd say the smart money is on the 'staying home' option."

"Uh-uhh, sweetie," declared Estelle. "You are going to the dance. But first, you and Connie and me are heading out on a little shopping trip in the morning."

Karen smiled warily. "Um, okay, I think. Sounds like fun, maybe. But I'm not sure how this is going to help the practice."

The two sisters exchanged edgy glances. Connie patted Karen's hand. "We'll explain all that in the car tomorrow, dear."

Karen turned to me. "What are these two up to?"

I held up my hands in a gesture of surrender. "My advice is to just go with it. In my experience, the Pillow sisters are not to be denied."

CHAPTER 29
The Perfect Moment

My plan was to go to Moon Lake, build a fire, and have a cozy evening of food and wine under a soft sky of pristine stars. At nine o'clock, provided Gene was in his right mind, "Over the Valley" would be playing on the radio and I would propose to an enchanted, radiant Christine. The plan was for us to share something sweet, endearing, perfect.

At least that was the plan.

That afternoon, winds of early autumn began to sweep down the high rim of hills that surrounded Watervalley. A cooler breeze blew in from the fields and brought with it the tender expectation of a beautiful twilight. But it also brought something rather unexpected. Rain.

Before leaving the clinic, I checked and rechecked the radar on my phone. A band of showers was moving through. With any luck, it would move out by eight o'clock, leaving a low, thick cloud cover. My plans were still intact, but now without the stars.

Christine had called me around four as she was leaving school for the day. At first she wanted to stay in and watch a movie, saying that she was tired from a very active week with sixth graders. Without showing my hand too strongly, I persisted with the idea of going out to the lake and building a fire. She finally acquiesced and told me to pick her up at seven.

But when I arrived at the farm, I found her sound asleep on the wicker couch on the front porch, curled up under a quilt. I eased in beside her and kissed her on the cheek. "Hey, Sleeping Beauty. Wake up. Prince Charming is here."

She opened her eyes slowly and stared vacantly for a moment. Then she pulled the quilt back over her shoulder and buried her face in the cushion. "Go away. You're still a frog. Come back in an hour and try again."

This was not in the script.

I bent over and kissed her again, applying slightly more pressure. She did nothing. Not a movement, not a sound, not even a demure and cooing moan. Nothing.

More aggressive action was needed.

I began to rub her back. Her face remained pressed into the cushion. "Sweetie, I think the pizza is getting cold."

"Let it."

"And the wine is getting hot."

"Fine by me."

"And we're missing the sunset."

"Whatever."

I was at a complete loss. She had yet to even open her eyes.

"Do you want me to leave?"

"No."

"So you want me to stay?"

"No."

"Do you want me to put my pants back on?"

That got her eyes open. She sat up abruptly and looked at me with something less than an adoring regard. "That wasn't even close to funny."

"Woke you up, didn't it?"

"I'm not liking you right now." She widened her eyes and inhaled deeply, lifting her arms above her head in a stiff, contorted yawn. Held by an elastic tie, her disheveled hair was pulled back and a little tousled to one side. She was sloppily attired in a sweatshirt and blue jeans. Sleep lines from the creases on the cushion were still faintly discernible on her face, and she looked at me in a drowsy stupor.

I spoke with a false earnestness. "Seriously, if you want to just pass on the evening and go back to sleep, that's fine by me. I'm sure Rhett would love the pizza."

"No, no, I'm awake now. Let's go."

Perhaps it was my predisposed mind-set for it to be a perfect evening, but I spoke the next words before thinking. "Do you need to go, you know, freshen up first?"

Her response convinced me that this was something you should never say to a woman, especially when she is still in the vexing fog of post-sleep. Christine dropped her chin in a look of sharp reproach. "Just what are you implying, Bradford?"

Now she was definitely awake.

I laughed at my own foolishness and ran my hand over the side of her face, smoothing back a stray lock of hair. "Okay, Sleeping Beauty. You are always gorgeous in my eyes."

"But what?"

"Well, as long as you're gorgeous in your eyes too, then we're good to go."

She frowned lightly and gathered up her hair, redoing the small elastic band. "Oh, you're probably right, but I'm too tired to care. It'll be dark soon, so just squint your eyes a lot."

By the time we loaded up in the Austin-Healey, the rain had completely stopped, leaving a fine, stinging mist. There was still something of a sullen, quiet reserve to Christine's mood. I had awoken Sleeping Beauty, but instead a fairy-tale character more like Grumpy had gotten into the car with me.

Enchanted and radiant no longer seemed part of the plan either.

At Christine's insistence, we stopped and picked up Rhett, taking him with us. Given the surprise visit we'd had on the previous trip to the lake, apparently Christine felt more secure having Rhett along. So the "we two" part of the evening turned into "we three."

Earlier, I had loaded some cordwood into the trunk. But it was soaked with rain, making for a difficult time starting a fire. I finally got a flame going by dousing on some gasoline I had brought along. Some of it got on my hands and, try as I might, I was unable to clean off the smell. This left me reeking with something less than a fetching aroma for the rest of the evening.

The orchard grass had been left uncut for quite some time and had fallen over in lumpy clumps, disguising the fact that the ground below was a mushy soup from the earlier downpour. I had innocently spread the blanket out near the fire, and Christine sleepily sat down and hugged her knees into a tight bundle. Suddenly she shrieked and popped up as if she had been stung.

"What's the matter?"

"My bottom's wet. Water must have leached through the blanket."

I bent down on one knee to feel the spot, only to discover that just as quickly, my knee was also soaked. Christine stood with her backside to the fire, none too happy. Ever the optimist, I was determined to salvage the moment and make the night magical.

I picked up the blanket and folded away the wet spot, placing it on the hood of the car. Warmed by the glow of the fire, we sat there, eating cold pizza and drinking red wine from Solo cups. I turned the radio on low and Rhett ventured into the darkness. In time, Christine again pulled her knees up under her chin and wrapped her arms around her legs in a tight ball. She snuggled in close beside me and rested her head on my shoulder, staring lost into the fire.

"You're awfully sweet, Bradford."

"And why is that?"

"You're trying really hard to make a nice evening out of a pretty dreary situation." She covered her mouth for a long yawn. Afterward, she shook her head briskly. "I'm sorry. I don't know why I'm so tired tonight."

"Oh, it's okay. It's been a while since we've been out here, and I just wanted it to seem special."

She took my arm and embraced it in a firm hug, pulling it tightly to her. I glanced at my watch. It was ten minutes before nine o'clock. Finally the moment and the mood seemed to be coming together. For the twentieth time that evening I put my hand in my jacket pocket and gently felt for the small case that held the ring. Satisfied yet again that everything was in place, I leaned over and kissed Christine's head, and we sat in silence. All we needed to do now was wait.

But Rhett had other ideas.

In the black of the night a short distance away, we heard a brief "woof" followed by a huge splash. Christine and I both sat up, looking at each other with quizzical faces. I called out to him, "Rhett! Come here, boy!"

There was no sound except for the faint lapping of water. I stood and called out again, imagining that Rhett would respond with some kind of bark that would signal the all clear. I mumbled under my breath, "I better see what's going on."

I grabbed a flashlight from the trunk, and we both walked toward the lake's edge, only to find the reflection of Rhett's eyes swimming toward us from about twenty feet out. He was carrying a large stick in his mouth. He proceeded to climb out of the water and, after a vigorous head-to-toe full-body shake, walked over and dropped the stick at my feet. Christine put her hand over her mouth, holding back a laugh.

I bent over and picked up the stick. "Nice job, fellow. Just whose car do you think you're riding in now?" We walked back, and I casually tossed Rhett's prize into the fire. We were about to sit again, when a thick pattering sound began to shimmer across the water. A chilly, biting gust of wind swept over us. We were being pelted.

It wasn't just rain; it was hail.

Christine frantically gathered the blanket and our things and threw them into the car while I fumbled to get the soft top pulled over and fastened. It was a brief chaos of shouts and movements under the barrage. Rhett casually made his way into the small backseat and plopped down quite comfortably while Christine and I plunged into the front seats and simultaneously rolled up our windows, finally closing off the onslaught. We both were partially soaked and took a moment to catch our breath. The fire had all but died out under the drenching rain and hail.

"Dang," blurted Christine. "That sure happened fast."

"Unbelievable," I responded, still somewhat rattled. Then I gathered myself and looked at my watch. It was three minutes after nine, so I instinctively reached over and turned up the radio. A commercial was playing.

"Are you listening for some kind of weather alert?"

"Um, yeah. Sure."

Christine exhaled a deep breath. "I think it's time for this girl to go home."

I needed to stall. Gene would be playing our song any moment now, and I was holding on blindly to the idea that all the cosmic tumblers would somehow realign.

"Let's give the storm a chance to blow over," I suggested.

We sat for a few moments longer, listening to what was now a pouring rain and the low squawk of the radio advertising the latest sale on canned goods down at the grocery store. The ideal mood of only minutes ago had all but vanished. As well, the charming air of romance was quickly being replaced by the permeating smell of wet dog. That along with the growing heat of Rhett's hot panting had promptly saturated the small enclosure. I started the car in a last-ditch effort to get some air circulating. And just as it roared to life, Gene Alley's smooth radio voice finally poured into our ears.

"We have a special request going out tonight for a special lady by a special fellow." Notably, Gene wasn't blessed with a diverse vocabulary.

"I'm not going to give out any names, but let's just say he's a doctor. A doctor of love, that is. This is WVLY, 'the Voice of the Valley,' and I'm your host, Gene Alley, hoping that tonight, all you lovebirds take flight and give a chance to a little romance."

At the mention of the word "doctor," Christine turned her head to the side and regarded me with surprise, as if I had made an unpleasant body noise. Undaunted, I began to reach in my pocket for the ring. The music started, and I was about to speak the endearing, magic words of love I had so meticulously practiced.

But instead of "Over the Valley" by Pink Martini, Gene was playing "Young Lust" by Pink Floyd, a song about a fellow who is new to town and looking for a dirty woman. I immediately froze with my hand holding the ring box in my coat pocket, my mouth dangling open, and my face in a locked panic. Christine's neck stiffened, and her scowl became even harsher.

"Wow, that's pretty sick. For a half second there, I thought Gene was talking about a song you had requested."

I jerked my hand out of my pocket and released a forced laugh. "What? Are you crazy? I sure didn't request that song." Not only was the moment blown; my evasive commentary was failing miserably. Christine lowered her head in a look of cautious skepticism.

The ring of her cell phone saved me. She retrieved it from her pocket and answered.

"Hello. Hey. Yes, he's right here." She smiled and winked at me. "Yes, he's right here too." She glanced back at Rhett. "Oh, that's really exciting." Christine was using her schoolteacher voice. "Uh-huh. Uh-huh. Okay, we'll be right there. Bye now."

She looked at me with a face of pure delight. "That was Will Fox. Dr. Davidson just arrived. Maggie is having her babies."

We drove back to Fleming Street. I had turned off the radio, and fortunately there was no further discussion regarding the song request. Oddly, I felt relieved. My best-laid plans had gone completely awry, and I had quietly decided that I would find a discreet moment after the dance the following night in which to propose.

We arrived at the Fox house in damp clothes but good spirits and found everyone huddled in the back utility room. Maggie had just finished delivering six perfectly healthy, squinty-eyed puppies. They had already instinctively moved toward the warmth of their mother and the hope of their first meal. Will and Louise were sleepy, but wrapped in a joyful, excited air. Karen smiled warmly at Christine and me.

Rhett seemed unusually subdued. He approached Maggie slowly, carefully sniffing his way. They regarded each other and eventually he lay on the floor just outside the whelping box, calmly keeping guard. It was all quite sweet and wonderful.

We chatted for a few minutes, but soon Christine and I headed back to Summerfield Road. As we made our way through the dark countryside, Christine sat consumed in thought. Eventually, I turned to her.

"Do you ever think about children, Christine?"

"Sure. I'm with children all day, every day. I think about them a lot."

"I don't mean in that way."

"In what way, then?"

"In the way of having some of your own one day."

"Sure. Although call me old-fashioned, but I've always had this silly notion about getting married first."

I grinned. "Probably a good idea." Silence ensued, and we continued into the solemn darkness, both of us feeling the sag of weariness. Faintly illuminated by the dashboard lights, Christine spoke guardedly, tenderly.

"So, Luke, what do you think?"

"About?"

"Children. Your own children, that is." We both knew in that delicate moment that the real topic was "our children."

I remained focused on the dark and narrow country road before me. My eventual response was certain and deliberate.

"This may come as a surprise to you, Miss Chambers, but I think that one day I would love to have five or six."

Christine gasped. "You're kidding, right?"

"Not in the least." The sincerity in my voice was unmistakable.

She stared at me wide-eyed for a moment before stiffly turning and looking forward, clearly needing a minute to process my declaration.

"I say something wrong?"

She exhaled a short laugh, shaking her head. "No, no, not at all. I think that's wonderful. But you're right. That wasn't the answer I was expecting."

We rode on in silence, neither of us choosing to pursue the subject further. But it was clear that Christine was a little stunned, because after I walked her to the door and we kissed good night, she remained studying me with a mystified face even after I had begun to step away.

I paused and turned back to her.

She wore a muted, probing expression. "Five or six, huh?"

I sank my hands into my coat pockets and smiled warmly. "Umm-hmm. Five or six."

Under the snug glow of the porch light, she stood silently. Then, ever so quietly and sweetly, a tender smile of acknowledgment spread across her face.

CHAPTER 30

The Swan

On Saturday I met Guy Dupree and the Night Owls over at the bandstand at four to coordinate their setting up. Connie was there along with the other volunteers to help with decorating. In an incredible last-minute transformation, the huge bandstand had been elaborately dressed in a Cole Porter theme of "Anything Goes." The idea seemed symbolically appropriate, given that this was Watervalley and everything from tuxedos to overalls would likely be in the mix.

Guy Dupree, a sprightly and lively fellow in his early fifties, was the band's piano and keyboard player. He was of modest height with a full head of neatly combed brown hair. While I was talking to him, a most ingenious idea occurred to me. "Guy, do you and the band by chance know the song 'Over the Valley'?"

"Absolutely, it's a Pink Martini standard."

"Well, I need to ask a big favor. Can you play it as the last song tonight?"

He lifted his eyebrows. "Trying to create a special moment for a certain someone?"

"Hmm, you might say that. Can you do it?"

"Piece of cake, Doc. Consider it done."

I thanked him and walked back to the car, rubbing my hands together in great satisfaction. The cosmos had sent a blunt message that the previous night at the lake was not the right time to propose. But tonight, as the band played our song, its music lilting through the autumn air, I would pull Christine away from the crowd for a short walk along the lake's edge. Under the romance and charm of the moonlit night I would propose. My private, intimate, perfect moment was finally going to happen. I knew it in my bones.

Around five thirty, a late-afternoon rain blew through quickly, leaving behind a clear, washed sky of cooler air and a soft twilight filled with delicate stars. A thin shaving of moon appeared against the blue, bringing a low luster to the warm and tender evening.

During my recent trip to Nashville, I had managed to purchase a classic black-tie tuxedo and candidly thought I looked rather dashing in it. Christine had dug into the boxes of clothes in the family attic and found a vintage black flapper dress from the twenties worn by her grandmother Cavanaugh to a costume party back in the sixties.

I arrived at the farmhouse early and waited for Christine in the entry hall. With her raven hair, red lips, and olive complexion, she descended the stairs as a woman at the flawless summit of her natural beauty. Every step she took was full of seductive grace. It would seem that by now I would have grown accustomed to these stunning moments. But the sensuous flow of her movements and her bewitching smile stole through me, leaving me breathless.

As we made our way toward town, it seemed the night was charged with an immense electricity, an incredible feeling of expectancy as all the headlights in the valley pointed toward the lake. By the time we arrived, the dance was in full swing. Everyone was captivated with the explosive sound of the Night Owls, the luminous glow of the bandstand lights, and the tingling promise of magic in the air.

The brassy, jazzy sound of the horns and deep, throbbing beat of drums permeated the night. Cacophonous voices and sparkling laughter rose everywhere. Couples were already crowding the dance floor, and small groups of onlookers claimed every inch of the huge bandstand's railing. As we made our way across the short entry pier, I began to feel a little overdressed. Yet we were warmly and enthusiastically received by shouts and raised eyebrows, as if the plain and simple people I had come to know expected nothing less than sartorial splendor from their town doctor and his beautiful date.

It seemed that all of Watervalley had turned out for the event, revealing the broad tapestry of small-town life. Some of the men were in their Sunday finery of gray suits and brown shoes. A few of the women wore stylish party dresses, albeit some of them looked as if they had dressed in their teenage daughter's clothes by mistake. Collectively, most strove toward the casual middle ground.

These were everyday people who were not too good or fine or proud to let loose and who made few pretenses to gentility. Nevertheless, they were unabashed about having a good time. As well, beer and wine were flowing readily, and I suspected that for many, more than their hair was well lubricated.

As we moved through the crowd, I noticed a number of bachelor farmers gathered in a clump near the concession table where they could easily assess everyone as they arrived and made their way up the short, narrow pier. The men were all scrubbed, starched, and clean-shaven. There was among them a bubbling camaraderie, a pungent brew of wit and humor as they nonchalantly surveyed the new arrivals for prospects of companionship. Then again, they also seemed to be completely entertained discussing the merits of various types of socket wrenches.

Towering over them all was Hoot Wilson, wearing a tie and sporting a clean white shirt that managed to contain his massive chest and overflowing midsection. He gave me an unreserved wave from across the crowd. I waved back but immediately noticed that one of his fellow bachelors was tapping Hoot's shoulder to draw his attention toward the pier's end and the shiny black BMW that had just arrived.

It was Estelle's car. The passenger side was facing the bandstand, and as the teenage valet opened the car door, what happened next brought all of the bachelor farmers to the railing in a gape-jawed silence.

From within the dark interior of the BMW, there appeared two long, slender legs above high heels that smoothly and enticingly touched down on the pavement. This was followed by the extension of a slim wrist adorned with a sparkling array of dazzling bracelets. The valet clasped the outstretched hand.

In a singular, fluid motion, Karen Davidson emerged into the evening, into the light, and into the wanton desires of all the frozen and gawking single men standing there.

Laughter and conversation fell silent as she made her way up the narrow pier to the bandstand. She was bare shouldered, wearing a snug black dress and a thin powder blue scarf with long ends that floated delicately behind her as she walked. It danced with her sensuous footsteps, seeming to bring with her on the night wind an invisible cape of enchantment.

Now, tightly wrapped in clothing that fully accentuated her feminine curves, her firm, athletic body moved with a rhythmic flow that easily drew a man's eye. Her Dutch-boy blond hair, which normally fell in an untidy shag, was pulled back and neatly pinned in a French twist, giving her an elegance that was nothing short of stunning. She walked with her chin slightly lowered and, along with her large blue eyes and splendid red lips, she was wearing a mirthful, confident smile that seemed full of secret warmth and surprise. She was fresh and pretty and seductively beautiful. And as I watched her, I was heartened by the delightful certainty that she knew it.

The crowd parted and, upon seeing us, Karen walked directly toward Christine and me. Elated, Christine hugged her and spoke while holding both of her hands.

"Karen, you are so beautiful! Just look at you!"

She smiled bashfully. "Yeah, quite the change, huh? I think Connie and Estelle are in the wrong business."

"All I can say is that you look absolutely spectacular."

The two of them turned to me, faces awash in pure delight. I smiled warmly at Karen and spoke with a bemused confidence. "Karen Davidson, you look perfectly gorgeous."

She nodded, her smile irrepressible. "Thanks, Luke."

As she spoke, I felt a large hand squeeze my right shoulder. "Evening, Doc. Quite a shindig, ain't it?"

It was Hoot Wilson standing there in his large and loud way. We shook hands, and the four of us exchanged enthusiastic greetings, after which there was a short, awkward pause. Hoot seemed to be wrestling with indecision. He finally spoke, fumbling through his words.

"Dr. Davidson, I was wondering, uh, if you would like to dance?"

She stepped toward Hoot. Her plain words didn't seem to match the dazzling and bewitching creature she'd become. "Sure, sounds good to me. But only if you call me Karen."

Hoot seemed almost surprised by her ready acceptance and

nodded briskly, bursting with the excited grin of a schoolboy. "Karen it is."

He took her hand and they moved to the dance floor, talking nonstop in a stream of conversation that seemed to flow effortlessly. A slow dance was playing. She looked small and demure as she pressed into him, but her eyes had an elfin sparkle. And as they began to dance, Hoot, who seemed to be in a state of euphoric wonder, closed his eyes and ever so gently placed his hand to her back as if he were tenderly and protectively holding a delicate flower.

CHAPTER 31
Over the Valley

Perhaps I should have caught on sooner, but as the evening progressed, I kept noticing that more and more of the women in the crowd, particularly the wives, were telegraphing brief smiles at me—the kind where they simultaneously squinted their eyes, scrunched up their noses, and raised their shoulders in a short, elated glance of excitement and approval. And while Christine and I were dancing, nearby couples were inconspicuously taking fleeting glimpses of her hand.

This was unnerving. No one, and I mean no one, knew of my plans to propose. And yet the nuanced looks, sky-high eyebrows, and secretive nods only multiplied as the night continued. Men and women of all ages subtly pointed at the two of us and whispered behind their hands, invariably followed by explosive wide-eyed responses.

Fortunately, Christine didn't seem to notice any of this. If she was aware of the ogling stares and cryptic messages that were flying around the bandstand, she was doing a good job of ignoring them. But I began to get a sick feeling. I so wanted the proposal to be a total surprise, yet all the covert signals suggesting that something was afoot were becoming impossible to dismiss.

The final straw came when I happened to look toward the small clique of jovial bachelor farmers. One of them took his little finger and did a pantomime of a hook in his mouth like a caught fish. This produced a chorus of shoulder-bumping laughter, and a couple of them shot subtle thumbs-up signs at me. A slow, smoldering resentment began to kindle within me. I liked the people of Watervalley. I really did. But they hadn't been invited to intrude upon this one intimate, private moment between Christine and me.

And how could they possibly have known? Who could have told?

The night had flown by, and there was still a quarter hour or so before the last song of the evening. Christine and I were on the dance floor, her cheek pressed to my shoulder. With what was likely a rather stern and unhappy face, I began to survey the room as we shuffled in a leisurely rotating circle. A few more bubbly faces winked at me, to which I gave an unkind scowl. Then it hit me. There was one person I hadn't seen all evening. I knew she was there, but she had carefully avoided me.

Connie Thompson.

The dance ended, and I asked Christine to excuse me for a moment. After a minute of weaving through the crowd, I found Connie on the level lawn just off the bandstand pier. She was engaged in a lively conversation with the mayor and his wife, but her face lost all animation when she saw me approaching with an unhappy glare. For the first time in our history, she wilted into a look of unadulterated contrition. I had found my culprit.

She did her best to choke out a cordial greeting. "Evening, Dr. Bradford. Certainly has been a lovely night, hasn't it?"

I stiffly greeted the mayor and his wife in a half smile and then turned sternly toward Connie. "Mrs. Thompson, a word please."

Connie nodded penitently, and we walked away from the bandstand for a half minute before stopping to ensure that our conversation was out of earshot.

"Constance Grace, for some odd reason I've been getting the impression that everybody here tonight thinks they know something about me, like I might have something big planned for this evening. Something I thought was very personal and private. Care to shed any light on what you know about this?"

To her credit, Connie didn't attempt to feign innocence. She nodded, exhaling a deep breath. "I happened to see the receipt from the jewelry store sitting on your kitchen table. Earlier this afternoon, I overheard Guy Dupree talking to the band about your request to play a special song to close out the evening. I guess I put two and two together and blurted out something in front of a couple of the ladies who were decorating. It was like throwing gasoline on a fire. I tried to get them to keep quiet about it, but this is Watervalley. One body always tells somebody."

"Connie! Good grief!" I said, consumed with a swelling aggravation. I knew her mistake was innocently made, but that was scant consolation. My plans had been put on public display and moreover, I had the nauseating thought that by now Christine had been made aware of them.

"I'm truly sorry, Luke. I really am."

I gave myself a minute to cool down and then spoke in a low, instructional voice.

"Connie, for some reason Christine loves this song called 'Over the Valley.' Why, I have no idea. I've never even heard it before. Guy Dupree agreed to play it as the last song tonight. And I just thought that it might be nice to tenderly and discreetly—and I do mean discreetly—ask the woman I love to marry me while it was playing. That doesn't seem too much to ask, does it?"

Connie looked down and nodded, humbly accepting the full weight of my admonishment.

"I wish I could fix this, Luke. I truly wish I could."

I blew out a final heavy sigh. "Oh crap, just forget about it. Look. My strategy is to bring her out here while the song in playing. I guess there's no reason it can't still happen. I just hope a crowd doesn't follow us."

Connie nodded, immediately in slightly better spirits. "If need be, I'll block the entrance to the pier while you two slip off."

I smiled in resignation. "Okay. Thanks. I hope that won't be necessary."

As we walked back to the bandstand, the mild sting of disappointment lingered. My plan was still intact, but I was a bag of nerves, my head in a spin as the final song approached. It was almost midnight, and even the old geezers who usually packed it in at sundown were still hanging around. They were all inconspicuously lingering, waiting, and staring with expectant faces. My trepidation grew.

Finally, the moment arrived, and Guy Dupree stepped to the microphone.

"Ladies and gentlemen, we have one final song to play to close out the night. But first, the band and I want to thank you for a wonderful time. You've been a great group, and we have loved being here."

His words were met with an enormous round of applause and loud cheers. "We have an unusual treat for you with our last number of the evening. We've had a special request from one of your very own to join the band and sing our final song."

A bolt of panic shot through me. This wasn't right.

"Ladies and gentlemen, please welcome Christine Chambers to the stage."

"What?" I blurted the word out loud and turned to Christine in a state of shock. A huge round of applause rose up as I grabbed her arm. "What's going on?"

She smiled sweetly. "While you stepped away, I asked Guy Dupree if they would play 'Over the Valley' and if I could sing it. He said sure."

I spoke before thinking. "But you can't!"

Christine looked crestfallen. "Why not?"

"Because . . ." I froze. I had no words, no response, only a foolish look of complete confusion. I stood there, gripping her hand in a speechless stupor. By now the applause had ended, and for the first time that evening, the bandstand stood in complete silence. I looked around and realized that the entire crowd was staring at us. That was it. I was done, defeated. A proposal just wasn't going to happen. I took a deep breath and smiled weakly. "Sure, go ahead."

Christine nodded hesitantly, then turned and made her way to the stage. All eyes followed her as she took the microphone from the stand and nodded to Guy Dupree at the piano. He struck the first melancholy notes of the tune, and Christine's rich, melodious voice filled the night with the words of the song.

Over the valley
I saw a silver cloud
With a pink lining
I said it right out loud
There's no denying
You are my one and only love
And we'll see over the valley
The moon rise above

I stood there for a moment, lost in a daze of bewilderment and disappointment. Couples began to gather on the dance floor, tenderly embracing and swaying to the silky lilt of the ballad. Even so, I felt that an ocean of eyes were still upon me, but I no longer cared. I took off my jacket and flung it over my shoulder, holding it casually by a single finger. Christine sang the second verse.

Over the valley
This house among the trees
Where we've been hiding
Making our memories
And I'm deciding
You are my one and only love
And we'll be over the valley
As the moon shines above

Her voice was sweet, lovely, perfect. But I was beside myself. I wanted to escape from all the gawking stares, the invasive scrutiny. I moved toward the concession table, bought a beer, and proceeded to walk away from the pier and into the gloom of the far parking lot. As I departed, I guess my grim, dispirited expression told its ugly story. Passing through the crowd, I was met with a host of silent and downcast faces. I stepped into the darkness and found the Austin-Healey in the moonlight. Leaning against the fender, I took a long draw of the beer as Christine sang the refrain.

The autumn breezes carry all the bluebirds
Down to where the sun still shines
If we could hold this day
In our hearts some way

We would never roam
Ever far from home

Footsteps crunched in the nearby gravel. I ignored them, gazing into the night stars as the person approached. It was Connie. I took another swallow of beer and cut my eyes toward her. "What?"

Her words were calm but laced with reproach. "You need to wipe the vinegar off your face, that's what."

"Meaning?"

"Meaning you've got a beautiful young woman back there who loves you from top to toe, singing a song that in her mind was written for just the two of you. And here you are, sulking in the moonlight because you don't like anybody knowing your business. Well, Luke, I've got a news flash. This is Watervalley, and things don't happen in a vacuum. You said it yourself. Your magic moment is while that song is playing. So you need to decide what's more important: avoiding a few well-meaning onlookers, or letting Christine know how much you really love her."

I stared at her in pursed-lipped silence. Her words washed over me. And I knew.

I knew in my bones she that was right. I took a deep breath of resignation, nodded, and handed her my unfinished beer. "Here, hold on to this if you would."

I began to walk with determined steps back toward the bandstand. Out of the corner of my eye, I noticed Connie briefly appraising the beer bottle before tilting it skyward and draining the balance of it. Her exuberant words floated behind me. "Go get 'em, Doctor."

As I briskly approached the narrow pier, Christine was finishing the second round of the song's refrain. All that remained was the repeat singing of the third and final verse. With each step I was energized with resolve, oblivious to everything but Christine and her lovely voice lilting sweetly in the night air, singing the closing words of the song.

Over the valley
Just above the fray
The sun is setting
And when we're old and gray
I'll still be betting
You are my one and only love

The band had paused as she sang the word "love" and held it in a long, delicate a cappella just as I arrived at the bandstand. The crowd parted in front of me, giving way to my clear, focused advance through the center of the dance floor and the band's elevated platform. Christine's face glowed when she saw me, and as I stepped toward her, she slowly, sweetly sang the words to the next line.

And we'll live over the valley

Without breaking stride, I tossed my coat to the side and dug my hand into my trouser pocket. In one fluid motion I came to a stop, dropping to one knee directly in front of her, and penitently bowed my head. I held the open ring case high in my right hand toward her. Christine gazed at me tearfully as she spoke the next words.

You'll always be with me

I looked up at her with an adoring, confident smile, bursting with delight. She responded with an enthusiastic nodding of her head before affectionately singing the final line of the song.

As the moon shines above.

I reached and grabbed her by the waist and lifted her down from the stage. She wrapped both arms tightly around my neck and whispered the words, "Yes, yes, yes," to me. And there in front of God and all creation, and about three hundred thunderously applauding citizens of Watervalley, we kissed lavishly.

I was engaged.

And most likely, there would be little need to put an announcement in the paper.

CHAPTER 32
In the Still of the Night

Guy Dupree and the Night Owls continued to play encore after encore as a line of well-wishers formed to congratulate us. Several patted me on the back, many of them hugged Christine, and all of them wanted to see the ring. Given that it was a two-and-a-half-carat stone, it was the focus of commentary.

More than a few of the well-meaning rural women commented, "Whoa, honey. What did you have to do to get that?"

John came and shook my hand, saying nothing and offering a mirthful wink. Hoot grabbed me in a jaws-of-life bear hug. He and Karen had spent most of the evening together, and she seemed delighted with his company. For Hoot, it was clearly a fortuitous match. They were roughly the same age, and Karen was likely one of the few women in the valley who wasn't put off by the smell of silage.

Connie and Estelle both came and hugged me, each with the remnants of elated tears staining their faces. Connie held my arm and whispered, "I'm awfully proud of you, sweetheart."

I regarded her with a rather puckish grin and whispered in return, "Thanks, for everything."

It was almost an hour before we made it to the car. It seemed that no one wanted the night to end and so many wanted to share in our excitement. But we were thinking differently. The furtive glances between the two of us clearly communicated our singular desire to get away, to be blissfully alone.

On the drive to her home, I shared with Christine all the painful details of my foiled plans to propose out at the lake and then at the dance. She laughed almost to the point of hysterics. And yet, oddly, my efforts seemed to engender in her an affectionate devotion beyond words.

"It was perfect, Luke. Just perfect," she assured me. It still amazed me that this beautiful girl who less than a year ago had so easily detested me now loved me so completely.

After we arrived at her home, Christine went upstairs and woke up her mother, Madeline, who had left the dance hours earlier. She came down in her housecoat and gave me a long hug as Christine told her about my center-stage proposal. I adored Madeline Chambers. She had married a farmer, but she had been a banker's daughter and was the embodiment of charm and graciousness. She was a lovely, engaging woman of incredible strength who had imbued her daughter with the best of her own qualities.

Madeline bid us good night and returned to bed. Christine grabbed a quilt, and we retreated to the quiet shadows of the moonlit front porch, sinking into the deep cushions of the wicker sofa. We sat tightly beside each other. Christine turned and brought her knees across my lap and draped her arms around my neck, occasionally kissing my cheek and nuzzling me with her nose when she wasn't gazing euphorically at the ring on her outstretched hand. It seemed she couldn't be close enough to me. It was heaven.

Despite the late hour, we were awash in a delicate euphoria, unable to stop talking and giggling in voices that were low and sweet, echoing musically against the quiet serenity of the night.

I spoke barely above a whisper. "So, Miss Chambers, when do you think you'd like to become a doctor's wife?"

"Mmm, I guess I'm kind of traditional. I've always wanted to be a June bride and get married at Watervalley First Presbyterian. That will give us time to plan the wedding. Besides, I won't be out of school until late May."

"June, huh. Seems like a rather long engagement."

"Is that a problem?"

"No. I guess not. It's just that I see engagement to be pretty much the same thing as marriage, except without the fringe benefits."

Christine laughed and shook her head, again rubbing her nose into my cheek. "Well, maybe we should just elope so we can get started on those six children you talked about."

"Okay, so what about all that? You seemed a little shell-shocked when I mentioned it last night."

"No, no, I love the idea. I really do. Look, you're an only child and I'm an only child. We have no first cousins. We're pretty much alone in the world, Luke. So the idea of a house bursting at the seams with little voices sounds absolutely wonderful to me. Although I have to admit, the thought of spending almost four and a half years pregnant is a little daunting."

"It will be fine, Christine. I will be right there." I paused a moment and looked into the darkness beyond the front porch. "You know, when I was little, I don't believe my dad ever missed a Little League or soccer game. He might have missed an inning or two, but he always showed up. He was my hero. And I never sensed he saw it as some obligation, I think he just loved me and wanted to watch me play. That's who my dad was, and that's who I intend to be."

"For all six?"

"For all six."

"Okay, this might be a silly question, but will we be able to afford that many?"

"They say that doctors make pretty good money, although granted, so far it's an unproven theory. Besides, the family trust comes into play in about three and a half years. So that should cover things like bicycles, braces, and your shoe budget."

She rolled her eyes at my teasing. "Easy there, Bradford. A girl has to keep her standards."

She leaned over and kissed me lightly on the cheek again. "I think it's wonderful. I love the idea of having six children."

I looked down and ran my hand along the curve of her hip and then under her delightfully rounded backside. "And I, Miss Chambers, love the idea of making six children."

Her eyes had a mischievous gleam. "Do you, now?"

"You know I do. Don't you ever think about it?"

She looked down, but her impish smile never wavered. "I think about it all the time."

It was not the response I was expecting. "Really?"

"Well, yeah. Really."

We sat for a moment, intimately holding tightly to each other in the autumn darkness. I placed my hand beside her face and gently kissed her forehead. "Christine, I'm in love with you—deeply in love with you. I think you know that."

She nodded. I looked down and spoke slowly, carefully choosing my words. "I've also come to understand from the things you've said that, well, you've held tight to a promise you made to yourself long ago, about waiting. And I love that about you too. But I won't lie about or deny my desire. So talk to me. Tell me what you want."

She searched my face, her piercing, luminous eyes reflecting her thoughts. And as I gazed at her, I saw all the strength, all the passion, all the tenderness of a woman who had clung bravely to an ideal that the larger world thought naïve and archaic.

Her words were soft, almost fragile, yet spoken with a full measure of certainty. "What I want is you, Luke. That's all I know." She paused for a moment before once again looking ardently into my eyes. "I want you. So I guess it's up to you. Perhaps I should feel differently, think differently . . . believe differently. But I don't. Not now. Not anymore. Not with you."

I nodded in understanding. Eventually, I leaned toward her and again pressed my lips to her forehead, leaving them there for the longest time.

CHAPTER 33

Unexpected

I arrived home around two in the morning. Christine had asked me to stay and sleep over in the guest bedroom, but I gently refused. I was exhausted and wanted my own bed.

Will and Louise had agreed to let Rhett stay with them for the night. So as I pulled in and parked the car at the side of the house, I was thinking of nothing more than collapsing into bed. But as I made my way to the front porch, something caught my eye.

I froze.

The porch light wasn't on, but the lamplight coming through the front windows dimly defined a large silhouette. It was a man sitting on the porch floor with his back against the house and his arms folded in front of him. His chin was down and his face was hidden under a ball cap. He wasn't moving.

My breath quickened as alarm raced through me. At this deep and desolate hour, nothing good could come of this strange presence. I stepped closer, my eyes straining to determine who this could possibly be. Then I heard a low wheezing sound. Whoever he was, he was asleep. But I was on edge, tense, alert.

I ascended the first step and leaned in, doing my best to be eye level with the ghostly figure. Within the frail shadows, the image was eerily surreal. But soon enough, I recognized him.

It was Clayton Ross.

I inhaled a deep breath and braced myself, unsure of what to anticipate upon rousing him. I stepped up on the porch and lightly tapped his foot.

In the flash of a moment he was on his feet and lunging at me like a tackling linebacker. But instead of throwing me to the ground, he slammed both of our bodies against the side of the house, using his to absorb the brunt of the crashing impact. His voice was thunderous, panic-stricken. "They're shooting, Jonas! They're shooting!"

"Clayton! Clayton! It's me, Luke Bradford."

He turned to me in wide-eyed terror. "Jonas, Jonas! Your face, your face! You're okay! Look, look. . . ." He stopped. His words drifted into the dark, and he slowly released his grip on me. He seemed lost, spooked, and he stared blankly into the night as he ran the palm of his hand over his forehead, obliviously pushing back his ball cap, which fell unheeded to the porch floor.

"Clayton, it's me, Dr. Bradford. I think you just woke from a bad dream." There was no smell of alcohol on his breath.

He stared numbly for another few seconds, his expression a picture of woe. For a brief moment, I saw in his eyes the half-captured image of a frightened child. His was a mind encased in fear and confusion. Awkwardly, he looked around, and I could see the light of reality begin to emerge on his face, leaving him in an embarrassed and lowly state. He glanced at me briefly and then carefully bent down and picked up his ball cap. His hands were trembling.

He spoke stiffly with downcast eyes. "I'm—I'm sorry, Dr. Bradford. I couldn't sleep tonight, so I started walking. I must have walked for miles, and somehow I got it in my head to come see you.

That maybe you could help me." He glanced up at my eyes, wanting to read something in my gaze. He looked down again quickly and continued. "After I got here . . . I don't know. Just knowing that I was close; knowing that I might talk to you and maybe you could help me . . . well, it made me relax, helped me to not think about things. So, I guess I fell asleep. I'm sorry. It's the middle of the night. I'll come back to the clinic sometime."

He offered a tight-lipped nod and began to step away. Despite my consuming exhaustion and a head floating in the fog and dullness of lost sleep, I lightly grabbed his shoulder. "Clayton, come inside for a while."

He paused for only a moment before nodding and following me. He took a seat on the large sofa in the living room while I walked to the kitchen and retrieved two bottles of water. I returned and handed one to him. I took off my tuxedo jacket, tossed it over the back of the large chair, and sat down.

He spoke politely. "I guess you went to the bandstand dance tonight?"

"Yeah, it was a good time." I paused and nodded thoughtfully. "A big evening."

He nodded in return, looking around the room, lost in uncertainty.

"So, I guess you opted not to go?" I said. "Veterans got in free, you know."

He smiled weakly and exhaled a deep sigh. "Probably best I didn't. I, uh, I don't seem to do well in crowds."

We sat looking at each other in an uneasy and appraising manner. The brooding air between us was thick, guarded, cautious. I lightly rubbed my chin.

"Who was Jonas, Clayton?"

There was a heavy pause at the mention of this name. At first, he spoke stiltedly, fumbling over his words and struggling through his sentences as if unsure where to begin. But in time, his low, husky voice poured out the long narrative of a buried desperation. He talked about the war and spoke of horrific, dreadful things: of terrified faces gasping for breath; of the warm, sickening stench of lacerated bodies; and of the gruesome business of wiping the remnants of his friend Jonas's face from his own uniform. His descriptions were grotesque and vivid. And yet I came to slowly realize the cathartic need he had to tell me. Apparently Clayton had determined that since I was a doctor, all the unspeakable gore wouldn't matter and that perhaps somehow I could dispassionately help him to understand, to find perspective. In reality, I could do little more than nod and listen.

It was the balance of his cheerless and somber words that convinced me there was a darkness in him that I couldn't begin to fathom. He told of how, since his return home, he had felt a stranger, always adrift, searching to find an entrance into his former life. Alcohol had become his refuge against the noise and confusion of the world. Ultimately, he told of a tremendous sense of failure and frustration, an obscure but consuming belief that his life would be forever tainted, restless, alone. His whole existence seemed defined by an epic sadness.

As I absorbed the full measure of his lament, I began to understand my disgraceful ignorance of post-traumatic stress. I was more comfortable with a disease process that presented itself with identifiable symptoms and a clear frontal wall of attack. In my discomfort in dealing with the elusive maladies of the mind, I tended to gloss over them, conveniently relegating them to some chemical imbalance or hormone deficiency.

I came to grasp how war makes tortured souls of its participants, often requiring them to live day by day, haunted by ghastly memories and tethered to cruel demons that fester like madness in their minds. It occurred to me that all who had been in battle had been forever changed by it. Some simply handled it better than others.

All of this contrasted shamefully with my joy of the previous hours. My consuming preoccupation with creating some perfect moment to propose now seemed frivolous when compared to the swallowing misery of this tearful young man. In my head I had invented a grand fiction about Clayton, assuming he was nothing more than a drunkard and a bully. I had been wrong.

Lost in thought, I now realized that he was asking a question.

"Is there some pill I can take, Dr. Bradford?"

I exhaled deeply. "Medications are probably part of the solution, Clayton. But I think it would be good for you to talk to someone . . . someone who has more experience with this kind of thing."

He shrugged his shoulders, not understanding. "We're talking here, aren't we?"

"We are, and as much as I want to help you, Clayton, I'm not the best choice." I paused for a moment, sharpening my gaze. An idea had struck me. "But I might know somebody who is."

Clayton sat despondently. Having poured out his story, he seemed drained. I was on the verge of collapse as well. "Clayton, I'm going to get you a pillow and a blanket, and you can bunk there on the couch tonight. In the morning, I'll give you a ride home."

He seemed slightly uncomfortable with this plan but ultimately responded with a muted nod. Another long silence followed, and I stared thoughtfully at him. "Clayton, you've been through a lot, and I'm sorry. But I'm going to do everything I can to help you get better."

"Thanks, Doc." His face was downcast, and it seemed he felt ashamed, embarrassed to admit to his pain. It made me all the more determined.

CHAPTER 34
Awakening

I finally managed to pull myself out of bed shortly before noon. Even the downtown church bells of Sunday morning had been unable to draw me out of my slumber. I ambled downstairs, and to no surprise, found that Clayton was gone. I was in the kitchen making coffee when my phone rang.

"Are you finally up?"

"Hello, beautiful," I responded sleepily. "Just couldn't wait to hear my voice, could you?"

"You know, I had the craziest dream last night."

"Oh, yeah?"

"Yeah. I dreamed this wonderful, sweet doctor asked me to marry him."

"Hold it. Shouldn't that be a wonderful, sweet, and handsome doctor asked you to marry him?"

"I thought the handsome part was understood."

"Nice save."

"What are you doing this afternoon?"

I conveyed the entire Clayton Ross episode to her, explaining that perhaps I had misjudged him. Without going into further detail, I told her that I was going to spend part of the afternoon looking into some methods of getting him help. She said she understood, and we made plans for later.

Karen Davidson answered on the third ring, pert and perky as ever. I asked her if she could meet me at the clinic in an hour. She agreed without pressing for further particulars. My plan was a long shot, given Karen's generally private nature. Having been an army medic for all those years, she might be able to relate to Clayton on a much deeper level than I could ever manage. It was worth a try.

When we met in my office an hour later, Karen was almost incandescent, wearing a radiant smile. Dressed casually in jeans and a flannel shirt, she was wearing a slightly less glossy version of the same hairstyle and makeup from the previous evening. She still had an unadorned demeanor and mild shyness, but simply put, she was pretty, very pretty, and she exuded a confidence that I had not seen before. She had clearly warmed to the idea of this bold new look, and I was delighted for her.

I couldn't help teasing her a little. "Dr. Davidson, you were quite the showstopper last night. I'm guessing you had a wonderful evening?"

"I doubt anything could top that final performance of yours, Doctor. Congratulations again, by the way."

"Thanks. So, Karen, tell me everything."

She sank slightly in her chair and gazed toward the ceiling, speaking with elation. "I had such a nice time with Hoot. Believe it or not, we talked shop most of the evening and, I'd have to say, I think he was pretty impressed."

"I think he was pretty impressed before you ever said a word."

Her face warmed into a wry grin. "Yeah, well, that too. But seriously, the conversation was great. We talked about herd management, nutrition strategies for improving milk production, vaccination scheduling. . . . It was wonderful."

"Wow. Be still my beating heart."

She laughed. "Okay, I get it. But it really was fabulous. Hoot introduced me to several of the other dairy farmers. Apparently they have a local dairymen association, and he wants me to speak at their next meeting."

"That sounds great. I'm really happy for you. So, what about you and Hoot? Looks like you two hit it off nicely. That couldn't all have been just shop talk."

A mischievous grin inched across her face. "Isn't he something? I like him. He's funny and so easy to talk with. He's a real sweetheart, despite being such a big bear."

"I think Hoot may actually be hairier than most bears, but it's a pretty good analogy."

Karen nodded, clearly walking on air. "He asked me to come out this afternoon and see his farm. He also wants me to meet his daughter, Wendy."

"You'll like her. Thirteen and smart as a whip. I think she's the real adult in that situation. Anyway, looks like the evening was a big success for the Davidson veterinary practice."

"It was incredible, crazy really. I mean, come on. Who knew?"

"Apparently Connie and Estelle did. You were pretty stunning."

"Yeah, I always figured I'd have to get cremated before anyone considered me smoking hot."

"Oh good grief, Karen. You're an attractive gal. Connie and Estelle just did a little polishing up."

"I guess the military years conditioned me not to care about my looks."

I planted my elbows on my desk, locking my fingers together. "I'm glad you brought that up. That's what I want to talk to you about. I need to ask you something, something personal and private."

"Okay."

"I heard from a discreet source that in the past you spent some time in an army mental facility. Is, umm, is that true?"

She was unfazed by this question. "That is very true."

"I have a reason for asking that I'll get to in a minute. But do you mind telling me about that chapter of your life?"

"Not at all. After all those years in the military, after all those deployments, I had become what I would call emotionally catatonic. I had just . . ." She paused for a second, collecting her thoughts. "I had just seen too much, been through too much. And it wasn't just combat wounds. A lot of my time was spent treating civilians—women and children who had been mangled by some homemade bomb or IED. Just caught in the wrong place at the wrong time."

She thought a moment. "You know, people see Hollywood violence all the time. So they think they understand it. The real thing is impossible to describe or fully comprehend."

She paused again, searching for words. "The explosions and the screams—it's overwhelming and terrifying, and you want to run away. The chaos of it all can just swallow you, all of you. But you have a job to do. So you learn to shut out the sensation, block them out. It works in the military, but it screws you up for a normal life. People don't know it, Luke, but every sixty-five minutes, a United States veteran commits suicide. I didn't want to become one of them. So, after I had made the decision not to re-up, I knew I needed some help. I went and got it."

"And that worked?"

She smiled weakly. "Some. Unfortunately, you can't seal up your memories. So you find a way to cope. Some pour themselves into the oblivion of work, some use alcohol, some bottle it up and nurse their wounds privately, and others wear everyone out, telling their troubled story to anyone who'll take the time to listen. And then, Luke, there are a lot of veterans who do just fine, who transition back and never have a problem. Everybody's different."

This part of the conversation flowed easily for her, revealing that this was a subject to which she had given considerable thought. I admired her all the more.

"And some," I said, "pour their hearts into taking care of animals."

Her warm smile returned. "Yes. Yes, they do." A light of higher purpose seemed to sparkle in her eyes. "And after last night, I'm realizing that maybe it's time I pour my heart into reconnecting with people a little bit too—time to come out of my shell, so to speak."

I smiled grandly, rubbing my hands together. "Well, Karen, I am really happy to hear you say that!"

We talked for the next half hour about Clayton Ross. Karen said she would be glad to speak with him. Granted, she had some reservations as to how much she might be able to help him, but I greatly encouraged her. My only other option was to send him to counseling several counties away. Karen was a promising first choice.

She also wanted to know how I had learned about her past and wasn't happy to hear my source was Luther. But I assured her that I thought he had told no one else. From my own experience, I knew Luther was a man who could keep secrets.

Soon afterward Karen left, but I remained, reflecting over all that I had learned in my conversations with her and Clayton. They had gone off to fight, done their duty, and returned. But the war had followed them home.

CHAPTER 35

An Interesting Request

The crisp, sunny days of September came and went. In the backyard I had abandoned the okra, which had now grown to the size of whale harpoons. The balance of the garden gasped its last breath with only a few cherry tomatoes still making their final stand. Slowly, the collage of orange, red, and yellow leaves began to spread across the yards of Fleming Street and against the distant hills. Cooler nights, thick with the pungent smell of woodsmoke, had become the norm.

For Christine and me, the days were golden. With the onset of cooler weather, she spent more and more evenings at my house, but she would never stay the night. It was a small town, and if sunrise found her car parked outside my home, it would ignite an explosion of gossip regardless of what had or had not occurred. Our relationship was our business alone. Given my penchant for privacy, I had no desire to serve up a savory dish for the local gossips to chew on. Like it or not, we were part of this community, and it would have been foolish to invite speculation.

She began to talk of wedding plans, a subject to which I quickly learned it was best for me to nod, agree, and say nothing. We talked often about children. Perhaps it was our way to inch toward the subject of physical intimacy. Ever since Christine's tender declaration the night we became engaged, the idea of making love with her often consumed me. Frequently in her absence, I would dwell on the possibility, resolving to act on these passionate emotions. But then, when the real situation presented itself, something held me in check, leaving between us a simmering tension.

The benefit dance had raised an impressive sum of money. But we were still short more than ten thousand dollars for the funds needed to build the memorial statue. When push finally came to shove, Connie and John would probably quietly come up with the rest of the money. But I knew that they had already donated huge sums, and I insisted that they hold off, believing that we needed to give the people of Watervalley more time to make up the difference.

Connie and the other volunteers continued to work on the list of names of fallen soldiers that would go on the memorial. All told, the list was nearing seventy men and women killed or missing in action during the wars of the last century. The volunteers had done exhaustive searches of local and state records as well as National Archives databases. Still, several names needed further information and verification. This required a trip to Nashville to the state's vital records office. On a Tuesday in late September, Connie stopped by the clinic around lunchtime to inform me that I was the one assigned the task.

"Give me one good reason why it has to be me."

Connie sat in the large leather chair across from my desk, indifferent to my whining. "Because the state of Tennessee has this funny little rule about privacy. Anyone can request information about a death certificate, but the state won't tell you the cause of death. The only people who can get that information are certain family members or a doctor. Now, sweetie, did that all make sense, or do I need to repeat it more slowly?" Her words were followed by a hard scrutiny.

I frowned and offered a reluctant grunt of understanding.

"Don't be sitting there giving me the stink-eye, young man. It won't hurt you to do this."

"When does it have to be done?"

"Within the next week or so. I'll get you a list of the names."

She left soon afterward, but within minutes, I had another visitor. It was Karen Davidson. Over the past weeks her business had turned around. By word of mouth, her incredible skills with animals and her progressive ideas of herd management were winning the confidence of the locals. I couldn't have been happier for her.

She was wearing jeans and a flannel shirt, her familiar uniform. But she had retained her newfound feminine panache. Her hair was longer, more stylish, and she radiated the alluring attractiveness of a confident woman. Her easy smile seemed perpetually touched with tenderness and humor.

We greeted each other warmly, and she took a seat in the chair Connie had just vacated.

"Karen, I'm going to be nosy. How are things going with you and Hoot?"

A mirthful look inched across her face. "We've been seeing a lot of each other. He's adorable, really. I told him that if he didn't quit treating me like a porcelain doll, I would give him a good old-fashioned army butt kicking."

"Well, aren't you just the charmer."

"Eh, he can take it."

"Sounds like he wants you to stick around."

"Yeah, he's got a little caretaker cottage on his farm that he's fixing up. He's invited me to move into it."

"Oh? And?"

"Well, I do need a place to stay. So I told him I would, but only on the strict condition that I pay rent. I like Hoot. And I really like Wendy. She's delightful. But, you know, things need to be taken a step at a time here."

I nodded.

"Besides," she said, "I've continued to stay at the B and B because Lida hardly charges me anything for rent. But I'm kind of glad to be moving out."

"And why is that?"

"That place is, well, different. Things go bump in the night."

"Yeah, I've heard that before. I guess every little town needs a spook or two. I don't put much stock in it, though."

"Anyway," Karen continued, "let me tell you why I dropped by. I need you to do something. It's regarding Clayton Ross."

"Okay, shoot."

"He and I have talked several times, and I think he's made some real progress."

"Good to hear. Thanks again for helping him."

"Sure. But here's the deal. He's actually a pretty sensitive kid, and he feels bad about that fight with the Mennonite guy back in July."

"Yeah, I remember it well."

"Clayton wants to find him and apologize. He figures you know who the fellow is since you sewed him up. So he wants to know if you will take him out to Mennonite country. He believes that if he goes out there by himself, they'll probably lock their doors and it won't go well. He's guessing that you might be better at approaching them. Some of them are your patients, isn't that right?"

"Yeah, they are." I thought about Karen's request for a moment. I admired Clayton for wanting to do this, and I saw little reason why I shouldn't try to help him. "Okay. When does he want to go?"

"Later this afternoon, actually."

"This afternoon?"

"Yeah, he works at the cabinet factory and gets off around three. He was hoping to come by afterward. You'd have several hours before dark."

The afternoon clinic schedule was light. "Sure. Tell him to come on."

Karen smiled broadly, thanked me, and rose to leave. It had been a good idea to bring Karen and Clayton together. This small request to accompany him was clearly the right thing to do. I didn't realize at the time that it would begin to unwind the spool of a much larger story.

CHAPTER 36
Making Amends

The best way to find Levi Beiler was to first talk to Jacob Yoder. Before Clayton arrived later that afternoon, I took some time to think about how I might approach Jacob. My eyes were drawn to the quilt he had given me. It was still draped over the arm of the office sofa where I had tossed it several months ago. With the onset of cooler evenings, it would be much more useful on the couch at home. So I walked over and was tucking it under my arm when there was a knock on the door. Clayton had arrived.

At first he regarded me with a rather stiff and awkward military politeness. We made our way to the Austin-Healey, where I laid the quilt on the small backseat. Clayton was quickly enamored of the sporty roadster. As we headed out of town, he seemed to relax.

"Man, this is quite the car, Dr. Bradford. How fast will it go?"

"You know, Clayton, that's a good question. Can't say I've ever tried to figure it out."

"Ah, probably just as well. If the sheriff catches you speeding in this thing, he'd probably throw your can in jail."

I spoke slowly. "Yeaaaaaah, I heard he does that."

He chuckled, making a grand nod as he gazed out the window. "That he does, Doc. That he does." An easy smile was etched across his face.

"Hey," he said, "I understand congratulations are in order. I hear you're marrying Christine Chambers."

"That would be true. And thanks."

"She was a senior when I was a freshman."

"So was she a pretty girl back then too?"

Clayton gave me an incredulous look. "Are you kidding, Doc? Look, she's your fiancée and everything, so I'm going to watch what I say here, but you can be she sure wasn't ugly."

I laughed. "Okay, good to know."

By now we were well into the open countryside. The day was warm for September. Decked in our sunglasses with the top down on the convertible, Clayton and I shared an unspoken exhilaration. He was six years my junior, but we enjoyed the camaraderie of two guys in a sports car cruising down the open road.

I half yelled above the rushing air, "I admire you, Clayton. This is a good thing you're doing."

He nodded. "Yeah, it feels right. Dr. Davidson encouraged me to do it."

"I'm glad you two are talking. Seems like that's been a good thing."

"Yeah, I gotta tell you, though, Doc, I've been through some stuff. But Dr. Davidson, she's seen some real crap."

"She works around cows. That's not too surprising."

Clayton looked over and smiled. "Nah, I'm telling you. Some of the things she's told me, jeez, I don't see how she got through it."

"Well, I'm coming to realize that Karen Davidson is tougher than the two of us put together."

Clayton nodded, his expression galvanized in agreement.

We had been traveling down Gallivant's Crossing and made the turn onto the narrow passageway of Mercy Creek Road.

"I don't know where Levi Beiler lives," I said, "but my plan is to go find his future father-in-law, Jacob Yoder, and ask for directions."

Instinctively, I slowed the car to a stop as we passed the small meadow with the old ruins. Something about it still seemed covered in essential wonder. Absorbed in thought, I looked over at Clayton, speaking hesitantly.

"Clayton, I'm going to ask you a question, and you're going to think I'm nuts."

He grunted a shallow laugh. "Doc, we're in pretty bad shape if I'm the sane one in the car."

"Here's the thing. You've spent a lot of time outdoors in the woods and fields of the valley, right?"

"All the time."

"Have you ever heard singing in the wind sometimes?"

His response was immediate. "Sure."

"Really?"

I turned to him, and he shrugged lightly. "Yeah. I remember even when I was a kid, I would be hiking across some field and I'd hear singing in the distant hills. The first time it happened, I ran home and told my folks."

"And what did they say?"

"Well, my dad thought I was imagining things. But my mom told me all kinds of old stories about how some people swore they could hear voices in the wind. I don't know. It's just Watervalley, I guess."

"So this happened to you more than once?"

"Oh, yeah. Quite a few times over the years. And you know,

it was never creepy or spooky. It was always pleasant and peaceful. Mostly folk songs. Sometimes it was old hymns. Why do you ask, Doc? Have you heard them?"

"Yeah, I have. What's that all about?"

"Beats me. My mom's always been kind of a religious person. She said they were angels, people who died with music still in them. And by music, I think she meant life." He looked out the window for a moment, seemingly uncomfortable with his own words, then turned to me with a shy uncertainty. "Kind of corny, I guess. I don't know, seems as good an explanation as any."

"Hey, works for me." I put the car back in gear and we pushed onward.

We topped the last hill before Mennonite country, and once again I was taken by the tranquillity of the pastoral scene before me. The houses were modest and cozy with orderly, unadorned yards that stood in the shadows of great barns. And gazing upon this quaint landscape, I became strangely aware that the Mennonite tempo of life was grandly measured by seasons and years and not by minutes and moments. Something in me envied them. I knew their work was hard and their days long, but admittedly, I was still fascinated by the certain rhythms of their world.

I pulled down Jacob's drive and parked some distance away from the house.

"Might be best if you sit tight for a moment while I find out where Levi Beiler lives."

Clayton nodded.

As I approached the house, I noticed that the boy of about twelve whom I had seen on my previous visit was washing apples in a large pail on the front porch. Upon seeing me, the limber little elf took off toward the barn. I slowed my approach, calculating that he had gone to bring back Jacob. Soon enough, five men in a tight group emerged from the barn and briskly made their way toward me.

This was not what I had expected, and I found their approach intimidating. Their determined gait continued, but as they drew closer, Jacob recognized me. An easy smile spread across his face, and without him saying a word, two of the men whom I did not know headed back to the barn. It was as if Jacob governed them unconsciously. Under their broad hats, I finally recognized the two men who had remained with Jacob as his father, Eli, and Levi Beiler. The boy who had retrieved them had followed at a distance.

As they approached, I noticed them scrutinizing my car in the distance. Eli had a sour face, and Levi wore an expression of strained uncertainty. They stopped some ten feet away and stood waiting in a patient silence while Jacob continued forward, greeting me in his familiar warm and reserved manner.

"Good afternoon, Dr. Bradford. You have paid us a visit." It was his curious way of invoking an explanation.

"Yes, Jacob. Good afternoon to you as well."

I went on to explain the purpose of the call. Pointing toward my car, I detailed Clayton's desire to apologize for his actions. Jacob nodded soberly. A knotty silence fell between us. He politely lifted his hand toward me, a gesture requesting me to stay while he walked back to the other two men. A huddled conversation ensued, and they looked at one another apprehensively, asking questions in a chorus of low voices. Finally, Levi and Jacob walked back toward me.

"What is the young man's name?" Jacob asked.

"Clayton Ross."

"Can you ask him to join us?"

"Sure." I turned toward the Austin-Healey and signaled to

Clayton, who got out of the car and began to make his way toward us. Levi stepped forward to meet him.

The two met some fifty feet away. Clayton extended his hand in greeting and, after a moment's hesitation, Levi took it and the two of them shook. At first they were awkward, uncertain of what to say or how to behave. Their conversation wasn't audible against the low breeze, but soon enough it was clear that Clayton was speaking in earnest. Levi was offering slight nods of his head in understanding.

Jacob's voice drew my attention away. "It is a fortunate thing that you have come, Dr. Bradford."

"Oh, and why is that?"

"I think it is time for Father to come and pay you a visit about his eyes. He has agreed."

We both turned toward Eli, who still stood a short distance away, staring at us with folded arms and a slightly sullen face.

I half whispered under my breath, "You certain about that?"

"Quite certain. Would Thursday afternoon of next week be an appropriate time?"

"I'm sure we can work it out. Come around three."

He nodded at me and then toward his father, who clearly understood what had just transpired.

As I turned back toward Clayton and Levi, the two of them were shaking hands again and walking back toward us. At this same time, I heard feminine voices emerging from around the back corner of the house. It was Jacob's wife, Hannah, and their daughter, Rebecca.

They had been thick in conversation as they turned the corner, unaware of Clayton's and my presence. Upon seeing us, they halted immediately. Rebecca had been smiling at something her mother was saying, but when she saw her fiancé talking with Clayton, her expression froze. They were now casting uneasy and troubled looks at each other.

Jacob gave Rebecca a reassuring nod, a simple sign that seemed to convey a full exchange of information. They approached cautiously. By now Jacob and Levi had joined us.

I introduced Clayton to Jacob, who regarded him with polite reserve. To his credit, Clayton spoke a respectful apology to Jacob, who in turn responded with a somewhat stoic but appreciative nod. An uncomfortable silence followed. It seemed our business was finished.

Simultaneously, Clayton and I both began to step away, but Jacob stopped me. "One moment, Dr. Bradford."

Clayton touched my arm. "I'll see you at the car, Doc."

Jacob turned toward his wife. "Hannah, bring a few of the apples." She walked to the front porch where a number of freshly cleaned apples sat on a table next to the water bucket.

Meanwhile, Levi shook my hand and stepped away toward Rebecca. As he approached, her mouth edged into a tender smile. And as I stood there and watched the two of them, an image was flickering in the shadowy corners of my mind. There was something about Rebecca that I was trying to recall. But whatever it was, it drifted just beyond the threshold of memory. I only half heard Jacob speaking to Hannah.

"Those are the red ones, aren't they?"

She was handing me four large, beautiful apples. I took them from her, but I was still lost in a mild fog. Something in my speechless and curious face prompted Hannah to politely explain Jacob's question.

"Jacob is like his father and has difficulty seeing certain colors."

I now realized my rudeness and thanked them profusely. Jacob thanked me as well and noted that he would see me the following week.

I returned to the Austin-Healey, and we headed back to town, talking easily about sports, the weather, and cars. But the entire way, I was plagued with the notion that somewhere in the exchange between Jacob and Hannah there was something I had missed.

CHAPTER 37
House Call

Rhett was now a regular fixture over at the Fox house, especially during the day when he and Maggie and their brood would eat, sleep, and frolic in the backyard. He seemed to be taking fatherhood in stride, generally lying with his head on his paws while some of the youngsters climbed over him during play. He was learning that parenting was not for those with short attention spans.

The puppies were now almost four weeks old, making more pressing the need to discuss future homes for them. Louise and Will wanted to keep one, and I was vacillating about keeping one myself. Two others had been spoken for: Hoot's daughter, Wendy, wanted one, much to Will's delight, and Nancy Orman, the clinic's administrator, also wanted one, saying that she and her husband had always loved golden retrievers. But that left two in need of homes.

Thursday morning I stopped by the diner and took my regular seat at the counter.

"Lida, you look like you are about to levitate. Have you been smoking some of Sunflower Miller's special tobacco?"

She winked and poured me a mug of coffee. I feigned a tone of further concern. "It's okay. You can tell me these things. I'm a doctor, you know."

Lida was incandescent. She leaned across the counter and spoke in an excited whisper. "I'm closing on the sale of the B and B this afternoon."

"Congratulations. I guess your Charleston buyer came through?"

"He sure did. Wonderful fellow. His name is Matthew House. He's a widower with the cutest eight-year-old twins, a boy and a girl. He looks to be early thirties, pretty close to your age. I think you'll like him."

"Sounds good."

"Oh, it is. He doesn't take possession until the first of December. Meanwhile, I've got to start moving everything out." She leaned even closer, cutting her eyes sharply. "Maybe I can get Casper the friendly ghost to move out too."

"Lida, Karen Davidson said something to that effect. Can't say I much believe in ghosts. What's the deal here?"

She shrugged. "Eh, let's just say that the old place has some long-term nonpaying guests."

"Fair enough. Does the new owner know about this?"

"First thing I told him."

"And?"

"He just laughed. He shook his head and said, 'Lady, I'm from Charleston. We've got so many phantoms floating around, we set extra plates at the dinner table.'"

"Lida, I'm happy for you. And I look forward to meeting the new owner."

I finished breakfast and headed to the clinic. It turned out to be a hectic day. Even so, we managed to stay on schedule—running late was one of my pet peeves, although the people of Watervalley didn't seem to mind either way. They kept a more tolerant pace and seemed to enjoy chatting in the waiting room, sharing a little gossip along with a few germs and the occasional virus.

However, one late-afternoon patient, Luther Whitmore, didn't show. He had a follow-up appointment for his macular degeneration. It was out of character for him to miss and not phone. So around six o'clock that evening, after finishing the day's paperwork and follow-up phone calls, I sat at my desk for a moment and brooded.

Luther's nonappearance troubled me. He was a punctual newspaperman. As much as I didn't like him, his blowing off an appointment sent a message. And I was his doctor.

I exhaled a deep sigh, knowing what I needed to do. But before grabbing my keys, I pulled open my bottom-left desk drawer and grabbed the bottle there. I locked up and headed over to his house.

As I parked in Luther's driveway, the last thin traces of daylight were slipping westward, leaving his imposing home in a cloak of gloomy shadows and sad whisperings. I stood quietly, absorbing the unsettling dreariness that permeated the air, before walking around the side of the house to the attached garage, where Luther typically found refuge from the boredom of his evenings. My intuition proved correct. I found him sitting on a folding chair near the partially open garage door, smoking a cigarette and staring vacantly into the oncoming darkness. I stopped a step or two away from him. Slowly, he turned his gaze toward me.

"Hello, Bradford. For some reason I thought I might be seeing you this evening."

"You missed your appointment today, Luther."

"So I did, so I did. Is that why you've come?" His question seemed in earnest, lacking its usual acidity.

"Not really. Just thought I'd drop by to get a dose of your charm."

"Sarcasm, eh, Bradford? Gee, that really hurt my feelings."

"For some reason, Luther, I don't take you for one of those tormented, thin-skinned guys."

He ignored me. "What have you got there?"

"Whiskey. It was a gift given to me last Christmas and has been sitting in my desk. I'm not a bourbon guy. It's Jim Beam, your brand of choice." I handed the bottle to him. This act of kindness seemed to throw him off his normal invective. With his cigarette locked between his knuckles, he rose from his chair to retrieve an empty Mason jar from a nearby shelf and poured a good two inches into it.

"So, what's on you mind?"

I folded my arms and shrugged, a gesture of honest confession. "Just checking in. Hoping to talk a little."

"How much time you got, Bradford? There might be a whole lot of words in this bottle."

"Luther, you mind if I push the garage door open a little more?"

"Suit yourself. But if all the cigarette smoke gets out, it will spoil the ambience."

In one tilt he drank a full inch of the whiskey and returned to his seat. I grabbed a small wooden chair, turned it away from Luther, and straddled it with my arms draped across the back.

"Look, Luther, I'm pretty sure we're not going to be tight chums any time soon. But the simple reality is this: you are one of my patients."

"Meaning?"

"Meaning my job is to give a damn."

Luther rubbed his chin slowly, assessing me in the dim light. "Yeah, I'll give you that, Bradford."

There was an accommodating tone to Luther's voice. His acknowledgment that he'd been expecting me spoke volumes. He was an intelligent, calculating man, blessed with a shrewd and detached ability to predict the actions of those around him. Something in Luther knew I would come . . . wanted me to come. Maybe, just maybe . . . Luther wanted to talk.

He held the Mason jar at eye level, studying it for a moment before taking another large swallow. Exhaling a contented sigh, he spoke lightly, clearly in a good humor. "Sort of brings a whole new meaning to the term 'Beam me up.'"

The last of twilight had faded, and we sat there in the black cloak of evening, illuminated only by the pale glow from neighboring houses.

"Luther, you want me to turn a light on?"

"Nah. I like the dark, Bradford." He put out his cigarette, crushing it into a small ashtray. "You were orphaned when you were twelve, weren't you?"

"Yes, I lost my parents, but I had an aunt who took me in and cared for me. Why do you ask?"

Luther had discerned my guarded attitude to his question. There was an obliging element to his response. "The point is, Doctor, everybody's life is a story. You just have to look for it. That's why I like the newspaper business. People don't just want information. They want a story."

"So, Luther, tell me your story."

"Why?"

"Like I said, my job is to give a damn."

He scratched his chin, amused. "You already know my story."

"No, not really. All I've got is information. You grew up on a farm, you lived in town as a teenager, and then you went to Vietnam, where, I might add, you were highly decorated. But you came back different. You fenced in Moon Lake and took over running the paper. And somewhere in the middle of all that, something happened. So, Luther, you can tell me to piss off like you have before, or maybe you can help me understand the larger story here."

Luther exhaled and leaned forward in his chair. Somehow over the course of my repeated visits it seemed that he had found in me a worthy delegate of his deeper reflections, a side of him that he kept carefully protected from the larger world. As he had done in July, he spoke with a moving eloquence, a somber and powerful voice that pierced the darkness.

"There's nothing unique about my story, Bradford. I came of age in the sixties, and the sixties were a troubled sea filled with wreckage. We were drops of blood upon the water, pulled apart by a world bound in fear, an unsettled and anxious generation split between old principles and new social and moral awakenings. Some of us stayed home and protested. Some of us went off to war. All of us left behind a past that was forever lost. We arrived in Vietnam believing in so many things—country, patriotism, service, God—and upon our return, we believed in one thing and one thing only: nothing. It was a wretched deterioration. First came disenchantment, then despair, then apathy. When it was over, there was no hero's welcome, no glorious return. America was indifferent; heaven was empty. It left us with hearts that would always know hunger." He paused before adding a final assertion to his soliloquy. "Hearts that would be forever stained by our stupid mistakes."

"How so?"

Luther sat brooding for a moment. When he finally answered, his words were grim, naked, penetrating. "In our hot youth, there was no life beyond the moment."

With that one comment, he had departed from a general summation about his generation. It was a small crack in the door to his personal life. I spoke innocently, endeavoring to hide my deeper interest. "Tell me what you mean by that, Luther."

My voice seemed to awaken him from some lost pocket of memory. From his hunched-over position he sat upright in his chair, stiffening his back in a gesture of resolve. "Oh, it doesn't matter, Bradford. The human mind's ability to adapt is formidable. We all came back and went about our days, our work, our lives, discreetly hiding our scars, covering them with the raiment of society." He took another large drink from his glass and sank back into a despondent brooding.

Once again Luther had been evasive, and I realized that my earlier assumption about his wanting to talk was wrong. I rose from my chair. "I think I've had all the fun I can stand for one evening. Call the clinic tomorrow and reschedule your appointment. We need to monitor your condition. Can't do that if you don't come see me."

"Bradford, I almost like you. Stick around and have a drink. We'll toast something."

"And what would we toast to?"

"To war and men and honor. To chivalry and when knighthood was in flower." He paused briefly to ceremoniously hold up his glass. He slurred drunkenly, halting over his words. "In fact, we'll do a toast to all the knights: the Teutonic Knights, the gin tonic knights, and the Three Dog Nights."

I smiled at Luther's cleverness and made one final probe into his well of secrets. "Luther, speaking of war and honor, why is it you don't want anyone to know about your medals of valor?"

At first he glared at me as if the question maddened him. Then his eyes drifted away, his face sullen. "Because, Bradford, the things I did in Vietnam, the acts of valor, as you call them, I didn't do them alone. . . . 'They also serve who only stand and wait.'"

I had no idea why he was quoting Milton or what it meant, and I saw little chance that he would explain further. "Call the clinic tomorrow. I'll toast to that."

I walked through the shadows to my car. Something about being with Luther always left me feeling empty, as if he drained the light and life out of me. And his talk of war and honor and chivalry made no sense. Still, I wondered about him. I had always thought the war had stained him with a lifetime of bitterness. I had assumed that in his youth, since he had believed so much, had trusted so much, the disillusionment of Vietnam had stripped him of all that he had previously held in wonder, leaving them ugly and common. And yet it gnawed at me that there was something more, some grand regret that haunted him.

As I walked up my porch steps under the stars of late September, one thing Luther had said still rang true. I didn't just want information; I wanted the story. I didn't realize at the time that in his own way, Luther was trying to tell me his.

CHAPTER 38
Pent Up

The following Saturday was the first of October and the Fall Festival. Ever since our engagement, Watervalley's regard for Christine and me was a testimony to the fabric of small-town life. Despite their firm disdain for anyone who made claim to pretentiousness, the plain and simple people of the town still wanted their champions. It seemed that by rules that were undeclared and vaporous, they bestowed on certain individuals an elevated social regard. Typically this involved money and lineage, although education was also a wild card that granted social esteem. As a physician, I had experienced that since the first day of my arrival.

Over the past month, I had begun to realize that along with Christine's gracious nature and striking beauty, in the eyes of Watervalley she was viewed as having all the social trappings of heritage and wealth. We were seen as the perfect couple, and it seemed to be a great point of pride with the locals that one of their own had won the heart of the town doctor. We were treated just short of nobility, a status neither of us understood or desired. The townsfolk couldn't get enough of us. It was both a blessing and a curse. But on this day, the Saturday of the Fall Festival, it felt like the latter.

Throughout the day, a growing tension seem to expand between Christine and me, and we argued over small things that didn't matter. As we moved among the throngs of people, we were constantly corralled by well-wishers who wanted to see Christine's ring, tease us about being engaged, and offer an endless encyclopedia of unwanted marriage advice.

By the time we arrived at the Fall Festival dance being held at the Memorial Building that evening, both of us were in a sour mood. Christine was distant, distracted, and my occasional inquiry as to whether everything was okay was met with immediate and curt dismissals. This fostered an impatient and brooding agitation between us. At the dance, the need to paint on a cordial smile for the endless stream of well-meaning townsfolk only exacerbated the situation. After thirty minutes of relentless interruptions, Christine turned to me.

"Can we go? Just, you know, leave?"

"Okay, fine." I set down my beer, took her by the hand, and we walked out. I didn't care about being at the dance anyway. But I was at a loss as to what could possibly be behind Christine's intolerant mood.

After getting into the car, instead of starting the engine, I draped my arms over the steering wheel. Fatigued and annoyed, I rested my chin on top of my hands. "So, what do you want to do?"

"I don't care." Her clipped words were dispirited, frustrated. "What do you want to do?"

"I wasn't the one who wanted to leave the dance."

"Do you want to go back?"

"Not particularly."

"So, what's your point?"

"My point," I said in a notably firmer but accommodating voice, "is that I don't care what we do. I'm okay with being at the dance; I'm okay with doing something else. I'm open. So, you just decide, and by golly, that's what we'll do."

A tense silence fell between us. Christine stared ahead in a brooding preoccupation: tight-lipped, pensive, caught in the shadow of some nagging worry. A moment later, she lifted her chin and exhaled deeply. "Let's go to your place and make love."

My blurted response was immediate, skeptical. "Is that what you want?"

Her boldness faltered. "Yes . . . no . . . I don't know. Maybe." She looked away. Her voice was timid, pleading. "Don't you want to?"

"Of course I want to. I wanted to make love with you the first time I saw you standing in your classroom door at school." I paused a moment, shrugging slightly. "Of course, back then it was probably for all the wrong reasons. But now, well, now it's for all the right reasons."

Her gaze probed mine. "Are there right reasons?"

"Sure there are."

She looked down and nodded delicately, still preoccupied and reflective.

"What's wrong, Christine?"

As soon as I pressed the question, she immediately fortified herself again, painting on a fainthearted smile, speaking dismissively. "I don't know. I've just been a bag of emotions lately." She sat, looking down. "All I know is that I love you very much." Again, she exhaled deeply and spoke with quiet resolve. "Maybe you should take me home. I'm just not feeling great."

"Tell me how you feel."

She looked up at me, searching my eyes, and seemed instantly comforted by the deep well of devotion she found there. Her mood lightened. Smiling warmly, she ran her finger along the back of my hand. "That is, take me home . . . unless, of course, you really would like to go back to your place and make love. I mean, I brought it up. I guess I'm not being very fair to bounce you around like that."

I almost laughed. Even I couldn't believe what I was about to say. "Christine, I'm pretty sure I'll hate myself in another hour, and I mean *really* hate myself. But, no. Not now. Not like this."

I reached over and held the soft contour of her face in my hand. I wanted her to answer my question, to talk to me, to tell me what was wrong. But she closed her eyes and rolled her cheek into my palm, breathing out a low murmur.

It had been a difficult, confusing day. The night was unseasonably cold and Christine shivered. I reached into the small rear seat and grabbed the Mennonite quilt that I had left there weeks before. I unfolded it and put it around her, then started the engine, turned on the headlights, and headed toward Summerfield Road.

As we passed under the streetlights, I reached over to hold her hand. But instead, she took my arm and wrapped it in a yielding embrace, holding it securely to her and resting her head on my shoulder the entire way home.

I walked her to the door and we kissed good night. But in the embrace that followed, she held me tightly, as if afraid to let me go. I was content to hold her as long as she wished. But in time, she took a deep breath of resolve, said good night, and disappeared behind the large front door.

The next morning, I texted Christine to see how she was feeling. Minutes later, she responded with a brief message. "Much better. Still sleeping. Will call later."

I was encouraged, thinking that possibly her curious malaise from the previous day was now past. Perhaps it had been a combination of weariness and stress mixed with who knew what. I had to laugh at myself. I worked all day, every day, in a building full of women. How come I still understood so little about them?

I gathered my coffee mug and stepped outside to take in the splendor of the unseasonably warm fall day, all the while thinking of Christine, ruminating on her offer of love the previous evening, toying with it, pondering it, and in time, becoming obsessed by it. The idea was consuming.

On the one hand, our restraint seemed absurd. We were in love, for heaven's sake, and engaged; fully committed to each other. A desire for total intimacy was completely natural. The previous evening's discord had precluded the possibility and had spoiled the moment. Even so, the thought of making love lingered. And that thought was powerful, delightful, and, more than I wanted to admit, irresistible.

I grew restless and wanted to get away, take a drive. After changing clothes, I grabbed my keys, started up the Austin-Healey, and headed out to the countryside. I drove for nearly an hour, aimlessly traveling the remote roads of Watervalley until I found myself on the east road headed toward the woods and Leyland Carter's secluded shack.

On the way, I made a brief stop at Eddie's Quick Mart to grab a soft drink and a couple of other items. The landscape on the east road seemed tangled and disfigured, broken up by overgrown, sagging fences and cluttered with the occasional abandoned building and weedy parking lot. In time, I was swallowed by thick woods.

I traveled down Beacon Lane and turned at Leyland's mailbox. After stopping in the small clearing in front of his house, I cut the engine and stepped toward the porch, calling out in a loud voice, "Leyland! Hey, Leyland! It's Luke Bradford, the doctor. Are you home?"

I waited and heard nothing. The house had the same deserted

appearance as on my last visit. Curtains still tightly covered the windows, and now a few errant tree branches had come to rest on the roof, providing a pocket for the accumulation of fallen leaves. I called out again, but there was still no sound save for the sporadic creak of the rocking chair, stirred by the occasional wisp of warm breeze. Otherwise, a heavy stillness permeated the air.

I walked around the side of the house, and toward the back, where I found a 1970s-vintage Ford truck parked in the weeds and gravel. It was beaten up and rusted.

The small back stoop was partially covered in leaves and adorned with an old pair of work boots that appeared to have been left in the weather for quite some time. I knocked loudly on the back door and still heard no sound. I thought about calling out again, but at this juncture, it seemed pointless. Leyland wasn't here.

I leaned on the fender of the truck for a few minutes and breathed in deeply of the rich, musty woods. Shafts of morning light filtered through the remaining leaves, warming the small backyard and illuminating small patches on the forest floor. The day had a dreamy, ethereal feel to it, and there was something comforting in the incredible silence. Even so, my thoughts troubled me. In time I ambled back around the house, looking down to carefully place my steps among the rocks and tall weeds. I was almost to the car before I heard Leyland speak.

"What's your hurry, Luke?"

He was sitting in the rocking chair, just as he had been in my previous visit. He was wearing a heavy, waist-length farm coat.

"How do you do that?"

"And what would that be?" His face was framed in the same grin as before.

I stepped onto the porch, folded my arms, and leaned my shoulder against the near column. "How do you sneak out here without making a sound?"

"Old is not the same as rusty, my boy."

I looked away, amused and not surprised that I wouldn't get a straight answer from him.

"What brings you out on this fine Sunday morning?"

"Seemed like a nice day for a drive. Catch a little fall color."

"You wouldn't have headed out the east highway for that."

"Yeah, but then I couldn't check up on you, could I?"

He nodded thoughtfully. "Well, you're a fine man for doing so."

"Since we're on that subject, tell me, Leyland. How have you been?"

"Pretty fair, pretty fair. I woke up aboveground this morning, which always makes for a good day."

"Can't argue with that, I guess. Are you getting along okay out here by yourself? You have everything you need, like food and medications and that sort of thing?"

"Seem to be. The well pump still works, I still hunt in the woods some from time to time, and I get to the store when I need to. And not to cut down on your business, Doc, but I feel fine. Don't take any medicine."

"Well, okay. I guess my work here is done."

I suspected Leyland knew I was joking, but he played along for sport.

"Ah, hang around. I'm sure you can think of another question or two."

I nodded and surveyed the nearby woods, which now seemed to have a warmth and brightness.

"If you don't mind my asking, Leyland, what do you do for entertainment?"

"Don't mind a'tall. I read, I listen to the woods, and when I get lonely, I hum a little tune."

I knew that for many of the older citizens of Watervalley, the pace of life was rather slow. But Leyland took this concept to an all-new level, completely detached from the fervor of the larger world. Still, he seemed content. "Well, I tell you, Leyland, I might get some of your well water before I go. Seems to keep you healthy, wealthy, and wise."

"Healthy and wise, maybe."

We shared a brief moment of mutual understanding before Leyland spoke again.

"So, what's troubling you today?"

I tightened my gaze at him. "And why do you think something is troubling me?"

"You seem wounded."

I stiffened slightly, amused and curious. "I don't think I follow you."

"When you were walking around the house just now . . . you seemed wounded."

I stood there with my hands in my coat pockets and shrugged. "No, Leyland. I feel fine."

He rubbed his mouth as if he had just finished a meal. Then he stood and, after steadying himself on the porch railing, he looked at the woods, seeming to search for a memory. "One time when I was a boy, I went with my dad to the store. It was a general merchandise where they sold everything: food, hardware, even clothing. Every time I had been in that store, the owner had told me to get a piece of peppermint candy out of the big jar. But for some reason, this time he didn't. Now, my dad needed a certain kind of rope. So he and the proprietor went back into the storeroom to look for it, leaving me all alone and standing next to that great big jar of peppermint candy." He paused a moment. "So, I had a decision to make. I knew I could take a piece and no one would ever miss it."

"But technically you thought that would be stealing," I said.

"Maybe, maybe not. The store owner had offered in the past."

"So, what did you do?"

"I took the lid off and put my hand in the jar. Then, after a moment, I just stopped. I pulled my hand out and put the lid back."

"Then what happened?"

"They came back out from the storeroom. My dad bought his rope. We left."

"And that's the end of the story?"

"Pretty much."

"Leyland, I think you lost me somewhere. I don't believe I see the connection between that story and your thinking that I look wounded."

"Because as we rode back home, I had the same look on my face that you did a few minutes ago. I wanted that piece of peppermint. It had been offered in the past, so I thought I could easily justify having it. I chose not to, and it was the right decision. But I had missed out on something really delightful. And frankly, I felt wounded."

I tightened my lips and thought about Leyland's words. He knew nothing about me or the desires swirling around in my head. But admittedly, his insightfulness was daunting.

Still pretending to be amused, I spoke cautiously, politely. "So, Leyland, tell me your point here."

He looked down for a moment, never losing his amiable smile. "The point, Doctor, is that in this life, just because you can doesn't mean you should."

His words hung heavy in the air. He gazed into the patchy sunlight of the woods. "It seems that within us are deeply buried notions. They well up from some ancient, hidden, half-forgotten, ancestral memory; they're woven into our very nature. Notions that we don't freely lay upon ourselves, yet notions that we feel we must obey. They confuse us, so we try to ignore them. But they hound us, chide us to weigh the moral quality of our actions."

"Not exactly a popular sentiment, Leyland, but I guess there may be some truth there."

He was half laughing under his breath. "The truth rarely gets applause."

He eased himself back into the rocking chair. He began to talk about his life, of how his favorite sandwich as a child was buttered white bread, of how he loved to work with wood and stone to build things, and of how his education at Vanderbilt had taught him a love of poetry.

Most of all, he talked about the land, of how the soil was his eternal kinsman, of how a life tilling the earth fostered a kind of wisdom and strength, of how the land was always beautiful, healing, full of adventure. It seemed that his was a contentment to be envied, and I found myself wanting to understand what had given his life such satisfaction and ease; what had made all the difficulties and disappointments of life seem so distant. He was a paradox to me: a life that had so little, yet a mind that had so much.

The noon hour approached, and he stood and stretched. "Son, I need to move around a little. You want to take a walk in the woods with me? There's a creek nearby with large rocks that form some shallow pools. I like to go to the water."

"Perhaps another time, Leyland. I probably ought to be getting back."

"Come again anytime. I should be here. If I'm not, I'm probably somewhere else." His eyes twinkled at his own humor.

I returned to the Austin-Healey and waved to him as I departed. He held up a hand in reply. I was lost in thought and was a half mile down Beacon Road when I noticed the bag from Eddie's Quick Mart on the passenger side.

"Crap," I said. I turned the car around and made my way back down Leyland's driveway. After parking, I reached into the bag and retrieved the five pieces of peppermint candy I had bought for him because he had asked me on my earlier visit if I had any. But he was nowhere to be seen.

I knocked on the door and called out, but received no answer. He had likely taken off into the woods and was out of earshot. I left the five pieces on his chair and headed back to town.

CHAPTER 39
Vital Records

Tuesday afternoon, Connie stopped by the office with the list of names for my visit to the Tennessee Office of Vital Records. The statue company was pressing for the names to be engraved as well as for the final payment. After talking with Nancy Orman about Wednesday's schedule, I reluctantly agreed to drive to Nashville the next morning.

I had already made plans to take Friday off and finally go to Atlanta, meet with the moving company, and arrange to transfer some furniture from storage. This unwanted trip to Nashville only complicated the week. But it had to be done.

I left early Wednesday, hoping to return in time to take care of any patients and then later meet up with Christine. We hadn't seen each other since Saturday.

The morning air was cool and sunny. Telephone poles flashed by in an endless blur as the roadster hummed across the hills and farmlands. I was restless, lost in thought.

A strange feeling troubled me that I had missed or forgotten something, and I began to randomly replay the events of recent weeks. For some reason, my mind kept returning to Luther and his odd desire to hide his heroism. I couldn't get his quote from Milton out of my head: "They also serve who only stand and wait." Presumably, he'd been talking about Eli Yoder, and yet, Eli's service hardly involved standing and waiting. Luther was more clever than that. I was missing something.

In time, I approached the familiar skyline of Nashville and made my way downtown to the Central Services Building and the state's vital records office. After parking, I grabbed the folder and headed inside. An hour later, the task was done.

But I wasn't the same. It had been deeply sobering to read the death certificates of the seven men on my list. They had been faceless names in a file folder, but now I knew part of their stories, and my efforts had insured that their names would appear on the memorial. It had been time well spent.

The day had warmed up, so I took off my jacket before getting into the car. I was about to toss it into the backseat when I noticed the quilt still there, neatly folded. Sunlight shining through the side window fell upon it, illuminating the vivid green and red patterns. Numerous times I had thought to take the quilt inside after arriving home. But it hadn't happened because something about it kept nagging me, pestering my subconscious, pleading for me to recall some conversation, some buried realization.

Then it hit me. I stood there stunned for several lost seconds. My mind raced; searching, probing, connecting the dots. I shut the car door, walked back inside, and returned to the vital records counter. There was one more document I needed to see.

When I arrived in Watervalley later that day, I drove straight to the offices of the *Village Voice*. I found Luther at his desk, seated in the middle of the modest-sized room cluttered with files, books, and old papers. He was reading something on his computer. I entered and shut the door behind me.

"Luther, we need to talk."

He was unmoved by the intensity in my voice. "Do I have a choice?"

"What happened the night of the fire?"

"You care to be more specific?"

"July fifth, 1968. The fire out on Mercy Creek Road. What happened?"

There was a subtle stiffening in his posture. By degrees his eyes grew more sharply focused. "Why do you ask?"

"Just humor me, Luther."

His expression turned crafty, undaunted. "We rode out there for nothing. The house on fire belonged to the Mennonites, and they didn't want our help. What of it?"

"Everybody knows that part. What I want to know is, what happened earlier that evening?"

Luther folded his arms and sat back in his chair. "I'm not sure I understand your question, Bradford."

He was stonewalling. "I think you do, Luther. I think you remember it vividly. It was the night before you headed off to war."

"Since you seem to be recently blessed with a dose of clairvoyance, why don't you tell me your theory?"

"Okay, fine." Once again Luther was at his game of cat and mouse. "Let's just say I'm spitballing here, but I'm guessing you knew that house well. I'm guessing that you were there earlier that night. You're a lot of things, Luther, but you're not a liar. So tell me. Yes or no?"

His haughty manner hardened to a low anger. "Why do you want to know, Bradford?"

"Because I want the truth. Because I think there is more to this story than even you know."

He stood heatedly and placed both hands on his desk as he leaned venomously toward me. "What do you mean, more than I know?"

"Just answer the question!"

"About what?"

"About what happened that night between you and Ellie Yoder."

His face went pale. His tall frame wilted before me, and he slowly eased back into his chair. For the longest time he stared vacantly, resurrecting the memories of a past decade. Eventually, he sighed deeply.

"You really want to hear all this?"

"Sure."

"Ellie Yoder and I had been secretly in love for years, ever since we were children. When we were kids, we promised to marry each other. That's why I know scripture so well. I was studying to become a Mennonite, so I could be accepted into their faith. When I moved to town, it was harder to see each other. We met secretly. We had been very careful, but I think Eli figured it out."

"What happened?"

"The war, the draft. I got called up, and it was a little late to claim that I was a conscientious objector. So we decided that I would serve my time and we would marry when I returned. The house on Mercy Creek Road was to be hers. We were going to live there until I had a chance to build a house at Moon Lake. Then she died. I didn't find out until two months after it happened. My mother mentioned her death randomly in a letter. Even she didn't know about us."

"So what happened that night, Luther? How did her house catch on fire?"

Despite his defeated tone, Luther scrutinized me sharply. "Bradford . . . I really don't get you. Why do you care?"

"For the moment, let's just say I'm curious and leave it at that."

This seem to satisfy him. His reflective voice filled the room. "It was my last night before leaving for the war. After it grew dark, we met at the house. It was abandoned in those days, and her family used it for storage. We were both eighteen—scared, uncertain, wholeheartedly in love. It was terrible. Somehow, we both had this desperate feeling we would never see each other again, that I would never return from the war. We were both in unexplainable tears."

He paused and stared at me. "Can you imagine what that's like, Bradford? To have the one person who is everything in your life standing before you, and to somehow know that this is it. To have the dreadful knowledge that after you say good-bye and turn away, you will never see them again?"

I let his question go unanswered, and Luther seemed to disappear back into his memories. "So, our emotions overcame us and we made love. We made love on a makeshift bed of burlap bags. At first we were both hesitant, unsure. Then one thing just led to another."

I let his words settle. "And the fire?"

Luther made a despondent shrug. "Eli must have found out what had happened. If he confronted her, Ellie wouldn't have lied about it. All I can figure is that in his anger, he came sometime later that night and set the house on fire. He had been my best friend and was going to be my brother-in-law. I'm sure he felt betrayed. I'm sure he blamed me, and I guess he should have. We haven't talked since."

Luther folded his arms and tilted his head to the side. He seemed oddly relieved to have finally told his story. "So when I came back, I fenced in Moon Lake. I wanted to close up the past, shut out all the memories. Shut out my shame."

"Your shame?"

Oddly, Luther grinned. "You probably won't understand this, Bradford. It seems the world has changed. But back then, Ellie and I had some deeply held beliefs . . . beliefs that in our desperation, we threw aside that night. We were young, foolishly trying to live inside some idealistic bubble. Our passion overcame our convictions. I blamed myself."

"Luther, why? You said it yourself. You were young. This was decades ago. Why bottle it up all these years?"

"I've never told anyone about why I fenced in Moon Lake or any of this because that would lead to questions. And one question would lead to another, and the last thing I was ever going to let happen was for anything to dishonor Ellie's memory."

I nodded my understanding. "So when you quoted Milton the other day, were you talking about her?"

"She told me she would pray for me every day. Pray for my safe return. Whatever courage or valor I displayed in Vietnam was because of her. Because I knew her prayers were protecting me. She was so much better than me. She was the brave one, the valiant one. That's how she served."

He looked up at me. "How did you figure this out? How did you know about Ellie and me?"

I thought about his question for a moment and then sat in the wooden chair across from his desk. "Because you told me."

"That's not true. I never spoke of it."

"Not all in one conversation, but in small pieces along the way . . . things you said."

"Such as?"

I waited before replying, contemplating all the things I knew and what I was willing to disclose. "In one of our conversations about Moon Lake, Luther, you said you had fenced in Eden. You're well versed in scripture, so that told me you saw something in your past as a fall from grace. Then the other night when you talked about chivalry and making stupid mistakes, about how in youth there is no life beyond the moment, an odd thought occurred to me. As much as you seem to loathe the Mennonites, you eulogized Ellie Yoder."

Luther nodded, but he was pensive, regarding me skeptically. "And you figured this out from that?"

I crossed my arms, deliberating. After several moments, I looked up at Luther and resolved to tell him what I had learned.

"There's more."

"I don't understand."

"I went to Nashville this morning to check on some records for the memorial project. While I was there, I looked up Ellie's death certificate. Being a doctor gives you certain privileges in regard to the Office of Vital Records, so I made a copy." I retrieved the paper from my coat pocket and handed it to him.

"Ellie didn't die of pneumonia. She died of eclampsia. It's a complication of pregnancy."

Luther's face lost all its color. "What are you saying?"

"It looks like you weren't the only one who didn't want to dishonor her name. As it's been told to me, Ellie went to live with Eli and his wife, Letta, shortly after he took his noncombat assignment. Apparently his service started right after you left for boot camp."

Luther nodded, affirming my assertion.

"A couple of months after you left, Ellie must have realized she was pregnant and somehow let Eli know. My guess is the Mennonites can be a pretty strict bunch, and Ellie was certain to be disgraced. But apparently Eli loved his sister more than he hated her transgression. I'm guessing the three of them worked out a plan claiming that Letta was pregnant. Since Eli and Letta would be gone from the Mennonite community for nearly two years with no family nearby, no one questioned Ellie's going to live with them and helping out. Then again, maybe everyone knew, and this was how the situation was worked out. But that seems far less likely."

"Are you telling me that Ellie and I had a child?"

"Yeah, I think so. I think Jacob Yoder is your son. At least, I'm pretty sure."

"Based on what?"

"Genetics, Luther. Eli is color-blind. I recently learned that Jacob is too. But color blindness is a sex-linked trait; it comes from the mother, not the father. That means Letta would have to be color-blind. Several months back, Letta instructed her grandson to go find a green and red quilt to give to me as payment for a house call. She's not color-blind, but I'm guessing that Ellie was."

Luther slowly nodded. "Yes, she was."

"There's more. Jacob and his wife, Hannah, have a daughter who is eighteen. She's very striking. But unlike her parents, she's also very tall. I've seen her on only a few occasions, and each time I kept thinking she reminded me of someone. And then today, when all this started falling into place, it hit me. She is the spitting image of your mother from her debutante picture. She's tall and willowy with an almost haunting beauty about her."

Luther leaned forward in his chair, rested his elbows on his knees, and sat gape-jawed in a mixture of astonishment and trepidation. "Are you certain about all this?"

"Not one hundred percent. Some of this is speculation. But for me, it all adds up."

After what seemed an eternity, he looked at me with a face that was searching, reflective, and oddly, serene.

"Bradford, I have a son?"

"So it would seem."

We sat in silence for another moment. There was little more to say, so I began to stand and make my departure. "Well, Luther. I'll uh . . . I'll let you get back to your day. And not to worry. I see no reason to breathe a word of this to anyone."

Luther offered an indebted nod. Then, uncharacteristically, he rose from his chair, walked around his desk, and extended his hand. "Thank you. Thank you for coming and telling me this." He looked down for a moment, his face penitent. "For some reason, Luke Bradford, you've been a friend, and I'm grateful."

"Sure. Just thought you'd want to know."

I turned to leave, but Luther stopped me. He stood for a moment, struggling to find the words. He seemed to have lost all of his haughty demeanor and spoke in a voice of complete contrition. "I'd like to ask you a favor."

CHAPTER 40
A Tenuous Gathering

The following day, Thursday, the clinic was remarkably busy. Since I was going to be out of the office Friday, two days of patients were being crammed into one. Late that afternoon, Nancy Orman caught me in the hallway as I exited an exam room.

"Dr. Bradford, the Yoders are here."

"How many of them came?"

"Jacob and his father."

"Okay, thanks. I'll take it from here." I'd told Nancy that I wanted to speak to Eli Yoder before they were shown to an exam room.

I took a deep breath, focused, and walked to the waiting area, where I found Jacob and Eli.

"Good afternoon," I said to both of them. I turned my attention to Eli. "Mr. Yoder, before we get started, I wonder if I might speak to you privately in my office."

He looked at me and then quickly to Jacob, who gave him a subtle nod. Eli rose slowly, regarding me warily. I extended my hand to guide him in the proper direction. He moved vigorously for a man of his years and once we were inside my office, I asked him to have a seat on the couch, where the quilt his family had given me was neatly folded on the cushion beside him. I pulled up a chair and sat across from him.

"Thank you, Mr. Yoder. I brought you here to ask you a question."

I was doing my best to stifle the timidity bouncing around in my throat. Conversely, Eli seemed perfectly relaxed, assessing me casually. He nodded his understanding.

"Can you tell me the colors of that quilt beside you?"

His eyes tightened and to my surprise, ever so subtly the corners of his mouth turned upward, revealing a buried amusement that was far removed from his customary stern countenance. "We both know, Dr. Bradford, that I am unable to see certain colors. What is your real question?"

His calm delivery coupled with his quick intuition threw me. I laughed. "Okay, fair enough." I studied him for a moment, rethinking my approach.

"Here's the thing. Jacob has the same condition. It's more commonly known as color blindness."

"Yes, that is correct."

"Well, that's the problem. Unless I'm mistaken, Letta is not color-blind, and that trait is passed through the mother . . . which leads me to believe that Jacob is not your biological son."

Eli stiffened. He drew in a long breath and cautiously chose his next words. "You seem quite certain, Dr. Bradford. Why is that?"

He had carefully avoided confirming my assertion. It was time to press the real agenda.

"Eli, I know that your sister Ellie died after complications of childbirth. I read her death certificate, which I found in the state archives. I'm also pretty sure that Jacob doesn't know that Ellie was his biological mother."

A long silence ensued as Eli looked to the side, his lips pressed firmly together. In time, he nodded in resignation and turned to me. "So, why is this important to you, Dr. Bradford? Do you intend to tell Jacob?"

I held up my hands. "No, no, not at all. I have neither a right nor a responsibility to do that."

"Then why are you asking?"

I was less sure of my response. "Because I'm a doctor. Because my job is to heal wounds."

"I don't think I understand."

"I need to ask you a favor, Eli. One other person knows the truth about Jacob—his father, Luther Whitmore. I told him yesterday. He doesn't want to cause any trouble, but he would like to meet with you. He didn't think you would talk to him, and I agreed to try to smooth the way for you to get together."

"And when does he want to meet?"

I shrugged. "Now, if possible. He can be here in a couple of minutes."

After a moment's hesitation, he nodded. "Perhaps it is time."

Luther had been waiting on my call and was soon at the clinic's back door. He didn't seem nervous, but I sure as heck was. We went to my office, where Eli was waiting.

Awkwardly, I endeavored to make introductions. "Mr. Yoder, I believe you are acquainted with Mr. Whitmore. I understand you two knew each other years ago?"

The two men stared at each other for the longest time, not with faces of anger or bitter assessment, but rather with a long-endured sadness.

"You look well, Eli."

"As do you."

"Not true. The years have taken their toll. You never were able to tell a lie."

A glint of amusement passed between the two of them, followed by another long silence.

Eli spoke calmly. "So, what is it you want?"

"I just wanted to say thank you, Eli. Thank you for protecting Ellie. Thank you for loving her despite . . ." He paused for a moment, weighing his words. "Despite our failure and our foolishness. And most of all, I want to thank you for raising our son. For loving him and for teaching him your ways and your beliefs. From what little I know of him, he's a very good man, a good husband, and a good father. He's that because of you and Letta."

Eli nodded his understanding.

As he spoke again, the poise Luther had so readily displayed moments ago began to falter. "You need to know, Eli. I have no intentions of saying anything. Not to Jacob, not to anyone. If he is told differently, then eventually everything will come out. You've taken great pains to keep Ellie's memory untarnished. All the kindness, all the light, and all the love that was in her shouldn't be tainted by one foolish act on my part. I should have loved her more wisely."

Luther's face tightened, and his chin began to quiver. He was fighting to keep his composure. "Just promise me, Eli. Just promise me that you've told Jacob how incredible, how wonderful, how beautiful, his aunt Ellie was. How she brought joy and splendor to the ordinary day." He looked at Eli humbly. "That's all I ask."

Luther's attempts to hold back tears had failed him, and a half century of pain and regret welled up in his eyes.

Eli looked down, seemingly unable to look at Luther. Now he seemed racked with woe, frail, and grief-stricken. After what seemed an eternity, he said, "I didn't start the fire."

Luther caught his breath. "Then who did?"

"Ellie did. After you left. She did it to punish herself for not being stronger. She never blamed you. Even months later, in her last hours, she never blamed you."

Eli paused and half sat, half collapsed into a nearby armchair. "After the baby was born, she kept insisting she was fine, stubbornly refusing to go to the hospital. Finally, I no longer believed her, and I ran as fast as I could to the nearest house so they could call for an emergency vehicle. But I was too late. By the time they arrived, she had already passed away. I blame myself."

He looked up at Luther. "You are not the only one with regrets. It seems we both should have been stronger and wiser."

Eli stood and faced Luther, searching his eyes. "Perhaps after forty-five years it is time Jacob knew the truth. Maybe it is time he met his real father."

Luther held up his hand. "No. No, Eli. You are his real father. And you always will be." Luther had regained control of himself. "One day, you and I will have to stand before our Maker and atone for our sins of omission. At least in that moment, we'll know that this time we were strong for Ellie's sake."

Eli absorbed Luther's words. "Perhaps you are right. Jacob is the best of us, Luther, your family and mine. Perhaps nothing is to be gained by burdening him with our mistakes."

"What about Letta, Eli?"

"Letta is a good woman," Eli said. "But, of course, you would know that from the old days. She was never able to have children and has seen Jacob as God's gift to her. She is at peace with all that has happened."

That being said, both men nodded to each other. It seemed an air of completion now washed over the conversation, and we all stood, silent and reflective. But Luther had one final request.

"Eli, do you suppose there is any chance I might meet him, and see his children?"

Eli thought for a moment. "Yes," he said quietly. "Yes, there is. Jacob's daughter, Rebecca, is getting married in two weeks." He shook his head, mildly amused. "Rebecca looks like your mother, Luther. She is an exact replica. I even called her Evangeline once in front of everyone. Letta nearly fainted." The two men shared an amused smile.

"Anyway," Eli continued, "Dr. Bradford is invited. Come with him as his guest."

It took a few seconds before I realized what Eli had said. "Oh, well, okay. I guess we'll be there."

Once again, the three of us stood silently. Then slowly, Luther held out his hand. Eli looked at it for a moment and then extended his. The two men shook, regarding each other with a quiet respect. And yet there was something else too. It was something in their eyes; perhaps a momentary spark, a subtle communication that only they understood. And in that moment, it seemed they were boys again, sharing the unspoken language of mischievous youth.

I led Eli to an exam room and checked his vision. It wasn't as bad as I had expected, but cataract surgery was still likely in his future. Afterward, I escorted him to the waiting room, where Jacob invited me to Rebecca's wedding, completely unaware of the conversation that had transpired minutes earlier. I asked if I could bring a friend. He agreed, they left, and I returned to my office, where Luther had waited to talk to me.

I took a seat behind my desk, delighted with the turn of events. Luther sat quietly in one of the wingback chairs. He allowed me a brief moment of smug but polite triumph before speaking. "I, um, I'm indebted to you, Doctor. Tremendously."

I nodded. Having Luther in my debt was such a splendid feeling, it was difficult to suppress the erupting smirk that so desperately wanted to emerge. But I managed. Luther continued.

"I've got a lot to think about, a lot of past mistakes to atone for. But, like I said, I owe you, Luke."

"Luther, you can start by keeping your eye appointments. I'm sure I'll think of something else along the way. But we'll start there."

I stood and we shook hands. But as I walked him to the door, he had a question for me.

"Bradford. I'm curious about something. How did you ever connect me with the cottage ruins on Mercy Creek Road?"

"The daisies."

"The daisies?"

"Yeah, from last May. I saw you walk out of the flower shop with a bouquet of daisies. Later that day, I saw daisies on the hearth at the ruins."

"Really? There were daisies on the hearth?"

"Well, yeah. Didn't you put them there?"

"Daisies were, in fact, Ellie's favorite flower. However, not to burst your bubble, but I buy daisies every May twenty-seventh to put on my mother's grave. It was the day she died. I haven't been out to Mercy Creek Road in thirty years."

Soon afterward, Luther departed, leaving me with many questions still unanswered.

CHAPTER 41
Bracken's Knoll

Later that day I left work shortly after five, delightfully anticipating meeting up with Christine. The hectic week had flown by, and the two of us hadn't seen each other since Saturday night and the abrupt departure from the dance. But seeing her wasn't going to happen. I called her while walking to my car, and she was on her way back to school for parent-teacher conferences that evening. I was leaving early in the morning to drive to Atlanta and planned to spend the night there. Our time together would have to wait.

There was something unsettling about our brief conversation on the phone. Christine's responses seemed clipped, distracted, and numerous times she told me she loved me. This was always wonderful to hear, but it seemed she couldn't say it enough. I told her I loved her too and asked if everything was okay.

"Everything's fine," she answered. "I just miss you a lot, that's all."

I was unconvinced, but there was little else I could do. "I'll be back early Saturday afternoon. We'll make up for lost time then."

"Yeah," she said sweetly. "That sounds great."

We hung up, and I considered driving over to the school to

catch her between meetings and surprise her with a hug and a smile. It was a pleasant idea, but I decided against it. She would be busy, and I needed to pack. Come Saturday, we would have the world to ourselves.

The next morning, the drive to Atlanta felt longer than it should have. Shortly after one o'clock, I met the moving company men at the storage facility. Several fifteen-by-thirty-foot climate-controlled rooms held all my worldly possessions, or at least all the worldly possessions belonging to my late aunt and parents. The storage units were paid for in a yearly draft out of my parents' estate. The summer before I had started med school at Vanderbilt was the last time I had been here. What with med school, residency, and my year in Watervalley, eight years had passed.

I had conveniently tucked away these huge chapters of my life, endeavoring to look forward rather than back. It had been my way of putting painful realities behind me. But as I rolled up the first of the large entry doors, the dormant air from all those enclosed years poured over me and brought with it a thousand memories. Oddly, they were sweet and comforting. And as the men moved patiently around boxes and furniture to locate the things I wanted, I began to understand the anchoring strength that these possessions had always provided me. The passing years had managed to ease the pain of my loss. But these things remained, and they served as reminders of the happy times of my youth.

In the years since I had last been here, I had been adrift, always scheming toward a richer, fuller tomorrow. Looking back, I realized that I had partly been in a great sleep, shutting off parts of my life. Yet now it seemed I had found my roots again, awakened to a world that had been strong and beautiful from days gone by. It was a strange and consoling revelation.

I pointed out to the moving company men the few pieces of

furniture I wanted shipped to Watervalley. Then I spent several hours rummaging through stacks of boxes, looking for the other items I wanted. In time, I found all of them: the family photo albums, my dad's journal along with my own journal, and my mother's jewelry box. It was nearing six o'clock when I pulled the last storage door shut and locked up.

I drove by my aunt's old house where I had lived as a teenager and past my old prep school where I had starred in basketball. Not surprisingly, they weren't quite as I remembered them. And yet, the memories were good ones. I grabbed some dinner and found my hotel, eager to spend time in a long conversation with Christine.

But she never answered the phone.

With the first call I left a message, assuming she would get back to me shortly. When an hour passed with no response, I called again, only to get her voice mail. I gave it a few minutes and called the landline at her mother's house. The answering machine picked up. I left a message there as well. I sent her numerous text messages, but these also received no response.

Slowly, the nagging progression of emotions began. First came curiosity, followed by worry, then anxiety and aggravation. I went to the hotel bar and drank a beer, searching for a way to occupy myself until Christine called. But she never did.

By now it was well past ten o'clock. I thought about phoning Connie. I doubted she would know anything, but she would calm my concerns and possibly offer an explanation. But the hour was late. I would just have to wait.

I was up and on the road by seven the next morning. There was an hour difference between Atlanta and home, so I waited patiently before calling. A little after eight o'clock Watervalley time, I dialed Christine's number.

Again, voice mail. It was maddening. My mind bounced between burning annoyance and sickening worry. All the possible explanations I could imagine went from bad to worse. I needed to be home, and now the long interstate miles seemed to drag on in monotonous, endless anticipation.

By midmorning I was two hours out and there was still no word. I pulled the car over and called Connie. At first she spoke lightly, endeavoring to mollify my feverish apprehension. But I persisted, and she offered to get in touch with Christine and have her call me. I thanked her and hung up, certain that soon my phone would ring and all would be fine. But another hour of driving passed in silence. I waited another thirty minutes and called Connie again. This time she didn't answer.

I scorched the road over the last miles into Watervalley, pushing the engine of the Austin-Healey to its limits. I was furious, scared, sick beyond words. I raced down Fleming Street and into my driveway. Connie's car was parked there. I was racked with the nauseating conviction that whatever the next minutes held, they would not be good.

Connie was sitting silently at the kitchen table, leaning forward and resting her elbows with her fingers slightly interlocked and tented, as if she had been praying. She turned and looked at me, her face framed in sadness.

"Sit down, Luke. I need to talk to you."

My fear and anger were obvious. "I'm not sitting, Connie. Tell me what's happened to Christine."

She nodded. "Christine is okay. But there's a problem."

"What?" I practically shouted. "What has happened that she can't talk to me about it?"

"After you and I talked, I called her. We spoke for quite a while. She got some pretty devastating news, and I think it has broken her in two. She didn't know how to tell you, especially not over the phone. I offered to talk to you. At first she said no, then she said sure. I believe she doesn't know what to think or say right now."

"Tell me what's happened, Connie."

"She's been having some problems lately; she's missed her cycle for several months." Connie paused and tilted her head slightly. "You're a doctor. . . . You understand what I'm talking about."

I nodded.

"Just before you two were engaged, she went to a gynecologist in Nashville, and they ran some tests. They found a problem with her hormone levels. They told her not to worry and to come back in a month so they could run a second set of tests. She didn't want to say anything to you before she knew there was really an issue. But she looked up the possibilities, and it's had her pretty worried this past week. Yesterday she went back for the second round of blood work, and the results weren't good. Apparently she has something called premature ovarian failure. Luke, she may never be able to have children."

I said nothing. After all the anxiety, all the fear, all the anguish of the last twenty-four hours, I simply shut down. It was my emotional fail-safe. I stared at Connie blankly. A thousand thoughts and feelings were pinging for my attention. I closed them out.

I spoke barely above a whisper. "Where was she when you talked to her, Connie?"

"Home. It was about an hour ago. She said she wanted to be alone and that she was going somewhere on the back of the farm."

I knew where Christine had gone. Without thinking to thank Connie, I turned and left. Numb to all the world around me, I started the engine and drove to Summerfield Road.

After parking the car at Christine's house, I headed across the open pastures and far reaches of the farm to a small rise called Bracken's Knoll. I had only a general sense of where it was located, so after crossing several broad fields, I called out for her.

"Christine, Christine, Christine . . ."

In the near distance, I saw her appear upon the crest of a low, treeless mound. I walked briskly up the slow rise and stopped several feet from her.

My words were wooden, void of emotion. "Why didn't you tell me?"

Her face was red and swollen from long fits of crying. The overcast October sky was cheerless, cold, unforgiving. She gasped deeply of the frigid air, heaving great breaths in and out. "Please don't be mad at me. Please don't be mad."

I said nothing. I only stared at her, standing there shivering in the tall orchard grass, frightened, distraught, waiting. The sleeves of her sweater were pulled over her hands, and her arms were folded around her stomach in an effort to contain her deep wailing sobs.

"Talk to me, Christine. Tell me everything."

CHAPTER 42
This Life

Her lips were quivering. Against her stilted, choppy breaths and the flood of tears, Christine bawled out her words. "It isn't fair," she cried. "It just isn't fair."

Weeping uncontrollably, she cupped her fingers over her mouth. I stepped toward her, but she held out her hand stiffly, signaling me to keep away. Her words were a muddle of defeat and rage. "I spent all these years trying to keep my dreams safe, trying to follow this—this ideal, and for what? I've just been stupid, completely, totally stupid."

"Don't say that," I said firmly.

"And why not?" she snapped back in her anger. "Look at the two of us. I mean, what's been the point of our holding off . . . like there would be some cosmic reward?"

I spoke calmly. "Is that what last weekend was all about?"

"What do you mean?"

"Is that why you were upset all day? Why you offered to make love? Because you were worried and angry at what the test results would show?"

She wiped the tears from her cheeks and folded her arms again. She said nothing but nodded her head in short, jerky movements.

I exhaled a heavy sigh and looked away. "You can't do that, Christine. You can't draw a circle in the dirt and leave me out of it."

"I was afraid."

"Afraid of what?"

"I didn't want to disappoint you."

"In what possible way?"

"By not being able to have children and then on top of that by being this foolish idealist. By cheating both of us out of so much. And for what? All these years of keeping this stupid promise to myself and the whole time the joke's been on me."

She burst into another gasping round of fitful sobs. Again, I endeavored to move closer, but she turned her back to me and stepped away. I stuck my hands into my coat pockets and stood there, giving her time. Finally, I walked around in front of her, crossed my arms, and stood patiently.

"What do you want, Christine?"

She gazed into my expressionless eyes, and her torrent of words poured out in an almost breathless whisper. "I want you to love me," she said. "I want you to please love me. Just as I am . . . broken, afraid, foolish. Because if you can't do that, if you think there's ever a chance that the day will come when you wake up and regret this moment, then I want you to just walk away, Luke Bradford. Just please, walk away."

I stood there like a ghost. Wisps of our breath vanished illusively into the frigid air, our voices swallowed into the vast landscape. The distant, shouldering hills, which had always been strong and protective, now seemed raw, cold, indifferent. She looked desperately into my face, searching. Finally, she could take it no longer.

The last of her anger had been wrenched from her, leaving her frail and vanquished. She pleaded, "Luke, talk to me. Tell me what will happen."

I stared for one final time into the far-flung expanse of Watervalley. Then I spoke the difficult words that needed to be said.

"This is our life, Christine. Despite all we do, all we plan, all we prepare, this stupid, broken world will find new reasons for us to say the hell with it and walk away." I folded my arms and paused.

"Ever since I was a kid and lost my parents, I've been either building walls or walking away. Eight years ago, I walked away from my parents' possessions because it was too painful to see them. I went to med school and built a wall of textbooks around me. Then I came here to Watervalley. And sure, I have to admit, every single day for the first six months, I thought about walking away. I thought about going back to Vanderbilt and doing research in a lab where I could control everything, where life could be planned out, made predictable." Still holding my emotions in check, I turned and looked into her eyes, so full of pain and loss.

"But then I met you. And that changed everything."

The broad, cold landscape of Bracken's Knoll was held in an echoless silence, awaiting my next words. I spoke with tenderness, with a voice that was unhurried, resolute. "So here's how it's going to be. You and I will get married, and if we never have children, so be it. If we never have money, so be it. If you get sick and I spend the rest of my life taking care of you, so be it. If all our days are filled with one hardship after another, so be it."

My emotions were overtaking me, choking me, consuming me. They welled up from all the buried years. I struggled to quell them, but it was little use. Tears rolled down my face, and I began to breathe in great gasps.

"If that is my fate, if that is my life, if that is my portion in this world, then so be it. Each night I will go to bed and count myself blessed."

Christine's tear-filled face was fearful, confused. "Why?" she whispered softly. "How can you say that?"

"Because I found you. Because out of the millions and millions of possibilities of where my life could have gone, I found you." I drew in a deep breath, probing her face.

"Don't you understand? There will never be another love. There will never be another life. There will only be you."

She glanced at me before looking to the side, speaking in a voice both uncertain and defiant. "You're just saying these things, Luke. I want to believe you, but I don't."

She was still consumed by her pain, desperately searching for some idea, some thought, some revelation that would suddenly reverse this harsh new reality and leave her dreams intact.

But there were none.

She spoke despondently. "Maybe you should just leave."

"That's not happening."

"What if I want you to?" she said.

"Then I'll wait."

She was still shivering, her arms folded tightly around her stomach. "I don't understand."

"I'll wait," I said gently. "I'll wait until you're ready. I'll wait until you're certain. I'll wait until you say yes again. I'm not walking away. I'm not leaving. For as long as it takes, I will wait."

Christine's face was drained and fragile. She spoke in a pleading whisper. "But why? Why would you want to? Why would you do that?"

I stepped toward her, smoothing the hair away from her face. "Because I've come to realize that waiting is the greatest test of love. You taught me that. You waited for me, Christine Chambers. So I will wait for you."

She wrapped her arms around my neck, weeping into my shoulder. I held her tightly and whispered the promises of my heart. "Sometimes, Christine, we just have to write our own happy endings."

With her eyes closed and her face pressed tightly against me, she murmured, "Tell me you love me, again."

"I do, Christine. I love you with all my heart."

In time her tears ended, and she reached up and wiped my face with her fingers.

"I've never seen you cry this way," she said hesitantly. "I'm sorry."

I nodded.

"How did you know where to find me?"

"Connie said you had gone somewhere on the farm. John once told me that when you were young you spent a lot of time at a place called Bracken's Knoll."

Her voice was low and soft. "I used to come here and write in my journal. It was always my favorite place on the farm, my safe place. I would sit out here and live in my dreams."

"What happened to them?"

"Oh," she said carefully, "I never really forgot them. I just got better at hiding them. Silly, I guess. But maybe that's what all girls do with their dreams."

Again, I smoothed her hair away and kissed her forehead before looking into the mysterious, undiscovered depths of her dark eyes. "I want to know your dreams, Christine. I want to be part of them."

She pressed her cheek against my chest and whispered tenderly, "You already are, Luke. You already are."

CHAPTER 43
Fathers and Sons

In the days that followed, I spent every spare moment researching premature ovarian failure. Given Christine's age and overall excellent health, there was still a reasonable hope that we might have our own children. But in the end, I told her it simply didn't matter. One way or another, we would have a houseful.

Even so, despite my constant reassurances and all the encouraging data available about overcoming the condition, the light in her eyes had dimmed. It seemed that there was now a small, buried sadness that would forever stain her, a faintly whispered voice of loss that could be triggered by a child's laugh or a thoughtless word. She would never speak of it, but I could read it in the tightening of her gaze or the line of her smile. It would remain a silent understanding between two people who shared the joys and tears of a joined life.

I found myself daydreaming of magically protecting her, of changing the world and shielding her from this grief. But that was far beyond any present ability. In truth, my heart was broken for her, but I never made mention of this. Somehow even the knowledge that I was saddened for her, that her perceived failure gave me any distress at all, only brought her further dismay. It was a testimony to the beautiful complexity of a woman's emotions. I only knew to love her.

On Thursday of the following week, at my request, John Harris stopped by my office during lunchtime. He made no mention of Christine, which to my mind confirmed that he was unaware of her condition. John was too good a man and loved his niece too dearly to say nothing if, in fact, he knew. The Chamberses were guarded people, and no doubt Christine wanted the matter to remain private, even from her uncle.

As he walked into my office, John was in a cajoling, jovial mood. "Well, Doctor. What bit of worldly wisdom do you have for me today?"

I directed him toward one of the wingback chairs. "Have a seat, Professor. I have good news."

"Oh," he said drily. "You're not about to tell me that I've won a golden retriever puppy, are you?"

"As a matter of fact, no. But it's not a bad idea. There are still two available."

"We'll table that motion for now. So, what's the news?"

"I have the rest of the money for the statue fund. It came from a donor who wishes to remain anonymous."

"You're kidding. The full ten thousand?"

"The full ten thousand, in cash. I deposited it yesterday afternoon into the fund's bank account."

John was stunned. "That's pretty amazing." He cut his eyes at me warily. "You didn't do this, did you, Bradford? You know, tap into the trust fund?"

I laughed. "John, I can't touch the trust fund for a few more years. You know that."

He nodded. "So no hints as to the donor?"

"You are familiar with the definition of 'anonymous,' aren't you?"

"Yeah, yeah. Fine, smart-ass." John grinned, awash with delight. "This gives me a great idea."

"Why do I already not like the sound of that?"

"We've got three weeks until Veterans Day. I'll call the monument company and have the statue installed in time to have a huge unveiling." John's face lit up like an excited child's. He clapped his hands together. "You can give the address!"

I didn't share his enthusiasm. "If I have to make another speech before the entire town, the only address I'm giving is a forwarding one."

John waved his hand in dismissal. "Oh, stop your whining. You did fine with the high school graduation speech earlier this year."

He was referring to the previous May, when I had been asked to give the commencement address to Watervalley's graduating seniors, a dubious task that had required a lot of long and anxious hours of preparation.

"You weren't even there," I retorted.

"I was afraid I'd get too emotional."

"Funny."

"Come on, you're perfect."

"Not happening, John."

"You'll do a great job, Doc." He rose from his chair and began to leave. "Well, gotta run. I need to get with the mayor and start the ball rolling."

I endeavored to offer some further rebuttal, but John moved too quickly, waving good-bye before I could utter a word. Just before departing my office door, he turned and scrutinized me. "Might be good if you keep it under twenty minutes. It'll probably be cold outside."

With that, he was gone.

"Great, another speech," I muttered. It was the sort of thing that made me want to sit in a dark corner and whimper.

The following week, Luther and I rode together in his sedan out to Mennonite country to attend the wedding of Levi and Rebecca. And as if going to a wedding with Luther Whitmore weren't weird enough, the time and day of the wedding made the whole affair absolutely bizarre.

It was at nine o'clock on a Tuesday morning.

Apparently, Old Order Mennonite weddings were all-day affairs and never held on Saturday. Doing so would require cleanup work to be done on Sunday, which was set aside strictly for worship. Luther picked me up at my house. He was in a lighthearted mood, which I found slightly unnerving.

As we headed down Fleming Street and out of town, Luther broke the silence. "So, Doctor, you get the money deposited okay?"

"All ten grand, Luther."

"Hope I didn't startle you Monday night. It was just easier to bring it by after dark. I figured no one would notice."

"It was fine, Luther. I put it under my pillow. Slept like a baby."

"Good to know."

"Word about an anonymous donor giving ten thousand dollars to the statue fund is going to cause quite a bit of speculation. You might want to think about putting an article in the paper just to draw suspicion away from yourself."

"Bradford, I doubt I'll be on anybody's top-ten list for suspected generosity. Still, that's probably not a bad idea."

"Oh come on, Luther. Don't sell yourself short. The sunshine factor always jumps up a notch or two whenever you walk into the room."

Luther ignored my jab. As we drove deeper into the countryside and passed distant farmhouses, he began to tell fascinating stories from his childhood about people who had lived on and worked these large, rich fields. I listened intently and realized that even Luther Whitmore had an abiding love of Watervalley, which had remained unvanquished by his years of bitterness. Within the realm of this wide fertile plain was an enduring strength that permeated its inhabitants, consoling them, whispering into their souls, and in time, providing a source of healing. Luther was no exception to Watervalley's influence.

Soon we made our way down Mercy Creek Road. I wanted to ask Luther about the old ruins site, but his mood had turned apprehensive and he hurried past it.

Unlike their Amish cousins, the Mennonites didn't always conduct weddings and church services at home. Years ago, they had built a small chapel in their community. Luther knew its location. Ours was the only car among an extensive gathering of horses, buggies, and wagons. After he parked and turned off the engine, he fell silent, clearly worried.

I cut my eyes at him. "You going to be okay?"

His words were laced with uneasiness. "I think so. Thanks for doing this, Luke."

"Not a problem," I said, sensing his apprehension. "Come on. You'll be fine."

It was already a splendid October morning, but as we emerged from the car, it seemed that a golden light displaced the air. The scene before us was quaint to the point of being surreal. The humble, starched white church was perfectly beautiful.

We made our way toward a small gathering of men standing near the front steps. They were all dressed in black hats, plain black clothes, and unadorned white shirts. We were met with polite but expressionless faces until Eli emerged from the crowd and approached us. He shook my hand and then Luther's. Then he gestured us toward the other men. I quickly recognized Jacob, who looked up as we approached. Eli made the introductions.

"Jacob, you know the doctor." We shook hands.

"And this is Luther Whitmore. He is a family friend from years ago."

Jacob extended his hand and regarded Luther with civility. Luther, however, was fixated, staring at Jacob. Finally, Luther reached and took his hand; in that moment, something rather indefinable seemed to pass between them. Jacob's eyes tightened, and he held on to Luther's hand, unable to let go. It was as though an unseen energy now connected the two men. Despite all my medical training, I couldn't help but think that there was much that the universe had yet to tell us about the primal bond between father and son.

Luther finally choked out a low response. "It's, um, it's good to finally meet you."

Luther looked at me awkwardly. I put my hand on his shoulder and gently guided him toward the steps. We took a seat on the back row, not wanting to draw attention to ourselves. Luther was clearly shaken but seemed to gather himself once we were settled.

In time, Levi emerged from a side door near the front. He was well groomed and eager, but stiffer than a fence post.

Minutes later Rebecca appeared, wearing a plain, light blue dress and a black bonnet; in keeping with conservative Mennonite custom, she wasn't carrying any flowers. Even so, she was radiant and Luther was visibly dumbstruck. His eyes were open, but he seemed to be looking at her from some great depth, lost in a welling-up of memories summoned forth in a grand moment of inexplicable peace. Ultimately, he looked at me with all-consuming gratitude. I was happy for him.

But I wasn't happy for me.

Mennonite weddings are largely church services, and they last three hours. By the time it was finally over, I thought that Levi and Rebecca had visibly aged in front of me. Afterward, Luther and I hung around outside to speak with the bride and groom, thinking it best not to participate in the reception at Jacob's home. To my surprise, as the couple departed the church, Rebecca was presented with a beautiful bouquet of flowers. They were daisies.

I shook Levi's hand, and he thanked me for coming. I started to take Rebecca's hand as well but stopped, unsure what was appropriate with Mennonite women. She read my hesitation and swallowed a short laugh, her dark eyes mysterious. She smiled at me, and I felt my face flush. It was easy to see that she had a beauty and a wisdom that belied her age, yet all the while I was reminded that she was the perfect replica of Evangeline Whitmore, Luther's mother.

Luther introduced himself, offering congratulations to Levi and making a few comments about having known Eli when they were young boys. He then turned to Rebecca and was uncharacteristically tongue-tied. Finally he said words that he'd clearly practiced, though they were still poorly delivered. "I knew your—your great-aunt Ellie as well. She was . . . She was a lovely and good person."

Rebecca nodded silently and respectfully. I couldn't help but wonder at her thoughts, and if she wanted to hear more about this lost person from her past. As well, I could tell that Luther desperately wanted to talk to her, to stare at her, his grandchild, to perhaps even hold her hand.

But he kept himself in check. He nodded to both of them and then to me. Before departing, I spoke to Jacob one final time.

"Congratulations, Jacob. It was a lovely ceremony."

He smiled at my poor attempt at diplomacy. "It was painfully long, Dr. Bradford. And you are kind for speaking considerately."

"Either way, I'm happy for them." We both turned and gazed

at the young couple, who were surrounded by well-wishers. "Jacob, I'm curious," I said, stepping closer to him. "Where did you find fresh daisies this late in the year?"

"Hannah grows them. We have a small greenhouse."

I nodded. "Levi told me they are going to build next year on the property along Mercy Creek Road."

"Yes, my aunt's place."

"Beautiful setting. I actually stopped and walked around the old foundation earlier this year. Wonderful place for a young couple."

Jacob nodded. A subtle question gathered in his eyes, as if he detected something intentional in my comment. There was.

"Funny thing, Jacob. When I stopped by there last spring, someone had left some freshly picked daisies on the hearth. Any idea who that might have been?"

He seemed slightly embarrassed. "That was me, Dr. Bradford. When I was a boy, each year around my aunt's and father's birthday, he and I would walk out to the old foundation. He would pick daisies, lay them on the hearth, and talk to me about his sister. They were twins, and I think he loved her very much. He has often said he wished I could have known her. So each spring I still put flowers on the hearth in her honor." He turned toward Eli, who stood several feet away talking to Luther, and added, "Over the years, my father has told me many things about my aunt, many stories, and many secrets from their childhood."

Jacob fell silent, and part of me couldn't help but wonder if he knew Ellie was his biological mother, if somehow over the years he had read the burden on Eli's heart to tell the truth, much in the same way Luther had unknowingly given me clues. His penetrating gaze at Luther seemed to confirm my suspicion, but he said nothing more. I would never know for sure.

I bid Jacob good-bye and joined Luther and Eli, who was

introducing Jacob's two younger boys to his old friend. The youths nodded politely and then dashed away, no doubt desiring to be first in the line for food.

As the two men shook hands one final time, Luther inquired, "Perhaps someday I can come and visit . . . for old times' sake."

Eli held on to Luther's hand and nodded. "Perhaps."

Even so, I could see in their eyes that both knew a return visit would likely never happen. There passed between these two childhood friends a final acknowledgment of who they once were and how their lives had been both wondrously and tragically entwined. But they belonged to different worlds, and both of them knew it.

As we walked back to the car, the crushing weight of Luther's painful life poured over me. To think that his son and grandchildren were living less than twenty-five miles away and yet he would likely never see them again seemed a terrible penance. But rather than looking miserable, Luther appeared divinely at peace, as if he were closing up a long-suffered wound. The one thing that Luther and Eli still shared was a love of Ellie Yoder. For her cherished and untarnished memory to remain intact, it was best to leave matters as they were. My heart went out to him.

On our return trip down Mercy Creek Road, I asked Luther if he minded stopping at the site of the ruins. He seemed glad to oblige.

He pulled only a few feet down the long drive and stopped the car. For a full minute we sat in silence, absorbing the view of this enchanted meadow and its surrounding hills.

"Levi told me that he and Rebecca are going to build here in the spring," I said.

Luther seemed pleased. "Ellie would like that. It's only right that her granddaughter should rebuild out of the ashes and live a happy life here."

A question struck me. "Luther, you know everything about this place. Who originally built this house?"

"No idea. It was abandoned for years before the Yoder family bought it. There's an old story that the guy who built it was at one time engaged to my grandmother."

"So I take it he wasn't your grandfather?"

"No, he was some fellow who died soon after their engagement. I don't know if he was killed in a farming accident or what. After several years, my grandmother met and married my grandfather. She died when my mom was three. Anyway, as the story goes, the fellow who built this place wrote her a bunch of poems. She had them made into a book. It's in the Watervalley library."

A memory fluttered. "What was the name of the book?"

"I believe it's called *Poems to Sylvia*. That was my grandmother's name."

"I think I've seen it. Will Fox was reading it on his front porch a while back."

Luther shrugged. "I remember seeing it once years ago, but I don't remember much about it."

"And you don't remember the name of the guy who wrote the poems?"

"Love poems from one of your grandmother's old boyfriends aren't exactly memorable stuff, Doctor."

"Point taken."

In time we left and Luther drove me to the clinic where, no doubt, a waiting room full of patients was anxiously anticipating my arrival. Luther got out of the car and walked around to shake my hand one last time.

"So, what's next?" I said.

"I'm leaving town for a few days. There's something I need to do. Someone I need to go see." His words seemed intentionally guarded, so I didn't inquire further.

Luther filled in the silence. "I know I've said this before, Luke, but I owe you. If there's ever anything you need me to do, just let me know."

I stared at him for a moment, and then a thought occurred to me. "Luther, you know there is one thing that does come to mind." Then another idea hit me, and I spoke hesitantly. "Actually . . . two."

CHAPTER 44

Beacon Road

The early days of November had been cool but unseasonably dry. My morning runs began in darkness, and along the way I would quietly watch the drowsy countryside awaken. As the first delicate light of morning pushed away the shadows, tatters of white fog could be seen nestled in the low-lying fields and along the creek banks. And by the time I made my way toward home, the sun had scaled the eastern hills, catching the morning sky on fire.

With each passing day, it seemed that Christine regained more of the joy for life that had always defined her. Despite the devastating news about her medical condition, she was courageously finding the resolve to hope. On a few occasions she even asked me about some of the articles she had read in online medical journals. Perhaps the best part of her willingness to talk was that she was beginning to understand the depth of my love for her, that this setback was our challenge together, not hers alone. On that heart-rending afternoon at Bracken's Knoll, I had never considered that this beautiful woman's greatest distress was her fear of losing me. It was a reality that I doubted I would ever completely understand.

Even so, she would occasionally tease that perhaps we should run off and elope so that we could start the whole baby factory process sooner. Admittedly, as a guy with a firm aversion to ceremony and on the heels of a three-hour Mennonite wedding, I found this idea had merit on several levels. Christine was as beautiful as ever, my blood was still decidedly red, and my passion for her was ever present.

On Thursday of the first week of November, Beatrice McClanahan came to the clinic complaining about an assortment of aches and pains. Her slightly disheveled appearance was a departure from her usual spruced-up and tidy manner. She was also quite liberated from her normally polite reserve and ranted on about everything.

She started with how stupidity was more and more in unlimited supply and how her neighbor had the brain-wave activity of a stapler. She progressed to the poor shape of her maple trees and when the sap would run, or not run, or simply jog in place. I listened as best I could but it was exhausting. Then a simple reality occurred to me. Beatrice was still full of life, but she was lonely and bored.

When she finally stopped to take a breath, I asked, "Beatrice, what would you think about providing a home to two wonderful puppies?"

Later that afternoon I brought the two remaining progeny of Rhett and Maggie's union to Beatrice's house. Earlier that morning, the friend who had driven Beatrice to the clinic had volunteered to take her by the Farmers Co-op, where she had loaded up on puppy food, puppy toys, puppy beds, and a fifty-five-gallon barrel of puppy love, figuratively speaking. As I handed the two squirming fellows to her, she was bubbling over with pure delight and laughing to the point of giddiness. Her animated face was a study of faultless devotion. She talked nonstop into the sweet, expressive brown eyes of her new canine companions. For Beatrice, it seemed like a day trip to heaven.

When I left her house, a good two hours of daylight still remained. The glaring reminder of Beatrice's loneliness made me think about Leyland Carter. He had mentioned having been in the war, and it occurred to me that it would be fully proper for him to be included in the assembly of veterans being recognized at the upcoming Veterans Day ceremony. After only a moment's deliberation, I headed out the east road to pay him a visit.

Twenty minutes later, I was inching the Austin-Healey down Leyland's ragged and partially washed-out driveway. I parked in the small grassy area in front of his house and, as I had done before, I called out to him as I approached the porch steps. The day was cold, but the late-afternoon sun was sharply bright, cutting brilliantly through the bare trees. The added light gave the dilapidated shack an eerie illumination.

More than ever, this rude cottage seemed to convey an air of desertion. I called out several times but was met with only the faint echo of my own voice resonating through the nearby woods. Repeated raps on the front door yielded neither sound nor movement from within. Leyland simply wasn't here; truthfully, the place looked like no one had been there for some time.

As I was turning to leave, I caught a glint of sunlight reflecting off the porch rocking chair. I stepped closer and was instantly dumbstruck. On the seat were the five pieces of wrapped peppermint that I had left there weeks earlier. This made no sense. Surely Leyland would have found them. A list of distressing possibilities began to nag at me. Had he fallen in the woods? Had he died in his sleep? No answers seemed like good ones.

I walked around the house and checked the doors and windows.

All were locked tight. His old truck still sat tiredly, covered in a blanket of rotting leaves. I stood silently, waiting, listening. Briefly, from somewhere in the distant woods I could have sworn I heard a man singing. It struck me as the same tune I had heard at the ruins on Mercy Creek Road months earlier. It lasted only half a minute and then faded. I called out a few more times, but to no avail.

I tried my cell phone, but there was still no service in this remote corner of the valley. I needed to contact Sheriff Thurman and get him along with the EMTs to investigate further. After stepping briskly to the car, I wheeled it around and bumped my way back out Leyland's driveway. As I made the turn onto Beacon Road, a car was approaching from the opposite direction. The driver recognized the Austin-Healey and pulled to a stop. I slowed up as well. It was Joe Dawson, the pastor from Watervalley First Presbyterian.

Riding in the passenger seat was none other than Leonard Lineberry, the full-time EMT and part-time preacher. In the past months the two of them had struck up a regular friendship based on their shared love of ministry. No doubt, Leonard found much to learn from Joe's seminary training, and Joe delighted in having a connection with someone who knew every soul in Watervalley, lost, found, or hiding. Joe rolled down his window, and we chatted in the middle of the remote highway.

Leonard spoke first. "Doc, what in the world are you doing out here and coming out of that old place? You trying to get a little gravel in your travel?"

"I came to see Leyland Carter."

"Leyland who?"

"Leyland Carter." Both men offered no response. "You remember, Joe. He was the fellow you asked me to check on when you stopped by the clinic last summer. We talked about him at the July Fourth celebration."

Joe looked lost and turned toward Leonard. Leonard placed his hand on the dash and leaned across Joe to speak to me. "Doc, are you looking for Lester Carter? He lives up the road a few miles. We're on our way to see him. Lester's pretty old and rusted out with lung disease, so Joe and I have made it a point to see him together."

"No," I responded immediately. "No, I'm talking about Leyland Carter. He's clearly an older fellow, but he definitely doesn't have COPD. Leyland is as fit as a fiddle."

Joe snapped his fingers and pointed at me. "You know, Luke, I remember the conversation you're talking about now. This may be my mistake. The fellow I was asking about was Lester Carter. I must have gotten the names confused."

"But that doesn't make any sense, because I've visited Leyland Carter out here a couple of times."

Leonard spoke cautiously. "Doc, are you talking about the place you just pulled out of?"

"Yeah, why?"

"Because that's the old Jamison place. Nobody's lived in that run-down shack for twenty years."

I shook my head. "Leonard, that can't be right. Like I said, I've been out to that house a couple of times before and talked with the guy who lives there. He said his name is Leyland Carter. And candidly, fellows, I'm a little worried about him right now. I just left there, and he's not answering the door. I'm afraid something may have happened to him."

Leonard was about to speak again, but Joe stopped him. He regarded me gravely. "Luke, I'm not sure how to tell you this, but whoever you were meeting with at that place wasn't Leyland Carter. I remember that name now. For some reason, Leyland Carter got left on the church rolls as an active member. But he died almost a hundred years ago."

CHAPTER 45
String of Pearls

We chatted for another minute or so before continuing on our separate ways, but I was resolved that some misunderstanding had occurred. Admittedly, Leyland Carter was a curious, elusive fellow, but he had been very real. It still troubled me that perhaps I should call the sheriff and investigate further. But with detached certitude, Leonard had reaffirmed his conviction that no one had lived at the old shack for some time. His steadfast insistence convinced me not to take immediate action. I looked at my watch and decided to head for home. For the first time since my return from Atlanta, Connie was cooking dinner for me. The two of us had much to talk about.

The slanting light of sunset spread before me as I made the lonely drive back to Fleming Street. The confusion of the previous hour troubled me. From deep within, the small, rational voice that served me so well in making patient assessments was casting doubt about all that I felt I knew regarding Leyland. I dismissed these thoughts, relegating them to the blur of a long and weary day.

Nightfall came quickly. By the time I reached home, a low

luster of moonlight had appeared. After pulling into my drive, the glow through the windows of my quaint little house, along with the anticipation of Connie's cooking, returned me to a lighter mood.

I found her in the kitchen, talking to Rhett and the newest member of my family, Casper, one of the male puppies. Rhett was lying forlornly on the kitchen floor and enduring an onslaught of nips and assaults from his wildly energetic offspring. Apparently, Connie shared my belief that Rhett had a full command of the English language. She was in rare form, preaching to him about the wages of sin.

"Umm-hmm, that's right, big fellow. You let a moment of unbridled passion get the best of you, and now look what 'chu got to put up with. I'm guessing the expression 'Every dog has his day' isn't such a proud mantra for you anymore. Humph, I'd say you need to be wagging your tail to the tune of 'Who's Sorry Now.'"

Rhett looked dolefully at me as if to say, *Please shoot me.*

Content that she had made her point, Connie turned to me. "Evening, sweetie. I was taking the opportunity to have a little teachable moment with Mr. Rhett here."

"So I heard. You know, Connie, I hate to tell you this, but I think Rhett operates on the theory that all dogs go to heaven. I'm not sure your lecture is going to yield the intended results."

"Humph," she snorted in response. "Doesn't hurt him to have someone hold up a light to his actions."

"You can't put all of this on Rhett. Seems to me the lady might have been willing."

Connie cut her eyes at me. "We're not going there, Luke Bradford. This is the South, and we don't impugn a young lady's virtue."

I laughed, holding up my hands in surrender. "Fair enough. I give."

Connie responded with a firm nod and seemed loaded for further evangelizing. I quickly changed the subject.

"So, what's for dinner?"

"Meat loaf, corn, and black-eyed peas. Get yourself washed. We've got a lot of catching up to do."

Five minutes later I was deep into the ecstasy of Connie's cooking. Having lured me into a state of slight euphoria, she went for the jugular with her first question. "So, Doctor, explain to me how it came to pass that you and Luther attended a Mennonite wedding together."

"I guess you saw where Luther put a short write-up about the wedding in the paper," I responded. I'd been as surprised as anyone to see the article. It seemed that Luther couldn't stop from making mention of his beautiful granddaughter's wedding, a relationship that was obviously not disclosed. Still, he clearly was risking the possibility that suspicions would be raised, especially given Luther's previous rants about the Mennonites.

"Yes, I did. What was that all about?" Connie persisted.

"I was invited and Luther wanted to come along. I guess he wrote the article as a piece of local color."

"Umm-hmm," Connie responded, unconvinced. "That's difficult to swallow. Usually Luther is more interested in off-color. He sure seems to have changed his attitude toward the Mennonite community."

I made no response, knowing that the least said was easiest defended. Still, Connie wasn't buying.

"Okay, tell me the real reason you took Luther along."

"Well, Mrs. Thompson, as you know, Luther was a boyhood friend with Eli Yoder. Years ago they had a falling-out. Both men have been to see me about problems with their eyesight. It occurred to me that along with their physical loss of vision, perhaps they had been blind to each other. So I arranged something of a reconciliation."

Having offered this information, I said nothing more, certain that Connie would understand two things. First, that I wasn't telling everything and second, that I couldn't.

Connie possessed an unfathomable capacity for insight. In the silence that ensued, it occurred to me that it was perhaps no accident that she was lecturing Rhett about his untimely consummation with Maggie at the exact moment I happened to arrive in the kitchen. This uncannily mirrored Luther Whitmore's story, even to the detail of not casting aspersions on Ellie Yoder. Yet again, it may have all been a coincidence.

Connie took a sip of tea and brooded. Then, it seemed, she deliberately turned and looked at Rhett for a few seconds. Afterward, she nodded her head lightly, signaling that the matter was closed. She spoke tenderly on a different matter. "Tell me how things are with you and Christine."

"It's been tough on her. There's a lot to process. But I've done everything I can to let her know it's all going to be okay, whatever the outcome."

"You know her aunt Molly, John's wife, couldn't have children and Christine is an only child."

"Yeah, I guess, considering her family history, her condition should have come as no big surprise."

"When she and I talked on that day you were driving back from Atlanta, she mentioned that you told her you wanted a lot of children. Five or six, I believe she said."

"That would be true." I hesitated a moment. "And one way or another, we can still have five or six children. I guess our home may end up looking like a miniature United Nations."

Connie's eyes softened momentarily, regarding me with clear admiration. Then she lifted her chin in an expression of hard resolve. "You're a good man, Luke Howard Bradford. This may sound awfully strange coming from me, but I'm going to tell you something, and, sweetie, you need to listen up good."

I nodded, curious as to what was on her mind.

"I didn't have four children by sitting in a pumpkin patch."

"Meaning?"

"Meaning, I've been reading up on premature ovarian failure. Youth is still on Christine's side."

I shrugged. "Yeah, that's largely true."

"Well, I know the two of you are trying to do the right thing and holding off till marriage. Don't ask me how I know. . . . I just know. Now don't get me wrong—I respect your choices, and I love you both deeply for it. But at the same time, part of me thinks that maybe the two of you need to just run off and get married, find yourself a room, and don't come up for air for about a week to ten days. Heavens, boy, your hormones are probably so backed up, I'm surprised you still have the power of speech."

I laughed outright, unable to contain myself from the odd mix of love and candor in Connie's words.

"Connie, the thought has crossed our minds." I paused for a moment. "But here's the deal. I'm in love with her. And I know she's always dreamed about having a big wedding with all of her friends and family present. Say we eloped and next June arrived and she still wasn't pregnant . . . then where would we be? As far as the two of us having our own children . . . well, that dream may be taken away. But the big church wedding is a dream of hers that I can help make happen. So, we'll wait until next June. At least, that's the plan." I paused, grunting a quick laugh. "Unless, of course, my hormones come up with a better one."

Connie patted my hand and nodded proudly. "All right then, sweetie. That's the way it will be."

The look on her face reminded me of something very important that I had failed to remember. "Oh my gosh. I almost forgot. Wait right here."

I went upstairs to search the boxes that I had brought back from Atlanta. After finding what I was looking for, I bounded back down the stairs and pulled my chair adjacent to Connie's. "I've got something here I want you to have." I placed the felt-covered jewelry box in her hand.

Connie looked at me dumbfounded. "Luke, what on earth?"

"Take it. Go ahead," I said.

She looked at me blankly before slowly opening the small container. Carefully, she lifted the long string of elegant white pearls. "Luke Bradford! Honey, I don't understand."

"They belonged to my mom. She wore them all the time, and I used to tease her about them. She wore them to church, to my ball games, everywhere. Anyway, I want you to have them."

Connie shook her head. "Luke, honey, I can't take these."

"And why not?"

Her words held a full measure of tender instruction. "Because these belonged to your momma." She slid the case toward me.

I smiled and gently slid it back. "They still do."

Connie stood and gave me a long hug. Tears welled up in her eyes.

"Besides," I said to her, "since all of my relatives are in the great beyond, come next June's wedding, you'll have one whole side of the church to yourself."

Connie laughed. "I'll be proud to stand in as your mom." She carefully placed the pearls back in the jewelry box and quickly regained her stern demeanor. "Now, be a good boy and help your momma clean up the kitchen."

As we worked side by side, we talked randomly about a number of topics, including the upcoming Veterans Day ceremony.

"So, do you have your speech prepared?" Connie asked, knowing I didn't.

"Nah, I figure if I do a lousy job, I'll quit getting asked to do these things."

"I can't say I approve of that attitude. Things happen for a reason, you know."

"Yeah, well, sometimes the reason is because you weren't paying close enough attention when a friend snookered you into doing something."

Connie grinned and let my comment sink in for a moment. "By the way, it turns out that seventy-two men and women from Watervalley have been killed in combat since 1900. Every one of them will have their name embossed on the statue base. The list is over there. The names are in chronological order as to when they were killed." Connie pointed to a manila folder on the kitchen counter.

Curious, I walked over and opened the file. But after seeing the first name on the list, a rush of panic seized me. "Connie, no." I looked at her, awash in disbelief and shock. "No, this can't be right!"

"Luke, what's wrong, honey?" She stepped toward me but stopped, staring in an odd mix of worry and astonishment. "Sweetie, you're as white as a sheet. If I didn't know better, I'd say you just saw a ghost!"

The first name on the list was a soldier killed in action, June 26, 1918, near Reims, France. His name was Leyland James Carter of Mercy Creek Road.

CHAPTER 46
Memorial

I will never understand how or why Leyland Carter appeared in my life as he did. I've never believed in ghosts and still don't. But as real as every fiber of my being wanted him to be, I had to concede that maybe he was just someone I created, some peculiar manifestation of my subconscious. I never shook Leyland's hand, I never saw him eat or drink, and I never saw him come or go. He just appeared. And all I could truly remember were his kind face and his temperate voice. As well, Leyland Carter had appeared to me as an old man, but he'd died a young soldier. Laughably, even when my mind created Leyland's imaginary ghost, I couldn't get his age right.

Still, something in my bones believed he was real.

Perhaps if our encounters had happened in the small hours of the night, or in the mystical half-light of sunset, I could have more easily relegated them to some fleeting trance or vaporous apparition. But they didn't. They occurred in broad daylight.

In hindsight, my conversations with Leyland held a singular quality that was grandly puzzling. Invariably, Leyland had told me things I didn't want to hear. But I had acted on his words and had made better, nobler choices because of them. And I could only wonder if in future days, during a morning run out Summerfield Road, or perhaps next spring while I was once again planting my garden, I would pause in my labor and suddenly catch on the lilt of the wind the sound of his spirited voice distantly singing a cheerful tune. I hoped so.

That night in the kitchen, I managed to regain my composure and dismiss the matter with Connie. She wasn't convinced, but she didn't pursue the subject further. I never spoke of Leyland to Christine or John or anyone. He would forever be a curious, yet oddly gratifying chapter of my life. I had no desire to spoil the richness of my experience with him or, for that matter, try to explain the unexplainable.

But I did have a passionate desire to know more about him. So in the final days before the memorial ceremony, I spent numerous hours at the Watervalley Library, digging through the archives and making discoveries that left me awestruck. Unlike the graduation speech earlier in the year, the Veterans Day speech was a story I couldn't wait to tell.

Despite the cool temperature, Tuesday, November 11, dawned bright and beautiful with a perfect blue sky. The air was filled with a strong, clean, alpine vigor. Red, white, and blue banners had been draped around the courthouse square, and flags hung everywhere. The world seemed dressed for a grand occasion. Rows of white wooden folding chairs lined the courthouse lawn, circling the veiled statue and the small podium in front of it. The chairs were for all of Watervalley's veterans.

Altogether there were more than one hundred of them. Among their ranks were Chick McKissick, Sheriff Warren Thurman, Maylen Cook, Clayton Ross, and Karen Davidson. These dozens of everyday men and women now went quietly about their jobs at the barbershop or the cabinet factory or the police station. Yet all of them had once put their lives on hold and served their country. Sitting near the podium and watching them take their places was possibly the most humbling experience of my life.

Then again, this was Watervalley, and humor was never far away. The veterans had been asked to wear all or part of their uniforms. Many did, with the exception of Gene Alley, who for some reason wore his old high school baseball uniform under his overcoat. Without a doubt, Gene was a little wacky due to the head trauma of his war wound. Then again, it occurred to me that he might simply be a living memorial to the long-term effects of questionable drug use. He was still a mystery.

Perhaps the most notable veteran in attendance was Luther Whitmore. His presence at the memorial service was one of the two favors I had asked of him. His uniform sagged a little, a testimony to the robust frame and stout fighting man Luther had once been. He had returned from his out-of-town journey, and to my surprise, seated beside him was his ex-wife, Claire. Luther had made peace with his past and had gone to California to find her. I didn't know if she had come for the memorial service, or for Luther, or for both, but I took it as a good sign that she was there.

Soon everyone was seated and assembled. John made a few opening remarks and then introduced me. I stepped to the podium, pulled my notes from my overcoat, and smiled warmly at those before me.

"I want to tell you about two soldiers," I said. "The first was a man born in 1894 several miles away in Maury County. His name was Leyland James Carter. When he was two years old, his family moved here to Watervalley. He grew up and went off to school at Vanderbilt University, where he earned a degree in classical studies. But he had a love of the soil, and after graduation he came back to

Watervalley, where he bought a small farm on Mercy Creek Road. There he built a house with his own hands. And, as often happens with men in Watervalley, he met a girl.

"Her name was Sylvia Bartholomew, and she was the love of his life. Then, in 1917 he was drafted. Before he left for France, he proposed and she accepted. She was seventeen years old. They were to be married upon his return and live in the cottage home he had built for them on Mercy Creek Road. While he was in France, he wrote her many letters, and it was clear that he missed her desperately. Leyland was also a man of wit and humor. In one letter, he wrote, 'Dear Sylvia: I have figured out how to make a small fortune in farming. You do this by first starting out with a large fortune.'"

A strong ripple of laughter swept through the crowd. I continued.

"Leyland also wrote poems in his letters to Sylvia. A few were about war, some were about home, and others were about the land. Leyland was one of the great company of men of Watervalley who lived by the soil and loved its mystery. For Leyland, the land seemed a source of essential wonder, and he took great delight in finding life in a handful of dust.

"But the most moving poems he wrote were about his love for Sylvia. One of my favorites is titled 'As Long As There Are Daisies,' in which he expresses the simple sentiment that as long as daisies bloom each year in the fields of Watervalley, so too will his love for her. It is clear that he loved Sylvia desperately and wanted nothing more than to return home, marry her, and live a quiet, peaceful life on his modest farm.

"But Leyland never made it back. He died in an attack at Bois Belleau near Reims, France, on June 26, 1918, and his is the first name on the memorial behind me. He was buried near the battlefield. Sylvia was heartbroken. She kept all of Leyland's letters and his poems, and eventually had them published in a small book, a copy of which can still be found in the Watervalley Library.

"In time, Sylvia married and had a daughter by the name of Evangeline, who was born in 1930. Evangeline was the mother of Watervalley's most decorated hero. This is the second soldier I want to tell you about.

"He joined the army in 1968 and, after undergoing basic training at Fort Polk, went to Vietnam, where he participated in multiple engagements with the enemy. At a time when most soldiers couldn't leave the war fast enough, he reenlisted twice and served until the close of the war in 1975. Along the way, he attained the rank of captain. He was wounded multiple times, for which he received four Purple Hearts. His acts of valor in combat won him two Bronze Star Medals, one Silver Star Medal, and a Distinguished Service Cross, the highest recognition a soldier can receive short of a Medal of Honor. It took quite a bit of digging through some military archives, but I finally uncovered that story.

"In 1971 while fighting in Quảng Ngãi Province, his patrol unit was ambushed, and he was shot and left for dead. But the wound only grazed his head. Upon regaining consciousness, he bandaged his injury. Then, instead of retreating to safe ground, he tracked his attackers back to a remote hut where two of his unit's men along with three other soldiers were being held prisoner. Single-handedly, he attacked, killing six of the enemy and freeing the five captives, two of whom had been beaten and had to be carried. All five of the rescued men survived the war."

I paused for a moment to look out over the crowd, wanting them to absorb my last statement. "After learning this story, I made quite a few phone calls. Each of the five men returned home, got married, and had families. Since then, two have passed away, one in an auto accident and the other from a heart attack. The five men had a combined eleven children and twenty-nine grandchildren; people who never would have lived were it not for the courage of one man. And I am pleased to say that at their insistence, the three surviving men are here today to pay tribute to this hero. They are the gentlemen seated to my right."

By now, many in the crowd were looking from side to side with curious glances. More than a few were staring at Luther Whitmore, who was sitting quietly, his face the picture of contrition and reserve. I paused and looked at him as well.

"Ladies and gentlemen, I know our memorial unveiling today is for those men and women who have died defending our country. But it seems both right and fitting that we take a moment to honor those who have served and are still with us, while they can hear our applause and know our appreciation. It also seems fitting to give a long-overdue hero's welcome to those who never got one and especially to Luther Allen Whitmore, Watervalley's most distinguished and most decorated soldier."

I fixed my gaze on Luther and began to clap loudly. The three men he had rescued immediately stood and clapped as well. Instantly and spontaneously the entire crowd stood and applauded in a thunderous ovation. Luther simply sat, holding Claire's hand. Tears welled in his eyes. He looked humbly up at me and nodded in a tight-lipped gesture of appreciation.

As the applause continued, I gazed around at all the lives before me, at the men and women in uniform. And I couldn't help but speculate that, just like Luther, there was in all of them something ruined, lost, or broken; that the unexplainable aspects of war had sealed up parts of their memory, robbing them of some irretrievable innocence, some unrecoverable sense of wonder. I gazed humbly at Karen and Clayton and so many others. For all of them, life had continued. Yet by some degree, war had changed them and taken from them something that they could never get back. Try as I might, I would never fully understand.

The applause ended and everyone sat again. I took a moment to smile warmly at those around me.

"I want to thank all of you who have given of your time and your money to make this moment and this memorial possible. I also want to thank you for giving me this opportunity to speak to you today so that those who have served, both living and dead, could be given the recognition and honor they are due. Let us never forget their sacrifice."

I pulled the rope to the veil covering the large statue. The fabric floated down gently, revealing a young man standing next to an army duffel bag. He was wearing a proud and expectant face of pure joy. Once again, the crowd erupted in deafening applause. And as I gazed at the large inscription at the base, I couldn't help but think of Leyland Carter.

The caption read, "Home, at Last."

CHAPTER 47
Dreams Come True

After the ceremony, I was seated in my chair, putting my notes back together, when Christine came up behind me. She draped her arms around my neck and pressed her cheek to mine. "You did great!"

"Thanks. It's a wonderful story. Although I'm not sure I did it justice."

"I think you did just fine. I'm very proud of you."

"Well, thank you, Miss Chambers."

"You're very welcome, Dr. Bradford!"

I stood and we walked a few steps. Christine hugged my arm as she spoke. "So, what's this big surprise you said you have for me when we talked on the phone earlier this morning?"

I reached for some papers in my coat pocket. "I was going to hold off for some special moment to tell you this, but I'm too excited to wait." I unfolded the papers and handed them to her.

"What is this?"

"It's a signed real estate contract, or more exactly, it's a one-year option to purchase. I've decided I'd like to own a piece of Watervalley."

Christine's jaw dropped. "Oh my goodness! You're kidding! Where?"

"Oh, it's just a fifteen-acre tract out past Gallivant's Crossing. Nothing too special about it. But I think everybody around here calls it Moon Lake."

Christine was completely speechless. She practically lunged toward me, wrapping her arms around my neck. Spontaneously, I lifted her in the air and lightly spun her around. After I set her down, she regarded me with rapt wonder.

"Luke! I don't know what to say. Does this honestly mean that one day we'll own Moon Lake?"

"Certainly looks that way. Of course, you'll have to actually marry me to own part of it. Although . . . even if you don't, you're still invited to come swim on the bathing-suit-optional days."

Christine was so ecstatic, she ignored my teasing and smiled with adoring wonder. She seemed incandescently happy.

"I can't believe you did this!"

"I figured that one day we'd build a house out there, so we can, you know, live over the valley."

Again, she hugged me excitedly. "I can't imagine how you pulled this off, Luke Bradford. I mean, how in the world did you get an old grump like Luther Whitmore to agree to it?"

"I beat him in a game of Twister."

"Bradford, you are unbelievable."

"Oh, well, gee, I don't know about all that," I said hesitantly.

But after a moment, I jokingly shrugged. "Okay, you're right. I am pretty unbelievable. Try not to drool."

She rolled her eyes. We were awash in a giddy foolishness. I took her hand, and we began to walk toward her car.

"So, Chambers, I've been thinking about the two of us. You? You're a smoking-hot girl. Me? Well, along with being unbelievable, I'm also the eventual owner of some pretty select Watervalley real estate. What say you and I get married next June?"

"Okay by me," she responded casually. "But I'm kind of high maintenance. You sure about this?" Her words were lighthearted, but there was also something of a searching, vulnerable quality to them.

I stopped and spoke slowly, resolutely. "Absolutely, positively, unquestionably, completely sure."

Christine ran her fingers under the lapel of my wool overcoat. "All right, then. I guess I'll say yes. But just so you know, my answer was kind of iffy before the Moon Lake deal got put on the table."

"Well, joke's on you, brown eyes. My Mennonite buddies tell me your family has a bunch of Holsteins. The handsome-doctor thing was just to lure you in. I'm all about snagging a dairy herd."

"Ugh, I knew it. I should never have fallen for you."

We laughed at ourselves. I loved her, and I saw in her eyes that she knew it. In that moment I realized the great responsibility I had to always assure her, to always protect her, to help her look beyond her broken dreams. It seemed that during our time together Christine had invariably been the strong one, the one with the emotional strength and courage to swallow pride, to speak softly against anger, to love unselfishly. Now it was for me to find the wisdom and the words, to be the one who stood against the storms that life would inevitably throw at us, and to be the one who, when necessary, would simply stand and wait.

I leaned forward and kissed her. "Okay, brown eyes, gotta run. I'm supposed to be part of some photo op over at the Memorial Building."

"Call me when you're done, and I'll meet you at your house."

"Right. And hey, if you don't mind, if you get there before me, check on Rhett and Casper? They may need to be let out."

"Sure."

I kissed her again and began to step backward, pulling my coat around me tightly to avoid the mild bite of the November air. Christine stood there and smiled sweetly, watching me leave.

"Don't forget, our dinner reservations are for six," she said.

"I won't."

"And it takes two hours to drive to Nashville."

"I know." I had continued walking backward away from her.

"And smile nice for the camera."

"I will." I turned toward the Memorial Building, not wanting to be late. But after two steps, Christine's warm, enchanting voice rang out from behind me.

"I love you, Mr. Wonderful."

"I love you too!" I echoed automatically, walking hurriedly.

But one step farther, I stopped abruptly. I stood frozen for a moment and then turned slowly around toward Christine. She was standing there in the crisp air and brilliant sun of that late-autumn afternoon, looking as radiant and beautiful as the first breathtaking moment I saw her in her classroom doorway more than a year ago. Her head was tilted to one side, and her face was framed in a soft, sentimental, affectionate smile. I stared at her for a few puzzled seconds before speaking with tender curiosity.

"What did you call me?"

POSTLUDE

Walking through the brisk November cold, Luke quickly made his way home from the Memorial Building. He was bubbling with anticipation. Both he and Christine were taking the next day off so they could go to Nashville that evening, grab some dinner, and then go hear Pink Martini play in a live concert. They would be late getting back to Watervalley, but the evening had all the potential to be nothing short of a fabulous time.

Before heading inside, he stopped at his mailbox and grabbed the envelopes that had accumulated over the last couple of days. While walking to the porch, he shuffled through a few familiar bills and became intrigued by a letter addressed to him from Vanderbilt University Medical Center. It was from Dr. Burns, his old med school professor. Consumed with curiosity, he stopped and opened it.

Dear Luke:

The medical center has recently been awarded a significant research grant to work in concert with Abbott Laboratories to perform alpha testing of a new fertility drug covering a range of reproductive disorders. I am searching for a candidate to head up the research team and thus am writing to see if this opportunity might be of interest.

It is my belief that this project would be well served by your considerable academic talents. While it may not avail the daily rewards of your present rural practice, it has the potential of bringing hope to innumerable women and couples struggling with infertility.

Please give this opportunity your fullest consideration and contact me at your convenience.

Sincerely,
John Burns, MD

Upon finishing the letter, Luke immediately wadded it up and stuck it into his coat pocket. But after taking two steps, he paused and stood for a moment, his mind racing. Then he carefully took the letter out of his pocket and neatly unfolded it. Smoothing out the crumpled edges, he again read Dr. Burns's words, "it has the potential of bringing hope to innumerable women and couples struggling with infertility." After standing there reflecting for a few seconds longer, he exhaled deeply and reached for his cell phone.

ACKNOWLEDGMENTS

Many thanks to my wife, Dawn, and son, Austin, for their continued support of my writing career. As well, thanks to Terri and Teresa . . . my amusing muses from oh-so-many decades ago.

A special thank-you to my mom, Sarah, whose beautiful mind has lost the light that so brilliantly inspired me during those tender years. Your love of words and the enchantment of story were matched only by your gift of hilarity. Thanks for always telling me I was your favorite. I promise not to let the brothers know.

And, as always, heartfelt thanks to my editor, Ellen Edwards, for once again chiseling at the words to render an extraordinary story about the splendor of ordinary days.

READERS GUIDE

THE SPLENDOR OF ORDINARY DAYS

A NOVEL OF WATERVALLEY

JEFF HIGH

READERS GUIDE

A CONVERSATION WITH JEFF HIGH

Spoiler Alert: The Conversation with Jeff High and Questions for Discussion that follow tell more about what happens in the book than you might want to know before reading it.

Q. It's terrific to be back in Watervalley with the characters we've come to love. This third book in the series explores, among other things, a military veteran who still suffers the effects of his service. What inspired you to tell this story?

A. Two different times in my life I went and talked to an Army recruiter. The first time was just before going to college. The recruiter talked me out of it because I was going to school on an academic scholarship, which the Army couldn't promise to duplicate. The second time was after I'd graduated college. This time I talked myself out of it. Although I have never served in the armed forces, I have always held a deep respect for the men and women who have. This story was my small way of expressing that admiration.

Q. Your original title for the book was They Also Serve. *What was the inspiration behind that idea?*

A. The original title was taken from Milton's poem "On His Blindness," in which the final line is "They also serve who only stand and wait." Among other things, it is a powerful statement about finding peace with one's lot in life, about how ordinary people doing ordinary work serve the ideals they hold dear. As well, the theme of blindness—physical, emotional, and even moral blindness—plays a huge role in this story.

Q. Four characters in the book are military veterans who still suffer from the effects of their service in one way or another. The book ends with the dedication of a new memorial statue to the local men and women who lost their lives serving their country in the last century. Can you tell us more about why you wanted to explore this theme, and what military service means to people in rural Tennessee?

A. In rural Tennessee—I am very proud to say—military service engenders a genuine respect that transcends boundaries of class, race, and gender that exist in all communities. I don't care if you are black, white, rich, poor, male, female, educated or not. . . . If you served in the military, and especially if you gave your life, we in Tennessee hold you in great reverence. When I was in grade school, a high school football star from my town was killed in Vietnam. Years later, as an adult, I happened to be in Washington, DC, and went to the Vietnam Memorial to do a rubbing of his name to give to his sister, whom I knew only secondhand. I intended it as simply a kind gesture. But strangely, the powerful, somber emotion of that moment brought me to tears. I was so struck with the young man's sacrifice.

Q. Luke and Christine face some significant challenges to their relationship in this book, not the least of which is Luke's thwarted attempts to propose marriage. What do you hope readers will take away from Luke and Christine's romance? And why was it important to include excerpts from Christine's teenage diary?

A. Luke and Christine's evolving relationship weighed heavily on me as I wrote this book. I wanted to portray two people who fall deeply in love and are clearly and naturally compelled by their desire for physical intimacy. But I also wanted to define them as two adults who have a moral compass, who struggle with their ideals in light of a larger world that overwhelmingly would think their choice to abstain archaic. The diary entries serve as a way of telling the reader more about Christine, who she is and how she defines herself. They also give the reader an enjoyable window into how close (or un-close) Luke comes to being the guy of her dreams.

Q. Luke's visits to Leyland Carter add an element of mystery, and even of the supernatural. Leyland acts almost as a philosopher whose questions help Luke to determine his course of action. The mystery surrounding Leyland makes him much more appealing than if he were just another wise old guy chatting on a porch. Can you share more about what you want to convey through this character?

A. Leyland Carter provides a means to reveal the struggles of Luke's conscience . . . to provide a monologue for working out his moral choices. As well, it is not by accident that it is Reverend Joe Dawson who brings Leyland to Luke's attention.

Q. Luke is the only one who sees Leyland, but over many years, others have heard the singing on the wind whose source remains unidentified. You suggest that such communion with the inexplicable is a feature of Southern life. Can you elaborate?

A. Few people in the South will admit to believing in ghosts . . . but then again, everyone in the South can tell you a personal ghost story. Religion and religious traditions run deep down here. By and large we are a people of faith, which requires that we believe in what we cannot see. We are also a region with a storied past. Great battles were fought in our backyards, battles in which young men were slaughtered, their lives ended before their time. All that loss and all that human agony leave the residue of a thousand stories about who died in this field, or near that house, or by that creek. Their spirits remain. Put together the two ingredients of faith and loss, and you have a culture in which the supernatural is part of the daily vernacular.

Q. I didn't know that there are Mennonite communities as far south as Tennessee. How long have they existed and what impact have they had?

A. Significant Mennonite communities can be found in Tennessee and Georgia (and perhaps other Southern states). There is a large Mennonite community in the county next to mine, and I often encountered them at the hospital where I worked. As well, my father ran a government-owned agricultural-research facility during my growing-up years. At a time when young men were being drafted for the Vietnam War, several Mennonite men worked at that facility in lieu of doing military service. That's where I got the idea for the story of Eli Yoder.

Q. Like Luke, do you believe that dogs can understand human speech? Or is Luke's golden retriever Rhett an exceptional case?

A. Let me just say this. . . . The original Rhett Butler, our family dog whose picture can be found on my Facebook page, without a doubt understood English fluently, especially Southern English. He would growl if you didn't say, "Yes, ma'am," or "No, ma'am."

Q. You include some quirky medical cases. Surely you've never met a man who spoke only in song lyrics or a blind woman who drove a lawn mower down Main Street. . . .

A. Actually, one story is completely true, and the other is partly true. In the little town of Spring Hill, where I grew up, there was an elderly lady who often drove her lawn mower down the street to the bank or the small grocery store. It was only a couple of blocks, and no one seemed to mind. There was also a fellow I knew while growing up who had a metal plate in his head after suffering a brain injury in a car accident. He swore the plate picked up a frequency from the local AM radio station, and he could hear what was being broadcast. We would test him against what was on the car radio, and sure enough, he could tell what song was playing. I don't just make this stuff up.

Q. You end the book with a surprise twist in which Luke is offered a new opportunity. Please don't keep us in suspense! Is Luke going to leave Watervalley? Can you give us some hints of what we can expect next?

A. For the answer to that question, you'll have to wait for book four of the Watervalley series.

Q. Your last book was honored as an OKRA Pick by the Independent Southern Booksellers. What has it been like for you to talk about the Watervalley series with booksellers and readers?

A. Of course it is a delight! As I have mentioned in earlier discussions, the Watervalley books are "glass half full" stories that seek to illuminate the sweet and decent things about Southern culture and the strong character of those who live there. But I would hasten to add that when I was travel nursing, I found these qualities in the people of small towns and communities all over America.

Q. So much about Watervalley seems timeless. In your day-to-day, do you see changes coming to the South that might become an ingrained part of Southern life? Do you anticipate working them into a future book?

A. I believe the South will become different . . . but its essence will not change. Our communities will become more diverse, and more and more of our jobs will be urban rather than rural. This is neither good nor bad, just different. What will not change is the Southern mind-set that invariably includes a devotion to our communities and our families. As well, the Christian faith comes in a lot of flavors in the South, including everything from the very traditionally devout to God's little goofballs. Even still, a belief in something beyond ourselves permeates our lives and speaks to defining qualities of our culture. I don't see that changing for a very long time, and clearly, I hope it never does.

QUESTIONS FOR DISCUSSION

1. What did you most enjoy about *The Splendor of Ordinary Days*? What made you laugh? What made you cry? Will anything about the book stay with you and become a part of who you are?

2. Name the characters who give Luke advice, wanted and unwanted, whenever he faces a dilemma. Do they help or hinder him? When is it right to step in to help advise a friend, and when is it better to stand back?

3. Luther Whitmore and Eli Yoder both want to keep pure the memory of Ellie Yoder, and decide not to reveal that she is the mother of Jacob and the grandmother of his children. In their situation, would you have made the same choice?

4. Is the Mr. Wonderful whom Christine writes about in her journal an unrealistic romantic idealization or a way of defining what qualities she considers most important in the man she marries? What did you write about in your teenage diary?

5. What was your response to Leyland Carter? What does he impart to Luke that Luke could not have learned any other way?

6. Luke feels compelled to resolve conflicts between people in town. Discuss the many ways in which he tries to bring about better understanding and reconciliation. Do you consider him a busybody who should mind his own business or a model for how the rest of us should behave?

7. Luke and Christine spend much of their courtship sitting and talking on her family's front porch. When was the last time you whiled away a summer evening sitting outside, watching night fall? Does Watervalley's slower pace appeal to you, or would it leave you bored? How much time do you spend outside enjoying the natural world?

8. Luke and Christine decide to abstain from physical intimacy until they're married. What do you think about that? What are some of the pros and cons of their decision? Does Christine's medical condition change that in your mind?

9. Discuss the various ghosts in Watervalley. Have you ever experienced an unexplained supernatural phenomenon? Or have you heard local stories about the supernatural? How do you explain the prevalence of such tales?

10. The Mennonite community in Watervalley lives largely apart, and sometimes tensions arise between it and the general population over their differing beliefs—regarding pacifism versus military service, for example, and over the role of government organizations such as the fire department. Is there a group of people in your community who live largely separate from the whole? If tensions exist, what have people done to resolve them?

11. Discuss Karen Davidson's reception by the town and what it takes for the situation to turn around.

12. Watervalley reveres its military veterans but doesn't always know how to meet their needs. Do you know a vet who could use some help? What are some of the factors that might complicate your community's efforts to help?

13. Will Fox has love troubles, but he finds a way to overcome his disappointment. Do you have any stories to share about youngsters you've known who have dealt with romantic complications?

14. Do you think Luke will leave Watervalley? Discuss the advantages and disadvantages of staying.

If you enjoyed

THE SPLENDOR OF ORDINARY DAYS

and want to know how it all began, return to Watervalley
by reading Jeff High's first Watervalley-set novel

MORE THINGS IN HEAVEN AND EARTH

available in paperback and e-book from New American Library.
Turn the page to read about Luke Bradford's early days in
Watervalley, filled with unexpected challenges
and charming surprises.

The first sign of a problem came when Wendy walked up to Nancy Orman, the receptionist, and announced in a small voice, "Mrs. Orman, something's not right with Daddy."

Nancy leaned over the counter and glanced at Hoot sleeping dreamily in the corner. She responded with an impish laugh. "Sweetie, I don't want to hurt your feelings, but we've all known that for years."

"No, you don't understand. I don't think he's breathing."

This got Nancy's attention. After a minute of shaking Hoot and fussing at him to "cut it out," she realized that something was drastically wrong. She burst into the exam room where I was taking a patient's history.

"Dr. Bradford, I need you to come to the waiting room immediately."

Her panicked tone told me more than the words themselves. I grabbed my stethoscope and followed.

A quick assessment told the ugly story. Hoot was in V-fib,

ventricular fibrillation. His heart was quivering, not beating. In a matter of minutes he would be dead. The clock was ticking.

"Nancy, call the EMTs over at the fire station. We're going to need them." I turned to the staff nurse. "Mary Jo, get the defibrillator off the crash cart. It's in exam room one."

Mary Jo didn't move. Her words seemed to ooze out one by one, thick with her dawdling Southern drawl. "Don't you want the whole cart?"

I responded firmly, calmly. "Mary Jo, if we have to run a full code on him, I don't want to do it on the waiting room floor. Go!"

She frowned and shuffled away.

"Cindy, go find the gurney and get it out here. We may need to move him to an exam room quickly." The frail little lab tech gave me a panicked nod and headed off. Meanwhile, I sent Camilla, the phlebotomist, to get the oxygen tank and bagging mask.

I enlisted some men from the waiting room to help me ease all three hundred–plus pounds of Hoot onto the floor, where once again I listened to his breathing, or lack thereof. One whiff and I shuddered. His gaping jaw emanated a toxic smell that could take the bark off a tree. I did a finger sweep, pulling out a large plug of chewing tobacco. My day just couldn't get better.

Cupping my hands over his mouth, I gave him two hard rescue blows, filling his lungs, and began doing chest compressions, hard and fast. Unbelievably, three more rounds of rescue blows and compressions ticked by and no one had returned. It was a damnable eternity.

"Where's the defibrillator?" I half yelled. People crowded silently around me, staring with anxious faces.

Mary Jo finally returned with it. She pulled up Hoot's T-shirt only to discover a chest hairier than a sheepdog. The shock pads would never find skin to stick to.

"Mary Jo, get the pediatric pads and put them on him first."

Again she argued. "Why? He's way too big for those!"

I was practically bouncing up and down doing compressions on Hoot's massive chest. I didn't need a debate. "Mary Jo, get out the pediatric pads and put them on him now!"

She reluctantly tore open the foil package and placed the two small pads on Hoot's upper right and lower left chest.

"Now rip them off."

Mary Jo gaped at me, confused.

"Go ahead—rip them off quickly."

She complied. It worked as a spontaneous wax job, leaving a clear surface for the adult pads.

It was time for another round of mouth-to-mouth. Two blows into the poor man's noxious oral cavity almost asphyxiated me. I looked up to see the arrival of the oxygen tank and had the fleeting notion that I might need it first.

"We had a hard time finding one that wasn't empty," said Camilla sheepishly.

Precious seconds were flying by. Still bouncing up and down, I snapped out instructions. "Camilla, hold the mask tightly over his mouth and nose and start bagging him."

She complied with a vengeance, squeezing vigorously on the oxygen bag, pumping him full of air.

"Camilla, we're not trying to inflate him like a flat tire. Just give him one slow squeeze every eight seconds." She was wide eyed and scared to death, but nodded obediently with quick bobs of her head.

Finally, the defibrillator was ready to analyze Hoot's heart rhythm. But when I stopped compressions to allow for the test, I noticed the valve of the oxygen tank sitting on zero. Camilla had been pumping him full of room air.

"Camilla, you need to cut the O_2 tank on, wide open." I was still calm but the aggravation was beginning to show. With quick, birdlike movements she looked back and forth between the tank and me, her face in a blank panic. I looked over to Nancy, speaking quickly.

"Nancy, turn the valve counterclockwise as far as it will go." She nodded and turned it so hard I thought she might twist it off.

Mary Jo hit the analyze button. Above the din of the small crowd the mechanical voice of the defibrillator announced, "Shock advised."

"Set it at two hundred fifty joules. Everybody step back!" I nodded to Mary Jo.

The shock caused Hoot's body to jolt, almost lifting off the floor. Finally, his quivering heart was getting smacked back into rhythm. All eyes were on the defibrillator, waiting, watching. Magically, after a few sputtering waves, it began to show a sinus rhythm, a normal heart wave. Once again Ol' Sparky had done his job. I exhaled a deep breath. Crisis over.

That is, until five beats later, when the rhythm went flatline. No quivering, no V-fib, nothing.

This was bad news—really bad news. The small voice of panic began whispering in the back of my head. For a moment I stood there, frozen in disbelief. All eyes were on me. The only solution for jump-starting a flatliner is drugs, delivered quickly and methodically in a timed sequence, and then shocking him. The voice was now screaming: *Get moving, Luke—Code Blue! Code Blue!*

"Camilla, keep bagging him." I searched the room and pointed to a lanky fellow in his late thirties. "You— Did you see the way I was doing those compressions?"

He nodded.

"I want you to start doing them just like I was. Press hard—he's a big fellow. Try to do a hundred a minute."

I turned to Mary Jo. "We need to get him to the exam room and run a full code. Where's our lift stretcher?"

"We don't have one."

"We don't have one?" I responded incredulously. We had to get him off the floor and onto the gurney, which, I now noticed, wasn't there.

"Where's the gurney?" I looked down the main hallway of the clinic. Nancy was waddling toward me, her short legs moving as quickly as they could. I met her halfway.

"Cindy's getting it. It was back in the storage room covered with the Christmas decorations. She's cleaning it up."

I pressed my lips sternly together, squelching back a fuming desire to scream, loudly and with gusto. "Nancy, I don't care if it's clean or not. Bring it now and bring an extra bedsheet."

I returned to the waiting room and recruited three men and two of the heftier farm women to help lift Hoot. We got the extra bedsheet under him just as Cindy arrived with the gurney. The air was thick with confusion and tension. Hoot's life was slipping away.

With three of us on each side, we yanked him up so hard he almost went airborne. Stepping quickly, we dished him onto the gurney in a smooth, sweeping motion that was perfectly executed—except for the small detail that no one had thought to lock the gurney's wheels. Upon landing, Hoot scooted across the floor like a roller skate, his massive limbs dangling from all sides. I dove and caught him. We moved swiftly.

Including the staff, about ten of us crowded into the small exam room. I stood at the head, calling out orders, timing the intervals, running the protocol. The passing minutes became a surreal blur as events moved with an unbelievable rapidity.

Everything imaginable went wrong.

Camilla, who normally had a rock-steady hand, was so shaken she took forever to get an IV started. This forced me to give the first two doses of epinephrine by direct injection into his jugular, creating no small mess of blood. No one could find a blood pressure cuff big enough to fit Hoot's arm. We pulled his boot off and put one at his ankle. I couldn't intubate him because the battery in the laryngoscope was dead. The only atropine available was a month out of date. I used it anyway. With no way to get quick lab results, I was left desperately short of critical metabolic information. It wasn't that the clinic's resources were primitive; they were nonexistent.

To top it all off, the EMTs had yet to arrive because they had been far out at a friend's farm helping to deliver a calf. Only in Watervalley.

Minutes passed. Numerous times the drug protocols sparked some sputtering waves. When that happened, we quickly shocked him, desperately trying to revive a normal rhythm. But nothing was working. Panic was seizing everyone, permeating the frantic voices of those around me. My frustration and anger mounted. Hoot Wilson was an otherwise robust, healthy man of forty-three. To my thinking, it just wasn't his time yet. But he was about to meet his maker because remote Watervalley lacked the fundamental equipment needed to keep him alive and all of my training couldn't make up the difference.

In my head I had been doing the math. It had been over thirty minutes since Nancy had first shaken him. By all the odds, he didn't have a chance. I needed to think about calling it, but I just couldn't. My irritation and fury surfaced. I took over doing the compressions and yelled audibly.

"Come on, dammit. Get a rhythm going." Sweat poured down my face. Everyone in the room was standing, staring with lost expressions. This ad hoc group had followed my instructions as best they could, but the drama had left them shell-shocked and exhausted. Everyone knew the inevitable was coming. We had given multiple doses of epinephrine and atropine, we'd done continuous compressions, multiple shocks, and yet nothing. No sustained rhythm. I had lost him.

Finally I stopped and stepped back, heaving deep gasps in and out, trying to catch my breath. I searched the long, somber faces of those in the room, particularly that of Mary Jo, the staff nurse. I was looking for confirmation. It was time to call it. That was when I noticed something that made me feel like an even grander failure.

It was Wendy, Hoot's daughter. All the while she had been sitting quietly in the corner of the exam room watching the terrible drama of her father's last minutes. But something was remarkably odd. Instead of being in a state of panic and tears, she looked placid, curious. She sat and waited patiently for me to break the silence. I needed to call it, but her presence stopped me.

Hoot was gone. At this point it made no sense to send her away, so I motioned for her to come closer. Her face expressionless, Wendy walked up to her father and with her pudgy hand she squeezed his large, bare foot and spoke in a soft and determined voice.

"Don't go yet, Daddy."

I exhaled deeply. It was the final straw, an epitaph to my failure.

And then I heard the beep, a singular heartbeat on the cardiac monitor. The room held its collective breath. The beep was followed by another, then another, then another. We all stood in stunned, shocked silence.

After ten more beats, Nancy Orman, a devout Baptist who for all of her fifty-three years had lived, walked, and breathed a mile away from the nearest known sin, blurted out in a low, weak voice, "Holy shit!"

Everyone else was speechless.

Miraculously, the heartbeat continued.

About this time the EMTs arrived. We loaded Hoot into the ambulance and I rode along for the forty-five-minute drive to the regional hospital in the next county. It was the closest facility available.

Hoot's heart rate remained constant. He even began to regain a drowsy consciousness on the ride over. A few days later he got a pacemaker and within a week he was back on the farm. It was a miraculous turnaround, one for the medical journals. But to the people of Watervalley, it seemed to be no big deal. To their thinking, it was just providential timing and grace.

For me, it was more complex, a combination of critical elements. Yet still, I couldn't completely account for it, just like so many other things about Watervalley that in time I would come to realize were simply not explainable.

Being dead on the exam room table for that long normally impacts mental function. But with Hoot's loud and happy personality, no one noticed a difference. He was just glad to be back among his cows and with the darling jewel of his life, his daughter, Wendy.

From then on, every day after school, Wendy would go and sit in the corner of the milk parlor and calmly do her homework while Hoot went about his work. Engrossed in her lessons, she would quietly study, seemingly oblivious to the incredible noise and clamor of the milk machines and baying cows. But every so often she would look up from her book, and sweetly, proudly gaze over at her immense father and, with a face of pure love, smile.

Hoot's Code Blue happened on the Thursday of my first week as the new doctor at the Watervalley Clinic, my first job out of med school. I'd like to be able to say that the days leading up to it since my Saturday arrival had not been quite so eventful.

Unfortunately, that just wouldn't be true.

Photo by Amanda Hagler

After growing up on a farm in rural Tennessee, **Jeff High** attained degrees in literature and nursing. He is the three-time winner, in fiction and poetry, of an annual writing contest held by Vanderbilt Medical Center. He lived in Nashville for many years, and throughout the country as a travel nurse, before returning to his original hometown, near where he now works as an operating room RN in general surgery.

CONNECT ONLINE

jeffhigh.com

watervalleybooks.com

facebook.com/JeffHighWriter